RUNNIN' NO MORE

RUNNIN' NO MORE

G.T. DÍPÈ

Copyright © 2024 by G.T. Dípè

Cover design © 2024 by Bidemi Hassan

ISBN 978-80-11-05828-9

The right of G.T. DÍPÈ to be identified as the author of this work has been asserted by her in accordance with copyright law.

All rights reserved. No part of this book may be reproduced in any form or by any electronic or mechanical means, including information storage and retrieval systems—except in the case of brief quotations embodied in reviews or scholarly articles—without permission from the author.

The characters and events portrayed in this book are fictitious or used fictitiously and are the product of the author's imagination. Any similarity to real persons, living or dead, is purely coincidental and not intended by the author.

All brand names and product names used in this book are trademarks, registered trademarks, or trade names of their respective holders. G.T. DÍPÈ is not associated with any product or vendor in this book.

 Created with Vellum

To the brave and beautiful souls of queer Nigerians, this book is for you. For every closet you've kicked open and every rainbow you've painted in a world that still prefers shades of grey. You are the poetry in a country that often demands silence, the defiant laughter in spaces that try to contain you. May your truth shine brighter than the ignorance that seeks to dim it. Know this—revolution is coming, and we'll be there, fists raised, fighting beside you. Because, darlings, freedom looks a lot like you—unapologetic, untamed, and completely unstoppable.

AUTHOR'S NOTE

My country, Nigeria, was once held in the grip of the British Empire, from the mid-nineteenth century until the dawn of October 1, 1960. Though we've been proudly independent ever since, it seems the British way of writing was one of our parting gifts. So, for readers who are neither Nigerian nor British (nor ever colonised by Britain), bear with me when you encounter an 'S' where you might expect a 'Z.' What can I say? Old habits die hard—and this Nigerian, she adores her 'SSSS.'

CONTENT WARNINGS

This novel is a work of fiction, but it contains themes and scenes that may be distressing to some readers, including:

- *Depictions of trauma and PTSD.*
- *Mentions of physical, emotional, and psychological abuse.*
- *Homophobia, attempted sexual assault, stalking, and other sensitive subjects.*

Thank you from the bottom of my heart for having saved me. I was drowning, and you threw yourself into the water without hesitation, without a backward look.

- Jean Cocteau to Jean Marais, 1939. Extracted from Henry's emails to Alex in *Red, White, & Royal Blue* by Casey McQuiston.

1
DECISIONS

*— Follow Your Fire
by Kodaline.*

Monday, 19th September 2022

ADE ADEOWO TILTS HIS HEAD, LETTING THE BITING Middlesbrough air flirt with his cheeks. The chill cuts deep, but not as deep as the truths he keeps hidden—buried in the dim corners of his soul, where pride smothers vulnerability, and shame persists like an opponent he can never outrun. He shakes his shoulder, straightens the sleeves of his green sweater, and swings open the passenger door of his bZ4X with the flourish of a seasoned valet.

Jola climbs out, the very picture of triumph—the sister whose tireless campaign (some might label it nagging) has finally worn him down, bringing him to Teesside University today. From the back seat, their friends—Ay and MT—tumble out in tow, huddled in trench coats and mittens. Ade thinks they look ridiculous.

"Doctor Adeowo, the newest assistant lecturer in town,"

Ade says with a half-bow, presenting Jola with a bouquet of red roses. "Courtesy of the elder Doctor Adeowo."

Jola inhales the delicate fragrance with all the grace of a queen receiving her due, the lines on her black suit sharp enough to slice bread. "Temmy does know how to spoil me. What an extraordinary brother."

Ade clears his throat, his voice drenched in mock indignation. "And I get no recognition whatsoever?"

"Maybe if you become a medical doctor like Temmy, you'll finally get some appreciation," Ay quips from the side.

"You sound just like a Nigerian parent," MT chimes in, shaking her head as they step into the Faculty of Science building. "Honestly, this doesn't feel too different from most Nigerian private universities."

Ade's steps falter as a sudden sharp ache wraps around his heart like a vice—his body betraying what he's trying to forget. Nigeria floods the edges of his mind, bright and relentless. The office he couldn't work in, the dream job that had dangled just within reach. Five gruelling interviews aced. He'd all but tasted it. And then, like a spineless fool, he gave it up. He could've stayed—should've stayed—to live the life he dared imagine. Bold. Unapologetic. Instead, he fled. Not gracefully, but like a thief sneaking out the back door, hoping no one would notice.

They make their way to the elevators, and Ade takes measured strides as if walking too quickly might shake something loose within him. His reflection in a nearby mirror is the same as ever: unruffled, collected, and almost artfully detached. Years of practice birthed this: his subtle, sly way of keeping the world at arm's length and himself blissfully and precariously afloat. He conceals himself in a veneer of calm while suppressing the unacknowledged darkness looming, waiting to be seen, waiting to be named. Ade is unaware—or perhaps unwilling to admit—that it is in the acknowledgement of one's deepest fears that the seeds of healing are sown and in the embrace of hidden sorrows that true strength is found.

He sighs inwardly and presses the button for the sixth floor, where "Environmental Science" is displayed; the lift hums and starts its ascent. When the doors slide open, Jola leads them down a long corridor, her footsteps confident. She makes a sharp right turn before stopping at the tenth door. Three names are boldly engraved on the door: *Jolade Grace Adeowo, PhD • Kurt Noah Sherwood, PhD • Chad Justin Morgan, PhD*.

"Pose in front of it, Jughead," he instructs, bringing out his phone.

Jola, ever the good sport, strikes a pose, her face a study in carefully managed pride and underlying tension. Ade watches her closely as the shutters click, silently observing the abstruse struggle between her confident exterior and what seems to be a swirling tempest of half-forgotten dreams beneath. Yet here she is, forging ahead with that stubborn determination that has always defined her. He silently hopes she allows herself room to breathe, feel, and simply *be*.

"Hand over your bag," he says, fully embracing his chief photographer role. Jola hands it over, rolling her eyes but going along with every pose they demand of her. "Point to your name," he suggests, trying not to grin.

"That's childish," Jola protests, but her hand reluctantly lifts to gesture at the door.

Once the impromptu photo shoot wraps up, Jola tries unlocking the door with her key but finds it unlocked. Before knocking, she pauses, and Ade gives her arm a gentle pat—a reassurance he knows she needs. Inside the office, two men are seated at two of the three desks. Both rise as the group enters. Jola walks over to the first man. "Jolade Adeowo," she says, extending her hand.

"Chad Morgan," he replies with a clean American accent. He is of average height, his black hair pulled back into a neat ponytail that just brushes the collar of his shirt.

The second man steps forward with a broad smile. "Kurt Sherwood here," he says, his British accent rolling smoothly. "Pleased to meet you." He's tall, with chestnut hair cropped short and humour in his grey eyes.

"These are my friends," Jola introduces, gesturing to Ay and MT. "And brother," she adds, nodding towards Ade.

Kurt's gaze lands on Ade, a flicker of curiosity there. "Are you all staff here?" The ladies quickly clarify that they're new graduate students while Jola explains Ade is visiting to decide if he should accept his offer of admission for graduate school here. Kurt's smile widens. "Fantastic," he says. "I've got a mate in Computing and Cyber Security. I can check if he's free to give you a tour of your department."

"That sounds perfect," MT chimes in. "I'm already enrolled in MSc Applied Data Science. Mind if I tag along?"

"Not at all," Kurt replies. "Shouldn't be a problem."

Ade glances at Jola, who slightly nods, understanding his unspoken question. "It'll be more helpful, I think," she says, settling into her desk chair. "They should be able to answer any questions you have."

With that, Kurt excuses himself to make a call, wandering over to the bookshelf as he dials. With only two guest chairs in front of Jola's desk, which Ade and MT have already claimed, Chad offers Ay one of his, and they settle into polite conversation.

A few seconds later, Kurt returns, his smile still firmly in place. "I've spoken to him. He's free for the next hour and can show you both around. You can find him in the Faculty of Engineering building on the third floor, the fifth office on the left. His name is Daniel Groza. Do you know where that is?"

"I have the campus map," MT answers. "And I was at the building last week for pre-registration."

"Brilliant," Ade says, shaking Kurt's hand. "Thank you very much."

"Anytime," Kurt responds, returning the handshake with a firm grip, then offering the same to MT before heading back to his desk.

"We'd better get moving," Ade says as he and MT head out of the office.

*

"We are lost," Ade declares, his tone laced with frustration as he mutters a series of *unprintable words* in Yoruba. His expression, however, seems more bewildered than wrathful, which is probably why MT remains unfazed by his outburst.

"*Se sùúrù*," MT snaps in Yoruba, demanding patience while she concentrates on the map.

They left Jola's office ten minutes ago, and by MT's calculations, they should have arrived three minutes ago. Yet here they are, wandering through what feels like the Bermuda Triangle of Teesside University. Ade is beginning to question whether he even wants to attend a university where it's so easy to get lost.

MT suddenly exclaims, yanking him from his thoughts. "Ah-ah, I told you we're not lost, just missed a turning. If we retrace our steps, we'll find the building quickly."

Ade sighs, half-turning back the way they came. "I think Kurt would've offered to take us there if we'd asked," he grumbles, starting to walk with his evidently mad friend.

"Oh, he would've offered, alright," MT snorts. "Maybe shove me down the stairs just so he could dazzle you into enrolling on the spot."

"What do you mean?"

"Oh my God, Ade. Did you not see him ogling at you?" MT states, like it was the most obvious thing. "Even though we were in the room, he was mentally undressing you," she adds, just as they finally find the correct turning.

Ade's attention drifts away from the directions, his arms crossing over his chest as if warding off an unseen chill. "When did you notice this? I thought he was just being nice."

"Òótó lo so, *my dear*—you said the truth," MT chuckles. "If his niceness will lead him to your pants."

"You are being ridiculous."

"Most times, I am," she allows. "But this time, I'm quite serious. We can ask Jola and Ay in the car. Now, look." She points with a satisfied smile. "We found it."

Sure enough, a massive building rises before them, with *FACULTY OF ENGINEERING* emblazoned boldly across the front. The interior of the building is almost a carbon copy of the science building they just left, right down to the similarly labelled elevator buttons. They exit the lift and find the right office with surprising ease. A man of average height opens the door, greeting them with a smile. "You must be from Kurt," he says, offering them the chairs in front of his desk.

About forty minutes later, they are heading out of the building, the autumn air crisp and carrying the faint scent of damp leaves. Ade crosses his arms, casting a wary glance at MT as she struggles to jam her hands back into the woolly monstrosities she calls mittens. They're enormous, puffy things in a shade of pink that could blind one at ten paces.

"Don't you dare put those back on," he commands, pointing at the mittens as if they're some dangerous contraband.

MT heaves a sigh, clutching the mittens to her chest like they're her only protection against the harsh, unfeeling English elements. "You know this is my *first time* leaving Nigeria. Do you want cold to kill me? Is that what you want?"

Ade gives her a bemused look, shaking his head. "Cold? You think this is cold?" He lets out a small chuckle. "It's not even November yet. What will you do in winter? Carry heater with you like a handbag?"

MT lifts her chin defiantly. "You don't want to know what Ay and I have planned for that."

Ade grins, a hint of wonder slipping through his amusement. "I still can't believe you two are actually here," he says, remembering how, only a month ago, MT and Ay had packed up their lives in Lagos and launched themselves into this damp and drizzly corner of England.

With her usual exuberance, MT intertwines their hands, tiptoes, and kisses his cheek. The kiss leaves a bright red smudge on his skin, which she promptly cleans with a wet wipe as if she's an artist correcting a minor flaw in her masterpiece. "Ade, Ade, my sweetheart," she croons, her voice honeyed with affection. "Feeling okay?"

Ade already has his answers locked and loaded for

questions like this. He's perfected the art of deflecting concern with a well-timed joke, a nonchalant smile, and a laugh that sounds just right. On rare occasions, like today, he briefly considers opening up, but the very thought of it turns his stomach. No, today isn't the day for such reckless honesty. Today, he is Teniade Adeowo, the embodiment of composure, here to tick boxes and choose a university. The rest—well, he can deal with that later. Or, knowing him, not at all.

So, he arranges his face into an image of ease. "Couldn't be better, sugar," he replies, his tone light as a breeze.

𓃡

Ade slouches in a chair in Jola's office, his eyes lazily scanning the room. It's spacious enough for three, the kind of space that begs to be filled with something more than silence. A couch lounges in front of the bookshelves, lined with books that are clearly well-read, their spines creased and faded. Some are stacked horizontally while others lean haphazardly, giving the shelves a sense of lived-in clutter.

Jola's desk, strategically placed by the window, is a sleek piece of dark wood, with two monitors, a laptop stand, a small potted plant, and a pen holder brimming with pens and pencils of varying colours and sizes. Outside the window, the city sprawls under a heavy blanket of grey clouds, the skyline softened by the overcast light that flattens the colours and dims the view. The faint hum of traffic filters through, just enough to remind Ade of life outside these walls.

Above the bookshelves, a small clock ticks away, its steady rhythm filling the gaps in the room's silence. Jola's scent lingers faintly—something floral and clean—mixing with the subtle musk of old books and polished wood.

Ade opens Twitter, and the first thing that greets him is a picture of an underwear model. *Typical*. He exhales, but the image drags him somewhere else. Heathrow. Six weeks ago. A face, a moment, a collision that seems to cling to his mind like static, much to the delight of Jola, who tease him mercilessly about his supposed gawking. Fine, maybe he was. But who wouldn't have stopped dead in their tracks? One minute, his nose was buried in his phone, and the next, he was face-to-face with a guy who looked like he just stepped straight out of a Renaissance sculpture. Ade hadn't just collided with him; he'd crashed into perfection.

The guy's face still hangs in his mind, like a portrait painted in painstaking detail: a face that looked like it was carved from marble, light-blue eyes that sparkled like sapphires when they caught the light, black hair framing his face in a cascade of perfect ringlets, and heart-shaped lips with a delicate curve. Even his nose was beautiful. *Kai, God dey create*. Ade groans inwardly, kicking himself for not at least getting the guy's name. How hard could it have been? Now, all he has is a ghost of a memory that haunts him every time. What's he supposed to do? Type "beautiful guy with sexy eyes and lips you want to worship" into Instagram's search bar? Yeah, that'll go well—maybe land him on some fan pages for Tyler Blackburn and Matt Bomer.

Jola's voice slices through his thoughts, pulling him back to reality. *Finally*. But then, another voice. A male voice. His heart stutters. It can't be. It's happening again, just like it has for weeks now—seeing people who look like him, hearing a voice that sounds just like his. He's hallucinating, he tells himself, creating illusions of things he wants but can never have.

And yet, here he is, torturing himself with the memory of a ten-minute encounter that, logically, should mean nothing. But logic has never been Ade's strong suit, especially when daydreaming is an option. Every morning for six weeks, those blue eyes return—the shade of a serene lake just before dusk. Every time, they rouse a feral gleam low in his navel, a spark that grows into a burn. He tells himself it's ephemeral, but who's he kidding? Ade still gives in to delusions sometimes, and he's already rewritten the encounter a hundred times in his head. Each version is more elaborate than the last—this time, he's charming, witty, and suave. The encounter ends with a flirtatious exchange, a date, and then a night he won't admit he fantasises about in detail.

His body stirs.

Gotta keep it together, Teniade. The last thing he needs is for Jola to walk in and notice his... predicament. But deep down, he knows his rearrangement is a hoax, destined to remain locked in the confines of his overactive imagination. Besides, what are the odds of ever running into the stranger again? About as likely as Jola winning the lottery.

"Here we are, gentlemen," Jola's voice rings out as she enters, flanked by two guys. She waves. "Hey, Ade."

Ade's heart lurches in his chest—hard. Did he wave back? He can't tell.

On Jola's left stands a tallish chap, good-looking, deep blue eyes, black hair cropped short, and obviously British—practically exuding tea and politeness. He's decked out in green cargo trousers and a black V-neck, the picture of effortless casual.

But it's the guy on her right who robs Ade of breath.

This one—this vision—wears a patterned purple shirt, meticulously tucked into tailored black trousers that sit with a sort of arrogant precision over polished Chelsea boots. The look is innocent, intentional. And yet Ade, with a single roguish glance, manages to mentally dismantle every layer, peeling back the fabric in his mind with an ease that feels almost indecent.

Ade then takes him in slowly. Those eyes, pale and piercing; that nose, just as well-constructed as he remembers; those lips, heart-shaped and curled slightly at the corners. And the hair—soft-looking curls framing his face like a halo.

It's him.

It's the airport stranger.

In Middles-fucking-brough.

2

REUNION

*— Beautiful Stranger
by Madonna.*

STEFAN WICKSTRÖM KNOWS ONE THING FOR CERTAIN: he is not a coward. Not even close.

He reminds himself of this, silently yet firmly, as he strolls through Teesside University's general library with his friend, Jason. True, he may have left Sweden to sidestep an uncomfortable situation, but that's not cowardice—it's a tactical retreat. After all, what's more pragmatic than pursuing his education and ensuring his future while leaving behind the ghosts of the past? If anything, it's multitasking at its finest.

The library tour is a welcome change from the frantic, touristy whirlwind Jason put him through in London after his arrival to England. London Eye, Tower Bridge, Big Ben, Sky Garden, and even Buckingham Palace—Jason seemed intent on cramming all of London's landmarks into one exhausting day. By the time they finally got to Kensington

Palace, with Jason speculating that it is "boring as hell to live in" now that Harry and Meghan had vacated, Stefan was ready to drop.

As they wander through the literary section, Jason grabs a copy of *Red, White and Royal Blue* from a shelf. "You've read this, right? What's it about?"

"Prince of England falls for the first son of the United States. That sums it up."

"Elaborate."

"Read it yourself." Stefan's lips curl upward, placing *A Little Life* back on the shelf. "No summary could do it justice."

Jason shrugs and returns the book, catching up with Stefan, who's been drawn to another shelf. "Is this the book where those two platonic paired warrior-like people," he says, plucking a copy of *City of Bones*, "slept together even though they know it's forbidden?"

"Trust you to have that story in your head. But no, you're thinking of Emma and Julian in *The Dark Artifices*."

Jason trails his hand on the books and promptly picks up *Lady Midnight*, flipping through the pages intensely. "Errr, but who is Mark? And Kieran? Why are they kissing? Where are the people who *should* be kissing?"

Stefan chuckles. "You cannot understand anything this way. But Mark is half shadow hunter, half-faerie, and Kieran is a prince of Faerie."

Jason continues consulting the book. "I found it. Wow, they're actually going to do it on a beach. Won't sand enter everywhere?" he gestures suggestively below his waistband, his eyes still scanning the pages. "Yes, I'm definitely reading this as well."

"About time you took my recommendations seriously."

Books are Stefan's lifeblood, especially anything by the

talented Cassandra Clare. The *Shadowhunters* series is his obsession, while Jason's literary experience is pretty much limited to *Harry Potter*. During their London tour, Jason had dragged Stefan to King's Cross Station, claiming he knew precisely how to find Platform Nine and Three-Quarters. Of course, he had refused to show Stefan because, as Jason simply put it, Stefan was "such a muggle." Typical Slytherin, that one.

As they leave the library, Stefan notices a peculiar event on his schedule: an introductory session not listed on Jason's. "What do you suppose this is for?" he asks.

"A cult initiation, maybe," Jason suggests. "Better brush up on your chants."

"Well, you're coming with me. If I go down, so are you."

"Or," Jason counters, "I could stay in the library. Being the brooding intellectual type might endear me to women."

"Stop thinking with your dick."

"Uh, rudeeee." Jason huffs, but he's grinning.

They walk down the hallway, and Stefan masks his unease with a brisk, purposeful stride. He's finally here, ready to start afresh. But despite his determined pace, his shoulders hunch slightly as if bracing against an invisible weight. And the noise of the hallway—a cacophony of laughter, chatter, and slamming doors—feels amplified.

For a split second, his eyes rest on a figure rounding the corner, and his stomach clenches as a flash of recognition sparks an irrational fear. He wills himself not to stumble, regaining his balance when he realises that the figure is a mere phantasm—not who he thinks it is. Stefan exhales, his shoulders easing as he and Jason enter the lecture hall. It's a medium-sized room, the chairs and tables arranged in a semicircle across five rows, each slightly higher than the one before. The stage, raised and curved, has a monitor and a desk.

"Really?" Jason groans as Stefan heads straight for the front row and sits down.

"I like to be attentive."

"You can be attentive over there," Jason suggests, pointing to the last row, where a beautiful lady is seated.

"You just want to flirt with her."

"As opposed to?"

"I won't be surprised if the Queen has caught wind of your reputation."

Jason is about to give a scathing retort when his phone rings. He answers it with a quick, "Hey, Benny," addressing his older brother.

Stefan scans the room, taking in the faces of his new classmates. These are the people he will spend the next year with. It wouldn't hurt to make a friend or two.

"Ben is needed in Newcastle," Jason informs, hanging up. "Something about documents that need his signature. Scott and Kiki are driving down with him. If we're not ready when he's here, he will drop the key and leave with them."

"Sounds cool."

"You know, I thought he drove us so he could meet that pretty faculty member."

About two weeks ago, while he was casually browsing his department's website, Stefan had stumbled upon the profile of one Dr Jolade Adeowo. Something about her face tugged at his memory, triggering a quiet yet persistent curiosity. In a bid to figure this out, he showed her picture to Ben and Jason, but neither seemed to recognise her. Undeterred, Stefan dug deeper into her professional page, discovering that her master's thesis on tropospheric ozone was strikingly similar to his bachelor's thesis. This fuelled his belief that Dr Adeowo could be an ideal mentor, especially given his ambitions of pursuing a doctorate.

"Um, why would he want to meet her?" Stefan muses, recalling how uninterested Ben seemed when they looked at her picture. However, there *was* that moment when Ben thought he saw her at a restaurant, only to dismiss it without explanation. "Is that why he's dressed like some fairy-tale prince today?"

It makes sense; Ben is definitely not dressed in that crisp Emporio Armani suit and Gaziano & Girling shoes for some boring meeting in Darlington.

Jason snickers. "I caught him checking her page on your faculty website," he says, wiping his eyes.

"Caught?"

"Yes. He closed the tab faster than if he was watching porn."

"Maybe he likes her?"

"Maybe," Jason concedes. "You never know with Ben." He glances over to the third row discreetly. "Do you think his *girlfriend* will be teaching you?"

Stefan's fingers drum absentmindedly on the table. "I do hope so," his eyes dart towards the door, but then he frowns. "When did we start calling her his girlfriend?"

"I don't know her name."

"You can refer to her as *her*," Stefan suggests dryly. "I'll know who you mean."

"We already have *her*," Jason points out, squinting at the screen as Stefan pulls up Dr Adeowo's profile. "How do you even pronounce the surname?"

"Ade-owo, I think."

"It could be Ad-eo-wo. Or Aeowo? Maybe the D and W are silent."

Stefan rolls his eyes. "That makes no sense."

Jason raises his hands in surrender. "Alright, we'll do it your way."

A man of average height enters the room and steps onto the stage. He introduces himself as Dr Chad Morgan and welcomes them before explaining that he'll be teaching Soil Chemistry, Ecology, and Climatology. He promises to send the study plans by the end of the day and throws in a reminder about thesis work. When the doors open next, Stefan hopes this is who he's been waiting for, but his crestfallen face makes Jason chuckle. "Looks like the lady might not be teaching you after all."

"I'll find her office."

"And if she turns out to be a snob?"

"She doesn't seem like the type."

Another man walks onto the stage. He introduces himself as Dr Kurt Sherwood and explains he is their Meteorology, Biometeorology, and Aerobiology lecturer. He advises them to read the first topic of the biometeorology study plan for tomorrow. The next time the doors open, Stefan doesn't even bother to look up, bracing himself for more disappointment. But then he hears the soft click of heels against the wooden floor.

He glances up as the newcomer connects her laptop to the projector, her head bowed in concentration.

"God, she's beautiful," Jason breathes.

She smiles as if she hears the compliment. But Stefan already knows who she is, even before she speaks.

⚘

Dr Adeowo scans the room, her gaze sweeping over the rows of expectant faces. Unlike the previous lecturers, who had a brisk, businesslike approach, there's a quiet grace about her—a calm that suggests she genuinely wants to be here, guiding this motley crew towards academic success.

"Good afternoon. I am Doctor Jolade Adeowo," she begins, her voice carrying a soft lilt. "My friends call me Jola, so if I can accomplish the Herculean task of befriending each and every one of you, you may call me that."

The room erupts in laughter.

"However," she continues, "you can call me Doctor A. Hi, everyone."

A thunderous "Hi, Doctor A!" echoes back at her as if they were greeting a favourite celebrity rather than an environmental science lecturer.

"I'm sure my colleagues explained this is just an introduction session." She gestures towards the last row. "If the person in the back could start us off with their name, country of origin, and pronouns, we'll work our way forward."

The introduction begins with the lady Jason has been staring at. "Jaklina Čizmić, Croatia, she/her," she says, setting the rhythm for the others.

Stefan listens attentively as his classmates introduce themselves, mentally ticking off names and countries. The room is a microcosm of the United Nations: Ghanaians, Nigerians, a few Europeans, Americans, a South African, and four non-binary students. The diversity in the room is something to behold—a vibrant mosaic of backgrounds and identities.

At the end of the introduction, Stefan raises his hand, prepared to clarify Jason's presence, just in case Dr A is keeping a headcount. "Yes, Stefan?" she acknowledges him with a nod.

"My friend here," he taps Jason on the shoulder, "is a student of International Management. Is it okay for him to stay just for today? He has to drive me home."

"He can stay," Dr A replies. "I know better than to annoy our drivers."

The room fills with a fresh wave of laughter, and even Jason can't help but grin.

"I'm British-Nigerian, and my pronouns are she/her," Dr A continues. "Now that we've gotten acquainted, I hope you all paid attention to each other. We're going to need to get along. I will be teaching you these three courses: Ambient Air Quality, Hydrological Components, and Environmental Protection." She pulls up the study plans on the screen. "These are now in your emails. We'll start with Hydrological Components tomorrow. Can anyone tell me the different HCs?"

Hands shoot up like rockets, eager to prove they've done their homework. Stefan leans over to whisper a component to non-student Jason, who, to Stefan's surprise, is called on to answer. "Rain," Jason says proudly.

"That's impressive."

"Stefan told me," Jason admits.

Dr A chuckles before calling on the other students: Motunrayo's answer is snow, Charles gives rain as his, dew from Jennifer, throughfall from Jaklina, and mist from Antwon.

"Very good," she says, beaming at the class. "Tomorrow, we'll dive into the components and their possible contribution to the water cycle." She checks her watch and frowns slightly. "I realise we've gone over time, and I apologise. Before we wrap up, here is a word about your thesis. Start preparing now, especially for those of you in the one-year programme. Senior lecturers will supervise, but you may choose an adviser between myself, Dr Morgan, or Dr Sherwood. I wish you a—"

Stefan's hand is up, almost involuntarily. He's unsure why he's doing this, but something compels him to make a lasting impression.

"Stefan?"

"I just wanted to thank you for this introduction session," he starts. "It is rare to have a teacher who cares about the individuality of their students. I feel obliged to point it out and thank you for it. I may not speak for the entire class, but I look forward to your classes. I—"

"You're speaking for all of us," calls Natalia.

"We are all looking forward to your classes. Thank you," Stefan adds with a small smile.

Dr A's grin stretches across her oval face. "Thank you, everyone," she practically sings. Then, turning to Stefan, she adds, "If you could wait for a few minutes?" He nods yes. "See you tomorrow at three. Goodbye, everyone."

"Bye, Doctor A."

※

Stefan shakes Dr A's hand, still grappling with that faintly disconcerting sense of familiarity. He can't quite place it but is resolutely confident he's seen her somewhere before.

"It's nice to finally meet you," he says.

"Finally?" she repeats as she shakes Jason.

They remain on stage, Stefan and Jason facing her. He'd ventured through her profile with the meticulousness of a detective, but now, facing the prospect of her judging him, he feels a pang of embarrassment. "Um, yeah. I went through the faculty profiles and was impressed with yours. I was hoping you'd teach me." He pauses, the next words nearly sticking in his throat. "I also think we've met before, but I'm at a loss as to where.

"Her expression softens, and Stefan now remembers to breathe. "You know, I had the same feeling when I saw you," she says. "Perhaps we crossed paths on a train?"

Stefan's eyes widen in disbelief, but it is Jason who replies with dry efficiency. "He hasn't been on the train since his arrival," he says, his phone chiming as he quickly taps away. "We'll need to crack that mystery, though."

"Indeed we shall," Dr A concurs. "I was hoping to discuss whether you'd be interested in collaborating on a review of fog chemistry. It's due for publication."

"Wow... Yes, I'm definitely interested," Stefan replies, his enthusiasm immediate.

"If you have about thirty minutes, we can discuss it in my office, I—"

The doors open, and she glances up. Stefan turns to see Ben approaching with an almost otherworldly poise. Once on stage, Ben focuses solely on Dr A, and Stefan has never seen him look at anyone with such intensity.

"Doctor A," Jason says, turning to her. "This is my older brother, Benjamin Brown. Benny," he directs to his brother. "Meet Doctor Jolade Adeowo."

Ben takes her hand with an air of reverence, lifting it to his lips and pressing a delicate kiss on the back. "Enchanted to meet you," he says, a hint of amusement in his eyes. "You may call me Ben."

"The pleasure is mine, and do call me Jola," she responds warmly.

"Jola? I like it," Ben smiles.

"I have a meeting with Doctor A," Stefan informs. "I'm to work with her on a publication."

"Right, let's go," Ben says.

Jason coughs. "Those documents of yours?"

"The documents?" Ben's demeanour shifts noticeably, a telltale sign of disappointment in his features. He hands Jason the car key. "Yeah, Scott and Kiki are waiting." Turning back to Dr A, he adds, "I hope we can meet again, perhaps become friends?"

"That would be lovely," she tilts her head, nodding in agreement.

"Have a splendid evening."

"And us?" Stefan demands.

"Farewell, kids." Ben turns on his heels and departs.

Stefan walks with Dr A and Jason to her office, their conversation still circling through potential places they might have crossed paths. But as soon as he steps inside the office, it clicks almost immediately. Seated in Dr A's office and staring directly at Stefan is the protagonist of his most vivid dreams—looking even more enthralling than he remembered from six weeks ago.

Stefan lands at London Heathrow Terminal Five and steps off the plane feeling smug about his shorts and plain V-neck—an outfit choice that quickly proves arbitrary given the sweltering heat. He joins the EU queue for passport control and retrieves his bags afterwards. Now, he's off to meet Jason, who is picking him up. As he walks, his phone vibrates and as he attempts to wrestle it from his pocket, he momentarily loses his sense of direction and crashes into someone, the jolt both jarring and surprising. An AirPods case skitters across the floor, and Stefan, in a flurry of apology, bends to retrieve it just as another hand reaches for it. He straightens up to offer the case to the owner but can only gape at the figure before him.

The guy—for he cannot be over twenty-five—stands tall and commanding. He's easily over six feet and has a stature that suggests he spends an admirable amount of time in the gym. His presence effortlessly draws the eye. He is obviously of African descent, with sleek melanated skin that is rich and radiant, neatly trimmed curls, and a clean-shaven jaw. His features are striking—his chiselled jawline is sculpted with the precision of a virtuoso, and his eyes hint at a world of untold stories, pulling Stefan in. The most captivating aspects are his chubby cheeks and perfect roseate lips, which add a softness to his rugged masculinity. This combination is utterly spellbinding and aligns perfectly with Stefan's preferences.

Later, Stefan would describe his reaction as akin to being hit with a stupefying charm from Harry Potter. He keeps his hand poised at his temple, hoping it conceals the look of sheer amazement on his face. He offers a small, apologetic smile and keeps his voice steady. "I am very sorry. I was distracted."

The guy's smile in return is like a burst of sunshine on a dreary day—radiant, sexy, infectious, and capable of melting the iciest hearts. "I," he clears his throat and smiles again. Stefan wants a tutorial on how to smile like that. "I was also distracted. I'm equally sorry." His voice is rich, smooth, and cordial, and his apology is unnecessary because he could do no wrong in Stefan's eyes.

"Here you go," Stefan returns the case. Their fingers brush transiently, sending an unexpected jolt through Stefan.

"Thank you... For picking this up," the guy says, his eyes searching Stefan's face as if trying to memorise it.

For a fleeting moment, the airport noise fades, and it feels like they are the only two people in the world. Eventually, they say their goodbyes, and Stefan watches him join a large group of people who regard him with barely concealed interest. Before disappearing, the guy looks back, their eyes meeting one last time, a hint of something unreadable in his eyes. Stefan turns to see Jason walking towards him with a big grin, dressed like someone who just sauntered off the set of 90210. Stefan knows how insufferable his friend would be if he saw the entire exchange and is not disappointed at all when Jason gets within earshot.

"Hey Stefan. Do you need that much time to return an AirPods case?" Jason asks.

Stefan sighs, "Nice to see you, J. Can we leave? I'm zero point one minute away from fainting."

"Your flight was less than three hours. Stop acting like you've flown in from Australia." Jason scrutinises him. "Or is this your attempt at avoidance? Because that won't do."

Stefan shrugs nonchalantly. It was worth the try. As they head out, he reflects on the encounter, struggling to explain to Jason the inexplicable rush of his heartbeat, the flush of heat to his cheeks, and the tingling sensation coursing through his body. He can't even explain it to himself.

Admittedly, the guy was undeniably attractive, the angels made sure of that. But hadn't he vowed to avoid attachments to steer clear of complications? Stefan might insist he's no coward, but he could easily be a fool. Otherwise, why would he replay the encounter in his head? What is this sense of loss? Why does he suddenly regret not getting to know a stranger with whom he spent less than twenty minutes? The stranger who hadn't even bothered to exchange names, let alone engage in a meaningful conversation. He is fairly sure the guy isn't dwelling on their brief, almost-did-not-happen encounter as Stefan is currently doing, lost in introspection. Realistically, he'll likely never see him again. After all, England is that big. He might even be on his way to Scotland or Wales. Better to forget him, his dazzling physique, and the entire episode.

They drop his bags into Jason's Infiniti QX80 and start the drive. Without any preamble, Jason turns to him. "The bloke is handsome."

Stefan tosses back his answer, light as a feather. "I didn't notice."

Jason's laughter rings out, loud and piercing. He then plays "Bad Liar."

Stefan might have thought he was stupefied six weeks ago, but right now, it feels like he's been struck by the Avada Kedavra curse. The entire airport déjà vu rushes back: heart skyrocketing, cheeks aflame, and those prickling little shocks dancing across his body. Add the fluttering in his stomach to that, and it's a recipe for pure chaos.

He's rooted to the spot, his eyes magnetised to the stranger before him, drawing him closer without a word spoken. An electric charge lingers between them, a silent agreement not to dare look away. The guy's expression alters, a glimmer of something familiar lighting his brown eyes. A slow, knowing smile begins to play at the corner of Stefan's mouth.

"Perhaps," Jason suggests with a hint of mischief, "we could all introduce ourselves?"

"I'll handle that. Jason, Stefan," Dr A gestures, "this is my brother, Teniade." She turns to him. "Jason and Stefan, I met them at the introduction session. Stefan is my student, and Jason is his friend."

Stefan already understands why Dr A looks familiar. The resemblance to her brother is uncanny; it's practically flashing neon. It doesn't even require a genius to figure that out.

"You can call me Ade," he says, extending a hand to Jason.

"Nice to meet you," Jason responds, shaking firmly.

Ade's smile is disarmingly charming. Stefan feels his heart tingle as he says, "Ade," clasping his long fingers around Stefan's smaller, delicate hand.

Stefan feels drunk on something potent.

They maintain their handshake, neither willing to let go. It must be the longest handshake in recorded history. The office fades into the background; all that matters is the sizzling air between them. They keep staring at each other, their eyes speaking volumes, and Stefan is instantly transported back to the airport, reliving that unforgettable first encounter and igniting a flurry of euphoria within him. Meeting Ade here feels surreal, like a scene lifted straight from a romance novel. It looks nothing like real life. It feels like he's alone with Ade in a universe of their creation.

"I have the table," Dr A breaks into their universe. "If you can come around, Stefan."

He would love nothing more than to drag Ade along, but reluctantly lets go of his hand and moves to the screen. Ade also seems unwilling to break their contact. Stefan finds this oddly reassuring,

"Can the title of the paper be added?" Stefan suggests, studying the table, "Not just the references."

"That makes sense," Dr A agrees, adding it. "Any other suggestions?"

"The sample collection year. It might differ from the publication year."

"I won't regret choosing you," she smiles warmly. "I'm sharing the document with you now."

Stefan glances up then, he sees Ade and Jason by the bookshelves, whispering and laughing about something.

"Um, I was wondering," he says shyly, "if it would be okay with you to be my adviser?"

"Of course. It is okay," she beams. "We're already going to be spending some time together. I will inform the head of department tomorrow." She sends the document to him. "Pardon my oversight. Do you think you can manage this alongside your regular coursework?"

He nods eagerly. "Yes... Absolutely. I mean this is a fantastic opportunity for me. I also need to build my publication list for PhD applications. So, thank you," he says, mirroring her smile.

Stefan thrives on busyness; idleness drives him mad. That's why he took a part-time role at Ben's company—his mind needs constant occupation because it is prone to wandering and getting ahead of him.

An idle hand is the devil's handjob, or is it playground? He'll have to google that quote later to be sure.

"We can work on more after this, and I can help you with your application." She looks up. "What are you both whispering about?"

Jason and Ade return to the desk. "Do you know?" Jason asks. "It was Ade you crashed into at the airport."

Of course, he knows, duh. And he's sure Jason knows

but has found a way to tease him. Stefan played right into his friend's callous trap.

Stefan's cheeks burn up again.

"That must be why I thought you looked familiar!" Dr A exclaims.

"You were there?" Jason asks.

"You were?" Dr A echoes.

"I witnessed the whole thing!" Jason boasts. "But I didn't see you."

"We were by the door, observing," she says, flashing a quick grin, her teeth gleaming. "Ade, where is my food?"

"In your kitchen," Ade says, rolling his eyes with a droll smile. "You're welcome."

Something he can't quite name courses through Stefan; his fingers twitching involuntarily, and his senses sharpen, all driven by an odd surge of adrenaline. *What's happening here, for God's sake?*

"Wow, I can't believe we're meeting you again," Dr A chuckles, "I tea—"

"Don't you need to eat?" Ade interrupts through gritted teeth.

"I'm hungry, truly," she says, turning to Jason. "Wanna join me?"

Jason considers. "What do you have?"

"Ade, what do I have?"

"Cheeseburgers."

"I shall join you." Jason follows her through a door by the bookshelves, leaving Stefan alone with Ade in the office. A moment later, Jason's head reappears. "Don't forget to get his mobile number this time," he practically shouts, his voice ringing through the room.

"I'll kill him," Stefan mumbles, his voice crackling with mock menace.

Ade's laughter ripples beside him, its seductive timbre hanging in the air.

Calm TF down, Stefan.

"I like him," Ade says, pulling out a chair for Stefan. He is pleased by this.

Stefan takes his seat. "I like him, except on days when he's driving me to homicidal thoughts."

"Is that standard advice?" Ade queries, his lips forming a tiny, cute downturn. "For you to obtain people's contact?"

How does a frown manage to look so charming? Stefan thinks he might need divine intervention to cope with this.

"This is the first time," Stefan replies, his smile crooked. "Maybe because Ben didn't get your sister's phone number."

"Who's Ben?" Ade asks, curiosity dancing in his eyes.

"Jason's brother," Stefan explains.

Ade leans forward. Stefan leans forward.

"Why should Jason's brother have Jola's number?" his eyes rove across Stefan's face, examining. "And why didn't he get it?"

A boldness overtakes Stefan from nowhere. It could be sheer recklessness or the knowledge that Ade hasn't forgotten him. "Give me your phone number," he requests, locking eyes with Ade. "And I'll explain."

"Wow," Ade's lips edge in a smile. "You're good."

"What's it going to be?"

Ade studies Stefan's face as if it holds the answer. "Give me your phone."

Ade takes Stefan's phone, types his number, and dials it before handing it back. Stefan saves the number with almost supernatural speed. Their conversation carries on—endless and delightful. They discover they were both at Tesco on Saturday and in the library today. Stefan begins to believe in the idea that the world is far smaller than it seems.

"Where are you from?" Ade asks.

"Sweden."

Ade's eyes gleam with triumph. "I guessed the Nordic countries when you bumped into me."

"I should apologise for that," he says with a wry smile. "Clumsy of me not looking where I was going."

Stefan is thoroughly enjoying their interaction, despite the brevity. There's something about Ade that outstrips mere physical appearance, a charisma that could enthral the soul of anyone fortunate enough to cross his path. It makes every moment in his presence feel special.

"You don't have to," Ade chuckles. "Don't think I don't know you're ribbing me."

"It's a newly discovered talent."

"How many minutes do you think it should take?" Ade glances towards the kitchen door, "to heat two cheeseburgers?"

Stefan scoffs. "You know they left us here on purpose?"

"You mean they don't care about our virtues?" Ade asks, feigning ignorance.

They lean even closer. Stefan feels Ade's breath on his skin, raising the hairs at the back of his neck. "Jason couldn't care less for my virtue," he says, biting the corner of his mouth. "Should I be scared for my virtue?"

Ade swallows, adjusts in his chair, and clears his throat. Stefan's lips curl into a satisfied smile as he notes the shift.

"Your virtue is safe," Ade replies with a slight cough, his voice laced with something intriguing. "For now."

Stefan's cheeks flush once more. It's no fault of his. Who turned up the thermostat? They're leaning in so close that Stefan can see the tiny details of Ade's eyes; he can sketch a map of his face. "For now," he repeats.

"I'm glad to meet you again," the words seem to spill out of Ade involuntarily.

Stefan then feels a sudden silly possession over him, a gravitational pull that defies explanation. His hand moves of its own accord, reaching out to grasp Ade's left hand. He relishes the comforting feel of Ade's skin beneath his thumb as he traces soft circles. Ade closes his eyes briefly, leaning even closer until their noses almost touch. The proximity sends a pulse through Stefan, stirring an intense urge to kiss Ade. The urge is so inundating that it borders on agony. But he holds back; they've only just met, even though it feels like they've known each other for ages. In Stefan's mind, however, he's lived with the presence of Ade for the past six weeks. He may feel reckless and bold, but Stefan isn't quite that brazen—at least not yet. He'll see how the rest of the day unfolds.

"I'm glad to meet you again, too," Stefan says in almost a whisper. "Do you go here? Or only drive your sister?"

"I enrolled a few minutes ago," Ade replies, his smile brightening.

"I feel like there's a story there."

"There is indeed. I may tell you later."

"Why not now?" Stefan asks, his eyes travelling over Ade's face, pausing on his eyes and lips.

Ade swallows again. Stefan's eyes trail the movement, tempted by the motion that travels down his throat, wanting to follow it all the way. Honestly, Stefan deserves an award for not jumping the guy: everything about Ade's demeanour practically screams, *kiss me, kiss me*.

"It's a rather long story," Ade says, squeezing Stefan's hand lightly.

Another set of tiny shocks rushes through Stefan's body. He needs to kiss Ade—in the next five seconds. It defies every rule he gave himself before moving to England, but one kiss shouldn't hurt—although Dua Lipa will disagree.

Ade's voice breaks him out of his wayward thoughts. "Will you be here tomorrow?"

"Yes, classes start tomorrow."

There's a specific kind of invitation in Ade's eyes as his head moves forward another centimetre. And it makes Stefan's decision for him. He throws caution to the wind, leaning in to bridge the gap between them until their foreheads touch. There is no hesitation on Ade's face. His lips part slightly, and his breath catches.

Stefan's heart thumbs wildly in his chest. *This is going to happen*.

Just as their lips are about to meet, a noise outside the door startles them. Stefan retracts with lightning speed.

3
INTRODUCTION

*— We're All in This Together
from High School Musical.*

"Ade, isn't that the car we admired this morning?" Ay's sharp eyes spot the car first, her finger darting out like a compass needle.

The evening sun bathes the BMW iX in a light that seems almost envious, as if the heavens themselves wish they could afford such a luxurious chariot. Ade squints, the reflection of the car glinting in his eyes. "I think you're right," he replies, half to himself, half to the universe, looking from his bZ4X to the iX.

"It's Ben's car," Jason supplies. "He dropped us this morning. Must have seen him on his way out."

"Tani Ben?" Ay and MT inquire, their synchrony almost suspiciously perfect.

"Jason's brother," Jola explains.

That piques Ay's curiosity. "How did you know Jason's brother?"

"Yes, Jughead, how?" Ade smirks.

"We met earlier," Jola says, vanishing into the car with all the mystique of a character from a noir film.

Ade laughs, walking Stefan to the iX. "We didn't see the driver, though, and she even missed the whole thing."

Stefan casually leans against the car. "Jason coordinated it for them to meet."

"Tell me the story. I need ammunition against her."

"Still not telling." Stefan's smile is so perfect, it makes Ade's resolve crumbles like a poorly baked scone.

Fuck my life.

"Are they watching?" he asks, eyes darting back to his car.

"They're not. Jason is weaving some of his dubious tales, I'm sure."

There's a gravity here, something magnetic that pulls Ade towards Stefan, like the universe is bringing them together for a purpose that is not yet revealed. It's impossible to ignore this connection—one that feels ancient and brand new, like rediscovering a favourite book on a forgotten shelf. Every fibre of Ade's being wants to rush, to dive headfirst, but his brain reminds him to take it slow, even as his heart rebels against such prudence. Frankly, if asked, Ade can mention a million ways he aspires to be close to Stefan. His body's reaction to Stefan is unmatched. It cannot be mistaken—the subtle roll of his eyes, the subconscious fluttering of his eyelashes, his contagious smile. They elicit a visceral response from Ade that he struggles to control.

"What time will you be here tomorrow?" Ade asks, lost in soft, pale blue eyes.

"Nine-thirty at the latest. Mine and Jason's classes start

at ten." Stefan pauses, considering. "Did you ask for a reason?"

"Yes, maybe we could have lunch?" Ade leans in, his voice dropping to a whisper. "If you wish."

"I'd like that. We can text about details later," he smiles, a promise in his expression. "Jason is here."

Ade opens the passenger door for Stefan and leans in when the window rolls down. "Wanna race to Newcastle?" he asks Jason.

"You have quite the interview waiting for you," Jason chuckles. "You're not up for a race, trust me."

There's no avoiding it, Ade knows—the inquisition awaits, and it's bound to be relentless.

"I'll see you both tomorrow," he says, lifting his hand. He feels Stefan's fingers brush his knuckles lightly. He couldn't help but smile, walking back to his car. By the time he climbs in, the iX is gone.

"Finally, he has our time," Jola announces as he drives back to Albert Road.

"You can't even pretend disinterest?"

"What would that achieve?" Ay says.

"*Tí mi ó bá wà interested, mo lè kú*—I can die if I'm not interested," MT says with a dramatic flair that would make a Shakespearean actress proud.

"Okay, okay, what do you wanna know?"

"Will you see him again?"

"What did you talk about?"

"Did he say he likes you?"

"Did you get his phone number?"

"How old is he?"

"Did you kiss?"

Ade sighs, regretting every life choice that led him to this moment. "Who asked the kiss question?"

"Jola," MT and AY chorus.

"What's wrong with you?" Ade asks his sister.

She has the decency to look abashed. "Jason planted it in my head. He said if he was left alone with someone he'd been thinking about for weeks, he'd be on his knees instantly. My first reaction was to ask why he would propose. It took me another five minutes to understand."

Ade laughs as he quickly tucks away that nugget about Stefan thinking of him, storing it for later analysis in the privacy of his own thoughts.

MT taps him and asks in the soft voice she uses when she wants something. "The question is hanging. You can as well answer."

"There was no kissing, people of God." He counts off his free hand. "Let's see. Will I see him again? I don't see how not to, considering we're enrolled in the same school."

"Free rides every day," cries MT.

"No smelly trains," AY sings happily.

"You enrolled!" Jola exclaims, her lips twitching into a brief smile. "My next mission is to make sure you become a lecturer."

That's classic Jola—everyone's a potential educator in her world. Her passions, though, don't stop at education. She's on a personal crusade to save the planet, recruiting her family and friends into an eco-army one by one. Ay is just as fervent, and together, they've roped in their other friends—Sasha, Priya, Peyton, and even Sasha's boyfriend, Martins. They're like an environmentalist Avengers team, minus the spandex.

"Moving on, what did we talk about? Random things. He's twenty-two, a—"

"You're only a year older! He looks so much younger" Jola cuts in. "Very appropriate."

"What is the next question?"

"If he said he likes you." MT supplies eagerly.

"Not in many words. We did just meet. Wouldn't it be weird?"

"Humph. There's nothing weird about it. We've heard of love at first sight," Ay insists.

"Theirs would be love at first crash," Jola quips.

Ade waves them off, his mind sojourning back to Jola's office. No, nothing that passed between him and Stefan could ever be weird to him.

"So, what's with you and Chad?" Jola turns her attention to Ay. "Should we start shipping?"

"We'll need to get to know each other, no?" Ay chuckles. "We can't all crash in love like Mr. Smitten here."

Ade knows there will be no end to this teasing. His doom is sealed.

"Oh God, you really have to be stopped," he groans.

"Nothing can stop me, baby," Ay pats his shoulder with mock seriousness.

MT gasps dramatically as though she's just uncovered a royal scandal. "I wonder what Kurt will do now that Ade is unavailable."

"Omg, you noticed also?" Jola turns back. "He even asked if you and Ade are together."

"Of course, I noticed. He wants to lather baked beans on Ade and eat him."

"Why baked beans?" Ade wrinkles his nose in distaste.

"I don't know what you British people eat," MT shrugs, unbothered. "And you didn't believe me when I told you."

"I believe you now," he admits. "He may have flirted with me while waiting for Jola."

"What happened?" three voices demand in unison.

"I may have flirted back."

"Tell us moreeee."

"Nothing much. I shut it down pretty quickly, and we returned to polite conversation."

Three collective sighs of disappointment signal the end of that chapter.

"By the way," Ay says, tapping Jola. "Do you know how you got home on Saturday?"

Jola scoffs. "I woke up yesterday in my bed. I remember nothing."

"I took her to bed," Ade pauses, frowning as the words hang in the air. "That didn't sound right. I mean I helped her to her room."

The ladies double over, laughing like they've just heard the world's best joke.

"Excusing the fact that she's my sister, so like, gross," Ade waggles a finger, trying to maintain some semblance of dignity. "The irony isn't lost on me if that's what you find funny."

But they don't stop laughing, and deep down, Ade knows he wouldn't have it any other way.

"Come in," Jola calls from the other side of the door. Ade enters the room with the faintest of sighs, knowing fully well what lies ahead. Jola stands by her bed, cradling a bowl of popcorn.

Of course, this is Jola—master of ceremonies when it comes to their 'TV sessions'. "I was getting everything ready for our sitcom time," she announces with an exaggerated sweep of her arm as if unveiling a grand masterpiece.

She had taken every opportunity to hound him during

dinner, gleefully recounting his reunion with Stefan, including some imitations and embellishments as she narrated the story. It's a wonder she didn't launch into a full theatrical performance, but there's always a next time. She'd then casually mentioned her *Seinfeld* rewatch, throwing in the invitation with all the grace of a general issuing a decree. Ade—shockingly—accepted without his usual grumblings.

Ade groans, the sound halfway between reluctance and surrender. "I should've expected this. You do take movie time seriously."

He's careful to sound inconvenienced, but he's quite pleased to spend time with her—he always is. Despite their six-year gap, Jola has never treated him like the annoying younger brother he secretly suspects himself to be. No, she's always been his friend, his confidant—the one person who never put him on some untouchable, unattainable pedestal. While they both love their older brother, Temmy, his mountain of responsibilities sets them apart. And even when Ade moved with their parents to Nigeria as a child, it didn't break the bond between him and Jola. That, it seemed, was immune to distance.

"See who's talking," Jola mutters. "You wouldn't be complaining if Stefan invited you."

He refuses to dignify that with a response and climbs onto the bed beside her. The room, in its riot of soft pastels, is something only Jola could pull off. What might have been garish in bolder hues is somehow calming, ethereal even, and exists in its own dreamscape—sea foam wallpaper meets lavender and beige furniture, while peach drapes frame the room. Even the floor, worn wood with character, seems to belong here. Ade's eyes flick to the photo frames on her chest of drawers, noticing two missing frames that had been there in April—replaced by empty space that says more than words could. But with her good mood tonight, he decides against asking questions.

The Netflix logo flashes on the screen, that little chime like a Pavlovian bell. And even though they've seen the sitcom and others alike more times than should be humanly possible, they still find themselves cackling. Ade especially loves this one—the semi-finale of season seven. By the time Kramer's ill-advised battle with a pair of too-tight jeans concludes, they're both clutching their sides, wiping away tears—of laughter, mostly. Jola places the now half-empty bowl of popcorn atop her drawer, turning to him with a face that suddenly has its serious lines drawn in. "Ade, are you okay? Truly?"

He once again reaches into his usual crest of well-rehearsed gems, but with Jola, lying is like trying to smuggle daylight past a rooster. She always knows, even when she pretends otherwise.

"I am, but I don't want to think about it. Not now," he breathes a heavy sigh, contemplating. "If I didn't have the support I've had, it would've been harder. But I'm sure time will lessen the blow," he adds with a small, forced chuckle. "Pun absolutely intended."

She gives a faint smile. "I suppose if you can joke about it, I shouldn't be too worried. But," she pauses, pursing her lips. "I'm worried, still. You gave up a lot to come back here. And I think you should consider therapy, please. Work through it. Keeping it all in is not how you heal."

Ade is silent for a moment, considering. He's not keeping anything in. He's *not* even thinking about it, not really. Sure, his plans might have taken a detour, but he has options—plenty of them, thanks to family connections. And if he so wishes, he wouldn't need a job. Not when God places him in generational wealth. If he insists, however, he could take up a cushy position in one of Nathan's parents' companies. But the thought of coasting through life on nepotism leaves a bad taste in his mouth. He's always wanted something of his own, earned by his own two hands. Maybe that's what stings the most, but what's the use of dwelling on things he can't change?

He squeezes Jola's hand reassuringly. "Are *you* also okay, Jughead?" he asks, cheekily steering the conversation away from him. "Did the nightmares stop?"

Jola glances at the drawer where the missing frames should be, then places her other hand over his. "Some days are better than others," she admits. "But I've had two years, and therapy helped. I know nothing will fix me completely, but maybe time will make it more bearable."

"And today? Did it go well?" Ade asks, peering at her face. "I know it's not exactly what you planned. I guess I'm just trying to make sure."

"It was great," she says, brightening. "The students are awesome. And this, teaching, is still my dream, even if I had to put it on hold. So, yeah. Time to get on with it." She pats his chubby cheeks. "You should consider therapy, Ade. Doctor Sparks is good."

He sucks in a breath. "I... I don't even know how to talk about it. I hardly did with you guys. It seems... shameful, to say the least."

Jola's eyes flash as she sits up straight, turning to face him head-on. "Listen to me, Teniade Adeowo," she says, her tone deliberate, picking her words carefully. "What happened to you is not your fault, and you have *nothing* to be ashamed of. We are who we are, what we are. And I have watched you grow into this amazing person. A caring, thoughtful, and responsible young man." She points at him. "You, my brother, are not defined by someone else's rotten opinion. Therapy shouldn't be something you shy away from out of shame. Do you hear me?"

Ade shuts his eyes, holding his tears at bay. "I hear you. Perfectly."

Tuesday, 20th September 2022.

"Nathannnnnnnnnnnnn," Jola shrieks with the enthusiasm of a teenager at a boyband concert, launching herself out of the car before Ade can even begin to park properly. She practically catapults into the open arms of Nathan, Ade's best friend and partner in crime.

Nathan catches Jola effortlessly, lifting her as if she weighs only a strand of wool, and spins her around with the sort of abandon usually reserved for children. When he finally sets her down, they lock into a hug that stretches on for what seems like several minutes. The hug is just breaking when Ade and the others reach Nathan's jet-black Range Rover Velar.

Ade and Nathan have always been each other's rock—strong, steadfast, and occasionally weather-beaten by the storms of life but always there. Nathan even had a say in Ade's return to England. It was his idea to apply for the master's programmes together. However, he's always viewed postgraduate degrees with the same enthusiasm one might have for a root canal unless, of course, you're an academic like Jola. But for Ade, Nathan is willing to make the exception, knowing the distraction will do him good after the turmoil of June. They'd do anything for each other, these two.

Nathaniel Dore is more than a best friend to Ade; he's the brother he chose, the one God forgot to assign by blood.

"Hello, little bro," Nathan pulls Ade into a hug that's just shy of bone-crushing.

"You are only a month older," Ade retorts, "and I'm taller than you."

"Go use am cash money for bank."

"I regret teaching a British man pidgin. No be your fault at all," Ade huffs, then turns to Ay and MT. "These are our friends, MT and Ay. You've already met them virtually, but this is the grand, in-person debut."

Nathan embraces them. "I've been looking forward to seeing you both. Apologies for not joining the airport welcome party. I was out of the country. And the minute I got back, this guy," he jerks a thumb at Ade, "turned me into some furniture-making workman."

"You didn't make the furniture, only p—" Ade starts but is cut off as Ben's iX purrs into a nearby parking space, diverting his attention.

"Oooohhhhh, Nathan, perfect timing," Jola interrupts, bouncing on the balls of her feet. "You'll meet Stefan."

Nathan shoots Ade an accusatory glance, the kind that says, *What have you gotten yourself into now?* Ade wonders what on earth that's about.

"So, it's airport guy," Nathan mutters, shaking his head in mock disbelief. "Jola mentioned him on our call last night. You chose a school because of a boy? I—" he cuts himself off as Ade steps forward to open Stefan's door. "I shall have stern words with you, Valet," he whispers menacingly just as Stefan emerges from the car.

Ade introduces Nathan to Stefan and Jason, though he

can't help but notice Nathan's eyes narrowing ever so slightly when they land on Stefan. As they begin the walk towards the science building, Ade falls into step beside Stefan, their fingers brushing lightly, sending sparks up Ade's arm.

"Hello," he mouths.

"Hello to you," Stefan mouths back before whispering, "We should have lunch with everyone, don't you think?"

Yesterday's lunch suggestion had been a private affair in his mind, just the two of them—was he not clear enough?

"Sure," he whispers back, the word slipping out more easily than he expected.

Before he leaves with Nathan and MT, they all agree to meet by twelve-thirty at the cafeteria near the library. By the time Nathan, MT, and Ade pick up their class schedules, they find out the only task for the day is a quick visit to the lab—which Daniel had already shown Ade and MT yesterday.

"Hi, Dr. Groza," MT says first, her voice sweetened by what might just be a crush on her thesis advisor.

In the lab, they meet two other classmates who promptly introduce themselves.

"Hiroshi Sode," the Japanese guy shakes them, "but I go by Rosh."

"PengFei Tang," the Chinese girl follows, her smile bright. "Peng is fine."

"This must be the best friend," Daniel says, shaking Nathan's hand before explaining that today's only purpose is for him to talk to students in groups and answer any questions. "I already covered that with you two," he adds to Ade and MT.

"So, this is our group, then?" Nathan says, his cheerfulness returning.

After leaving the lab, they invite Rosh and Peng to join them for lunch, to which they agree. Walking into the cafeteria, they spot their friends at a table with three extra seats. On seeing they are five, Jason adds two more. Ade sits next to Stefan, making introductions once again. He's lost count of how many people he's introduced since yesterday.

Jason clears his throat in a manner indicating an announcement. "Before I forget, we have a party on Saturday."

Saturday, 24th September 2022.

"It's called legwork," Ade explains with the patience of a man who knows his audience might not pass this dance examination. "You've got to loosen up. Relax your body. Your feet should be a shoulder-width apart, then bend your knees slightly to stay flexible. And let the rhythm do the work."

By the end of his tutorial, Rosh is the only one who's managed something that even vaguely resembles legwork, though it's more like an awkward shuffle than anything that can be seen on a dance floor in Lagos. Ade can't help but burst out laughing as he retreats to the couch with Stefan, still catching his breath. "Zlatan shouldn't see that. The song is called 'Zanku' for a reason."

They sink into the soft couch, Stefan turning his body towards Ade and draping his legs casually across Ade's lap. "We gave it our best shot," Stefan says with a chuckle. "But that's a complicated dance. I'd love to see you try Vals or Slängpolska."

Ade raises a confused brow. "What on earth are those?"

"Swedish dances," Stefan explains, a hint of pride in his voice. "Vals is similar to waltz."

"Well," Ade says with a grin, "if you're willing to teach, I'm sure I'll execute them with perfect form."

"Are you asking for dance lessons, Mr. Adeowo?" Stefan's voice drops into a seductive murmur.

Ade swallows. "Maybe," he replies, nodding towards the dance floor. "Or get Jason and Jaklina to teach me whatever *that* is."

Jason and Lina are dancing to "Despacito". Or rather, engaging in what can only be described as an enthusiastic and public display of almost affection. It's salsa in the loosest sense of the word, though Ade is pretty sure salsa usually involves more rhythm and less horizontal intent. The dance floor is also populated by Nathan, MT, Rosh, and Peng, all lost in their own worlds of swaying hips and questionable moves. Meanwhile, Jola's friends and Martins are parked at a nearby table, keeping the drinks flowing. Ben exited earlier with his friends, and Jola disappeared soon after. Neither has resurfaced.

"I think your friend doesn't like me. Nathan, not MT," Stefan says suddenly, his tone matter-of-fact, as if commenting on the weather.

Ade whips his face sideways to look at Stefan. "Did he say something to you?"

"No, nothing like that. It's just a feeling," Stefan replies, his words starting to slur ever so slightly. "Don't worry about it."

"I'll definitely worry about it," Ade insists, lifting a hand to Stefan's face, intent on some small gesture of comfort.

Stefan flinches.

It's a subtle movement, the kind that most people might overlook, but Ade is not most people. He wonders if it's the alcohol or something else entirely and hesitates, letting his hand fall back to his side.

"Is Jason invited next week?" Stefan asks, shifting the conversation as if eager to move past whatever just happened.

"Of course, everyone is invited. We informed Sophia."

"Who's Sophia?"

"My sister-in-law."

"Is she Nigerian?"

"Yes. But originally British before we poached her."

"What's your brother's name?" Stefan chuckles, leaning in closer. "And your nephews?"

"Temilade," Ade says, leaning in as well. "And the boys are Ademide, Eniade, and Adedeji."

"Ages?" Stefan asks. "Your nephews, I mean. Not your brother."

"Thirteen, twelve, and almost four."

Stefan nods. "They're kissing," he says, looking at the dance floor.

Sure enough, Jason and Lina have moved from dancing to something far more intense, their passionate embrace almost making the rest of the room disappear. Ade watches, amused but not entirely surprised. If they weren't surrounded by friends, he's sure they'd be well on their way to abandoning clothes altogether.

"They could hit it off," Ade says.

"Hope it doesn't get messy," Stefan mumbles. "She's the only friend I have from class. I should have known this was his plan when he made me invite her."

"Is he that notorious?"

Before Stefan can answer, his attention is diverted. "That's my jammmm!" Stefan exclaims, springing to his feet with the kind of energy only good music can conjure.

He grabs Ade's hand, dragging him towards the dance floor as "Pepas" blares through the speakers. Ade barely has time to protest before he's swept up in the rhythm, the conversation about Nathan and the mystery of Stefan's flinch pushed to the back of his mind.

For now, it's just the music, the dance floor, and Stefan.

4

THE PARTY

— Turn Up by Olamide.

"We should stop meeting like this," Ade quips, his hand gently massaging Stefan's temple.

It's the kind of touch that doesn't demand relief but offers it, nonetheless, leaving Stefan's brain to grapple with the very notion of the distance he promised himself he'd keep. The promise, it seems, hasn't quite reached his body, which is already betraying him by craving Ade. It's been seven weeks since they first collided at the airport, surrounded by a crowd of curious onlookers, but now, without an audience, the sensation is more intense.

On Monday, Stefan had made a pact with himself to maintain a respectful distance until they know each other better. He'd even orchestrated lunch plans involving other people to act as buffers because being alone with Ade might prove too tempting. Yet here he is, close enough to count the hair on Ade's head, his self-control dangling by a thread.

Despite his carefully laid plans, every brush of their

fingers, every eye contact, every accidental touch only heightens Stefan's awareness of Ade. Once, Stefan had even plucked a stray fibre from Ade's neck, a brief but charged contact that sent a jolt through him like a bolt of lightning. So, at night, when he replays their interactions, coupled with flirting with Ade via texts and calls, and his body tightens, demanding release, he has a vivid image to help himself.

He clears his throat, trying to gather himself. "Hi," he manages, though his voice is more of a croak than he'd like.

Ade smiles in that disarming way of his, and Stefan feels like he's been hit by a pleasant, slow-moving freight train. "Hi," he replies, his hand lingering on Stefan's temple just a moment longer than necessary before reluctantly pulling away. Stefan, however, would rather that hand stayed exactly where it was. "You look good."

Stefan's fingers instinctively reach for the gold chain on Ade's neck. "You are not bad looking yourself," he murmurs.

Ade's nostrils flare subtly as he leans in to sniff him like a police dog. "Ombré Leather?" he guesses.

Stefan nods, a faint smile tugging at his lips. "Correct." His fingers trace the chain absentmindedly. "This is nice."

Ade could just say "thank you" and leave it at that, but he doesn't. Instead, his hand closes around Stefan's wrist, and all of Stefan's senses go haywire. Ade's steady gaze reminds Stefan exactly why he thought buffers were necessary.

"Ben got a DJ?" Ade asks, his head tilting slightly as the music from the patio wafts to the base of the stairs.

"And a bartender," Stefan adds, a soft chuckle escaping him.

They both laugh, but the distance between them shrinks imperceptibly—or maybe it's Stefan's doing, his hand still hanging onto Ade's chain, pulling him closer? There's no way to tell who's closing the gap, only that they're now so close that Stefan is staring at Ade deep in those sexy eyes of his, framed by long, lush lashes. Despite the dimness, they have a subtle shine, like stars in the night sky—bewitching Stefan. Suddenly, Stefan is back in Jola's office on Monday, where the air felt misty with unspoken need. His heart pounds, his stomach flips, and the urge to kiss Ade is almost overwhelming. It's as though an invisible force is pulling them together, a silent proposition hanging in the air, Ade's eyes drawing him inexorably closer.

"Can I k—" Stefan begins but is abruptly cut off by the sound of the patio door opening, shattering the spell like a dropped glass.

Jason appears, looking down at them from the top of the stairs, a grin plastered on his face. Perfect timing, as always.

Now is not the time to make an appearance. Fuck off, but like in an "I love you" way.

Jason smirks. "The offer still stands," he says before retreating back to the party, leaving a frustrated Stefan and a curious Ade behind.

"I'll kill him," Stefan mutters under his breath.

"What offer?" Ade looks genuinely curious, but his smile is crooked.

Stefan sighs, letting his head fall against Ade's chest in mock defeat. "You don't want to know."

Ade chuckles softly, the vibrations rumbling through his chest. "I think we should join the party," he suggests, his hand moving to Stefan's waist, massaging it in a way that's far too distracting.

"I need five minutes," Stefan mumbles, lifting his head. He knows his face is flushed, and not just from the proximity. "And you need to stop that if you're serious about joining the party."

"What party?" Ade probes, a slight curve at the corners of his mouth. Stefan is seconds away from abandoning all pretence of propriety and dragging Ade upstairs to show him exactly what he's been imagining since Monday. But Ade pulls back slightly, concern flashing across his face. "You okay?"

"Yeah," Stefan nods, biting his lips.

"I was going to invite you to my brother's place next Saturday before I got... side-tracked."

Stefan rolls his eyes. "What for?"

"It's my nephew's birthday," Ade explains. "Since it is also Nigeria's Independence Day, we're throwing an after-party. The kid's party ends by five, and the adults' party starts then."

"Adults party?" he quirks a brow.

"Stef, your mind is dirty."

"Stef?" he chirps, momentarily distracted. "I like it," he adds, a slow smile spreading across his face.

"Has no one ever called you that?"

"None," he confirms, his eyes drifting over Ade's features. "You should call me that."

Ade laughs, shaking his head. "So, are you free?"

Internally, Stefan shouts, "Of course!" but outwardly, he keeps his cool, leaning back slightly. "I'm free," he says with a nonchalant shrug. "What does your nephew like?" At Ade's confused look, Stefan clarifies. "It's his birthday, right?"

"Cars," Ade says, grinning widely. "He's obsessed with them."

Stefan nods, making a mental note. "We can go up now, I think."

"Here they are," Rosh announces, gesturing to Ade and Stefan as they stroll in, hand in hand. Stefan heads straight for Jason's side while Ade detours the refreshment table. After snatching up two sandwiches, he reclaims his spot beside Stefan, right next to Nathan, who, from Stefan's perspective, seems to regard him with a haughty disdain before muttering something to Ade.

Stefan takes a moment to survey the patio of Ben's house at Twenty-Four Darras Hall, where they are having the party. On one side, a teal-green medium-sized couch with incredibly soft cushions sits resplendent, flanked by high-backed chairs of the same colour. Soft peach blankets drape over the furniture, with a small glass stool between them adorned with a beautiful vase of red roses—Jola's favourite. In the middle of the room is the party table, surrounded by twenty comfortable-looking chairs.

After Ben introduces Ade to Scott and Kiki, he heads to Theo, the bartender. "He makes the best cocktails," Ben booms, handing out the drinks menu.

Sasha and Priya whisper conspiratorially, with Jola's eyes trained on them like a hawk. Clearly irked by their secrecy, she demands, "Come out with it."

"I'm already out," Priya replies with a faux innocent look.

"Good one, babe," Peyton praises her girlfriend. "They think Ben is the gorgeous man they saw at Neely's last Saturday." She reports happily.

"We were there last Saturday," Jason declares, slamming his hand on the table as if it were a gavel of truth.

Ben was correct then about seeing Jola, but Jason's

dramatic table slam is a tad much. "Must you be so dramatic?" Stefan inquires.

"Ben is the beautiful man you were sad not to have seen?" MT ask, turning to Jola.

The conversation explodes with overlapping voices, and Jola's friends start laughing until Theo appears.

"We should order drinks," Jola calls above the commotion, sounding remarkably unperturbed.

"Coward," Ade mutters, causing Stefan to chuckle.

"Hi, Theo," Sasha raises a hand, squinting at the menu in her hand. "What's in an old-fashioned, darlin'?"

"Whiskey, ma'am."

She nods. "Which brand?"

Ben and Jason chorus, "Tullamore Dew."

"It's a mighty fine whiskey." Theo laughs, defending his country's product. "What are the lads having?" he asks after taking the ladies' order of old-fashioned, with two for Sasha.

Nathan taps Ade, who disregards his own list and is reading with Stefan. "There's Azul."

Ade brightens. "I'm driving, so I can't drink, but I'll handle the presentation." He then regales them with tales of Nigerian high-end clubs where tequila is brought out with Afropop and fireworks—a display of opulence and extravagance.

Ade walks to Mike, the DJ, before accepting a bottle of Azul from Theo. With Ameno Amapiano Remix playing, he launches into his demonstration. Their new friends, including Stefan, bring their phones out, taking pictures and videos of Ade, who is beaming like a proud showman.

Jola waits until they're done chugging down the whiskey, then goes to the refreshment table. "I need help here."

Ben springs into action. "What do you need?"

Together, they carry two boxes, a flask, soup bowls, and cutlery to the table. "These," Jola says, opening the boxes and flasks, "are some Nigerian delicacies."

"Isn't yellow rice the Nigerian delicacy?" Rosh queries.

"It's Jollof, but we have quite a lot," MT responds.

Jola begins distributing the food. "Please try them slowly to gauge the spice level."

Jason looks up, his eyes watering. "Should've led with that," he says after biting into a stewed turkey. Ben's turkey drops from laughing so hard at his brother. Seeing Jason's plight, Jola opens a bottle of water for him. "It's very spicy but also delicious. I find it impossible to stop eating." Jason admits, sniffling.

"*Olamide, gbémi débè*," Ay shouts as something called "Turn Up" starts playing.

"What does that mean?" Stefan asks Ade.

"Take me there," Ade replies, standing up and joining the other Nigerians as they enthusiastically demonstrate how to properly revel in a party.

Saturday, 1st October 2022.

Stefan arrives at the Bower-Adeowo's party with Ben and Jason, and they are immediately drawn to the football game unfolding before them. As he scans the crowd, Stefan notices Ade's absence. The players, all under five, are intent on their little game, led by a serious-looking referee who Stefan guesses is Ade's older brother.

"They all can't be over five," Stefan says, impressed, as they join Scott and his wife, Carol, by the sidelines.

"They're playing well," Jason agrees. "I'd watch them over Arsenal any day."

Carol doubles over with laughter while Scott and Ben glare at Jason.

"I forgot the gift," Stefan says, gesturing for Ben to give him the car keys before heading back outside.

As he returns to the driveway, Stefan's eyes roam the surroundings with habitual vigilance. The music from the party pulses through the air, its steady rhythm juxtaposed with the frenetic beating of Stefan's heart. He is finally free, a reality that has slowly dawned on him since arriving in Newcastle. It's time to stop looking over his shoulders and embrace the life he's been missing for the past four years.

But just as he starts to relax, he spots a figure in the distance—one with an eerily familiar silhouette. A jolt of nerves spikes through him, and for a heartbeat, his breath catches. He focuses on the figure as the familiar shape walks closer with a casual stride, and a rush of anxiety floods Stefan's senses. He steps back instinctively, gripping the door handle as if it might anchor him amidst the rising tide of panic. But instead of coming fully into view, the figure pivots into a turning and vanishes from sight.

Stefan exhales in relief and retrieves the gift bag from the car. As he straightens, he notices a red Ford in the distance, looking out of place, its tinted windows shrouding the occupant. Without a second thought, Stefan hurries towards the car, nearly dropping the gift in his haste. The car speeds off before he's halfway there, and he shakes his head, reminding himself that this is a party, not a private investigation. The Adeowos seem to have quite the guest list; Stefan shouldn't make this about himself.

After the game, Scott's second son, Ewan, leaves with his parents to find his brother. Ade's brother approaches with a little boy, clearly the birthday boy. "Stefan, Jason and Ben," Temmy shakes each of their hands, introducing himself. Stefan isn't surprised by his recognition; Ade had mentioned he'd shown their pictures to his family.

Adedeji looks up at Ben with bright curiosity. "You are Aunt Jola's boyfriend?"

"Adedeji!" Jola exclaims, appearing with her friends, who are struggling to suppress their laughter. "You can't ask our guests if they're my boyfriend." She ruffles the boy's hair.

Adedeji, unfazed, replies, "I didn't ask everyone. I asked him," he points at Ben. "I didn't even ask the other two uncles."

"And we take no offence," Stefan says, handing him the gift. Ben and Jason do the same.

After Adedeji thanks them, they move to the cake table, where they meet his brothers. "I got a BMW from Uncle Ben, a G-wagon from Uncle Stefan and all the Avengers from Uncle Jason," he announces happily, as if they aren't toy cars. "You are never getting in my car."

Walking to the Independence Day party area, Stefan notices the green and white decorations reflecting Nigeria's colours. Little flags adorn each table covered in white tablecloths, while the chairs are covered in green—artificial flowers in green and white sway in the breeze. Theo and Mike are also here at Jola's suggestion. It is last week all over again, only in a different location. Stefan looks around again, searching for a tall, dark and handsome individual, which he's seen several of—who knew all Nigerian Men are attractive? But he hasn't seen his. Not that—he reminds himself—Ade is his.

In the party area, everyone clusters in small groups, engaging in polite conversation. When Nathan joins them, he asks Ay about MT, who informs him she's on a date and will arrive later. For some inexplicable reason, this titbit puts Stefan's mind at ease. He knows Ade and MT are just friends, but what right does he have to be jealous, even if they aren't? In reality, there's nothing concrete between him and Ade. Only a force he's decided not to name because naming things makes it real.

Ignorance is sexy, as the saying goes.

Another curiosity is Nathan's odd behaviour, which has been akin to a death scare every time Stefan is near. However, Nathan's ominous vibes are notably absent this week, but the feeling that Nathan doesn't like him is still there. So, it is with great surprise that Stefan doesn't collapse from shock when Nathan walks up to him with a polite smile—a genuine smile, not a grimace. "Ade had to change, maybe even shower," Nathan whispers. "The kids got paint on him," he gives his phone to Stefan, grinning maniacally. Stefan doesn't believe this is the same guy. "I have it on video."

Stefan's laugh attracts Jola, who snatches the phone and starts watching with her friends, laughing at the paint-streaked Ade. "Thank you," he says.

Nathan winks, and Stefan wonders if the apocalypse might be on the horizon. Can the day get any stranger?

"I have his phone, in case you've texted him," Nathan informs.

Stefan did. It may have added to his worries, but no one has to know that. Jola edges closer to them to return Nathan's phone. She then holds the hem of Stefan's shirt, examining the *MALEC* written on it with wide eyes.

"Don't tell me you're a *Shadowhunters* fan?" she asks, still holding his shirt as if intending to take it off.

Recognising another fan, Stefan smiles. "Okay, I won't tell you."

Jola drags him to a table, where they sit on two chairs facing each other, chatting animatedly about their mutual love for the fictional group of super warriors created by Cassandra Clare. "Sophia is going to love you. We're both obsessed with the books," Jola beams.

Very good in Stefan's opinion: the more people in Ade's family that love him, the better his chances.

Calm down, Stefan.

He returns her smile. "We should definitely organise a day to discuss the books," he suggests, then asks for directions to the bathroom.

On his way, he finds himself thinking about his messages with Ade and the nasty turn their conversations always take. As usual, Stefan's wayward body reacts to his thoughts. He's diagnosed himself properly: he is horny. And not just for anyone; his horniness has a name, a face, and a body. A body he aches to have on his. During the week, a stunning babe from class had flirted with him mildly, and he would've flirted back if his mind isn't otherwise occupied with chubby cheeks and pink lips. Although his plan to keep their meetings strictly among friends has worked so far, he wonders how long it can last. He sighs inwardly, ascending the stairs, wondering if there isn't any restroom downstairs, when he hears a soft voice.

"You should look where you're going."

Stefan lifts his head. Standing just a few metres away, as if he appeared there by apparition, looking directly at Stefan with his beautiful eyes, his lovely smile on his face, and in a purple unbuttoned shirt is Ade.

5

GOD BLESS NIGERIA

— Geng by Mayorkun.

Saturday, 1st October 2022.

ADE WALKS WITH NATHAN, TRAILING BEHIND THE KIDS as they head out from the party room on the third floor of the Bower-Adeowo's house at Sixteen Stamfordham Road, to the outdoor part of Adedeji's birthday party.

"You almost kissed him?" Nathan says, casting a sidelong glance at Ade, after hearing him explain the reason behind his lateness to the patio last Saturday. "What happened to," he air-quotes, "I'm just getting to know him."

"It's part of the process," Ade says, grinning like a Cheshire cat.

Ade is still puzzled by Nathan's coldness towards Stefan, but during their brief discussion last Saturday, Nathan had the grace to look solemn and apologetic, but all Nathan promised was to stop his death glares.

"If you insist," Nathan says in a clipped tone.

"Why don't you like him?"

Nathan looks momentarily taken aback. "I have nothing against him, but I don't know him or his intentions. And neither do you."

"Isn't that what I'm trying to do?"

"Yeah, right. Trying to kiss him, that's for sure."

Ade cackles. "Do you not remember asking me to kiss Jeffery?"

"You're foolish," Nathan laughs. "We were nineteen, and you wanted to be sure." He waggles a finger at Ade. "And I have known him for three years already. Don't forget, he also told me he likes you."

Jeffery was Ade's first and only kiss. When he came out to Nathan, his friend set him up on a date with one of his old classmates and told Ade to kiss the boy, and he would know because Ade wanted to be sure before telling his family. The date with Jeffery went well; the kiss was great, but distance was the issue. About four months after they started dating, Jeffery moved to Australia for school and is still there. There was almost someone else after Jeffery, but that turned out to be bad news, which, thinking about it now, may have contributed to Nathan's current behaviour.

"So," Ade bumps his shoulder into Nathan's. "If we wait three years for you to know him, and he tells you he likes me, you will approve?"

They're now in the backyard. Ade surveys the scene: kids grouped around the bouncy castle with Jola and her friends, others enchanted by the magician, and some at the face painter and petting zoo.

"My approval isn't the issue here, and you know it," Nathan says seriously. "I don't want a repeat of this summer. I know it's your personal experience, and I can't begin to understand what you went through," he exhales heavily. "But don't you see? That when you are hurt, those who love you are also hurt. Hurt that you don't deserve, and it's painful for us to see you suffer and feel powerless to help."

Ade deflates. Nathan's words ring true. He knows his loved ones were deeply affected by the incident in June. While he's aware of their unconditional support, Nathan's raw emotion and visible affection are profoundly humbling. "I know. I," he attempts, but stops when he realises Nathan isn't done.

"I guess what I'm saying is, I need you to be careful," Nathan continues. "If this is someone you want to have some fun with, I won't even bat an eyelash," he pauses. "But I've seen how you look at him. It's not some fling, which gives him the power to hurt you," he looks at Ade, afraid he's overstepped, but Ade nods for him to go on. "I'm not saying everyone you meet will be a bad sort, but they can't all be good."

Ade sniffles, then takes Nathan by the arm and clasps him in a hug. "I love you. You know that, right?"

"I should think so," Nathan pats his back. "We're brothers, after all," he adds, making a heart shape with his fingers. Ade hugs him again.

They walk to the football field, Adedeji's big request for his birthday, but the game hasn't started yet despite the little rascal hurrying them out of the house. Ade reflects on Nathan's words. Everything he said is spot-on. He returned to England in part to avoid romantic entanglements, but what can he do when he crashed into it on his very first day back? He isn't confused; this is not confusion. He wants something with Stefan. The way he feels around him, and even in his absence, can't be set aside. But the ultimate question is if it is worth going for. If there isn't a possibility that it will end up as another colossal pile of failure. There are decisions to be made and questions to be answered, but this is not the day for that. Today, he thinks with a sense of relief, is about unwinding with friends after a stressful week.

"Hey there, you two," Jola calls out, approaching with her friends, all of them laughing at something.

"What's the display of affection for? Priya asks, turning to Nathan.

"He needs to stake his claim on me so none of you can snatch me, apparently." Nathan shares.

Ade rolls his eyes. "When is the drinking supposed to start, please?"

Peyton snorts. "Do you need your booze up to smooch pretty boy?"

"How do I even know you people?" Ade mutters.

Stop, guys," Ay interjects sympathetically. "He's perfectly capable of smooching without inhibition."

"Drinking can start once the kids leave," Jola finally answers.

They wander around the party before stopping at a crafts table where Ade finds Ademide and Eniade with Scott's sons—Ethan and Ewan, and Kiki's daughter—Anwuli.

"Ewan," Carol calls, walking to the table. "Do you want to play football? One of the kids is tired."

The boy drops the paper boat—or could it be a sailor's hat?—and follows his mom. Ade can't help but wonder at the changes that are happening in their lives. People they didn't know a month ago are here celebrating with them, and that he has somehow found himself in a large friend group.

"Uncle Ade, Uncle Nathan," Anwuli looks up, "Come

make handprints with me." She brings out the paint from under the table.

"Good luck." Jola and her friends escape before they get an invitation.

Ade and Nathan sigh before kneeling by the table. It was mascara on his lashes inside. Now it's handprints. Being an uncle can be exhausting.

"When's he getting here?" Nathan asks. "You know, pretty boy."

"Should be here before the kids leave," Ade responds, with a slight roll of his eyes.

"The rest of them?"

"After five. Carol will also be driving Ethan, Ewan, and Anwuli home by then."

At the mention of her name, Anwuli looks up and smiles falsely before smearing handprints on Ade's cheeks. On seeing this, the others join in, with Nathan cheering them on as they smear Ade with paint. He even has his phone out, making a video. Before Ade can say "Jack Robinson," he's covered in paint from head to toe.

🏃

Ade jogs upstairs for a quick shower, glancing out the window to check if Stefan has arrived. Seeing no sign of him, he steps into the shower, the warm water cascading over him like a blessing. Naturally, as these things tend to go, his thoughts drift towards Stefan—because really, where else would they go? This leads to other musings about Stefan, and, unavoidably, some of his body parts, and what Ade could do with those, which—to be honest—leads to a shower far longer than even the most generous environmentalist could approve of.

Buttoning a grey shirt in front of his mirror, Ade glances out again, and sees Stefan walking towards the house. For reasons best known to Ade, he dashes back into his closet and rummages for a purple shirt, to match Stefan's t-shirt. He steps out to the corridor just in time to see Stefan, whose eyes, of course, are glued to his phone like it's the Holy Grail. It must be a habit of his, Ade concludes.

Stefan stops short at the sound of Ade's voice, lifting his head as if surprised to find that the real world still exists. "What are you doing here?" he asks.

"I live here," Ade chuckles, a sly grin forming as he imagines all the different ways this could have gone. "You were about to walk into me. Again."

"Third time would've been the charm," Stefan smirks before continuing down the corridor. "Where's the restroom?"

Ade's eyebrows arch in suspicion. Did he really climb all the way up here for a restroom? There's a perfectly good one by the backdoor.

"Jola directed me up here," Stefan adds, pausing in front of Ade.

Ah, now it makes sense. "She's shameless," Ade mutters under his breath.

"What?" Stefan asks, clearly confused.

"She sent you up here on purpose," Ade clarifies.

Stefan's blue eyes crinkle in that way they do when he's halfway between amusement and confusion. "I was wondering why there were no toilets downstairs when you appeared," he says, following Ade into his room. "She isn't subtle, is she?" he asks, his lips curving into a perfect, inviting arc.

"I can't say that she is," Ade agrees, moving to lock the

door behind them with an almost ceremonial flourish. "You can use mine," he gestures toward the bathroom door.

He stands before the mirror, buttoning his shirt with deliberate slowness, and whistling a tune—something light and careless that matches his current mood. Stefan joins him, positioning himself by the mirror, their reflections blending in the soft light.

"You can see the entire party from here," Stefan comments, his eyes scanning the scene below. "They're by the buffet table."

Ade moves behind him, picking up his brush and running it through his hair. "My room has a pleasant view," he murmurs, his voice low.

"It does," Stefan agrees, peering out the window. "Can you see what they're having?"

"Let's see," Ade edges closer, their proximity so narrow now that a secret couldn't be slipped between them. "Jola is loading Ben's plate with Jollof rice, fried rice, and," he squints, trying to make out the details, "that should be turkey, th—"

"I was worried when I texted you and got no response."

"I'm sorry," Ade replies, inching closer. "Nathan has my phone."

"He told me later, and about the paint," Stefan says, his tone lighter, almost teasing.

"He did?"

Stefan nods. "He has a video, you know? We all saw it. I thought the little handprints were adorable."

"Now I wonder why I washed it off," he mutters, still brushing his hair—the repetitive motion grounding him.

Stefan turns to him, his eyes sparkling with a touch of playfulness. "Can I do that?" he asks, pointing to the brush.

Ade hands him the brush and lowers his head so Stefan

can brush his already maximally brushed-out hair. "Thanks," he says, feeling giddier than he has any right to.

"It's so soft," Stefan observes, running his fingers through Ade's hair. "What do you put in it?"

Ade rattles off a list of products. "Cantu conditioner, shampoo and shea butter, Vatika coconut oil, SheaMoisture enhancing smoothie and others."

"That's why it smells like coconut," Stefan says, nestling his nose into Ade's hair. "I like it." He returns the brush. "I think it's done."

Ade takes the brush and pulls Stefan closer by the waist, their eyes locked in an intense, unspoken connection. "Thank you."

"Nice shirt." Stefan splays his hands on Ade's shirt, feeling the fabric beneath his fingers.

"I changed to this when I saw you coming."

"I appreciate the honesty," Stefan grins, his pristine teeth gleaming against the light.

Ade's eyes roam over Stefan's face, drinking in every detail like a man at an oasis. *Boy, he is pretty.* His eyes, nose, mouth—everything about Stefan screams perfection, and in this moment, Ade can't help but be submerged in the sheer beauty before him.

"Your hair is longer," Ade notes, the observation almost reverent. "Almost falling into your eyes."

Stefan holds a strand of his hair, smiling. "Isn't it good?"

Stefan's smile tugs at Ade's heart, and a few other places as well. It's perfect, in Ade's opinion. The hair on Stefan's forehead frames his face in soft curls, rendering him even more beautiful. "It's good, I like it," he says, lifting his hand to touch Stefan's face.

Stefan flinches.

Ade is almost certain Stefan hasn't taken alcohol today,

so this reaction is perplexing. He searches for a way to ask about it, but every approach in his mind sounds intrusive.

"Hey," Ade drops his hand, leaning in to press his forehead against Stefan's. "You okay?"

"I'm fine," Stefan responds, his breath warm against Ade's skin.

Ade brushes their noses together, the touch tender and voltaic, sending sparks skittering through his veins. Then, as he cannot help himself, he kisses the tip of Stefan's nose. Stefan's sharp inhale reverberates deep within Ade. He kisses Stefan's right ear, his words tumbling out like a confession. "What are you doing to me?" he whispers, licking the edge of Stefan's ear, each word an invocation. "You've been flirting with me all week."

Stefan's breath catches again, and he encircles Ade's waist, his light blue eyes darkening to a deeper shade, almost navy. He bites his lower lip, a slow, tantalising smile curving his mouth. "I didn't hear you complaining," he replies, his voice a soft tease.

Ade's body tightens.

He trails kisses from Stefan's forehead down to his chin and along his jawline, and when he reaches Stefan's mouth, he gasps into Ade's mouth, the sound of a whispered "finally." Their lips meet, delicate and cautious at first, a tentative exploration—a moment suspended in time. But soon, Ade pulls Stefan closer, intensifying the kiss into something more passionate, more urgent. Ade feels dizzy with the thrill of it—Stefan's mouth on his, kissing him as he has dreamed, savouring Stefan's luscious lips. Stefan slides his hand from Ade's waist up to his arm, stopping at his biceps, and squeezes lightly. The hairbrush clatters to the floor, freeing Ade's hand to tangle in Stefan's hair. The soft, raven strands are finer than he imagined, silky and smooth to the touch. He prods Stefan's mouth open with his tongue, and it's open, hot and willing on his.

They explore each other's mouth extensively, leaving no part untouched, as if drinking from the well of life. Ade tightens his grip on Stefan's hair, his body responding in ways he never thought possible. And when Stefan takes Ade's upper lip between his teeth, grazing it before biting down lightly, Ade's body tightens even further, and the need to be closer—closer than close—overwhelms him. He manoeuvres them to the bed, sits on the edge and pulls Stefan to his lap. Stefan bestrides him willingly, and for a moment, it feels like they might actually merge into one being.

"You have no idea what you're doing to me either," Stefan whispers, his breath hot, giving Ade goosebumps.

Ade grunts—a sound he didn't know he could make. He pulls Stefan closer by the hips, his hands travelling back to squeeze his arse—Stefan's unbelievably soft arse. Stefan gasps into his mouth again, and Ade is utterly lost. Stefan's fingers dance over the buttons of Ade's shirt—why did he bother to button the damn thing—shrugging it off him and discarding it on the floor, his hands roam the length of Ade's arms, and Ade dissolves at each caress. He feels it through his body like electrical currents.

He pulls off Stefan's t-shirt in a swift movement, joining his shirt on the floor. Ade opens his eyes to marvel at the sight of Stefan's chest, a landscape he longed to explore, but only for about a second, before Stefan's lips reclaim his own in a kiss that steals his very breath away.

His jeans are growing uncomfortably tight—clearly, he didn't think this through when he got dressed. Stefan pulls Ade's undershirt from the jeans adeptly, soon joining their shirts on the floor. His tongue trails a path of fire down

Ade's shoulder and neck, igniting a primal longing within him that he never knew existed, and can barely control.

"Damn me. Can't get enough of this," Stefan puffs, his tongue finding its way back to Ade's mouth.

Ade has never thought mere touches or whispers of sweet nothings could be as pleasurable as this. Stefan's hands move to the band of Ade's jeans, fingers deftly finding the buttons with an expertise that sends a thrill straight through Ade. But Stefan pauses, leaning in to nibble on Ade's earlobe before asking, "Do you have a condom?"

Ade's heart skips a beat—then two. His eyes fly open, a silent expletive running through his mind like a ticker tape. He shakes his head, cursing his lack of foresight in the most colourful terms imaginable, though he manages to keep those particular thoughts to himself. Stefan masks his disappointment with a resigned sigh. He bites his lips—the only lips Ade wants to kiss till the end of time—and reluctantly moves his hands to rest on Ade's chest, their earlier urgency ebbing away. They collapse onto the bed, Stefan's head finds a comfortable space on Ade's chest, Ade's hand threading through Stefan's hair.

"That was..." Ade trails off, searching for a word that could encapsulate what just happened. Great? Fantastic? Intoxicating? Divine? But none of them seem to do justice.

"It was," Stefan breathes as they lie tangled together in a bed that now feels far too big and yet, just right.

And then, as if released from the burden of unspoken words, they burst into laughter. It's the kind of laughter that keeps going, mixed with relief, giddiness, and the absurdity of the situation.

"We should join the party." Ade breaks the companionable silence. But he makes no effort to move, his hand still in Stefan's hair, a satisfying anchor to this private world that feels far more important than anything beyond the door. Nothing compares to Stefan's warm body on his.

"But it's so comfortable here," Stefan whines.

Ade rolls him gently, so they're lying on their sides, facing each other, their bodies still pressed together, the soft silk caressing their skin. "You're hungry. I can hear your stomach rumbling."

"My stomach did no such thing," Stefan interjects, looking down at it with a mock scowl. "Betrayer."

"I'm hungry. Actually, starving," Ade admits, although he's inclined to devour Stefan more than anything from the buffet downstairs.

"Well," Stefan concedes, standing up. "Wouldn't want you to starve to death."

Stefan regards their clothes on the floor before picking up Ade's undershirt for him. After slipping into his own t-shirt, Stefan gestures for Ade to open his arms. He then picks up the hairbrush and brushes Ade's hair. Ade pulls him back in his lap, willing to starve. "So, you start work on Monday?" he asks, massaging Stefan's back.

Stefan's mouth opens slightly in disbelief. "Yeah," he smiles radiantly. "I'm looking forward to it." Ade nods and tangles his hand back in Stefan's hair, feeling the strands. "You're obsessed with my hair," Stefan teases.

"It's good hair," Ade says, kissing the curls on his forehead. "I love the feel of it."

Stefan briefly closes his eyes, when he opens them, a flicker of nerves pass over his face. "Um," he says, his lips curling upwards hesitantly. "Do you maybe want to go out with me?" his cheeks flush, but it only makes him more endearing. "Like on a date?"

Ade wasn't expecting this—he'd imagined himself asking first, perhaps with a grand gesture or at least a bit of smooth charm. But here Stefan is, beating him to it with all the awkward charm of a rom-com hero. He thinks back to his conversation with Nathan, about needing time to think things through, but something in his gut tells him this is right. He wants to try this with Stefan. It also helps that things between them seem effortless; nothing is forced, and there is no weirdness. Maybe he should try leaving his fears aside for now and control his fate. Perhaps this obvious connection they share will lead to greatness. It has to.

Instead of saying yes like a normal person, Ade grins devilishly, then flips Stefan to the bed, supporting himself over him using his elbows, his eyes roaming Stefan's face seductively. "I find that," he says, dragging out each word. "I do want to maybe go out with you," his voice is laced with an undertone he isn't aware of. "Like on a date."

"You're a fool." Stefan says, mirroring Ade's grin.

Ade nods, accepting the title with a happiness that feels almost royal. Stefan pulls Ade down and he collapses on him. their mouths finding each other with a hunger that, for the moment, eclipses any need for food. They descend the stairs minutes later, holding hands, finally joining the party.

"When should we go?" Ade asks, the eagerness in his voice unmistakable.

"Next Saturday?"

"We're in London next weekend to visit the Bowers. Sophia's mom is sick."

"You mentioned it," he allows. "We can decide when later."

Outside, walking to the party, Ade leans in. "You know, the others think we were having sex, right?"

Stefan lets out a scoff that's half-laugh. "Well, it wasn't for a lack of trying on our part."

🏃

Ade is too stunned to speak.

He really shouldn't be, though. As he's come to learn these past few days, Stefan has a knack for impeccable timing, like a cat who knows the precise moment to pounce. And, honestly, there's no lie in what Stefan said—things spiralled the way they did because Ade was utterly powerless to stop them. Not that he wanted to, of course. But his lack of preparedness promptly threw a spanner in the works.

Lack of planning: 1—Ade: 0.

"That mouth of yours," Ade says now, the only retort he can manage.

Stefan doesn't miss a beat. "You wanna know what it can do?" he deadpans.

God, he is on a roll today, but that's an easy one. "I have a fair idea."

Sound the bells; Ade won this round.

"Oh honey," Stefan says, full of cheeky confidence, "you don't know the half of it."

He deserves points for that. Ade has reasons to know that there's no stopping him once Stefan gets started. There are texts and phone calls to back it up.

"I yield to the master," Ade hails with his hands up.

"I'll pity you 'cause we're almost there," he grins, then stops walking. "Um, did you say something to Nathan?"

"Why?" Ade asks carefully.

Stefan shrugs. "He's nicer."

Ade grins, lopsided and amused. "How about we discuss this later?"

"Always later," Stefan mutters as they resume walking, clearly unimpressed.

"Look who's here," Jason slurs, sighting Ade and Stefan.

The group is evidently soused—tipsy, at the very least. Ade has lost track of time in his room, but the night is still young. Only the bulbs hanging above illuminate the space now that darkness has settled in, and the chill of autumn creeps through the air.

"Sophia has your food," Nathan informs.

As if on cue, Sophia walks to them with Temmy. "Thank you again, Stefan," she says, "for Deji's gift."

"You got him a gift?" Ade asks, raising an eyebrow.

Stefan ignores him. "I hope he likes it?"

"I'm pretty sure there's a place for it on his bed," Temmy says, placing a stack of plates on the table.

"I'm not sure what you like," Sophia hands Stefan a five-tiered steel food flask, "but there are options here."

"Thank you." Stefan accepts the flask.

"And am I to starve then?" Ade frowns at the second flask with Sophia.

"Yes, my dear," Sophia answers.

"I'll just eat from Stefan's flask."

Stefan hugs his flask to his chest and shakes his head like a child guarding his favourite toy. Sophia laughs and gives Ade the other flask before joining Jola and the others. Ade opens the flasks, and there are indeed options: fried rice, jollof rice, poundo yam, egusi soup, and one bowl is full of proteins—turkey, chicken, peppered snail, goat meat and fried fish.

"What's this?" Stefan points at the white rounded lump in one bowl, eyeing it warningly.

"It's called poundo yam," Jason supplies beside them. "Jola explained the difference between this and pounded yam earlier. It's tasty. You eat it with that," he points to the egusi soup. "And you eat it with your hand."

Ade retrieves two bowls of clean water and a hand wash gel from the buffet table. "In case you want to try the poundo," he says, indicating the bowl of water and the hand wash. "Or do you want me to feed you?"

It slips out before Ade can catch himself, but Stefan nods eagerly, agreeing to be fed. Ade washes his hand, takes a morsel, dips it in the soup, and feeds it to Stefan, who has his mouth open. To Ade's surprise, Stefan swallows it whole, not bothering to chew—a rarity for first timers.

"How is it?" Ade asks, half-expecting a grimace. "Good?"

"Spicy," Stefan gulps down water, "spicy, but good. More, please." Ade obliges, feeding him four more morsels before Stefan drains another glass of water. "There's something in the soup," Stefan says, pointing to the bowl "you call it?"

"Plenty," Ade says, happy to explain. "They're cut into small pieces. There's crayfish, locust beans, ponmo, giz—" He stops when he sees Stefan's bemused expression. Clearly, locust beans are an unknown entity in Stefan's world. "Give me your phone."

Ade googles each ingredient and shows them to Stefan. "That's tiny shrimp," Stefan laughs, pointing to the crayfish. "I'll try the other meals," he says, after examining all the pictures. "You should eat as well."

They're so absorbed in their exchange that they temporarily forget the presence of others—until someone coughs pointedly. They both look up to find everyone watching them with amused expressions. Stefan blushes faintly but then focuses intently on his fried rice, as if it's the most engrossing dish in the world.

Ade, however, doesn't bother with subtlety. "What?" he demands, glaring at the onlookers.

"Nice show," Jola comments.

"Interesting," Temmy mouths to Ade.

Ade narrows his eyes at his siblings but resumes eating without further comment.

"Do you guys want anything to drink?" Theo asks, appearing by the table.

"Stef, what do you want?" Ade asks.

Stefan doesn't look up from his plate. "Are they still here?"

Ade knows Stefan can be shy, but this seems different—could he be embarrassed? Ade glances around, but no one is paying them any attention anymore.

"No," he replies. "Is anything wrong?" he wants to take Stefan's hands; the urge to do so is powerful, but he figures that might be counterproductive.

"I just wasn't expecting the attention," Stefan says in a low voice.

Ade wasn't either. He dread the numerous ways Jola and Nathan will undoubtedly satirise him later. But when he's with Stefan, the world and everyone in it simply disappear, leaving just the two of them in their haven of bliss. *My God, what is happening to me?*

"Jameson is fine," Stefan says to Theo, who returns with two bottles shortly after.

When they rejoin the others, Sophia, Temmy, Scott, and Kiki have already left, leaving the party to the same group as last Saturday, with the addition of Kurt and Chad.

Mike, the DJ, is strictly spinning Nigerian hits. When "Love Nwantiti" starts playing, Stefan asks how it's pronounced, because it's popular on TikTok.

"Nwan-ti-ti," Ade teaches, enunciating carefully.

"Nawa-tin-tin," Stefan, the student, attempts after ten failed trials.

"Close enough," Ade allows.

The music choice is excellent, even by Ade's standards. From Burna Boy's "Ye" to Olamide's "Wo", Lojay's "Monalisa", "Baby Hello" by Wande Coal, Joeboy's "Baby", "Jealous" by Fireboy DML, and Davido's "Damiduro"—the hits keep coming. When Mayorkun's "Geng" blasts through the speakers, Jola and Ay leap up, shrieking.

Ade knows Afropop has a way of unleashing the wild side of Nigerians, but he didn't expect it to have the same effects on foreigners.

"You need to dance to this," Jola urges Ben, who dutifully joins her to dance, though he has no clue how to dance to the song. Waltzing is clearly off the table.

"Pepper dem, geng," Jola shouts, turning her back to Ben and grinding against him.

"What the hell is an akube Balenciaga?" Stefan whispers in Ade's ear, his hand snug around Ade's waist.

Ade laughs. "It means anything used, second-hand. The general classification of second-hand products in Nigeria is called akube."

"And how does one dance to this? Is it still Zanku?"

Ade loops his arms around Stefan's neck, still chuckling. "Just shake your body."

The music keeps morphing from one hit to another. "Gbese", "Anifowoshe", "KPK", "Imagine That", and "Like To Party", among others. Ade, his sister, and their friends can't resist singing along, whooping with unbridled joy.

They finally stop dancing about an hour later so Theo and Mike can start packing up. Jola takes the opportunity to announce the Halloween party at Ben's on the Twenty-Ninth.

"Wait, there's no party before then?" Rosh inquires, dismayed. "I thought this is an every-weekend thing."

"We've been introduced to a wavelength they can't keep up with," Peng complains, patting Rosh's arm.

"We should drink more," Sasha suggests, sinking back into her chair.

"You plan to get thoroughly foxed, yeah?" Ben asks.

"We are celebrating our liberation from your forefathers after all," Sasha, a Canadian, declares. "God bless Nigeria."

"Is it?" Ben inquires dryly. "What's playing, then?"

Ay snorts. "Colonial master dey ask question."

"Descendant of colonial masters," Jola corrects.

Ben shakes his head as Theo serves them more drinks before leaving with Mike. Soon, their guests have all left, except for Ben and those returning to his house since the Uber XL is taking its time. Ade walks with them to the gate to wait, holding Stefan's hands.

"I'll call you tomorrow to start planning," Ben says to Jola.

"The party isn't until another three weeks," Jola points out.

"When should we start then, princess?"

Ade almost stumbles but recovers swiftly. Stefan and Jason exchange a flabbergasted look, clearly having heard Ben as well. But Jason quickly composes himself and looks away. Jola, however, either didn't hear Ben or isn't fazed by the pet name. Ade steers Stefan a few metres away from the others, trying to conjure an excuse to make him stay longer, but finds none. "I'll see you on Monday," he says.

Stefan nods. "Mm-hmm, Monday," he echoes, drawing Ade closer for a kiss.

The Uber finally arrives and Stefan climbs in, cheeks flushed. He waves goodbye to Ade and Jola before the car pulls away. Ade remains standing there, watching wistfully as the vehicle disappears down the road.

Jola turns to him. "Are you in love with him?"

Monday, 3rd October 2022.

Ben swings open the front door of Twenty-Four Darras Hall just as Ade and Jola approach. His impeccable timing makes Ade wonder if Ben has been waiting in the entryway, like a dutiful footman, anticipating their—or, to be accurate, Jola's—arrival.

"Hi guys," Ben greets. "Jason is checking if Rosh and Peng are ready."

Ade glances around the room. "I got a notification from the vendor."

"I don't think he's even up yet." Ben says, guiding them to the living room, its serene all-white décor highlighted by the view of the pool through the expansive glass doors. "But Sonia called me. It's in his cubicle."

"Isn't he supposed to start work by nine?" Ade asks, smiling. "And he's still sleeping?"

"He might be awake, but I haven't seen him. Go see for yourself." Ben suggests, offering directions to Stefan's room.

Ade approaches Stefan's door and knocks once, hoping not to disturb him if he's still asleep. He listens attentively until he hears footsteps. Stefan opens the door a few seconds later. "Jason, why are you knocking?" he starts, then blinks in surprise. "You are not Jason." His face lights up with a smile as he steps into Ade's open arms.

"Disappointed?" Ade whispers in Stefan's ears.

"To see your handsome face?" Stefan lifts his head, eyes twinkling. "No one could be disappointed to see you." He steps back, gesturing for Ade to enter. "Come in."

Ade follows him into the room, closing the door behind him. Stefan is clearly awake and even partially dressed, his lean form accentuated by black trousers. A selection of shirts—royal blue, peach and green—are laid out on the bed like a painter's palette.

"You're here for Rosh and Peng?" Stefan asks.

"Yes," Ade replies, removing an envelope from his pocket. "And to give you this."

Stefan's fingers brush Ade's as he accepts the envelope, their eyes meeting for a moment longer than necessary. "It has my name," he says, opening the envelope with interest.

"That's because it's yours," Ade points out.

Stefan ignores him. "It's a barcode," he says more to himself, holding up the business-size card. He removes his phone from his pocket and scans it. His eyes soften as realisation dawns on him. "Wow, you made me a playlist."

The joy in his voice is all Ade needs. "Turn it over."

"Stef, I made you this for your first day. Teni," Stefan reads aloud.

Stefan had mentioned his fondness for the first part of his name—Teni—so Ade had written it out and taught him how to pronounce it. Hearing Stefan say "Teni" with his sweet little Swedish accent, the one word, two syllables that is his own name, stirred something deep within him.

"I hope you like it," Ade says, needing him to.

Stefan's eyes light up with genuine delight. He slips the card and phone in his pocket, then bridges all gap between them, his hands encircling Ade's waist. He tiptoes and brushes his lips lightly across Ade's earlobe. "I like it very much," he whispers. "Thank you, Teni."

He pronounces it "Te-nie," and Ade, already spellbound, can feel the effect. He's had this name all his life, but never has it sounded so seductively, as though wrapped in the promise of driving him delightfully mad. Stefan presses up against him, wedging one leg between Ade's thighs, feeling him up as he trails his tongue along Ade's ear.

"You're welcome," Ade manages to croak out, his voice betraying his breathless state.

"And I like this very much," Stefan's breath hot in Ade's ears. "And I haven't even touched you."

"*Stef*," Ade whispers, feeling his pulse quicken with every teasing caress. His entire body is taut from only tongue and whispers; Heaven knows what more would do to him. Is this the norm for everyone caught in the throes of attraction? "*Stef*," he whispers again as Stefan replaces his leg with his hand between Ade's thighs, trailing the length of him—the very taut length of him.

"Hmmm," Stefan moans. "You'll ruin me."

Ade stares at him, incredulous, as if Stefan isn't the very architect of Ade's current state, his hand still continuing his sensual sensation. "The same can be said about you," he says, pressing a kiss on Stefan's shoulder.

Stefan's hand moves to Ade's waist. "If I start what's on my mind, I won't go to the office today." He smiles impishly. "And there's the playlist to listen to."

Ade swallows, mesmerised. "Yes, there's the playlist to listen to," he repeats in a trance.

"What shirt should I wear?" Stefan returns to regarding his shirts.

"You... You're asking me about a shirt?" Ade's smile is wickedly amused.

"I may have to jump you otherwise."

In a flash, Ade takes two strides, pulls Stefan from the bedside, and has his back against the wall. He pauses just long enough to appreciate Stefan's pretty face before clamping down his mouth on Stefan's in an impassioned kiss, pouring all his arousal into it. His tongue invades every corner of Stefan's mouth, while his left hand tangles in his hair and his right hand travels to Stefan's thighs, repeating his earlier gesture, and Ade is gratified to feel Stefan's taut response. "Today makes it two months," he pants into Stefan's mouth, "since you crashed into me, you know?"

Stefan nods. "It's been two months since you took my breath away."

"And you took mine as well," Ade murmurs, his tongue languidly duelling with Stefan's. "You're straining against your trousers," he teases, his fingers tracing the outline.

Stefan pulls hurriedly at Ade's shirt, his hands finding skin, tightening his grip. "Take it off me."

Ade undoes his button with deft fingers. "Tell me what you want me to do," he asks, eager to comply.

"Touch me. *Please*," he begs, "I want you to touch me."

Ade obliges, kissing his way down Stefan's neck and chest, pausing to minister to each nipple with a teasing flick of his tongue. "Yes," Stefan moans. "Just like that," his hands cradling Ade's head, "damn."

Ade sinks to his knees, his hands on Stefan's waist, kissing the flat panes of his stomach down to the band of his trousers, one hand poised at Stefan's zipper.

A sharp knock at the door, followed by Jason's voice. "Ade, Rosh and Peng will be ready in a minute."

"Okay," Ade calls to Jason.

Stefan pulls him up, panting. "You have to go?"

Ade nods, his heart pounding hotly. "You'll let me know what you think of the playlist?" He grabs the peach shirt from the bed and helps Stefan into it.

"I'll see you tomorrow?" Stefan asks, his tone subdued.

"It's labs week."

"Okay," Stefan says dully.

Ade lifts Stefan's chin with a finger. "How about I text if I have any free time?"

Stefan splays his hands on Ade's chest, fluttering his eyelashes. "How about," he purrs, "you text me how it would've ended if Jason didn't knock?"

Ade swallows thickly. "I'll text you every detail," he promises, sealing it with another kiss.

6
SUNFLOWER

— Sunflower, Vol. 6
by Harry Styles.

Monday, 3rd October 2022.

How's Stefan supposed to concentrate at work when the only thing filling his head is his Ade? *Okay, maybe not mine yet.* But the plans to make Ade his man are well underway. Stefan must either find a way to stop daydreaming about Ade during work hours or embrace the fate of Monica in the pilot of *Friends*.

"Here we are," Ben announces, rudely jolting Stefan back to reality.

They are now parked in the underground lot of the M.B.L building on Abbey Road. Stefan, blissfully preoccupied, had paid little attention to the drive. Is there such a thing as *blissfully preoccupied*? If not, Stefan is quite prepared to pioneer its existence.

They part ways once they exit the lift. Stefan's only a

few metres away when Ben's voice calls out, "Something's waiting for you," before he turns a corner and disappears.

Stefan chuckles, musing on how Jason and Ben are like two peas in a pod, though neither brother will ever admit it. He hurries his steps, wondering what could be waiting for him, but meets Sonia, Ben's executive assistant, midway to his office.

"Morning Stefan," Sonia chirps

"Morning Sonia. How's it going?" he replies.

"Can't complain," she says. "The package is q—" She suddenly claps a mouth over her mouth. "Byeeee," her mumbles through her fingers as she scurries away.

Stefan hurries, eager to uncover the mystery of what's waiting for him. The Research and Development office is an expanse of modernity: floor-to-ceiling windows, plush cubicles, a rainbow of couches, two massage chairs, and a whiteboard near the window. The space practically screams "new age". Mr. Ray Sommersfield, Stefan's manager, approaches with a firm handshake and a warm smile.

"Welcome, Mr. Wickström. Come with me. Before you settle to your workspace, I'll introduce you to the others."

Stefan follows, though he's itching to see his workspace right this minute. The office houses around twenty-five cubicles, but by the end of the introductions, he's only met six colleagues.

"This is my office," Ray points out a space with his name boldly displayed on the door. "I'm here if you need anything."

They walk a short distance to Stefan's cubicle labelled "S. Wickström". There, on the table, is indeed a package, but Stefan strives to remain calm, not losing his equilibrium in the presence of his boss.

"Here we are," Ray says, pointing to Stefan's workspace.

"For the first month, you'll be reading the training materials, shadowing your colleagues, and participating in various in-house training sessions." He nods towards the laptop. "Your email is set up, and the training documents are ready. I wish you a great first day."

Stefan's heart does a sweet and weird acrobatics, an odd yet exhilarating flip, as his fingers close around the bouquet resting on his desk. The flowers are an explosion of golden yellow—fifty sunflowers, give or take a few. Each one a tiny sun in its own right—arranged with such meticulous care that he momentarily wonders if he's stumbled into a dream. It's not so much just the bouquet or the playlist, but the gesture itself, the thought that went into the planning.

A smile breaks across Stefan's face, starting slow, then spreading wider, like sunlight creeping over the horizon. He can't help it—he's positively glowing. There's no need to guess who the sender is; he knows already. But still, his fingers fumble with a sudden eagerness as he tears open the note nestled in the bouquet.

> Stef,
> I believe our favourite things bring us luck. So, here's one of yours in my hope that it not only brightens your space, but also bring you luck.
>
> - Téní.

Stefan reads the note, his eyes skimming over the words not once, not twice, but about a hundred times in the span of a minute. Each time, his smile widens, and his stomach flutters in such a way that no amount of deep breathing could settle. The words on the page seem to shimmer, each letter sparking joy so profound it feels almost ridiculous.

There's a lightness to it, a sense of inevitability that feels as thrilling as it is terrifying.

Omg, I'm falling in love with him?

Stefan quickly pulls out his phone, his fingers flying over the screen as he texts Ade: *Wow. Mind blown. Love it, thank you. It's called "solros" in Swedish. Add to your dictionary.*

Stefan is going about his day in a daze, lost in the fog of melodies and trying to decipher any cryptic message behind each track. Listening to "Self Control", his mind whirls—did Ade choose this song for a reason? Shouldn't he be the one sending it? Ade, who had taken his carefully guarded willpower and snapped it like a twig—in two equal halves. All of Stefan's buffers and previous resolutions—take it slow, don't be rash, avoid meeting Ade alone, blah, blah, blah—seem laughably naïve. The only thing Stefan wants now is to meet Ade privately, even if just for a stolen ten minutes. It doesn't even matter if the privacy is the windshield of a car. He needs to get his hands on Ade. It is an absolute necessity at this point.

A chime drags him out of his wayward thoughts, a series of responses from Ade to his earlier messages: *Glad you love it*, followed by: *apologies response is late. Crazy day*, and then: *I miss you.*

Stefan's face breaks into a grin so wide it feels perpetual as he types back: *I miss you, call you later*.

He makes his way to Ben's office when he sees it's lunch time. "What are you grinning about?" Ben asks.

"Oh, wouldn't you like to know?" Stefan smirks.

"I can guess what it's about, you know? And you're still grinning."

Stefan is fairly certain he might never stop. He doesn't even know how to turn it off. "I'm not grinning."

"If you say so."

Stefan walks a few metres from the office building with Ben to DINE, a place that could easily be mistaken for a quaint tea room rather than a restaurant. The space is medium-sized, with about ten total tables. Ben and Stefan settle into a two-person table by the widow. Ben scans the barcode on the table and gives his phone to Stefan. "Go through the menu and add what you want."

"Very Wendy's style," he comments, scrolling through the menu. After about five minutes, he gives the phone back.

"BLT and orange juice?" Ben asks, one brow sceptically raised. "That's all?"

Ben complains all the time that the amount of food Jason and the other Gen Zs eat will send him into poverty, but he's still such a grandma when you don't eat enough.

"I'm not very hungry," Stefan assures him.

Ben nods. "Should be here in ten." He looks up from his phone. "So, you've seen your package?"

Stefan loads the pictures and shows them to him. "Here."

Ben studies them, then hands back the phone with a nod. "He knows his stuff. His sister thinks he's quite serious about you."

"And what do you think?"

Ben looks genuinely surprised at being asked for his opinion, as if he hasn't realised that Stefan sees him as more than just Jason's brother. "Well, he does seem to really like you," he says thoughtfully. "And from what I've seen, you like him, right?"

Like? Stefan's on the brink of saying *love*, but settles for a cooler, "I do."

Their conversation is interrupted by the arrival of their food. With a polite nod, Ben excuses himself to the toilet. Stefan inhales the rich aroma of their meals before reaching for his phone to snap a picture of his lunch to send to Ade. It's become a sort of ritual, a little way of saying, "Look at this. Wish you were here." But before he can hit send, a voice, unmistakable and unwelcome, cuts through the air behind him.

"Well, hello there."

Stefan's heart thuds, and not in the good way. It can't be. What would he be doing here in England? And in Newcastle, of all places? But Stefan knows with sinking certainty that he's not imagining things. This isn't some bizarre auditory illusion. The person behind the voice steps into view, and standing before Stefan is a man of below-average height with an unimpressive stature and distinct Central European features that are always overshadowed by the idiotic permanent grin plastered across his face—a grin that could win an award for the most obnoxious expression ever worn by a human being. Where is Ben? Stefan thinks with a pang of desperation. His day has been going so well, but his string of perfect moments are now teetering on the brink of ruin.

"What... What are you doing here, Honza?" Stefan asks, mustering a voice as icy as he can manage, though the coldness is more for show than anything else.

"Now, come on, my dear Omar," Honza says with mock reproach. "That's no way to greet your boyfriend."

7

LABYRINTH

— Demons by Imagine Dragons.

Tuesday, 18th October 2022.

"You seem distracted," Jola says, her voice casual yet perceptive as Stefan walks beside her into her office. "Anything wrong?"

"Not at all," Stefan replies quickly, his eyes flitting around the room. "Just thinking of NRWIs and your lecture, that's all."

Jola chuckles, all too familiar with Stefan's attempts at nonchalance. Distracted indeed. The truth is he's barely holding it together. The last encounter still leaves his pulse jittering. Honza, all cool and unnervingly polite, had vanished with just a nod after Ben returned to their table, leaving Stefan scrambling for explanations. "He just said I looked familiar," he'd told Ben, improvising poorly.

Stefan hates lying, and he's not even good or talented at it. But talking about Honza? Now, *that* is a curse of the highest order. The man is more than a thorn in Stefan's flesh—he's far more insidious. And the very idea that Honza might be following him here, creeping into this part of his life is nauseating. It's like waiting for a storm that cannot be outran. At least Ade's London trip has been a reprieve. If Ade had been around, he would have caught on instantly—the darting eyes, the stiff shoulders, the way Stefan jumps at shadows. Ade is surprisingly attentive.

What must i do to get that aspect of my life off my back? Although Honza hasn't reappeared since two weeks ago, Stefan can't quite shake the suspicion that he is lurking and watching his every move again. It's maddening, really—like living under a microscope held by someone with far too much time on their hands. Sharing this with Ade is, of course, out of the question. How would he react? Probably with more questions than Stefan has answers to, and that's a conversation Stefan would rather dodge like a poorly thrown frisbee.

Jola's voice pulls him back to the present, mercifully. "I've seen your additions to our document," she says, connecting her laptop to the monitor. "Can we go through them together? Saves me adding comments."

"Sure," Stefan walks over to join her.

"I like that you've only included dominant ions. That's impressive. But," she pauses and gives him a look that's equal parts impressed and questioning. "When did you have the time to add results from twenty articles?"

"Over the weekend," Stefan laughs. "I skipped my sleep meds."

"Stefan!" Jola's eyes widen in horror. "Don't do that. Only work on it when you have free time."

Stefan didn't intend to alarm her but cannot tell her the real reason he'd been up all night involved after-hours dealings with her brother—their own personal *digital liaison*. Now *that* information would be the actual alarm. "I skip them sometimes to avoid dependency," he says, placing a hand on his chest in mock humility. "I'm touched you're concerned for my health."

"You and Ade are the same," Jola rolls her eyes. After a thorough run-through of their work, she nods approvingly. "We can leave it here. Everything's in order."

At that moment, the door swing open, and in walks MT with Nathan and, as if summoned by a wish, Ade himself.

"Kurt and Chad?" MT asks.

"We didn't meet either of them," Jola replies to MT.

Ade's eyes light up as soon as they lock with Stefan's, the kind of look that could turn the gloomiest day into a sunlit garden. "You good?" he asks, leaning in.

"Yes... Why'd you ask?" Stefan replies, startled by the sudden inquiry.

"Nothing," Ade replies, slipping his fingers into Stefan's hand like they belong there, perfectly intertwined. "Just thought to check."

And just like that, Stefan's anxiety ebbs away as if Ade's presence alone could smooth the rough edges of his thoughts. He pulls Ade closer, wrapping an arm around his waist in an easy, sideways hug. "I'm okay, thanks." It's a half truth, but one he's hoping will suffice for now.

Nathan catches sight of them, smiles, but wisely holds his tongue as the group begins making their way to the parking lot. "Where's Ay?" MT asks, scanning around.

"Will join us in the car," Jola replies.

"Jola said you're reading the Shadowhunters books?" Stefan says.

"Jola cannot keep a secret," he gives Stefan his phone. "She gave me quite the list."

"Wow. She's the golden fan. I would've never thought of this."

"I read the first three stories on the list already, that Magnus Bane is hilarious."

Stefan laughs. "He's my favourite character." He gives back Ade's phone. "Can you unlock this?" Ade tells him his password instead. "And what genres do you like?" he asks, airdropping the list to his phone before returning Ade's phone.

"I read a lot of smut," Ade says, chuckling. "Then some Queer African books. I love *The Death of Vivek Oji*. Have you heard of it? Oh, and the *Twilight* books, they're my favourite."

"No, I haven't but I will check it out. If Jola has the same version of *The Mortal Instruments* books as mine, there should be a Stephenie Meyer recommendation on them," Stefan says, grinning like a proud dad.

"You're serious?"

"My favourite author is your favourite author's favourite author."

"*O lénu pa*," Ade salutes with both hands up.

"Tell me what that means," Stefan asks, his eyes shining.

"You're mouthed. It's a form of hailing in Nigeria." Ade says, opening his car's boot. "I forgot to give you lunch."

Stefan grins, remembering their kiss in the car earlier. The small pause when he got into the backseat beside Ade, them grabbing each other, not knowing who reached out first. The way their mouths moved in holy synchronisation. "You did," he deadpans.

Ade chuckles. "You're incorrigible."

They wave to Jason and Lina, who predictably start

kissing. Stefan lets out a laugh, shaking his head. "Do they ever stop kissing?"

Nathan scoffs. "One can say same for present company, but I'll refrain from mentioning names." With a mock salute, he climbs into his Velar and drives off.

"I've got something for you," Ade says, pulling out a gift bag with the flourish of a magician revealing his greatest trick. "The best shortbread in England, no less. Baked by Stella, the Bowers cook."

Stefan sticks half a biscuit in his mouth and motions for Ade to bite the other end. The biscuit is undoubtedly delicious, but he has only a second to savour the taste before Ade's mouth is on his.

"So…" Ade says between kisses, pulling Stefan closer by the waist, "I've found a list of restaurants we could try on Saturday."

"Yeah? Or should we have it at the loft? I could cook you something."

It's a spur-of-the-moment suggestion, one he almost takes back.

"Can I watch? Or participate, if you tell me what to do." A faint smile flickers across Ade's face. "I can't cook shit."

Stefan's heart spurs, it soars, it does an Olympic-worthy somersault, and a thousand other things. "Sophia told me if you boil water, the kettle will burn," he teases, laughing freely and without restraint.

"Sophia's a show killer," Ade pouts with the kind of adorable indignation that would melt iron. "Isn't she supposed to embellish my ratings?"

"Why do you need embellished ratings?"

"You'll see," Ade flashes a devilish grin.

Saturday can't come fast enough, and the anticipation is enough to drive Stefan to distraction. "Looking forward to it," he grins. "Before I forget, you mentioned Nathan's family owns some dealerships. Do they have any here?"

"You want to buy a car?"

"I'm considering it."

"They have in London and Manchester, but the others are outside England. Although I—" he trails off as if hesitating.

"What?"

"I can always drive you," Ade offers with a nonchalant shrug, as though he hasn't just proposed something that sends Stefan's heart into a sprint.

"I-I," Stefan stammers, throat dry. "I wouldn't want to burden you."

"Stef, it's not a burden. I'd be happy to."

Stefan can't suppress the smile spreading across his face, feeling lighter than he has in days. Maybe, just maybe this time won't be a disaster. He's counting on it not to be. "You're fast becoming my favourite person, you know?"

"And you, mine," Ade replies, his lips brushing Stefan's in a kiss that speaks of promises unsaid.

They reluctantly pull apart and make their way to Jason's QX80. "Where's Lina?" Stefan asks Jason, who stands alone, looking unbothered.

"Has something to do in the library."

"I'll text you when I'm home," Ade says, leaning in through the passenger door to steal one last kiss. He then plants a final one on Stefan's forehead for good measure. "Wanna race, Jason?"

"Bring it on."

Ade grins, and winks at Stefan before walking back to his car.

"He's clearly smitten," Jason comments.

"And you?" Stefan throws the question back.

To Stefan's surprise, Jason didn't even try to evade the question. "I don't know. I do like her, though."

"Have you told her that? Define things?"

Jason snorts. "Define things with him," he nods towards Ade, "and lead by example."

"Maybe I will," Stefan chuckles. "This weekend."

He glances towards Ade's, but the Toyota has already disappeared from view. Instead, the clear line of sight reveals the red Ford parked a few spaces away, its windows rolled down. Stefan's stomach drops. Despite the distance, he'd recognise the man behind the wheel anywhere.

It's Honza.

Wednesday, 19th October 2022.

Stefan is still plagued with that nagging feeling, the one that crawls beneath his skin, whispering of eyes on his back. Always watching. Always waiting.

I already left my country, my home, for Godforsaken Honza. Must I now pause my life too? He sighs, frustrated, as if the answer might drop from the ceiling, but it's as elusive as ever. What *can* he do?

And yesterday didn't bring clarity. Just more unease. Before he could approach the red Ford, Honza drove off in the other direction. When Jason asked why he looked like he had seen a ghost, Stefan improvised—yet again—and told Jason he thought he saw someone familiar. Stefan had told Jason a little about Honza, it was even his suggestion for Stefan to relocate for time being. But if he tells Jason that Honza may have followed him to Newcastle, he'd only get the same advice he's been dodging for years: "Report it to the police." But how can he report the situation without sounding like a pathetic fool? Besides, it's a mess of his own making, isn't it? People always pay for their choices, and this is his tab.

He sighs again, deciding to call his friends back at home. Żaneta, especially, might be able to fetch him some answers.

She picks up, sounding drowsy. "Are you in love with me?"

"I might be," Stefan chuckles. "But don't tell Edwin."

"I heard that," comes Edwin's voice before he joins Żaneta on the screen.

"Why are you calling so early? Should you not be in school?" Żaneta inquires.

"I only go on Tuesdays and Thursdays, and I am calling to ask if there's any new info about Honz."

They both pay full attention to that. "Is anything wrong?" she asks.

"And why would you want to know that?" Edwin asks, already suspicious.

Stefan explains the two instances of seeing Honza, and how it cannot be chalked up to mere coincidence. He's sure Honza followed him.

"Give me a minute," Żaneta says. "I saw something from Marek the other day, but my TL refreshed... Wait, let me find it."

Marek is a guy they went to Uni with. While they aren't so close, they hang out sometimes with him and their other classmates.

Żaneta lets out a small "Oh," then sighs. "They have a picture together."

"They know each other then," Edwin lets out a low groan. "It makes sense since they're both Czechs. Do you have Marek on IG?"

"What's his username, Żane?" Stefan types it in on IG. "Shit, I'm following him."

"Block him," Edwin advises sagely.

"Yeah, but the deed is done," Stefan sighs, raking a hand through his hair. "Honz may have targeted him for this exact reason."

Żaneta is not one to handle such things with grace, she explodes in Swedish. "*Jag bryr mig fan inte!*" She's turning crimson now. "I don't fucking care. And I'm going to *kill* that worthless bastard. What does he want? Stalking you like some second-rate Bond villain?"

Stefan can't help but try for humour, though it feels weak on his tongue. "Ludvin will get you off the hook."

Edwin cracks a small smile at the mention of his older brother, the criminal defence lawyer they always joke about. "By the way, are you coming to the Advokat's wedding?" he asks, sidestepping the rage brewing from his girlfriend.

"I'll let you know in two weeks."

Żaneta is not easily swayed. "Go to the police, Sigvard," she pleads.

Sigvard is the name his paternal grandparents gave him. It is a traditional Swedish name that means 'victory guardian.' No one but them called him that until they died, but Żaneta deplores it when she is persuasive.

"And tell them what?" Stefan sighs. "There's this guy who I *think* followed me to England?"

"Confront him then," Edwin suggests. "Record your conversation, and you can have something to give the police." He breathes out a heavy sigh. "God, I hate the man," he avows.

Żaneta, still visibly fuming, asks, "Are you going to tell Ade?"

Stefan is silent for a moment. "Isn't it too early to burden him with this? When it might eventually come to nothing."

Edwin fixes him with a look. "Nothing that concerns Honza comes to nothing. You know that, Stefan."

He obviously misunderstands Stefan's point. "That's not what I mean," Stefan clarifies.

"You mean you and Ade?" Żaneta presses.

"Yeah."

"*Men du gillar honom, villa du slänga det?*—but you like him, do you want to throw that away?" Żaneta asks, clearly surprised.

Stefan pinches the bridge of his nose. "*Det är inte det—* it's not that," he exhales deeply. "I don't know if I can commit to him if this still lurks behind me. I never thought Honz would track me. He was supposed to be in fucking Prague."

Edwin scoffs. "Stefan, you've fallen for the guy. You don't have to tell him now, but at least tell Ben and Jason if Honza approaches you again."

Żaneta nods vigorously. "You really have to trust people to help you. There are things you cannot solve all on your own."

This is not the first time Stefan has heard this, but it feels heavier now, more real. He had thought leaving Stockholm would free him from Honza's persistence, but actually following him across borders? This is new. And new means action.

"Who told you I've fallen for him?" Stefan says, ready for the conversation to go in a different direction.

"Oh come on. Ade this, Ade that. Our ears are full. Ade made me a playlist. Ade brought me shortbread from London," Edwin smirks.

"Don't forget the solros!" Żaneta adds.

"You're insufferable," Stefan says, trying to suppress a laugh. "How do I tolerate you?"

"Because you love us," they say in perfect, mischievous unison.

Stefan shakes his head, laughing at last. "God help me, but I do."

"Be watchful, okay?" Edwin's voice softens as he pivots back to seriousness. "If you confront him, make sure you have it on record."

"And we love you," Żaneta says before they end the call.

🏃

Stefan steps out onto his balcony, the morning air kissing his skin. "*Kall*—cold," he mutters to himself, a shiver darting through him as he scans the car park, half-expecting Honza to emerge. But there's nothing, just the empty expanse of cars.

He retreats inside, shutting the door with a sigh, his robe falls to the floor in a heap as he collapses on the bed.

It was different before and the situation was simple—he had nothing Honza could touch, nothing precious enough to lose, no one Honza could hurt except him. Now, he has Ade. Ade, with his disarming smiles and quiet presence, the one thing in Stefan's life that actually makes sense. If Honza decides to sink his claws in, Stefan could lose something irreplaceable.

As a decision starts forming in his mind, he unlocks his phone and, almost without thinking, opens his gallery. The recent photos are a testament to just how quickly Ade has woven himself into his life in such a short period. In each picture, Ade looks effortlessly handsome, even in the candid shots where he's unaware of the camera—laughing, lost in thought, the silly selfies they took at Ben's. He stops at the ridiculous video Nathan had sent of Ade feeding him at the Independence Day party, the pair of them so wrapped up in each other they barely noticed the rest of the world. A smile creeps across Stefan's face, despite the dread twisting in his gut.

Why is my life so complicated?

The thought lingers like a bad aftertaste. He knows what needs to be done. Honza has to back off, or Stefan risks losing it all. Ade can't be dragged into this mess—not when they've barely had a chance to build something together. And Stefan cannot let Honza ruin this—ruin *them*. With a resigned breath, he sets his iPad to record and unblocks Honza's number, his thumb hovering for a second before pressing dial.

"It's so nice of you to call me, Omar." Honza's voice slithers through the line, smooth but unmistakably smug.

Stefan clenches his jaw. *Why do I always feel like I need a shower after hearing his voice?*

"I've told you to leave me alone. What else do you want?" His tone is sharp, cutting through any niceties.

Honza chuckles. It's the sound of someone who's been told no but refuses to listen. "What I've always wanted."

"*Dum*—stupid," Stefan thinks, muttering it under his breath. "Aren't you with Marek?" It's petty, stupid even, but Stefan wants him to know he found him out, however unhelpful or unnecessary it is.

"Marek?" Honza spits the name. "I don't fucking want Marek. I want *you*."

Stefan rolls his eyes, his patience thinning. "Honz, you and I are done." he says, exhaustion lacing every word. "We've been done for *years*."

"But I apologised to you!" Honza yells. "I apologised for everything. What else do you want? I'll do anything."

Except leave me alone. It's like trying to reason with a brick wall.

"Meet with me, Omar. *Prosím.*" Honza pleads, trying a different tactic. "My hotel is just by the railway station. One meeting, that's all."

Stefan feels the bile rise in his throat. "No." The word is final, and this time, he means it.

Stefan shudders at the thought of ever laying eyes on Honza again, whether in a public square or a private room. The memories are still too raw, too close to the surface. Back then, when the incessant calls grew unbearable and Honza cornered him in every part of the city, he'd agree to meet him. It was illogical, almost comical in hindsight—Stefan knew that, but he figured out a bargaining chip. It was a dangerous game, a flawed strategy to keep Honza at bay. A promise to meet was nothing more than a distraction, a trick to lure Honza into leaving him be. Stefan didn't know better then, but he does now. He is no longer the same guy. He has a life here, one with a future he can actually picture—a future with Ade, who makes Stefan's heart race just by existing. A life he wants to see through without running.

The mere idea of being separated from Ade is too much too bear. And he never thought he could have this: someone he is head over heels for, someone he wants to worship the very ground he walks on, someone he wants to cherish and protect. And this realisation toughens Stefan, making it clear that he no longer needs to play Honza's games. Enough is enough.

"Omar," Honza says pleadingly. "Just for us to talk it out."

"I won't meet with you, ever. And if you follow me and

my friends again, I will report you to the police. For real this time."

There's a heavy pause on the other end of the line. Then, finally, a sigh. "Just know I love you," Honza says, the words hollow, like a badly delivered line in a cheap drama.

"Fuck outta my phone, *Galning*—maniac," Stefan swears as he ends the call. He saves the recording and sends it to his group chat with Żaneta and Edwin.

TÉNÍADÉ 😊 >
Wed 19.10 at 10:22 PM

> Why'd you leave Nigeria?

Because I miss Jola. She is miserable without me

> I can understand that.

Are you saying you'd be miserable without me?

> I don't give answers to rhetorical questions.

Smart boy with a smart mouth.

> And can do smart things with said smart mouth.

Describe them.

> ▶ ·ıl|ı|ıl||ıı|ıl|ıl|ııl 15:23

Damn, that's hot.

Happy to please.

Thur 20.10 at 08:45 PM

Do you have any allergies?

None that I know of. Want me to bring anything?

Your dick.

Can't leave it behind if I tried.

Gospel.

8
THE DATE

*— I Wanna Be Yours
by Arctic Monkeys.*

TÉNÍADÉ 😇 >
Today 08:40 AM

Jem and Tessa >>>>>>

Why did Jem have to become a silent bro?

> LOL. I prefer Jem and Tessa as well.
>
> You said no spoilers.

How did you know about Jem? Are you done reading?

Jola told me upfront lol.

Only a few more chapters to go. Will already went after Tessa.

> You can finish reading from my copy.

> There will be time for reading?

> You know what? No. You will be occupied.

> Doing what?

> Get here and you will find out.

> Little slut.

Saturday, 22nd October 2022.

THE MOST ANTICIPATED DAY IN STEFAN'S LIFE IS finally here, like the opening night of a long-running play he's convinced is about him. He walks regally into his bathroom, buoyed by a sense of anticipation, the kind that makes even a dreary Monday feel like a Friday in the summer. After today, he won't remain hopelessly and tragically single. No, he would've joined the ranks of love-struck fools.

"Siri, play 'Lovefool' by The Cardigans."

First order of business: shaving. Stefan has never been exceptionally gifted in the facial hair department—or anywhere else. Frankly, it's a small miracle there's anything sprouting atop his head at all. Still, he makes sure to attend to the areas that might later, if all goes according to plan, face invasion prim and proper. Thoroughly satisfied with his grooming, he steps into the shower. There's a very real chance, he muses, that he won't be showering alone tomorrow. The thought spawns a delicious little fantasy:

him, lathering Ade with shower gel, his hands sliding over every inch of skin—his chest, his arms, his legs, and—

"*Whoa.*"

His body makes its appreciation known in no uncertain terms, but that does little to deter Stefan's thoughts. Oh no, now he's imagining having to tiptoe to reach Ade's face, because of course, Ade insists on being taller. And yes, there would be hair-washing too. Ade's hair will require a *special* attention. After scrubbing Ade clean, there would be... rewards. He can see it all: Ade, on his knees, lips parting—

"Whoa," he repeats before addressing his increasingly impatient dick with a pointed glance. "Be patient."

The rest, Stefan decides, is best saved for the main event. Out of the shower, he slathers on his skincare products—one mustn't neglect the face on a day such as this. He then moves to his closet, dons a wool sweater and jeans, and leaves for Tesco. On his way, he reviews his need for a car, and concludes he doesn't even need one. After all, Jason drives him to campus, Ben drives him to work, and Ade drives him to distraction.

Wait. His thoughts are wandering again.

He surveys the area briskly as he walks but sees nothing suspicious, which is quite the relief. His phone call with Honza must have worked a miracle. After four fucking years. "*Galen pojke,*" he mutters, calling Honza a crazy person in Swedish.

Stefan was right—so right—to ask Ade out. It wasn't just a stroke of luck; it was one of those rare cosmic moments when the universe gives a firm nudge and mutters, "Well done." For once, his instincts hadn't been playing tricks on him. No, he had finally managed to get something spectacularly right.

In their exchange of glances, those awkward chuckles,

hilarious conversations, and insanely amazing kisses, he saw it—a connection worth chasing. Not some crush or half-hearted fling destined to fizzle out by next weekend, but something that has roots, depth. Something that settles deep in Stefan's chest, claiming him in a way he didn't know he needed. And it is also in the way Ade's presence steadies him, even when his heart threatens to flutter out of his chest. And then there are those conversations—or rather, those *not* conversations—the ones where they say absolutely nothing but seem to communicate everything.

And now here he is, standing on the cusp of everything he's ever wanted, trying his best not to burst at the seams with anticipation. His mind keeps spinning around the idea of looking Ade straight in the eyes and finally—*finally*—telling him. That he's in love with him. But it's not just about saying the words, is it? No, it's about that moment—that gloriously cinematic moment—when the words are out there, floating between them, and they're no longer dancing around it like two bashful teenagers. No more skirting the edges. No more hiding behind clever banter, coy flirtations and *accidental* make out sessions. Just them, standing in the open, touchy-feely and electric. And the promise of it sends Stefan soaring. He's floating well above the mundane realm now, up in the rare air of cloud nine, where nothing can touch him. For once, everything seems to be tilting in his favour. Now all he has to do is hold his nerve long enough to tell Ade what has been waiting, quietly and patiently, in his heart. And if his heart doesn't beat right out of his chest before then, well, that would be quite the bonus.

🏃

TÉNÍADÉ 💀 >

Today 11:24 AM

> Come with your haircare.

Wanna wash my hair?

> Wanna wash the whole of you.

Is this a date? Or a sex party for two?

> Sex party for two sounds cool. I like it.

Will pack an overnight bag.

Looking forward to SP42.

> I need you to come fast.

Really? Fast?

> Get your mind out of the bin.

Says the one with the invitation for SP42.

🏃

"Siri, play 'Take Me To Church' by Hozier," Stefan instructs as if Siri could ever understand his preparation for a night of risqué revelations and whatever comes after.

The kitchen becomes his sanctuary as he busies himself with the chopping and dicing of ingredients, slicing not just the vegetables but also any errant thoughts of Ade and what the evening may entail.

After Hozier, the music is unending, it shifts through "So What," followed by "Secrets." He's deep into "Life for

Rent" when Ade text arrives. Stefan immediately covers the bowls, tucks away the excess in the fridge, and washes his hands before heading upstairs to change into a more comfortable, indoor-friendly outfit. He steps onto his balcony, his fur robe cinched tight, and scans the parking lot, waiting for Ade to drive in. Soon, Ade's bZ4X drives into view, and Stefan's heart makes a predictable but no less dramatic leap. There's Ade, pulling up, beaming that devastating smile of his as he bobs his head to music. He watches as Ade opens his door and reaches back to grab a bouquet and gift bag. But then Ade pauses, drops the items on the passenger's seat, and lifts his phone to his ear.

"Oh, he has a call," Stefan comments to himself, mildly annoyed at whoever has the audacity to delay his man.

He should go downstairs and open the door. But... he can't. It's too much fun watching Ade, each second teasing him with the promise of what's come. Just as he's about to turn and make his way down, something stops him: Ade drops his phone, the smile abruptly vanishing, replaced with a look of utter distress. And before Stefan can even blink, Ade is hitting his head against the steering wheel.

What the actual fuck?

Panic rises in Stefan's chest. He bolts inside, sprinting down the stairs in such haste that he's barely aware of anything around him. He grabs his phone as he rushes out, his brain half-shouting at him for still being in flip-flops, of all things.

"Can't go back upstairs," he huffs, yanking on his coat and slipping into crocs.

He hurries, his pulse loud in his ears as his mind races to fill in the blanks of what he's just witnessed. He jabs the elevator buttons with far more force than necessary, anxiety crawling up his spine as the lift inches its way down.

He has to be okay. He has to be.

He crashes out of the front door, into the cool evening air, but when he reaches the parking lot and skids to a stop, there's nothing. No bZ4X. No Ade. Only the blank, indifferent stretch of tarmac where his car once sat. It's as if he was never there at all.

🏃

Stefan whirls around the parking lot like a man possessed, eyes darting left and right, his breath rising in quick, white puffs against the cold. His eyes sweeps over the parking lot, searching for a sign—any sign—that Ade hasn't simply evaporated into thin air. But a few stray leaves, tossed by the wind, are his only company.

Where is he?

His heart does that annoying plummeting thing hearts do in situations like this. Could Ade have actually left? Surely not. Stefan pulls out his phone, fumbling to dial Ade's number with trembling fingers. He mutters a string of increasingly desperate, "Come on, please pick up," pacing in tight circles as if this will summon Ade back by sheer kinetic energy.

The phone rings. And rings. *And rings.* Stefan's hope deflates like a punctured balloon with each unanswered ring, the cold creeping in despite his coat. After what feels like a lifetime of fruitless pacing, he pauses, eyes narrowing at the AMG parked before him. He absurdly crouches down and peers underneath the car—just to be sure Ade and his SUV didn't shrink and are hiding there. His mind spins through a maze of worst-case scenarios, each more troubling than the last. He stops dialling Ade now to order an Uber. The idiot who accepts the ride is still twenty minutes away and completing another trip. *I should have bought a darn car*. Stefan cancels, reorders, and gets the same fool again. "Fuck off."

He gives up on Uber and resumes dialling Ade, still pacing around the parking lot, but there is no response. He orders another Uber, this time a measly eight minutes away. Progress, at least. Stefan concludes calling Ade is useless and dials Jola instead, but there is no response either. When his phone finally rings, he fishes it out of his pocket, hoping it is Ade calling him back, or even Jola, but it is Ben.

"Hi Ben," he says, trying not to sound too panicked.

"Hey Stefan, what's up?"

"Are you with Jola?" Stefan skips the pleasantries, heart beating out a frantic rhythm.

"Yes, do you know what happened?"

"I'm almost there."

Stefan is already halfway out of the Uber before he even registers leaving it, racing up the stairs two at a time. He bursts into the Bower-Adeowo's living room where he finds Ben.

Ben greets him with a bear hug. "You look harried. What happened?"

Stefan clings to Ben, and catches his breath for a minute. "I don't know," he says, voice strained. "Something agitated him, but he was gone when I got downstairs. Did he say anything when he got here?"

"The only thing he said was to tell you he's sorry," Ben says.

Stefan's confusion grows at Ben's words. *Why would Ade apologise?* Jola enters the room before he can voice his questions, followed by Temmy and Sophia.

Jola rushes to Stefan immediately, radiating concern.

"My God, Stefan, are you okay?" She inquires, pulling him into another hug.

Stefan's throat tightens. She's worried *about him*? How can she be thinking about his welfare when Ade's the one who should have all her attention. "I'm fine, Jola," he croaks, though his voice barely gets the words out. "How's he?"

"He's sleeping," Temmy replies.

Sophia offers a hug next. "He did say to tell you sorry, whatever for?"

"I have no idea. He didn't even come upstairs. I saw him from the balcony, and he..." he says in a rush. His throat hurts like hell.

Temmy pats his arm. "Why don't you sit down? And you can tell us the bit you know after you rest."

Stefan nods, sinking into a nearby couch. He accepts a glass of water with thanks from Jola, who settles on the arm of his couch. He then explains everything he saw earlier. From Ade driving in, the mysterious phone call, the hitting of the head, and how he wasn't in the parking lot when Stefan ran out. "Did you see his phone?" he asks, thinking the call could've been about a family member. "Or did you get any call?"

Temmy seems to have reached the same conclusion. He is already dialling a number. "*Maami?*" he says once the call connects.

Stefan figures it means mother in Yoruba.

"I'm fine, we're all fine, ma," he says and pauses. "Did anything happen? How's dad?" Temmy listens for a minute, then mouths, "Everything is fine at home."

The rest of the call is in rapid Yoruba. Stefan understands nothing.

Temmy sighs. "He's sleeping. I'm telling the truth," he gives the phone to Sophia.

"Mumsy, he's okay. We're just trying to understand what call he got," Sophia says and listens for a beat. "Stefan told us. He's here."

Stefan is shocked by this. Did Ade tell his mom about him? He dreamily thinks about meeting Ade's mom for a second, then snaps out of it. *Now is not the time.*

"I'll switch the call to video and show him to you," Sophia says, leaving the room with Temmy.

"We should check the car," Stefan suggests, springing to his feet.

Jola grasps his hand. "Thank you for coming."

They fan out with a sort of silent choreography—Stefan to the passenger's seat, Jola to the driver's, and Ben to the back seat. Stefan see Ade's phone almost immediately, resting forlornly on the floor beside a card. "Found it," he announces and gives the phone to Jola before turning the card over. "Beautiful lilies for my beautiful boy." The words twist his gut in the sweetest, most painful way, like bittersweet honey poured over a wound.

"It's locked, and he's asleep," Jola makes a disgruntled noise. "I have to wait."

Stefan takes the phone back from her. "I know his passcode," he says as a way of explanation.

The look on Jola's face would scare anyone less used to her—shock, surprise, and something resembling admiration. But she takes the phone without comment and begins scrolling. Five minutes later, she lets out a scream that could wake the dead. "Temmy!" she screeches, bolting from the car. Ben and Stefan exchange a wide-eyed glance—silent communication for, *What fresh hell is this?*—and then they're both scrambling after her.

Inside, Jola's already mid-rant, her voice reaching the

entryway from the base of the stairs, her words a furious blur of, "I found it. Mom and dad should've let me treat his fuck up." Stefan catches up just as she drops an "*Omo àlè yen ni*" with the kind of venom that would make any recipient need an antidote. Stefan—thanks to Ade—knows the phrase roughly translates to "that bastard." It's oddly comforting at a time like this, realising that he's even learned Ade's bad words. Small victories.

Ben, jacket now hanging neatly by the door like a man preparing for battle, looks at Stefan. Neither of them moves. It's painfully clear that they've stumbled into a family moment, a private one. Should they retreat, fade into the background like the outsiders they are? Or would that be more awkward than staying?

"We can think of fuck ups and whatnot later," Temmy says, his voice low and controlled. "Right now, Ade needs help. Proper help. And I don't know how we can make him see that."

"He refuses," Jola says. "I've tried to convince him countlessly."

Feeling like eavesdroppers at this point, Stefan and Ben drift towards the group. The conversation stutters to a halt as they approach. Stefan, driven by curiosity and worry—against his better judgment—asks, "What's going on?" He regrets the question almost immediately, but it hangs there, impossible to unsay.

Temmy gives Stefan a polite, if slightly patronising, smile. "It's something from the past. Ade is in the best position to explain." His words are vague and offer no real insight. He gives Ade's phone to Jola. "Unlock this."

Jola shakes her head. "Stefan unlocked it."

Temmy's expression shifts, not hiding his surprise, he gives the phone to Stefan without further comment. Stefan tells him the passcode instead. "I want to see him," he informs. "You'll be able to unlock it if it locks again."

"Thanks. You can stay for as long as you'd like," Temmy says with the authority of someone used to managing crises.

Stefan nods in thanks, his mind already half upstairs with Ade. "Where can I get a vase?" he asks as he waves the bouquet a little, feeling slightly foolish. "I want to put these in his room."

"There is an empty one on the table by the entryway," Sophia informs.

"Thank you," Stefan says, already heading for the door.

Stefan ascends the staircase, Temmy's words echoing in his mind: *Something from the past.*

"What's in your past, Teni?"

But the idea of the past resurfacing to wreak havoc on the present strikes an uncomfortable chord with Stefan. He knows that tune far too well. Hadn't he fled from the past just this year to seek solace in the anonymity of new beginnings? But whatever this is, at least Ade doesn't have to face it alone. Ade has him now.

The door clicks shut behind him, and he steps into Ade's room where he sees Ade sleeping like his brother said. Stefan pads across the room, silent as a cat, and makes for the bathroom. The vase in hand, he fills it with water, then sets it on the chest of drawers as if he's performing some delicate ritual, because in a way, he is. He kneels beside the bed and reaches for a towel, tenderly wiping the sheen of sweat from Ade's forehead. His fingers linger, tracing the elegant arch of Ade's brow with the kind of reverence usually reserved for rare books.

After a few minutes, Stefan rises with a quiet efficiency and rummages through Ade's closet for a new pair of pyjamas. He steps back into the room, plucks *Ace of Spades* from the bookshelf and sits with his back to the headrest. He switches on the reading lamp dimly, and begins to stroke Ade's hair absently, fingers moving through soft coils like they're a part of him.

But his mind is wandering. What's that old saying? *Man proposes, God... discards? Dissociates?* He's fairly certain it's not *composts*, though given Stefan's day, that too might be appropriate.

Their plans lie in a heap somewhere, but it doesn't matter—Stefan is here, beside Ade, where he needs to be. That's the bit that counts, surely. With a barely-there sigh, Stefan opens the book and begins to read.

9

THE AFTERMATH

— Futile Devices
by Sufjan Stevens.

Saturday, 22nd October 2022.

As the final credits of *The Mortal Instruments: City of Bones* roll across the screen, Ade rises from his bed. He decides to hold off on any commentary about the movie until their ritual of post-viewing debate—after all, Stefan's the expert on urban fantasy and shadowy teenagers. Though, Ade grins to himself, that debate might just have to wait, because, well, he and Stefan may have other pressing matters to attend to. Movies—*even* Stefan's favourites, may have to take the back seat.

Sauntering into his closet like a dark prince, he makes an executive decision: he will pack a bigger luggage instead of his backpack. It is practical to leave it in Stefan's loft permanently to avoid the hassle of repacking a bag when he spends the night at Stefan's because—he grins again—there's a *lot* of spending the night at Stefan's in his future.

By the time he's done rummaging through his closet, he's pulled together a selection that could clothe a small city: sweatpants, jeans, tailored trousers, shirts, round necks, pyjamas, socks, towels, and of course all necessary skincare and haircare products. He then pauses mid-thought—ah, underwear. Slightly important.

He tosses those in alongside a new bottle of Tobacco Vanille, the perfume he's convinced makes him smell like sophistication wrapped in a hug. Then he's off to the bathroom for a quick shower, emerging minutes later dressed in a light blue round neck and black tailored trousers. He is checking himself out in the mirror when he remembers the most crucial items of the day, he heads straight to his drawer to retrieve them.

"Never to be caught unfresh *or* unprepared," he chortles, a little bit proud of himself.

He wheels the bag over to his room before returning to the mirror for one final, slightly panicked touch: rehearsing his declaration. "Stef, before anything happens between us, I want you to know I'm in love with you," he tries aloud, then cringes immediately. Too stiff.

Okay, maybe a simpler approach? "I love you, Stef." Short. Direct. About as romantic as a post-it note.

He frowns and tries again. "Stef, I love you so much that I feel my heart expanding as your love grows." Ade wrinkles his nose. Now it actually sounds like a heartfelt confession *and* an impending heart condition.

"*Wo, mo ma pada improvise ni,*" he mutters in Yoruba, deciding that his best bet is to wing it.

He follows the sound of chatter to the living room where he finds his siblings and Ben. "Are you moving out?" Sophia asks, as if already planning to give his room to one of his nephews.

"Just when we were hoping to charge you and the other rascal here rent," Temmy adds.

Jola points to Ade's luggage. "What's that?"

Ade grins with a touch of malevolence. "Charge rent, dad will pay," addressing the couple before turning to Jola. "This," he gestures dramatically to his sizeable luggage, "is an overnight bag."

"More like an over-year bag," Ben comments.

Naturally, the room erupts into fits of laughter, as if Ben is the king of comedy. Ade rolls his eyes but can't help chuckling. "I'll be back... whenever," he announces, making a quick exit to the garage before anyone can delay him further.

He texts Stefan: *on my way*. He then slides into his car and heads off, Katy Perry's "Roar" blasting through the speakers.

Ade's first detour is to the wine store on Ponteland, where he takes his time, deliberating over the bottles like he's selecting rare jewels and not booze. He handpicks an array of fine wine, a choice that will make even a sommelier nod in approval. Satisfied, he moves on to his next stop: the florist on Middle Dr and Rotary and collects his order of a bouquet of lilies. He smiles, thinking about Stefan's list of favourite flowers. Ade, bless him, intends to buy every single one—possibly more flowers than Stefan can fit in his loft, but there's no no half-measures when it comes to love.

He reflects on the different tasks on his to-do list today, many of them for the first time, and he is bursting with anticipation. When he'd gone out with Jeffery, things had been... fine. Pleasant, even. But this is worlds apart. With

Stefan, it's as if his heart was locked and abandoned like a long-forgotten chest in an attic, has now been found, opened, and brought back to life. Ade is high on love, utterly intoxicated. He imagines capturing its essence in poetry, singing ballads in its honour to the moon, or even grabbing a megaphone and announcing it to anyone who will listen. How could he not? When one finds something as profound and precious as this, hiding it seems criminal.

He drives into the parking lot of Stefan's building and finds an empty space to park. He's halfway out of the car when his phone rings. He fishes for it, thinking it's Stefan calling. After all, he's set the ringer just for Stefan's calls, lest he miss it. That's love, isn't it? Taking your phone off silent for someone. But the caller ID isn't Stefan. It's not anyone he knows, actually. It's an unsaved Nigerian number. Ade's first thought is that it might be his parents—new SIM, maybe? There's no real reason for them to call from a different number, but better safe than sorry. He answers. "Hello?"

The voice on the other end is one Ade is not prepared for. "Don't you miss me?" The drawl is unmistakable, sending a chill through him like ice slipping down his spine. Ade's brain momentarily freezes, his fingers unable to act, trapped in some awful paralysis.

"I just heard you fled because you couldn't handle me breaking your heart," the voice barks a harsh laugh. "Such a pussy."

Ade barely whispers, "Yinka?" as though saying the name might make it less real.

Yinka's laugh comes again, harsh and twisted. "Don't you want to fuck me? Kiss me? Stupid fag. Your kind should be beheaded. Imprisonment is not en—"

Ade's brain thaws. Memories rushing at him like a

raging river—cheap liquor in his hair, eyes burning, taunts ringing in his ears, the cracks in his phone, the shame, the humiliation, the indignity of it. His chest is suddenly tight, constricted by an invisible force around his heart, squeezing it without mercy. His hand trembles as he silences his phone and throws it onto the passenger seat. His skin is slick with sweat, his whole body vibrating with the rawness of it all.

"WHY?" he bellows. "Why, why, why?" He pounds his head against the steering wheel, over and over, in a frenzied attempt to drown out the pain. In a blind rush, he shuts the door and speeds off.

Later, Ade won't remember the drive home, won't recall a single detail of the drive. Somehow, the car finds its way into the driveway. He doesn't even bother with the garage. He needs to get out. He feels like the enclosed space is suffocating him. Without a second thought, he rushes out of the car and into the house. In the entryway, the puzzled stares of his siblings barely registers because Ade's heart is currently shattering painfully.

"Tell him I'm sorry," he manages to choke out before fleeing to his room.

He storms into his room and collapses to the floor, knees up, chin resting on them, his body shaking violently as though it might shatter from the inside. He doesn't even notice his siblings have followed him until Temmy scoots down to him. "Ade, what's wrong?"

Ade can't answer. It is difficult to breathe. Temmy sits behind him, cushioning him till the trebling begins to subside. Ade raises his head then, eyes red. "I couldn't do it," he laments. "I couldn't go in. You have to tell him I'm sorry."

"Ben probably called him already," Temmy says in a calm and gentle tone. "Can you tell us what happened?"

Jola kneels in front of him; mirroring the pain Ade feels. The pain is so raw, it cuts through his heart. "Teniade, *kílóselè?*—what happened?" she takes his hand, her voice pleading. "Please tell us."

Ade presses a hand to his chest, grabbing the flesh as if trying to claw his heart out from inside and to stop it from beating. Tears spill down his face, unchecked.

"It's okay. You can tell us later." Temmy removes Ade's hand from his chest.

Sophia enters the room with a tray—water, a glass, and a small tablet. She sets it down on a bedside drawer and kneels beside Jola. "I brought you something to help you sleep, hon. Will you take it?"

Ade nods weakly, and Temmy helps him get to his closet to change into Pyjamas. The tablet kicks in quickly, pulling him down into sleep where, mercifully, the pain doesn't follow.

⚘

Sunday, 23rd October 2022.

Ade wakes up slowly, his senses gradually tuning into the world around him.

As he gets more conscious, he feels a familiar hand threading through his hair. He doesn't need to open his eyes to know whose it is—Stefan's touch is as unmistakable as it is calming, a mixture of tenderness and quiet strength, the kind of touch that says, "I've got you," without making a fuss about it. Ade's chest tightens, and not just because he's been lying awkwardly on his side. The memories of this afternoon flood back, uninvited and insistent. *Did Stefan come for me?* He wonders. *And he's still here?* Despite Ade's disappearing act, complete with no calls, no texts—just radio silence, ruining their whole day. And yet, here Stefan is, right by his side.

In this precise moment, Ade's love for Stefan deepens, like roots finding richer soil. But how can he explain without sending the poor guy running for the hills? Ade is usually articulate, but regarding this particular issue, he finds himself at a loss of words, unable to be coherent. It's shameful and he struggles to even think about it. The thought of revealing it makes his skin crawl with embarrassment. It's not exactly the sort of thing you drop into casual conversation—"By the way, I have this unspoken affliction that makes me want to curl up and disappear, but fancy a cup of tea?" No, that won't do at all.

Or is Stefan here as a courtesy? Ade frets. He could just be a nice guy who feels obliged to come after him out of decency. Maybe he's mentally composing his escape route—something polite and well-rehearsed before vanishing into the night, never to be seen again. Ade shakes his head, trying to banish the thought. *No*, he tells himself firmly, *Stefan is here because he cares*. It's the only lifeline he can hold onto right now.

"Stef?" His voice breaks the silence before he even realises he's spoken.

"Yes, it's me." Stefan's voice is soothing, reassuring, and just a touch amused—as if to say, *who else would it be, the postman?*

Ade rolls over, finally opening his eyes. The room is dark, except for the lamp, which appears to be set at dim, but he sees Stefan clearly—he's sure he'd see him even if it's pitch dark, he will see Stefan's face even if he goes blind.

"I'm so sorry," Ade blurts out, voice cracking. "I shouldn't have left. I couldn't think. It felt like I was choking. I'm sorry."

"Shhhh," Stefan hushes him with a gentle finger to his lips. He stretches out fully on the bed beside him. "You don't have to be sorry, and you don't have to explain anything right now. Okay?" He leans in, planting a soft kiss on Ade's forehead. "Do you feel better? Can I get you anything?"

And for the first time in forever, Ade feels a glimmer of peace. Stefan is here. His beautiful boy is here. And that's enough to keep the demons at bay, at least for now. His eyes blur, an unruly mix of relief and gratitude. Knowing that Stefan is here, not out of a sense of obligation, but because he wants to be.

"What time is it?" Ade's voice is quiet, more out of awe than fatigue.

Stefan squints at his phone screen. "It's just past two in the morning."

"Why aren't you asleep?" Ade edges closer to Stefan.

Stefan shrugs with that easy grace of his. "Didn't bring my sleep meds. Could've borrowed some of yours, but I decided to stay awake in case you wake up.."

Ade's heart practically jumps. It seems impossible—quite unbelievable—that someone like Stefan would go through such lengths for him. It makes Ade feel like he's won a prize he never even realised he was in the running for. "Thank you," he nestles in, the way one might sidle up to a warm cup of tea on a cold day.

Stefan tilts his head. "Are you sure you don't need anything? Water, maybe?"

Ade's breath hitches, words spilling out before he can second-guess them. "I need you," he whispers. "Only you."

In the next second, Stefan closes the distance, capturing Ade's mouth in a kiss that feels both familiar and urgent, as if every kiss before this one had only been practice. Stefan's hand grips Ade's arm, and soon, his tongue is exploring Ade's mouth with the kind of fervour that makes time irrelevant. His hands roam over Ade's body, tracing every line, every curve, and the soft, breathless moans that escape him set a fire under Ade's skin, melting away the last remnants of his anxiety. Ade kisses him back with equal enthusiasm, his fingers diving into Stefan's hair, feeling the way it tangles through them, messy and wonderful. Every touch, every sound from Stefan, has Ade dissolving into him—completely and irrevocably undone.

Stefan's hands hover just above the collar of Ade's pyjama shirt. "I want you," he murmurs, his voice thick, dripping with need.

Ade's breath turns ragged, his pulse drumming wildly beneath his skin as a fiery heat floods through him, leaving nothing but desire in its wake. "I want you, too," he murmurs against Stefan's mouth, the words slipping out like a confession he'd held on to for far too long.

Stefan's fingers fumble, a little trembly, as they begin undoing the buttons of Ade's pyjama shirt.

"I've wanted you since the moment I met you," Ade continues, as though he's only just realised it himself. "Even when I didn't know who you were... I wanted you."

There's something deliciously reckless in the way Stefan nips at Ade's upper lip, almost like he's making up for lost time. "You are always in my dreams," he whispers, his voice rough. "Always." His hands, now bold, push Ade's pyjama shirt from his shoulders, as if shedding the last vestiges of restraint.

Stefan's lips trail from the corner of Ade's mouth to his

jaw, then lower, each kiss a scorching little promise. His tongue carves a hot, moist path down Ade's neck, chest, stopping just at the peak of his nipples. Ade's fingers curl into Stefan's hair, gripping tighter, desperate for more. He silently urges Stefan on, the feel of his tongue and lips against his skin making him shudder.

When Stefan's mouth finally returns to his, it's more frantic than before, as if they might somehow devour each other whole. "I can never get enough of this," Stefan breathes between kisses, "I can never get enough of you."

Ade's hands are already working on Stefan's pyjama shirt. "It's the same for me," he mutters, fingers gliding over Stefan's chest and down to the band of his trousers. His hands wander further back, slipping inside to cup Stefan's bare arse, squeezing it with a wicked grin as Stefan gasps into his mouth.

"Damn, Stef," Ade whispers in a low, appreciative growl, "so soft."

He hastily pulls down Stefan's pyjamas bottoms, leaving him exposed. Ade's hand finds its rhythm, stroking Stefan with the kind of intent precision that has Stefan's voice quivering. "Yes," Stefan pants. "Yes, *Teni*."

"I want all of you," Ade breathes, the raw hunger in his words conspicuous.

Stefan opens his eyes, dark with longing, that unmistakable smoulder. "Then take me."

Ade, completely unravelled by the hankering coursing through his veins, skittishly reaches into the drawer at his bedside, hands moving faster than his brain. He tosses a bottle and packet onto the table, never for once breaking eye contact. With exquisite care, he rolls Stefan onto his back, his hand never losing its rhythm.

"You're so beautiful. You're perfect."

But just as he is on the brink of transcendence, an unwelcome intruder—doubt—creeps in. It sweeps through Ade's mind like a gale, all dark thoughts and sharp pangs, impossible to ignore.

His heart clenches, but he pushes it aside, choosing, for now, to focus on Stefan. He moves over him, supporting his weight on one elbow as he dips down to capture Stefan's mouth once more, getting lost in the way Stefan's body responds to his touch, arching into him. He lets his lips travel up to Stefan's forehead, his breath coming in uneven gasps, and kisses his way down Stefan's face, from his nose to the sensitive shell of his ear. But when he's at Stefan's neck, Stefan's voice breaks through the haze.

"Teni," Stefan whispers. "We can stop if you want."

Ade blinks, confused and lost. "I don't wanna stop."

Stefan's fingers gently brush his own neck, then reach out to smear something wet across Ade's arm. "But you're crying," he says, pulling Ade down on him, his fingers running through Ade's hair. "I thought it was sweat at first, but you're crying. It's okay... we can stop if it's too much."

Ade's head spins. *Crying?* He hadn't even noticed the tears, nor when they began to fall.

"Hey," Stefan's voice is so commiserative it threatens to undo Ade entirely. "Are you alright?"

Ade can only nod. His throat feels tight, and his mind is a whirlwind. He *wants* to say something, to tell Stefan that he loves him so much it wrenches his heart. That this—he—means more to him than anything. That loving him is the easiest thing in the world, even when everything else feels impossible. But the words remain stuck in his throat.

There is something inside him, a darkness within, something that's been hiding in plain sight, something he can no longer ignore. He's scared of it, and scared of what it might do to someone as good, as kind as Stefan. And others may call it denial, but to Ade, it's more like a finely tuned survival instinct. He's constructed a cage around himself, fully aware that the world seems hell-bent on breaking him, piece by fragile piece. So, naturally, Ade does what any reasonable person would do: he runs. No, *sprints*—from the dreary feeling of being lesser, of being weak.

In avoidance, he finds a strange, stubborn strength, a way to stay afloat in a sea of challenges. It's not that Ade doesn't see the harsh realities—oh, he sees them all too clearly. But here's the thing: by shoving them aside, he carves out just enough space to breathe, to endure, to live another day.

He rolls off Stefan, embarrassment now replacing the earlier fire. "I can... I can continue till you..." but the words fall flat.

Stefan pulls his own bottoms back up and wraps his arms around Ade, holding him close, providing him a sanctuary. "It's okay," Stefan reassures, his lips brushing against Ade's hair. "We don't have to do anything."

Ade leans into the comfort, holding on to him tighter, his heart pounding in his chest. "Thanks, Stef. For being here."

"I'll always be here," Stefan says, stifling a yawn. "I'd do anything for you."

My God, I need to get help. I cannot give him half a heart; he deserves better than that. He deserves so much more.

By the time the first light of dawn creeps through the curtains, Ade knows precisely what he must do.

10
THERAPY

*— Mystery of Love
by Sufjan Stevens.*

Ade barely slept. The night had been a series of half-conscious turns. He's wide awake when the soft knock on his door comes, and Jola's voice follows. "Ade?"

"Come in, Jughead," Ade's tired voice calls.

Jola steps in, her eyes immediately catching on the way Ade's fingers lazily comb through Stefan's hair. "I told him to do that for you yesterday," she whispers.

Ade forces a weak smile. "He did. Woke up around two. He wasn't sleeping then."

Jola nods, coming closer. "I just wanted to check on you," she says, her hand cool as it presses against his forehead like she's measuring something. "See if you're alright. Need anything?" She reaches for the bedside drawer, but her eyes flick away almost instantly.

"I'm fine," Ade assures her, though there's a slight crack

in his voice, like he's holding something back. "Still in one piece."

"I can see that," Jola chuckles. "And *so* is he, but don't let me wake him." She gestures towards Stefan's peacefully slumbering form with a mock attempt at discretion.

"Wait." Ade's voice catches her just as she turns to leave. "I need to talk to you. In your room." Carefully, he lifts Stefan's head onto a pillow before standing up, as if he is handling the most precious thing in the world. He grabs two pyjama shirts from the floor, folds one neatly beside Stefan and slips the other over his own tired body. For a moment, he stands there, staring at Stefan with an unguarded, almost raw yearning, completely forgetting why he wanted to talk to Jola in the first place.

"You'll see him after. Stop staring like you want to pounce on him," Jola teases. Throwing him a look over her shoulder.

Ade doesn't laugh, not even a hint of a smile. Instead, he sighs, leans down to kiss Stefan's hair and forehead, before straightening up again, trying to keep the conflict within him from seeping out. But Jola already notices his downturned lips, downcast eyes, and slumped shoulders. "What's wrong?" she asks, her teasing gone, replaced by concern. "You said you're okay."

He waits until they're in her room, then sits on the bed, exhaling like he's been holding his breath for hours. "I don't think I'll be okay for a long time, Jola."

"Talk to me," she says, sitting beside him. "Why would you say that?"

Ade takes a deep breath, his eyes clouded with something deeper than exhaustion. "Remember in June, when I told you I didn't feel anything about what happened? That I was fine because, you know, crazy things happen all the time?"

Jola nods, her hand finding his, giving him something to anchor himself to.

"I lied," he says, his voice cracking slightly. "I wasn't fine. I felt humiliated... worthless, even. I-I just shoved it to the back of m-my mind, pretended it didn't matter. As long as I didn't see or hear from any of them, I could ignore it, move on. And I tried. I thought I could just meet new people, hang out, and have fun. Nothing serious." He lets out a small, bitter laugh. "But I fell in love, Jola. I fell hard. And now... I can't be with him. Not like this."

Jola snatches her hands from his and stands abruptly. "You *can't* be with him?" she echoes bewilderedly. "B-b-but you slept with him?"

Ade shakes his head. "I didn't. I mean... I couldn't."

"You *couldn't?*" Her voice lowers, like she's tiptoeing around something delicate.

The question in her eyes is clear, so Ade spares her the awkwardness. "Not couldn't... I cried," he admits.

"Is that why you think you can't be with him?" Her voice softens, and she reaches out, her hand back in his.

"I can't, Jola," he repeats, wiping away a stray tear. "I can't be with him like this."

Jola dials Temmy, telling him to bring Sophia. In a few minutes, they appear, walking into the room with curious but worried expressions. "What's wrong?" Temmy asks, looking between Jola and Ade.

Jola sighs, gesturing towards Ade. "He doesn't want to be with Stefan."

"What?" Temmy and Sophia echo in disbelief.

"Did something happen?" Temmy asks, directing the question to Ade now.

Ade shakes his head. "No... I just... I can't look him in the eyes and," he pulls the flesh at his throat.

Temmy takes Ade's hand, squeezing it gently. "Did he say anything to you?" he turns to Jola.

Jola shakes her head. "Nothing he isn't saying now. He cannot be with him, not like this."

Sophia sits beside Ade. "Not like how, honey? It's obvious you both love each other."

"I do love him," Ade whispers. "But I need to be better for him. I want to be better for him. I need to start therapy."

"It's not that you don't want to be with him," Jola says, piecing it together. "Like this. You don't want to be with him when you think there's something broken about you?"

"Yes," Ade nods, a tear slipping down his cheek.

"But don't you think being with him will do better to help you heal?" Sophia asks.

"I understand better now," Jola says. Sophia and Temmy turn to her. "He mentioned he couldn't be intimate with him an—"

"What do you mean couldn't?" Temmy interrupts.

"I'll explain properly," Ade sighs, "but can I see Sparks today?"

"I'll go call him," Temmy says, leaving the room.

"You'll be okay, hon," Sophia hugs Ade sideways.

"He'll be here before noon," Temmy informs, dragging Jola's work chair to sit in front of Ade. "He doesn't work today but understands why it's important."

"Thanks, Temmy," Ade says.

Temmy takes Ade's hand again, offering a small smile. "You know there is nothing you can't tell us, right?"

Ade clears his throat, voice steady, and launches into a detailed explanation.

"I had no idea I was even crying until he pointed it out," he says, sucking in a deep lungful of air. "I knew then that I needed help. If I don't get a grip on things, this will keep happening, and it won't be fair to him." His voice wavers but doesn't break. "Wouldn't it be better to be with him when I rid myself of these burdens?"

He winces, and presses a finger against his temples, rubbing circles to massage away the worry lodged there. What he really wants, craves even, is Stefan's touch—the quiet reassurance of his presence. But this decision, this one, is his alone. Ade knows he must heal first.

The room falls into a heavy silence that stretches until Temmy, in his no-nonsense manner, slices through the quiet. "So, let me get this straight. You think if you tell Stefan what's going on, he'll not want to be with you?"

Ade nods, his eyes fixed stubbornly on the floor. "Yes."

"And your plan," Temmy continues, incredulous but calm, "is to fix yourself, get help, but in the meantime, just not see him? Avoid him?"

Ade's head snaps up, caught off guard. He shrugs, helpless. "Yes?"

Temmy, arms crossed, leans forward slightly. "And what exactly do you plan on telling him? 'Sorry, I'm off on a little self-improvement holiday. See you when I'm less of a mess'? How do you think that will go?"

Ade falters, thrown by the bluntness. He hadn't thought it through—not really. He had convinced himself that absence would be better than inadequacy, but now... now, he can see the gaping holes in his logic.

Temmy groans, his head tilting back in exasperation. "Ade, seriously, are we supposed to go tell him to shove off because you're 'working on yourself'? The guy came here yesterday looking like his heart had been run through a shredder, and you think he's going to just walk away?"

Sophia leans in, her voice gentler, more like a caress than a reprimand. "I said the same thing to Temmy yesterday. Anyone else would've been livid with you for driving off without a word. But Stefan? He was all nerves and heart eyes, worried sick about you."

Jola reaches and takes his hand. "He was the one who suggested we search for your phone, you know? He was frantic when you left, called you forty times, no exaggeration. Forty!"

Ade's stormy mind calms. Hope swells in him, cautiously at first. Could it be true? Could Stefan really understand, not view him as irreparably broken? Maybe, just maybe there's room to breathe. Room to heal and love, wholly, with no holdbacks, with no discord in his mind.

Jola presses on. "And he called me as well. I saw it later. Like I've told you, don't give unworthy people control over your life and choices. They are irrelevant. You can unpack, unburden, and get better while with him. He's choosing you. Let him."

Temmy leans back, arms crossed but the hard edge in his voice softens. "It's a wonderful step to want to be better for him. That shows you love him, and you know he deserves all of you. The whole nine yards." A beat passes. "If you stop seeing him now, if you tell him you can't be with him, you can't be sure he will want to be with you after you think you're ready to love him as he deserves."

Sophia nods in agreement. "If you're overwhelmed and can't be intimate, it's normal. Tell him. Lay it all out, darling."

Ade nods, feeling the weight on his chest begin to lift as

his siblings weave a net of support beneath him, ready to catch him if he falls. It's as if their collective strength is transferring into him, fortifying his will to finally face the things he's been avoiding. He looks around at them—Temmy, Sophia, Jola—and can't help but feel a deep, unspoken gratitude.

They've all been nudging him gently, persistently, to get help since June. Every conversation, every quiet check-in, had contained the subtle but steady encouragement to stop pretending he could carry the burden alone. And yet, not one of them had thrown an "I told you so" in his face.

Their patience astounds him. It would've been so easy for them to give up on him or grow tired of his avoidance, to get frustrated with his stubborn refusal to face his own pain. But they never did. They stood by him with quiet, steady loyalty, like lighthouses on a stormy shore, waiting for him to find his way home. Ade smiles, a genuine, grateful smile that pulls at the corners of his mouth, lighting up his tired eyes.

A lump forms in his throat, but it's not the kind of pressure that threatens to crush him. It's the kind that comes from being overwhelmed by love, from realising how lucky he is to have them—his siblings who see him, truly see him, in all his messiness and fragility, and love him anyway. "Thank you," he says. "I love you."

Jola sighs with relief and kisses his cheeks. "We love you too."

Temmy stands up, a sense of finality in his movements. "Remember what mom and dad always tell us. Love is the one thing you can't screw up unless you don't try," he says, clapping his brother on the shoulder.

Ade rises too, stretching out his limbs as if the conversation has left him lighter, more alive. His lips curl into a grin. "Right. Well, speaking of love... I think I'll go have sex now."

Jola rolls her eyes but can't hide her smile. "Sparks is going to have his hands full with you. And I'll be breaking into his office to read your file, just for fun."

Temmy points at Ade. "You go do that," then at Jola, "I won't bail you out." He takes his wife's hand, "Come along, baby."

Jola makes a disgusted sound, watching them leave her room.

With a spring in his step, Ade makes his way back to his room, mind abuzz with everything his siblings said. He's going to tell Stefan everything—every bit of pain, every crack, every flaw. He's going to tell him how much he loves him and—he grins devilishly—he's going to finish what they started earlier.

He pushes open the door, careful not to make too much noise in case Stefan is still asleep. But as he steps inside, his smile fades. The bed is empty. Stefan isn't sleeping. In fact, Stefan isn't there at all.

"Stef?" Ade calls, knocking on the bathroom door, hoping for the familiar sound of Stefan's voice.

Silence. Not a peep from the other side. A pit forms in his stomach as he glances around the room. Something's off. It takes him a second to notice—Stefan's pyjamas, neatly folded on the floor, like an offering to the gods. Panic, swift and unyielding, wraps its icy fingers around Ade's chest.

In a blur, he bolts out of his room, voice echoing through the house. "Stefan?" His shout ricochets off the walls, far louder than intended. Somewhere in the back of his mind, he remembers his nephews are still asleep. Well, were asleep, most likely.

"Ade?" Temmy appears in the corridor, closely followed by Sophia and Jola, all looking mildly alarmed.

Ade's already halfway to the stairs, his feet barely touching the steps. "I can't find him. He's not in my room!" he yells, the words spilling out as he skids dangerously close to tumbling down the stairs. "Shit, shit, shit."

He flings himself into a berserk search, checking every room. Living room? Empty. Kitchen? No sign. Dining room? Nada. Playroom? Full of toys, no Stefan. His heart pounds in his ears as he sprints towards the party room, praying that Stefan's just gotten lost in the house's labyrinthine halls. Then, he hears a car outside in the driveway. Could it be? He rushes to the entryway, nearly crashing headfirst into Ben.

"Ade, what happened to Stefan?" Ben skips the greetings, straight to the point, his expression not giving anything away.

"You've seen him?" Ade's voice rises in pitch, a note of pleading creeping in. "Please, take me to him."

"Did he say anything to you?" Jola asks, walking to Ben.

"Only wants Jason," Ben replies.

Ade's heart drops to somewhere near his knees. He lunges for the door, but Jola grabs his arm. "You're in PJs and slippers. Go change"

"I have to go now," Ade protests, his throat tightening.

Jola hands him a jacket. "Ben, please take him."

Ade nods gratefully, slipping on the jacket, not bothering to zip it up. He's out the door before anyone can say another word, slippers slapping against the pavement, heart hammering in his chest, hoping against hope that it isn't what he thinks it is.

A heavy numbness paralyses Ade as he steps back into the house, feeling as if every breath takes twice the effort. His siblings are already gathered in the entryway, a silent chorus of concerned faces as they take in his wet cheeks and swollen eyes, and though they don't say a word, their arms encircle him in warm, familiar embraces.

Jola peels off his jacket. "We'll talk later. Go. He's in the study."

Ade shuffles towards Temmy's study, dread pooling in his gut. He's already ruined everything before it even began, hasn't he? *Brilliant strategy, Ade.* Why hadn't he thought it through? Why hadn't he waited until Stefan left before opening his big mouth to Jola? Why, for heaven's sake, can't he just see five minutes into the bloody future? *Why? Why? Why?*

Fuck my life.

Inside the study, Dr. Sparks sits on a couch, the very picture of British calm—a man in his mid-fifties with a reading glass perched on the bridge of his nose, like some professor about to crack open a dusty tome. Sparks is practically the family shrink by now, having guided Sophia and Temmy through postpartum depression after the birth of Demmy, Jola also became his patient two years ago. Now, it's Ade's turn. *Welcome to the club*, he thinks, *membership: one miserable Adeowo at a time.*

"Hi doc," Ade mutters, shaking Sparks' hand numbly.

"Hello, Ade," Sparks replies with his characteristic serenity, gesturing towards the couch. "Please, take a seat. I understand you've asked to speak with me today."

"Yeah. I did," Ade says, sliding into the seat, the words feeling like pebbles he's about to choke on.

"And what might have brought this on?" Sparks asks, his tone gentle but probing, eyes as calm as a still pond.

Ade knows exactly why he's asking. Jola had tried to rope him into therapy right after the incident in June, practically pleaded with him to speak with Sparks. But he had refused, convinced he could bury the whole thing, pretending it hadn't shaken him to his core. Classic denial; a textbook case. But now he understands. He can see it in the faces of his family, hear it in Nathan's voice when he'd told Ade just weeks ago that what happened affects everyone who loves him, not just him. *Should have listened.*

Ade takes a deep breath, as if that alone will still the hurricane inside. "Because I've come to realise what happened to me this June is not 'nothing,' as I've been telling myself, and everyone else, for the past few months."

Sparks nods thoughtfully. "And this decision. This choice to come to me, was it entirely yours?"

Ade sighs, running a hand across his face. "Partly, yes. I decided to talk to you today on my own, but, well, something pushed me to finally face it."

He's surprised by the steadiness of his voice, though his insides feel anything but calm. He had imagined he'd crumble the moment he walked through the door, fall apart at the seams. But then he remembers Stefan. Not the version of Stefan he'd just seen, heartbroken and distant— No, that image tears at his heart, ripping it into a thousand pieces. Instead, he thinks of Stefan smiling, laughing, teasing, kissing him, saying he'd do anything for him. And that's why Ade is still able to speak, to find coherence. *I have to do this*, he tells himself. *For him. To see him smile again.*

"What brought you to this decision?" Sparks prompts calmly.

Ade inhales slowly, trying to steady the rising tide of emotions. "Well, I thought if I didn't dwell on what happened, I could just forget it. You know, it wouldn't have any power over me if I ignored it long enough." He swallows hard. "But yesterday, I got a call and it just... triggered everything. All those things I'd pushed down came flooding back, overwhelming me. I felt like I was drowning."

He places a hand over his chest to somehow ease the pressure. "About two months ago, I met someone... someone I connected with in a way I've never experienced before. It's like there's this force pulling me towards him. And, well... I couldn't help myself. I fell in love with him," he smiles, a bittersweet expression as memories of Stefan flash through his mind—their collision at the airport, their unexpected reunion on campus, the little moments that followed. "Yesterday," he continues, "I realised I couldn't be with him, not properly. Not while every little thing might send me spiralling b-back into th-that suffocation."

Sparks nods, the calm in his expression unchanging. "So, you think that in order to move forward with this person, you need to confront what happened in June? Not simply dismiss it?"

"Yes," Ade affirms, his voice steady with determination. "I need to understand it. And overcome it."

Sparks leans forward slightly, pen ready, eyes holding Ade's gaze with quiet intensity. "I need you to tell me exactly what happened this summer."

Ade takes a slow, deliberate breath, trying to steady his heart. Every inhale feels jagged, as though the very air he draws into his lungs might tear him apart from the inside. He braces himself, summoning the strength to say aloud the thing he's buried for months, the thing he's avoided thinking about in any real sense. He never thought he would have to say these words. But here he is.

Ade opens his mouth to speak, but nothing comes out at

first. Instead, his mind rushes back to that day and how everything changed in a heartbeat. He can feel it all over again: the pure terror that engulfed him, the cold sweat that broke out on his skin as he was surrounded. The sharp sting of their fists, the sickening crunch of his body hitting the ground, the confusion, the helplessness, the raw, primal fear. The unspoken words behind their action.

Abomination. Disgrace. We'll show you.

Ade squeezes his eyes shut, pushing the memories away. His fingers curl into fists as though holding on might somehow keep him from falling apart. He forces himself to breathe. Forces himself to return to the present, where the room is calm, and Sparks is waiting.

Finally, he opens his eyes and speaks. "On the nineteenth of June, I was attacked by a group of four men in Lagos, Nigeria," he pauses, his throat tight. "For being gay."

11
FIGHT OR FLIGHT

— *Pompeii by Bastille.*

"Stefan?" Jason's voice is soft as silk, with a cautious hand patting Stefan's arm. "Stefan, what happened?"

Stefan rolls onto his back, blinking up at the ceiling. His face is undoubtedly a mess, his eyes swollen like a boxer who'd gone one round too many. Not his finest moment, he knows.

Jason's eyes widen like saucers, shock painting his features. "What the bloody hell happened?" His usual humour has scampered off somewhere. "Who do I have to murder?" His arms circle Stefan, protective as ever. "Was it Ade?"

Stefan holds him, trying to wrestle words from the fog clouding his mind. Despair is such an uncooperative bastard when it comes to forming coherent thoughts.

"It's okay if you don't want to talk now," Jason reassures him, almost as if coaxing a kitten. "You can tell me later."

Physical touch has always been a cornerstone of Stefan's life, grounding him in ways words never could. His family, especially his grandparents made sure of that. Even among his closest friends—Edwin and Żaneta—touch had always bridged gaps that conversation sometimes couldn't. They always understood that sometimes, all he needed was someone's quiet presence. Jason is no exception. In fact, Jason's easy, unforced affection had become a lifeline for Stefan over the years. It's the kind that doesn't demand anything in return—a casual arm slung over his shoulder, or an effortless hug after a long day.

But with Jason, it's not just about physicality. His respect for boundaries runs deeper than hugs or pats on the back. He knows when to simply be there, leaving the space for Stefan to decide what he needs. That patience, that quiet understanding, makes Jason easy to confide in. Stefan never feels rushed or pressured with him, never feels like he has to explain himself right away.

Stefan has always liked to take his time, to let his thoughts simmer before they become words. It's not that he doesn't trust people, but rather, he's never been comfortable with the idea of burdening others with his problems.

"I *want* to tell you," Stefan manages to say. "That's why I'm here."

He spills it all—Honza following him, his strange attempt at confrontation via a phone call, Ade and the situation back at Stamfordham Road. Every detail pours out, until all that's left is the hollow ache in his chest.

"He was the lad at school, yeah?" Jason connects the dots, worry lines creasing his forehead. "Stefan, you shouldn't have kept all this to yourself. Dad's got mates in the police. We could've sorted this."

"I think he means it," Stefan says quietly. "That he'll leave me alone now."

"We can come back to that. Did Ade say that?" Jason's disbelief mirrors Stefan's inner anguish. "Maybe you misheard? Or is there a context to it?"

Context. Right. Even though he doesn't want to, the cursed memory replays in Stefan's mind like an awful film he can't pause. The quiet unsettling stillness of the house as he left Ade's room, eager to find him, check on him. But before he could even find Ade, Jola's voice had sliced through the air like a blade—

"He doesn't want to be with Stefan."

The sentence rings out, sharp and jagged, as if flung into the air with the sole purpose of shattering him. Stefan freezes, his heart instantly crashing against his ribs, each pulse a violent, disorienting lurch. For a moment, he can barely comprehend it. His legs feels like lead, his joints stiff and uncooperative as if his body suddenly forgets how to function.

Then, Ade's voice breaks through, and somehow, it's worse. So much worse.

"I just... I can't look him in the eyes."

It feels like a punch to the stomach. A wave of pain slams into him with the force of a storm, leaving him stunned. Tears spring to his eyes, hot and stinging, and he stumbles backward, nearly losing his balance. This isn't real. It can't be. How can Ade say that? The person who's made him feel seen, now saying he can't even look at him?

He staggers back into the room, body on autopilot. His mind swirls with confusion and betrayal, but his hands move with desperate, furious energy. He yanks off the pyjama, flinging it aside like it is the source of all his misery, as if it is to blame for his heart splintering like brittle glass. He dresses quickly, almost mechanically.

The tears come fast now, slipping down his cheeks in hot, relentless streams, but he doesn't stop to wipe them away. He can't afford to. He has to move, has to leave. He returns to the pyjama he'd thrown, snatches it up and neatly folds it, placing it on the floor with a bizarre sense of care. It doesn't matter, none of it does—but his mind clings to the task. And then he flees. His movements are a blur, a desperate dash out of the room, down the stairs, through the house and out the door.

"I know what I heard," Stefan says, his voice barely more than a rasp. "His sister said it, and then he confirmed. It's just... I don't know. I had to leave."

"I don't get it!" Jason exclaims. "Ade's always like *obsessed* with you." He catches Stefan's sniffle then stops. "I don't want you to be stressed about this. I'll get you breakfast."

Stefan tried to engage his brain, to be analytical. Was chasing after Ade a mistake? Had Ade misunderstood everything? But *he'd* been the one to say it was okay to stop. Why would Ade make such a cutting statement? What context could there be?

"Frustrerande," Stefan mutters.

"I know that one," Jason returns, bearing comfort in the form of hot chocolate and biscuits. "Frustration, right?"

"It's one of the easy Swedish words to guess," Stefan manages a small smile. "Thanks."

"Listen," Jason sits down beside him, all serious now.

"You need the facts before you jump to any decisions, yeah? Don't go making things worse by guessing."

"I just. I," he lets out a long exhale. "I don't want to repeat past mistakes, giving benefits of doubt to someone who may not deserve it. Making up for their lapses with excuses I created for them and filling the gaps with whatever makes it hurts less."

Jason leans back, looking helpless. "I'm not the right guy for this. Maybe we can call mom?"

Stefan chuckles. "Because she's a psychologist?"

Jason shrugs. "I plan to ring her for something. Might as well do it together."

Before they can dive deeper into psychoanalysis, a knock interrupts. And then, of all people, Ade's voice drifts in from the hallway, calling Stefan's name.

Stefan's heart thuds loudly, then does something horribly out of sync. "What's he doing here?"

Jason makes a small, uncertain gesture. "What do you want me to do??"

"Get him to leave," Stefan says automatically. He doesn't trust himself around Ade right now.

"Maybe hear him out?" Jason tilts his head thoughtfully. "There's got to be a reason he's here."

"No, no," Stefan disagrees, shaking his head frantically.

As Jason leaves to deal with Ade, Stefan begins to pace the room, his body unable to stay still. His mind keeps churning out questions, each one more disorienting than the last. *Why is Ade here? Did he come all this way just to repeat it? To say to my face what he couldn't say before? Or is he here to take it all back?* He can still feel the stab of the pain that had ripped through him earlier, like a dagger plunged straight into his chest. It had been so immediate that he didn't even have the space to think, only react.

"You alright, Stefan?" Ben asks, walking towards him.

"Is he gone?"

Jason walks behind Ben, sighing like he's just dealt with a particularly stubborn toddler. "Won't leave. Says he needs to talk to you."

"He explained some things," Ben says, his voice pacifying. "You don't have to listen to him now, but you could see him just to tell him that."

"He looks miserable," Jason adds, trying to sound neutral but not entirely hiding the satisfaction in his tone. "And he's in his PJs."

Stefan sighs. "Fine."

Ade walks in a few minutes later. Jason wasn't lying—he looks miserable, clad in crumpled pyjamas, eyes red-rimmed and pained. Stefan's heart twists involuntarily at the sight. *Damn it*.

"Stef, I'm so sorry. I—"

Stefan cuts him off, his voice cold. "You say that a lot."

Ade closes his eyes slowly, as if bracing himself for an impact, but Stefan couldn't care less. The rage swirling inside him is a wildfire, untameable. His chest heaves as he tries to rein it in, but it is futile. It's taken on a life of its own, careening wildly through him like an uninvited guest he can't evict.

"I don't know the extent of what you heard, but," Ade begins, voice so quiet, so small. It's a tone Stefan might have found pitiable under any other circumstances.

"I heard enough," his words are sharp, glinting with hurt and fury. "Do you know how it feels? Waking up, searching for you, worrying myself sick, a-and," his voice falters.

The sting of tears makes him want to punch something —anything. He *detests* crying, and he's damn good at not doing it. Not even Honza, with all his cruelty, could drag a tear from him. So why—*why*—is he falling apart now? Over a guy he's known for, what, a month? Less than two months of knowing Ade, and suddenly his world is upended. It's absurd, and yet here he is, breaking down like some tragic character from a cheap romance novel. Another tear escapes, and the disgust he feels for himself only intensifies. Furiously, he wipes it away.

Who cares if Ade doesn't want me?

The thought should be empowering, liberating even, but instead, it strikes like a fist to his gut, knocking the wind out of him.

Ade detaches from the wall and drops to his knees in front of Stefan, his own face a mess of tears and anguish. There's no hesitation in his movement—just pure, unfiltered desperation. "Stef, please don't cry. I-I want to explain everything," he says, hands hovering near Stefan's, not quite touching, as if waiting for permission.

Stefan knows, with a dreadful certainty, that if Ade touches him, even for a moment, he'll unravel completely. Every last thread of control he's holding on to will snap. His body, however, has other ideas. It *craves* Ade's touch, yearns for the comfort of it. "I don't want you to touch me," he snaps, his skin prickling with the paradoxical motive to both push Ade away and pull him close, and the contradiction makes his head spin.

Ade's hands drops to his sides as if it's been slapped. He doesn't flinch, but something in him visibly deflates. And if he looked miserable before, he now looks broken, as if the very life has been siphoned out of him. His eyes latch onto Stefan, pleading silently. And damn it all, but Stefan can't bear it. Can't bear that he's the one causing this pain. But it doesn't change anything—not really. He can't afford to let

Ade in right now, not when the wounds are still fresh, still bleeding.

Ade stays rooted to the spot, hands limp at his sides, as if to say, *Look, I'm not touching you. But please, let me fix this.* His voice, when it comes, is barely audible. "Please, let me explain."

Stefan folds his arms around himself to ward off the chill settling in. But it doesn't help. The cold has now burrowed deep, lodging itself in his bones. "I don't feel well."

Ade's about to respond when they hear a knock. Ben's voice filters through the door. "Ade, Jola says Dr. Sparks is at the house."

Ade sighs—a deep, weary sound that seems to drain the last of his energy. He rises slowly, as if every movement is an effort, like gravity's taken a special interest in making his life difficult. His face is streaked with tears, but he doesn't bother wiping them away. "Stef, please know I would never do anything to hurt you," he says, and there's something almost painfully sincere about the way he says it.

Stefan doesn't respond. What's left to say? He watches as Ade leaves, the door closing with a soft click. The moment Ade's gone, Stefan's legs give out, and he collapses into the bed, curling into himself. The shivering starts almost immediately, and he buries his face in the pillows, trying to block out the world.

12

ACCEPTANCE

— Someone You Love
by Tina Dico.

Friday, 28th October 2022.

Ade finds himself in a reclining chair, not lounging about like Joey and Chandler, but sitting rather more stiffly in the decidedly less fun setting of Dr. Sparks' office. Therapy. He's come to view it as less of a last resort and more of a lifeline, though he'd never have admitted that a week ago.

"How're you feeling today, Ade?" Dr. Sparks asks in that infuriating way therapists do, as if waiting to catch something in mid-air.

He's been seeing the doctor daily since their Sunday's session, and though he entered the process sceptically, he's now a fierce advocate for therapy. Turns out, talking about your feelings doesn't actually cause spontaneous combustion.

When Sparks had asked him on Wednesday if he could

finally admit to being traumatised, Ade's answer had leapt out before he'd even had time to censor it. There was no room for denial anymore, no pretence left to cling on to. He knew, without a shadow of doubt, that what he had been grappling with had a name: trauma. It was a dormant beast he'd shoved into the farthest, dustiest corner of his mind—stuffed into hibernation that even he had almost forgotten it was there. Or at least, he had hoped he could forget. Foolproof, right? But that wasn't the case. And Saturday? Well, Saturday was the grand awakening—a roaring, clawing, full-blown rebellion that almost broke him in half.

Ade spent so long pretending the beast wasn't there, believing he could outsmart it, or at the very least, outrun it. But no one really outruns a beast, do they? Not unless you're in a Hollywood blockbuster, and even then, things tend to end badly. For months, he's buried it under his study, under social niceties, under the quiet little lie he told himself every morning: *I'm fine.* Ross Geller would be proud of him.

Now, with Sparks guiding him through the wreckage, he is finally sorting through the rubble. But this is just the beginning. Admitting the trauma exists? That's the easy part. Understanding it, confronting it, healing from it? Well, that is the real work—and, knowing his luck, it is probably going to get messier before it gets any cleaner.

"As okay as I can be, doc," he says with a half-hearted shrug.

"And have you spoken to Stefan yet?"

"No."

He winces as the word leaves his mouth, a sharp reminder of the distance that's been widening with each passing day. Stefan has been sick since Sunday, and Ade has tried to see him, tried to call, but Stefan's been as elusive as a rare bird. He's always asleep or unavailable, his phone perpetually off like a 'do not disturb' sign.

"And how does that make you feel?"

Ade clenches his jaw, feeling everything at once—a bitter blend of uselessness, rejection, anxiety, and something that tastes a lot like heartbreak. "Anxious," he finally says."

"What makes you anxious?"

"That he might not want to hear me out. Or worse, if I do get to talk to him, he won't want to be with me."

Sparks nods, scribbling something in his notepad. "Let's take it one step at a time," he advises with the patience of someone who's seen a lot of Ade. "We talked about your tendency to overthink yesterday, remember? Focus on yourself first, then the conversation. Have you figured out what you want to say?"

"Everything. I see no reason to hide anything now."

The session slips into a deeper discussion about how to approach Stefan, how to balance honesty with sensitivity. Ade knows he didn't mean to hurt Stefan, but intentions don't always shield people—he's learned that much, at least. But no amount of talking with Sparks can fully smother the fear growing in him—that Stefan may never look at him the same way again. That fear is the foundation on which all his others are built. This week has proven to be a monumental struggle for Ade, the sort that might make even a seasoned veteran reach for a stiff drink. And it's not just about confronting the attack with Sparks; that part, grim as it is, has yielded some positive outcomes.

As the session winds down, Ade recites his new mantra. "Got it. Be understanding. Don't overthink."

Sparks smiles in a way that says, *you're getting it.* "And

be patient. If you do get the chance to talk, don't push. Keep in mind, he may need time to process."

"Understanding, no overthinking, and patience. Easy peasy," he mutters, but even he knows it's anything but.

"If you need me, call over the weekend. Otherwise, I'll see you Monday."

"Thanks, doc."

Ade walks out into the world, where the real work begins. Back in his car, he adjusts the vase of flowers on the passenger seat—this has become his daily ritual. He's been delivering bouquets to Stefan's room at Ben's house, with cute little *get well soon* cards in them. With "Heavy" playing on his stereo, he drives out of Sparks' office on Orchard Street, and merges into the traffic on the A695, heading towards Darras Hall.

He knows he should manage his expectations and give Stefan space, but Ade's life feels like it's hanging by a thread. One that could snap with a single word. A part of him wishes he could erase the whole mess, take back the careless words that sparked this week of hell. Yet, another part of him knows this path, painful as it is, might be the better one.

Why is everything so heavy?

He drives onto the quieter Scotswood Road, his mind playing over memories of Stefan's smile—that soft, radiant smile that melts every defence Ade ever had. He would give anything to see it again, to make Stefan laugh, to hold him, to remind him how good they were together, to love him so fully that it erases everything else. Because Ade knows one thing for sure—whatever is broken inside him will be fixed. For Stefan, he'll make sure of it.

His thoughts carry him all the way to Darras Hall. As

he walks in, he finds Ben in the living room. "Hi, Ben," he greets. "What are those bags in the entryway?"

"Hey, Ade. They are Halloween décor," Ben replies. "Jola and her friends are having a sleepover tonight. Don't tell me you forgot."

"Right," he says, distracted, already halfway to the kitchen.

"He's awake by the way," Ben calls after him.

Ade nearly trips over his own feet. "I can't go in?"

"He said it's okay," Ben informs. "Like we've been able to hide your visits. What with all the flowers?"

Ade smiles for the first time in days—his first real smile all week. "Thanks, Ben."

He hurriedly fills the vase and arranges the flowers with a speed that could rival a Formula 1 pit crew, before practically flying up the stairs. He knocks, heart in his throat, and enters when Stefan's voice invites him inside. The sight of seeing Stefan's eyes finally open after days feels like the world's axis has shifted. Stefan's face still bears the evidence of the flu: his skin is paler than usual, with a slight flush on his cheeks, his blue eyes are red-rimmed and watery with dark circles underneath. It's a far cry from the distressing image of Sunday morning, when his nose was swollen, and the area around his nostril was chafed. But beneath all that, it's still Stefan—his Stefan.

"How're you feeling?" Ade asks, carefully placing the vase on a side table.

"I feel better. Thanks for the flowers." Stefan replies, though his voice lacks the tenderness it once held, there is no coldness either—just a strange, careful distance.

Ade swallows hard. *Do not overthink.*

"Stef," he begins, the words sticky and slow, but Stefan sits up, cutting him off with a slight wave of his hand.

"Can you get me some water, please?"

Ade nods and all but bolts to the kitchen, returning quickly with a glass of water. "Here you go."

"Thanks."

"Stef, I want to explain everything to you," Ade blurts out, the words tumbling out faster than he can control.

"You can," Stefan replies, setting the empty glass down. "But it won't be today."

"When?" Ade's voice is almost a whisper, his heart hammering in his chest.

"I don't know," Stefan sighs, rubbing his temples. "I'm still trying to process it all. Listening to you... it might be too much right now."

"Are you upset?"

"I don't know what I feel," Stefan says, his eyes drifting shut. "You clearly said you didn't want me a—"

"I *want* you," Ade interrupts, his voice urgent, almost pleading.

"Okay. But you don't want to be with me?"

Ade, somewhat befuddled but driven by an instinct he can't quite pin down, climbs onto the bed and kneels beside Stefan. "I want to be with you. It's all I've wanted since I met you," he declares, fingers twitching as if they might break free and touch Stefan. "But there are things I need to s—"

"Okay, okay," Stefan interrupts weakly. "Tomorrow. I need to rest now."

"Okay, thanks," Ade responds, preparing to remove himself from the bed, but Stefan's hand on his arm stops him.

"You can stay a bit longer."

Ade's heart lifts, a faint but hopeful flicker. "Anything you need?"

Stefan leans back against the pillows, his back turned to Ade. "Hold me."

Ade holds him.

Saturday, 14th May 2022.

Lagos.

"Adeeeeeeeeeee." MT shrieks, her voice slicing through the air like a siren's call, eyes alight with the glee of a child on Christmas morning. She fumbles with her birthday gifts, both wigs held high as though they were the crown jewels.

"*Ma pariwo*—don't shout," Ade chuckles.

"Two! You got me *two?*" MT exclaims, as she dramatically inhales the scent of the wigs like they're the finest perfumes from Paris.

"Well, you *did* have two on your Wishlist," he points out.

She throws the wigs aside, flinging herself into his arms with the enthusiasm of someone reuniting after a great war. "Thank you so much, honey!"

"Anything for you, sugar," he says, his words soft, like the kiss he plants on her forehead.

MT is, after all, Ade's only friend in Nigeria who knows the whole truth about him—the full, uncensored truth. They've been close friends since their first year at university, but it was at the start of their third year that MT had declared, with a heart full of hope and maybe something more, that she liked him. Ade, flustered but honest, had told her in a hurried breath: *It's not you, it's...*

me. Not the sort of phrase that inspires confidence, but honesty tends to do that. He blurted out the reason almost as if he were diving into cold water—quick and necessary. He didn't want her to doubt herself, didn't want her to feel less because, in a world like this, especially in Nigeria, how often does a woman take that brave first step?

Now, MT looks around the bedroom in the serviced apartment her parents rented for the grand event—her twenty-third birthday bash worthy of a mini carnival. Downstairs, the sound of laughter, music, and the general murmur of too many people who've had just enough to drink wafts up. The pool is the star of the evening, with a few of their schoolmates lounging around it, looking as though they're in an advert for some luxurious life that only exists on Instagram.

MT leans in, dropping her voice to a conspiring whisper, "Did you meet anyone this time?"

Ade chuckles. She always asks after his trips to England, as if one day he'll say, *Yes, MT, I met the love of my life at the corner shop, buying crumpets.* "No, still no one since Jeff."

MT's eyes light up, as if she's suddenly been hit by an epiphany. "You will meet someone *amazing* soon, I just know it. Someone handsome, sexy… Ooooh, maybe one of those Scandinavians! I read they're the most gorgeous people in the world," she sighs, staring off dreamily as if she can already see him emerging from a snow-dusted forest. "If visas weren't so impossible to get from Nigeria, I'd be in Denmark right now with a bottle of Jack Daniels."

"Sure, sure," Ade chuckles at her enthusiasm. "Sexy guy from Denmark is in my future. I see it."

"You laugh now," she rolls her eyes with exaggerated

exasperation. "But when you're strolling arm in arm with your tall, Viking boyfriend, don't say I didn't call it."

He grins. "I'll be sure to send you a postcard."

"Come on, let's go eat before the vultures downstairs finish everything."

They step out into the party, and as if on cue, Ay appears, gliding in through the gate. "Welcome to the always lit party," Ade calls out, pulling her into a quick hug.

The three of them gravitate towards a table, reminiscing about MT's previous birthday extravaganzas—stories that grow more exaggerated with each retelling—until MT suddenly jumps up, declaring with queenly authority, "I have to talk to *everyone*, not just you two!" And with that, she flounces off.

Ay soon follows suit, excusing herself to the restroom, leaving Ade alone with his thoughts, until Halima—an old classmate—approaches, accompanied by someone Ade doesn't recognise.

"Would you ever stop growing more handsome by the day? Ehn, Ade?"

"And who would I have to keep me humble if not you, Halima?" Ade chuckles.

"Ade, meet my friend," she gestures towards the man beside her, who stands out with a complexion so fair it flirts with the idea of albinism.

The stranger extends his hand with the confidence of someone who knows his introduction will make an impression. "Olayinka Oguns."

Ade shakes his hand, offering a smile that's equal parts polite and curious. "Teniade Adeowo."

13
HALLOWEEN

— Hearts by Jessie Ware.

Saturday, 29th October 2022.

ANXIETY COILS TIGHT IN ADE'S CHEST, A RELENTLESS serpent threatening to consume him as he powers through the Halloween party at Ben's house. He had hoped that his discussion with Stefan would top the evening's agenda, only to be met by Stefan's absence, which fuels Ade's mounting panic. Is Stefan even well enough? Or did he leave to avoid him? Stefan's arrival offers no relief. When he sees Ade, he quickly looks away without so much as a nod. The snub leaves Ade reeling, feeling like a jittery marionette on the edge of a string.

Now, Ade feels feverish as he prepares to approach Stefan despite the chill in the air—two degrees Celsius and still, he's sweating as though he's stepped into a sauna. He inhales sharply, willing his limbs to obey, and mentally repeating his mantra. Nathan squeezes his hand reassuringly before he leaves.

"Need a drink first," he mutters, ambling to Theo at the bar. "Hi Theo."

"Hey, Ade. What can I get you?"

Ade surveys the array of bottles behind the bar like they do in movies. He's not aiming for inebriation, just enough of a liquid courage to assist him. "Jameson will do."

"On the rocks?"

"Neat."

Theo hands him a glass, which Ade drains in one swift gulp before gesturing for a refill. With the drink now coursing through his veins, he picks up the glass and walks to Stefan and Jola, who are engrossed in conversation.

"I almost choked laughing when I read your shirt," Jola is saying as she takes his hand. "I love how the voyance rune looks on your hand." She then looks up and sees Ade. "I need to get my dancers before they get too drunk. Look behind you."

Stefan turns, his eyes lingering on Ade's robe a beat longer before he looks up. "Nice costume, brother Zachariah" he says, fingers grazing the fabric. "Jola said I'd be impressed."

Ade offers a tight-lipped smile, his stomach somersaulting with nerves. "Are you?"

"Maybe," his tone cryptic, his eyes squarely on the robe. As "Bones" starts playing, he releases the robe. "There's a dance?"

"Yeah, she made them learn it this afternoon."

Stefan removes his phone, switches it on and begins recording. The choreography is surprisingly good, if one overlooks Sasha's laughter, Kurt's scowl and Rosh making his moves a minute too late. After a resounding cheer from the non-dancers, the dancers disperse as the intro to "Cake By The Ocean" begins.

"They did quite okay," Stefan observes.

"I'm glad I didn't have to dance, though," Ade says, pointing to Stefan's empty glass. "Want another drink?"

"No, I'm good."

"When can we talk?"

"Come with me," Stefan says, his voice low and inviting.

They walk in silence—down the wooden stairs, through the dimly lit corridor, and then up again to Stefan's room. The journey feels endless, Ade's steps getting heavier as they approach Stefan's room. This is it, he thinks, his thoughts whirling in a tumult of apprehension. He is on the brink of unveiling everything that makes him cringe with deep-seated shame. His family and Sparks insist that this isn't his burden to bear, but their reassurances do little to dispel the shame he feels.

A week of therapy, they say, is but the beginning of a long, gradual journey. Ade knows that healing cannot be rushed or forced; it is a painstaking process that demands patience and persistence. Each step towards the door feels like a step into the unknown, and as he steps through the door ahead of Stefan, he chants his mantra silently. *Be understanding. Don't overthink. Be patient.*

Stefan locks the door and turns to enter the room, but stops short when he sees Ade. They simply stand there, an awkward tableau of unspoken words. Despite having articulated all he wants to say, despite knowing he will sound petulant and childish, Ade blurts out, "You cut your hair?" the words eluding him before he can stop them.

May 2022.

Lagos.

Ade stands amidst the party of the year, where the chatter flows as freely as the cocktails, and the Afro-beats vibrate through his bones with a baseline that practically rearranges internal organs. He watches MT work the crowd like a social maestro, tending to her guests with care and a little joke here and there. It's almost a shame to leave, but there's only so long a guy can take before the wave of introductions starts to feel like a compulsory networking event.

"Great party as always, sugar," Ade says, his voice drowned out by the noise. "I'm seeing you both this weekend, right?"

"Of course," Ay chirps from beside MT. "I've missed your chef's delicacies," she adds, pinching his cheeks. "It's why you didn't lose this."

As he steps outside, the hot Lagos air slaps his skin in the most unwelcome way. The street is almost comically still in contrast to the riot of music and laughter behind him. He's halfway to his Mercedes Benz 4MATIC, when a figure materialises in front of him.

"Ade, you're leaving?" the guy asks, sounding like he's genuinely surprised. Which is odd, because if anyone had been watching Ade's entire mental exit strategy unfold over the past ten minutes, this wouldn't come as a shock.

Ade nods, his mind flickering with the vaguest recollection of being introduced earlier. *Ah, yes, he was with Halima.* What was the guy's name again? Yomi? *No.* Yetunde? *That's a girl's name* but something with a Y for sure. He offers a polite smile, already kicking himself for what's about to come out of his mouth. "I'm sorry. What's your name again?" *Smooth, Ade. Really smooth.*

"I'm not that memorable if you've forgotten my name," the guy replies with a sly grin.

Ade suppresses a laugh. He likes this one. Quick on his feet. "How about you remind me? And as an apology for my terrible memory, I'll give you a lift home. That is, if you didn't drive here."

"It's Yinka. Olayinka Oguns," he says. "And no, I didn't drive."

"Where do you live?" Ade asks, pulling away from Ajose Adeogun Street.

"Akoka," Yinka replies. "I'm a four-hundred-level Architecture student at Unilag. You graduated with Halima, right?"

"Yeah, in 2019."

"Where did you serve?" Yinka asks, diving into what every Nigerian knows is the go-to conversation filler.

"Ministry of Finance, Abuja," Ade says.

"Seems you're a hotshot then."

Ade laughs, giving a humble shrug that feels more like a formality. "Why do people keep saying that?" he asks, his tone mockingly incredulous.

Yinka gestures vaguely at Ade's car and probably the entire aura Ade unknowingly radiates. "Seems obvious," he says. "Do you visit the mainland often?"

"No, I'm barely in Lagos," Ade replies. "But I hang out with MT and Ay in VI when I'm in town."

"The celebrant and the tall lady you were hugging?"

Ade blinks, surprised. "You were paying attention."

"I've been paying attention to you since we were introduced," Yinka says, matter-of-factly.

Okay, hol' up. Ade cannot help but wonder if he's misreading things here. Then again, Lagos is always one giant grey area when it comes to social cues. You can never tell if someone is flirting, networking, or just making polite conversation. Sometimes it's all three.

"And I thought the tall babe, Ay, right?" Yinka continues, "was your girlfriend."

Ade laughs, shaking his head. "No, no. She's my sister's best friend. We're tight."

Yinka doesn't seem convinced, though his smile stays put. "Do you have any male friends?"

Ade is mildly thrown by the question's sudden pivot. "Uhm, yeah. My best friend, Nathan," he says, slowing down as they approach Gbagada. "You might have to direct me from here or," he gives Yinka his phone, "type your address here."

Yinka's eyes gleam with something Ade can't quite place. "I can direct you," he says. "How about I input my number instead?"

Oh, there it is. And it is enough to leave Ade uncertain whether this is platonic or something else entirely—is Yinka flirting, or is this just a particularly confident student angling for some kind of mentorship? In Lagos, the lines blur like the traffic at Ikeja-Along.

"That'll be okay," Ade says, trying to sound neutral but ending up somewhere between curious and amused.

"This Nathan, he's in Lagos as well?" Yinka asks, indicating a right turn ahead.

"No, he isn't."

They approach Yinka's house—a tall, hazardous structure that looks like it could collapse in fifteen minutes or less. Ade parks in front of the house, keeping his judgment to himself. *No way this thing is safe to live in.*

"I can't seem to find myself on your WhatsApp. Or did I not do it right?"

Ade quickly checks the connection, because of course, his Smile NG modem has chosen now to disconnect. "I'll need to reconnect," he mutters, fixing the issue. "There, I've sent you a 'hi' on WhatsApp."

"Is this a UK number?" Yinka asks, glancing at his phone. Ade nods. "What if I want to call you? Don't you have a Nigerian number?"

Ade sighs, waving a hand dismissively. "I keep losing those SIM cards. You can FaceTime me instead."

Yinka laughs, holding up his Infinix. "I don't use an iPhone."

"Pardon me. I can dig out an old SIM or buy a new one, I suppose."

There's a brief, charged pause, and then Yinka's tone shifts, more deliberate. "I hope you won't think I'm being forward if I say I want us to know each other better?"

Ade looks at him, caught between genuine surprise and a feeling that's... well, something he'll unpack later. The guy seems harmless enough, and turning him down feels unnecessary, especially with Lagos' unspoken hierarchy at play. He doesn't want to come off like some snobbish islander who won't mix with the mainlanders.

"That'll be fine," Ade says with a carefully polite smile.

What's the worst that could happen?

🏃

No unholy gridlock on the Third Mainland Bridge, no inch-by-inch crawl while Lagos pulses with its usual unrelenting impatience. For once, the city's hustle and bustle has given

Ade a pass, and he steps into his room with the quiet relief that comes with an early evening.

A quick shower washes away the day. *Who knew a party could be so exhausting?* Not that he didn't have fun—it was MT's bash, after all, always an explosion of people, booze and chaotic energy. By the time he's out, the faint scent of coconut mixed with sandalwood fills the room, and his muscles feel loose, like they're finally convinced they belong to a human again. He picks his phone and there it is, a message from Yinka: *Nice meeting you today, Ade.*

A simple message, but there's something about it that makes him pause. Ade stares at the text, thumb hovering, running through possible responses. *What's the right response here?* Should he keep it light? Friendly? He considers being clever, something witty, but instead, he sighs and types back the safest option: *Same here.*

Wow, Ade, what a conversationalist you are. Truly riveting stuff.

But it's enough, apparently. This small, seemingly forgettable exchange with Yinka becomes something of a seed. And it begins to grow. One minute, it's the usual pleasantries: *How was your day? Have you eaten?* Next, they've got a regular streak going as their conversations pick up pace, expanding beyond the surface-level exchanges into something far more comfortable. And then there are the memes. Oh, the memes. They range from the absurd—some ridiculous picture of a passenger pressing down on a danfo's brake while the driver goes to fight with touts—to the downright hysterical: Nigerian Twitter threads that spiral into chaos, TikToks about the daily struggle of surviving in Lagos, even the hilarious videos from comedian Sabinus that had them both cackling.

Ade finds himself laughing more than he has in a while, the kind of laughter that comes out unexpectedly, spilling out even when he's trying to keep a straight face. And it's not just the memes. Slowly, their conversations start dipping into other areas: Life, school, politics. Sometimes Ade gets a voice note from Yinka, talking about everything from the state of the country to some random philosophical question, and Ade finds himself enjoying the way Yinka's mind works, sharp and quick but with a certain softness around the edges.

Yinka's got a cheeky side, no doubt about that, and every now and then, he tosses out a line that floats right on the edge of a joke and something more—something that feels just a touch too intimate to be brushed off as mere jest. Like when Yinka sends a voice note with that teasing lilt in his voice, "You know, if I weren't such a gentleman, I'd say you've got me wrapped around your finger, Ade," and then quickly follows it up with a laugh. Like a cat playing with a string, Yinka dangles his words in front of Ade, teasing, tempting, but never pulling too hard. And Ade? Well, he's gotten good at side-stepping these moments, casually bobbing and weaving, keeping things light.

But it gets Ade thinking. Does Yinka know? *No, no, how could he?* Ade reassures himself, fingers drumming nervously on his thigh as the thought snakes through his mind. He's careful—*always* careful. He's built his life like a fortress, every door locked, every window closed, every secret tucked neatly behind layers of charisma. There's no crack in his armour, no loose thread for anyone to tug at.

Ade's dealt with it before—guys who flirt without meaning it, pushing boundaries for the fun of it, with no intention to step over the line. It's the kind of thing you brush off with a grin and a quick joke. And Lagos? In this city, you don't just *come out* in casual conversation—not unless you have a death wish or are in very, very trusted company. Here, you play your cards close and careful, like a magician keeping his sleight of hand hidden. People guess, sure, but no one ever says it. Not outright. *And yet...* something about Yinka feels different. There's an audacity to him, like he knows something he shouldn't, and he's daring Ade to acknowledge it.

Could he be? Ade wonders. And if Yinka is like him—if Yinka knows—what does that mean for them? But even as these questions swirl in his mind, Ade shoves them aside. *No, no, don't get carried away.* Yinka's just being Yinka— bold, curious, maybe a little too observant for his own good. He *couldn't possibly* know. Because that's the thing, isn't it? Ade has lived his life by a strict set of rules. Keep your head down. Don't let anyone in too close. Be friendly, but never too familiar. And above all, never, ever let anyone guess the truth about you.

Then, in the last week of May, Yinka disappears.

One moment, Ade's phone is alive with texts—memes, voice notes, links to the latest Twitter outrage, all laced with Yinka's signature humour. And then, just like that, nothing. Radio silence. His phone number is unreachable, and his WhatsApp messages didn't deliver. No more *lmao, can you believe this?* Or *check this out, it's killing me* 😂. Just... quiet. At first, Ade brushes it off. *Maybe he's busy.* It happens, life gets in the way.

But when a day passes without so much as a *Good morning, bro*, Ade starts to feel a tiny, unfamiliar knot of unease form in his chest. Yinka, of all people, is never the type to ghost—not without a reason. He's the type to broadcast even the most mundane happenings in his life. Got stuck in traffic? Expect a voice note complaining about it. Didn't get enough sleep? Prepare for a deluge of sleepy face emojis.

By the second day, Ade finds himself checking his phone more often than usual, waiting for that familiar notification to pop up. *Any minute now*, he tells himself. But the screen stays blank.

Or maybe something's wrong? The thought worms its way in on the third day, that creeping suspicion that maybe this isn't just a harmless disappearing act. Ade tries to shake it off. *He's probably fine, right?*

By the time a week has slipped by, Ade has left more undelivered messages than he cares to count on WhatsApp, debating whether to text one last time or just let it go.

Just as he's about to give up, his phone rings.

It's Yinka.

"Sorry, Ade," Yinka's voice comes through the speaker, equal parts apologetic and weary. "Dropped my phone. Total write-off. I'm using a friend's phone to call my parents. Thought I should also call you."

There it is again—that ease with which Yinka slots Ade right into the list of important people. *The parents, and me. Interesting.*

"I'll send you a phone," Ade says, without even thinking.

A stunned pause on the other end. "What? For real?"

Ade's already scrolling through his phone, searching for the latest iPhone on Jumia like it's an errand as routine as ordering lunch. "Yeah, you'll have it by tomorrow."

Yinka's laugh is half disbelieving, half grateful. "Wow, Ade. You're too kind."

Am I? Maybe he's just ridiculous. But he hits 'purchase' anyway, and the next day, Yinka calls him on FaceTime with the wide-eyed glee of someone who's just found out he's won the lottery.

"Wow, Ade, seriously," Yinka says, holding up the shiny iPhone 13 Pro Max like it's a newborn child. "I can't believe it. Thank you."

"It's nothing," Ade brushes it off, though he can't help but enjoy the way Yinka beams. And just like that, their routine picks up again, uninterrupted, as if the brief silence had never happened.

But then, one morning in early June, Ade wakes up to a missed call from Yinka. At first, he blinks groggily at the time the call came in. *Three a.m.?* He frowns and dials back. Yinka picks up after a couple of rings, his voice hesitant.

"Wossup? You know my phone is always on silent."

"It's nothing," Yinka mumbles.

Oh, no you don't. Ade sits up. "Nah, it's something. You wouldn't call me at three in the morning just to chat. Do I need to come to Akoka and drag it out of you?"

There's a brief pause, and then Yinka's smile sneaks back into his voice. "I need you to promise something first."

Ade's mind kicks into overdrive, sifting through the possible 'talk' that could warrant this kind of hush-hush tone. *Is he in trouble? Is this about his studies? Have I somehow offended him?*

"As long as you didn't murder someone, we're good."

There's a soft laugh on the other end, but it quickly dissolves. Yinka's voice drops. "What I'm about to say, I don't want it to change anything between us."

Oh God, what is this? Ade wonders. "Alright, alright, spill. What is it?"

"You haven't promised," Yinka presses.

"I promise," Ade says calmly.

What on earth is this about? Their conversations have

been breezy, light-hearted, nothing that should lead to *this*. For a brief second, Ade thinks he might just hang up to avoid whatever's coming.

But then Yinka speaks, his voice small, as if it's curling in on itself, like he's bracing for something that might break him. "Ade, I'm gay... and I'm in love with you."

Enipé?—You say?

14

RUNNIN'

— Runnin' by Adam Lambert.

Saturday, 29th October 2022.

"Is that what you want to talk about?" Stefan asks, a laugh bubbling up his throat, despite his best efforts to stay composed. "My hair?"

Stefan tries to hold on to his indignation, but it's a losing battle, especially with Ade standing there in that ridiculous robe Jola got for him, looking unfairly attractive. It clouds Stefan's thoughts entirely; he wants to know what, if anything, Ade is wearing underneath that robe. And if time permits, he fully intends to find out—by removing every last piece of Ade's costume.

Ade shrugs, his smile small but infuriatingly charming. "I couldn't help but notice. You look more beautiful." His voice dips into that familiar low, velvety tone, a caress in itself, turning Stefan's already fragile resolve into a warm, formless puddle of want.

Great. Just great. How is he meant to survive this

conversation if Ade insists on being this hot, and, worse, calling him beautiful with that voice? That voice that practically makes trousers optional. Stefan takes a reflexive step backwards, hoping distance will help clear his head. But of course, Ade misreads the move.

Ade's hand shoots out, grabbing Stefan by the arm. "Stef, wait."

And here's where things get blurry. If this semester's grades were based on his ability to describe what happens next, he'd be staring down a spectacular failure. At some point, maybe, he leapt. Or perhaps Ade lifted him bodily—both are possible, neither is entirely clear. All Stefan knows is that one second he's contemplating an escape route, and the next he's firmly in Ade's arms, pressed to the door like it's all he's ever wanted in life. Ade's arms wrap securely around Stefan's waist with Stefan's legs already coiled around Ade's waist, and they're kissing with a ferocity that makes it seem like the world is about to end.

Wait, no. Scratch that. Ravaging each other's mouths is more accurate. It's like every pent-up emotion, every unsaid word, is translating into this kiss—fiery, all-consuming, almost-violent, and oxygen-obliterating. Ade's hands grip Stefan's hips, pulling him in like he's afraid to let go. *Ah, there goes self-control*, Stefan thinks, half-lost in the heady sensation of Ade's mouth against his own, the taste of him, the heat of his body. Ade kisses him like he's parched, and Stefan is the only drink in sight, like his mouth is made of every flavour Ade's ever craved, and God knows Stefan is drowning in it. It's excruciatingly scrumptious, and, if Stefan is honest, he's not sure he'll survive it.

"God, Teni," Stefan whispers breathlessly between kisses, voice barely holding together. "Can't get enough."

"Stef," Ade grunts, voice rough, hands gripping tighter. "My Stef."

Steady, Stefan. Stay sharp. Don't get lost in—Nope. Too late. He's gone. That low possessive tone—like it's some kind of claim—is just enough to make Stefan's brain misfire. After what feels like an eternity—it could be hours, days, months, or even a century or two—Stefan pulls back, just barely, chest heaving with exertion. He blinks up at Ade, his lips tingling, and manages a hoarse, "Bed."

Ade, without missing a beat, scoops Stefan up and begins walking towards the bed. Stefan knows he's small, but he's not that small. Certainly not light enough to be carried like *this*, but apparently, Ade thinks he's not more than a featherweight. Somewhere along the way, Stefan's fingers struggle to find the knot on Ade's robe. A tug, a pull, and the robe slides soundlessly on the floor as Ade lowers him onto the bed with the kind of gentleness Stefan isn't quite prepared for.

When he opens his eyes, he sees Ade in nothing but a red round-neck and black sweatpants. For a moment, Stefan's heart does a double take. *Really? That's all he's wearing under that damn robe?* Yet, the simplicity of it is devastating. *Why does this guy look so damn hot even in basic clothes?* It's really not fair. His eyes hungrily trace the lines of Ade's body, practically burning a path down Ade's chest to between his thighs. He watches as Ade slowly peels off their shoes before crawling atop him, pressing Stefan into the mattress with his weight.

Ade stares down at him, eyes dark with not only want, but hesitation too, his hands resting on either side of Stefan's head. And Stefan realises Ade is waiting. Waiting for... permission?

"Can I touch you?" Ade's voice, usually so steady, shakes with a trace of fear.

Stefan's throat tightens at the memory of Sunday morning, the way Ade had looked at him—hurt, confused, blindsided by rejection. God, how it had torn at Stefan, how badly he had wanted to take it all back the second he saw that look in Ade's eyes. Stefan had felt rejected too, but hearing it in Ade's voice now makes something in Stefan's chest ache.

"You can touch me," Stefan breathes, leaning up to kiss Ade's cheek, his lips brushing against the stubble. "I want you to touch me, Teni."

Ade doesn't need further encouragement. His hands are on him in a heartbeat—weaving through Stefan's hair, roaming across his body as if he's memorising every inch of him again, the way a blind man rediscovers an old, beloved map. "I miss you," Ade whispers. "I miss you so much, Stef. I miss this."

Stefan arches into his touch, forgetting everything else—feeling it as the last vestiges of his anger and uncertainty disappear. Stefan can't think straight anymore. He is melting under the waves of sensation, until all that's left is need—pure, unadulterated need. He feels Ade's hands everywhere, undoing him slowly, tracing every line of muscle, tugging off Stefan's shirt, reacquainting himself with every inch of skin. Ade dips his head, teasing Stefan's nipples with his tongue, drawing out a moan Stefan couldn't suppress if he tried. His mind fractures, utterly blissed out, lost in the sweet torture, and all he can think of is: *If I die from this, so be it.*

Stefan manages to divest Ade of his round-neck then reverses their positions, perching on top of Ade. His knuckles drag languidly down Ade's chest, stopping just shy of the waistband of his sweatpants. "Tell me," he whispers against Ade's neck, trailing his tongue to Ade's ear. "How does my body feel on yours?"

Ade grunts, his voice husky, raw. "It feels right," he says, barely able to get the words out. "It feels perfect."

Stefan's hands move blindingly quick, pushing Ade's sweatpants down and watching with a mix of fascination and satisfaction as Ade's very impressive length springs free. Just as he reaches for him, Ade grabs his wrist, his voice coming out in a strained whisper. "Stef," he says, fighting for control. "I want this. I've wanted nothing more. But... we need to talk."

Stefan groans in frustration, even as his hand strokes Ade. "I don't want to talk," he whines, feeling Ade twitch beneath him. "I want this."

"Stef," Ade breathes, his voice laced with barely restrained desire. "Stef, yes... I mean, after."

Stefan lets out the most exasperated sigh in human history, his head dropping forward dramatically. "Fine," he mutters, fingers stilling, but not before one last teasing stroke. "But you're putting your pants back on."

🏃

Ade clasps Stefan's hand with a tenderness that belies the adrenaline rush that had him almost bouncing off the walls mere seconds ago. His body settling into a more serene state brings with it a realisation of the urgency to steady his thoughts and truly listen. Yet, even as he strives for calm, a wry suspicion begins to emerge—one that has been nagging him since Sunday. Stefan wants to—no, needs to—decipher the reason behind Ade's statement, that infernal context which seems to remain out of grasp. To Stefan, this entire situation hinges on this elusive piece of puzzle, and without it, he is afraid they cannot find a clear path forward.

"You'll be the second person I've told this to," Ade begins, "The first is Dr. Sparks, who I started seeing on Sunday. I didn't tell my family, but they figured out enough."

Stefan draws in a shuddering breath. "Can you start with Sunday?"

Ade eye's shift, a moment's hesitation clouding his eyes before he meets Stefan's again. "Stef, you need the whole story to understand," he insists.

"I want to know about Sunday."

Ade's shoulders sag as he exhales sharply. "Okay. After you fell asleep, I realised I couldn't continue like this. I have to fix what's wrong with me. I told my family that morning I needed to start therapy."

"Did you plan to tell me what happened?" Stefan asks, a knot forming in his stomach. "Is it related to Saturday?"

"It is," Ade admits.

"Did you plan to tell me on Sunday?" Stefan presses.

Ade's eyes flicker with contrition. "I wanted to tell you after I'd started therapy. I thought it was best."

Stefan's heart plummets, his voice shaking with an unspoken fear. "So, what did you plan to tell me?"

"Stef, please understand that I was freaking out," Ade says, his voice edged with frantic urgency. "After you pointed out I was crying, I couldn't sleep. All I could think of was that you deserve better, that I need to be better," he sits up and squeezes Stefan's hand. "For you."

"I understand that, but I was right there in your house on Sunday. My question is simple."

"I-I. I don't know," Ade stammers. "I didn't think a-a-about it."

Tears sting Stefan's eyes as he snatches his hand away and stands. "You were going to leave me there in your room? Tell Jola to ask me to leave?"

Ade scrambles off the bed, standing in front of him. "Stef, I wasn't thinking right. I need to explain it all, not just bits and pieces."

Stefan shakes his head, the realisation cutting deep. "You know what I thought that morning?" He sniffs. "That whatever the problem was, I could help you, be there for you. Not knowing," he sniffs again. "The whole time, you were planning on how to get me to leave. To discard me?"

He'd imagined the grim possibility of Ade leaving him stranded in that room, waiting until he gets the cue to leave. The thought is both unbearable and profoundly cruel. To be left there, an unwelcome guest in the space they had just shared so intimately, forced to read between the lines of unspoken goodbyes. Or something along the line of *Don't let the door hit you on the way out!* The idea that Ade might have planned not to only disappear from his life, but also leave him to stew in his own bewildered solitude feels like a gut-wrenching betrayal. This is not just about the absence of words or gestures; it is the stark chilling reality of being rendered worthless, unwanted, and alone.

"And what do you expect to happen when you get better?" Stefan continues. "Pick me back up? Snap your fingers," Stefan snaps his fingers for emphasis, "and say, 'Stefan, now I want to be with you'? And then I'll say yes, sir?" He shakes his head. "No. No, you didn't think. You did not think of me."

"Stef, I'm sorry. Temmy pointed out all these to me, and I came back to the room to tell you everything. To tell you, I'd start therapy. To tell you that I—"

"That's not important now," Stefan cuts him off.

"Temmy had to tell you to think about me. You couldn't realise that on your own?" He picks up his shirt. "And what do you expect to happen during? That you'd still be able to touch me? That we'd keep talking, huh?"

Ade brushes away a stray tear that slips from his eye. "No, Stef, it isn't just about touching you to me," his lips trembles as he speaks. "I stopped just now because I don't want anything to pass between us based on half-truths. I want to lay myself bare for you."

Stefan's laughter bursts forth, sharp and bitter. "Well, congratulations then," he says, clapping pointedly. "Is that what you want?" Each clap punctuates his words. "You and I planned to be together. Isn't that what Saturday was for?"

Ade moves a step closer. "It was. It is. Stef, I'm sorry."

"Don't tell me you're sorry, Ade," Stefan snaps. "Tell me what was on your mind when you decided to go back on a path we were on. Were you just going to leave me hanging? That's what I need to understand."

Ade closes the distance between them and takes Stefan's hands. "Stef, it was incredibly stupid of me. I know now. But maybe subconsciously, I thought we might remain friends while I worked on my issues, and after, I may be lucky enough to convince you to be with me. The better me I worked on for you."

"Friends, huh?" Stefan smiles sadly.

His heart feels like it's been dropped from a great height, shattering into a thousand irreparable pieces. The galling part is Ade's readiness to let him go, without so much as a conversation, without trying to understand what Stefan is willing to offer—his unwavering dedication, his constant presence, the emotional energy he is ready to pour into their relationship. Stefan is not foolish enough to believe that love is some sort of magical fix-all. He knows better than to clutch at illusions when the reality is that sometimes, one's deepest desires can slip through one's fingers like sand. Perhaps this whole affair with Ade was nothing more than a grand chase after a will-o'-the-wisp, a fruitless pursuit leading straight to a dead end.

Life, Stefan realises, is riddled with harsh and painful realities.

And though it's a bitter pill to swallow, Stefan has to admit they missed their chance on Sunday—a tragic case of two dancers moving to entirely different tunes on a stage far too small for missteps. How can they ever hope to align their lives if their thoughts, their intentions, keep veering so wildly apart? If Ade is so quick to retreat at the first hint of turbulence, what's to stop him from leaving over something trivial next time? A bad day at work, a flat tyre, or even a burnt dinner—will that be enough to send him packing again? To anyone else, this might sound a bit melodramatic, but Stefan can't shake the growing feeling that it's somehow his fault. Perhaps there's something inherently off about him, some invisible defect that's driving sane people away.

"I could never be friends with you, Teni," Stefan says, struggling to get the words out. He gestures to Ade's clothes scattered on the floor. "I want you every time. And it can't be said for sure that you would still want to be with me after you get better." He wears his shirt. "So, what happens if I remained friends with you, but you change your mind la—"

Ade kisses him, a heartrending and urgent plea evident in the touch of his lips. With each brush against Stefan's, there's a silent prayer for understanding and forgiveness. "Stef, I would never. I couldn't. It is only you for me."

Stefan kisses him back. Of course, he does—how could he not? It's his Teniade, and Stefan is in love with him, head over heels, in a way that feels inevitable. But even in the passion of the kiss, his mind is a swirling mess of tangled thoughts and unsettling what-ifs. And at the heart of it all lies a single excruciating truth: when it mattered most, when everything hung in the balance, Ade made his choice without even pausing to consider how his decision would carve through Stefan's life like a dual blade. That's the unacceptable part—the thoughtlessness and the casual disregard. It's like dancing in a dream while knowing there's a crack in the floor. It's something Stefan can't shake, because how can love coexist with betrayal on the same fragile thread without it snapping?

Stefan breaks away, his chest heaving. "I couldn't be just friends with you because I wouldn't have been able to stop falling in love with you, and where would that have left me after you get better and decide you don't want me after all?" he hurries out of the room as the first tear trickles down his cheek.

15

REFLECTION

— WILD by Troye Sivan.

Saturday, 19th November 2022.

"Hey, love," Jola breezes in, her presence a sudden swirl in the stillness of Ade's room. She spins around, presenting her back with her usual demand: "Help with the zip, please."

Ade, half-propped on his bed, carefully slips a bookmark into *Chain of Iron* with the exaggerated care of someone who'd rather not be moving at all. He rises to his knees, fingers grazing the cool metal of the zipper. "Is Ben here?" His voice is low, like the room itself, steeped in a quiet hum.

"Nah, in another thirty minutes or so," Jola says, spinning around to face him. Her eyes dart across the room —cluttered, dark, an ode to disarray—but she remains tactfully silent.

"What's going on between you two, anyway." Ade ventures, half-absent.

Jola's eyes flit away, almost evasive. "We kind of kissed," she admits, dropping the words into the silence like an unexpected pebble into still water.

Ade digests this with the slow precision of someone mentally chewing a particularly unappetising bite. "Did you talk about it?"

She gives a casual shrug, as if discussing the fate of a stale croissant. "Yeah, we pretty much did. And it led to the bigger talk of me telling him we can only be friends. He seems okay with the idea," she tongues the corner of her mouth. "I don't think he wants anything more himself, so cool."

"How did you come to that conclusion?"

"Well, he didn't resist the idea or anything. And there's something about him. I think it's connected to the death of his sister."

"Did he tell you anything about that?" Ade's voice is cautious now.

"Not much. Just that they were in London last month for her remembrance."

"And you're sure... you're not ready for...?"

"No." A firm line, drawn in sand.

Ade sighs, a soft puff of air escaping the tight knot in his chest. He decides not to intrude further. "We're a pair, aren't we? You and I."

A wry smile curls on Jola's lips. "You know, I was thinking the same thing earlier. To be raised in so much love and then be made to doubt and fear the very foundation on which you grew up."

For a moment, something inside Ade unwinds, loosening the knot, just a little. Trust Jola to articulate what he barely understands himself.

"I look at mom and dad, and marvel at the extent of

what they share. They are so in love, it borders on ridiculous," he says, a reluctant smile forming. Their parents, in their boundless love, had always made sure their children knew it was okay to love, however and whomever they chose. Ade feels nostalgic remembering the things his parents impacted on him since he was grown enough to understand the way of the world. "I remember mom telling me this summer that what is the point of a world where we cannot love who we want, however we want. Why should some people get to decide what love is?"

"We won the jackpot of parents," Jola says, her laugh light but sincere.

Ade cannot disagree. Their parents' love has been a shelter—no, a fortress. But even fortresses can't keep out life's claws. They've both had to swallow hard truths and grow up in a world that rarely offers the kindness their parents so freely give. Jola, for all her charm and wit, learned her own painful lessons—different from Ade's, naturally, but cruelty doesn't particularly care for details. It takes whatever shape that suits the moment.

"I shouldn't have left," Ade blurts before he can reel it back in, the words tumbling out awkwardly.

"Wh—" Jola starts, then pauses. "Ade, I thought we were past this?"

"I know," he flops back on the bed. "It's just... never mind. I'm being silly."

"Hey," Jola sits on the edge of the bed and nudges his leg with her elbow. "Talk to me."

This is usually where Ade would deftly sidestep, firing off a clever joke or a witty retort—a sharp comment ready, a smirk playing on his lips to deflect the gravity of the conversation and maintain his façade of easy-going nonchalance. But now, all those carefully crafted masks seem to have slipped away, like autumn leaves caught in an unexpected gust of winds, leaving a stark void in their wake.

His final exchange with Stefan keeps replaying in his mind like a record that's stuck in an eternal loop of regret. It's as if every word he wishes he could retract has left an indelible mark, like graffiti on the walls of his soul. Daily, Ade wrestles with the question of whether it is too late to repair the damage. But like he's come to know, some things, like spilled milk or broken hearts, may not be so easily mended. Denying this truth feels like trying to ignore the inevitable British rain—it's pointless and bound to drench one in misery.

"If I had stayed in Naij, I wouldn't have met him. Wouldn't have known what could've been. What I let slip away. And th-that's what's killing me."

"Ademi," Jola's hand tightens on his. "You were exposed, at risk. We had no choice."

"They could've thrown me in prison for all I care," Ade replies with a bitter laugh. "Wouldn't have stopped me from sucking dicks."

Jola giggles, despite herself, but the levity doesn't last. Her face sets into something more serious, more weighted. "I still don't think it's too late, Ade," she says, her voice carrying the kind of conviction Ade wished he could borrow for a bit. "Starting therapy when you did? That was brave, and it matters. It really does."

Her words float in the space between them, offering comfort, though they sting as they settle. "But if I'd just listened to you back then... maybe I wouldn't have pushed him away. Maybe I'd still have him."

The silence that follows is dense and tangible, like fog settling heavily over a moor. The pain in Ade's heart is a dull, throbbing ache that won't be erased by time or distraction. He thought he built those walls to keep others out but in reality he had meticulously crafted an elaborate maze with no exit, a cell where he is both warden and prisoner.

Jola's voice cuts through, rich with empathy. "Ade, you can't change the past. But you can stop punishing yourself for it. What matters is you're finally getting help."

He feels the tightness in his chest return, his breath shallow as he struggles with his own self-loathing. "I should have explained to him that midnight. I can't cope with him thinking it was easy for me to leave him. It was the most difficult choice I made, because I thought that was the only option. And now, I can't even tell him how sorry I am."

Jola, bless her, doesn't let him wallow long. "You might not be able to tell him," she says, "But you can still tell yourself. And maybe one day, you'll get the chance to apologise, or maybe he will see the changes you're making and reach out. But even if that doesn't happen, Ade, you're doing this for you. You deserve to be happy, to feel okay again.

Happy. The word flutters through his mind like a forgotten tune, one he used to hum along to but now struggles to recall. It feels like something out of a half-remembered dream, foreign and out of reach. He contemplates how different his life might be if he's acknowledged the cracks in his own façade earlier, instead of insisting on his own brand of stoicism. It makes him ache to think about how much pain he could have avoided—for himself and for the guy he loves.

"I just... I miss him, Jola. I miss him so much. And I hate myself for not doing this sooner. For ignoring everything"

Jola embraces him. "Ade," she says, her voice steady and unwavering, "self-forgiveness is a journey, not a sprint. It takes time. And it's not your fault, but I'm proud of you for taking this step, even if it feels like it's too late. You're doing something good for yourself, and that's never too late."

"Maybe Ben can talk to him again?" his voice wobbles with the kind of desperation only siblings can bear witness to.

Jola nods. "I can ask him. But Ade, Stefan probably needs time. Just like you did when you realised you needed help. It might be the same for him, and hounding him will not help us get there."

Ade smiles, albeit faintly. "I know," he mutters.

"How's it going with Sparks?"

Ade shrugs. "As well as it can." A non-answer, but it's all he's got.

Her phone chimes—perfect timing, always—and she taps something out before standing. "Ben's here," she announces, already halfway out the door.

Ade leans back into his pillows, watching her go. "Jughead?" he calls after her, layering just enough mischief into his tone to cover the jagged edges beneath.

"Yes, if I see Stefan, I will discreetly snap his pictures and send them to you," she tosses back, without missing a beat, because she knows him well. Too well.

He sighs, eyes drifting to his phone, the screen dark and silent. He picks it up and opens the email in his draft—the one he's rewritten a dozen times, always stopping just short of sending. His thumb hovers over the send button. But before he can hit send, there's a knock at his door.

"Ade. We're leaving," Sophia's voice filters through. "The kids are in the playroom."

"Brilliant," Ade mutters, dragging himself out of bed.

He enters the room to find Demmy sprawled on the sofa, full of teenage disdain. "I am too old to have a babysitter," he declares with the flair of someone who truly believes he's a Disney teen star.

"You were less exhausting at one," Ade sighs. "Those were the glory days."

Demmy cracks a grin, opening *Under The Udala Trees*, which he stole from Jola. "Yeah, but one-year-old me couldn't roast you."

"Touché."

From the floor, Deji, already knee-deep in plastic bricks, pipes up. "Is Uncle Stefan visiting today?" His tone is so hopeful it's painful.

"No. I've told you ten times," Ade almost snaps.

Deji sulks for all of two seconds before shrugging it off. "Enny, wanna build a castle?"

"Sure." Enny drops his iPad and joins his brother on the mat.

Ade attempts to continue *Chain of Iron*, flipping to his marked page, but the words refuse to settle. They slip and slide around his brain like rain on a windshield. He tries to focus—really, he does—but his thoughts keep curling back to Stefan, like a ribbon left untied. It's not the grand moments that gnaw at him, not their first kiss or whispered confessions. No, what Ade misses most are the small things, the tiny rituals they'd shared as naturally as breathing. The long winding walks where their conversations ebbed and flowed like the Thames at low tide. Their absurd video calls where they'd try to outdo each other with terrible accents or impromptu karaoke. The ease of it all, the way Stefan's laugh would vibrate down the phone, warm and unguarded—

His attention shifts to the squabble brewing between the boys. "Where do I put my G-wagon, then?" Deji demands, pointing to the car with far too much pride.

"On your bed, like you've been doing since your birthday," Demmy replies cooly.

"When did you join the castle-building, Mr Too-Old-For-Babysitting?"

Demmy shrugs, inspecting the structure. "They were doing it all wrong. I had to intervene."

Ade takes in the wonky structure on the floor, and indeed, one side of the castle is no different from the Leaning Tower of Pisa. "So, you want to demolish it?"

"They leave me no choice."

Ade lets out a long-suffering sigh. This is *not* how he envisioned his Saturday going, but somehow, it's fitting.

Sunday, 19th June 2022.

Lagos.

Ade stands in front of his wardrobe, observing his row of clothes with the same focus a chess grandmaster might give an opening move. He shakes his head, still trying to get his mind around preparing for a date—with a guy. In Nigeria, of all places. A quiet laugh escapes him, the folly of it all tasting faintly sweet.

He pulls out an outfit, absentmindedly replaying Yinka's mad confession. Yinka had blurted out his feelings and promptly ended the call. Typical. Ade spent the next few hours calling him back, each call unanswered, as if Yinka had sprinted for cover the moment he'd hung up. When he finally called the next day, he mumbled an apology, and asked to meet. But Ade was due in Abuja for some interviews.

Ade admires Yinka's courage. It takes a special kind of nerve to confess your feelings, especially in a country where doing so could be the equivalent of jumping into a crocodile-infested river and hoping they're feeling vegetarian that day. That sort of honesty, uninhibited and bare, had intrigued Ade—a bit more like curiosity, a bit less than love, but definitely more than casual infatuation. There may be a potential here. Perhaps if they're careful—oh, *how* they'd need to be careful—this could blossom into something significant, something with substance.

Of course, careful is an understatement in Nigeria, where even ghosts gossip. Every move, every word, every side-glances could be fuel for a scandal. Still, he lets his mind wander to places far removed from Lagos, and pictures possibilities that feel worlds away. Maybe he could help Yinka get a UK visa, or a Schengen one. There's freedom in Europe—a kind of liberation neither of them can fully taste in Nigeria. London, Paris—cities where love between two men isn't a political statement or a death sentence. Imagine that—two guys strolling without looking over their shoulders. Maybe a stolen kiss in a Parisian café or lounging together in some forgotten corner of London, without worrying about a neighbourhood uncle catching them from behind a suspiciously placed newspaper.

But reality has a way of pulling him back, and Ade knows he has to be strategic about this. He can't afford to be reckless, not with the family's name attached to him like a badge of honour and burden all at once. The Adeowos are not just any family—they're practically an institution, and if there's anything Nigerians love more than a scandal, it's a scandal involving public office holders and celebrities. And the consequences wouldn't just fall on him—they'd ripple outwards, tainting everyone, from his parents to his siblings. Yes, his family is fiercely progressive in many ways, outspoken against the rampant homophobia that infects the country. His mother, a high-ranking supreme court judge, has even given passionate speeches against Nigeria's anti-gay laws, and his father has voiced his disgust at the way the government scapegoats the LGBTQ+ community.

But still, they don't know about him. Not yet. Ade hasn't had the courage—or audacity?—to bring up the small matter of his sexuality. Not that there's a logical reason for his delay, mind you. His parents are not the conservative, pearl-clutching types; they wouldn't disown him, or throw a Bible at him, or faint dramatically onto the nearest piece of furniture. If anything, his mother might start planning his wedding the next day, all the while making sure to invite twice as many guests as absolutely necessary.

So why hasn't he told them? Maybe because once he says it, once it's out there, the gears of his world will shift and there'll be no turning back. The moment will arrive—he's certain of that. He'll know when the time is right, when he's sent some sort of poetic signal. Perhaps a rainbow bursting through the Lagos smog or his mother's sudden declaration that she's redecorating the house in pride colours. Until then, well, there's no harm in waiting, is there?

Ade gets dressed and minutes later, he's seated in his 4MATIC, with Taiwo, his mom's driver, behind the wheel. Since there will be drinking involved tonight, a sober drive home seems like a good precaution. First stop: Yinka's parents' place in Iyana-Ipaja. Then, they'll head to the serviced apartment Ade rented in Magodo. Except Yinka isn't waiting outside when they pull up. Ade calls him, barely registering the distant voices that leak through the line. "I'm here. Where are you?"

"I'm not ready yet," Yinka's voice comes thin and strained. "Come to me. I'll give you directions."

Ade sighs, questioning why Yinka isn't simply outside like they agreed. He follows the directions begrudgingly, which lead him to a football field. A dry, patchy excuse for one. "There's no house here," he says into the phone. "Maybe I missed the way somehow?"

Before he can receive a response, a sharp pain explodes through his leg, sending the world spinning. The ground rises to meet him with brutal force, and agony shoots through his body. He thinks it's a mugging at first—Taiwo did warn him about this area's reputation. He is ready to offer money to be left alone when he hears a voice.

"Yinka, na him be this?" a voice asks in pidgin English.

"Na him," Yinka's voice confirms.

Ade tries to stand, legs wobbling beneath him like a newborn foal. He wants to demand an explanation—surely this is all some horrid misunderstanding. Why is this happening? Why Yinka? But before a single word escapes his mouth, a hard punch sends him reeling. He barely registers the pain before the onslaught begins—fists and feet raining down on him from all sides, relentless and unyielding. His body instinctively curls in on itself, trying to shield the most vulnerable parts, but the blows find their mark with terrifying precision.

He tries to fend them off, flailing like someone who has seen many boxing matches but never quite mastered the choreography. His arms, heavy with exhaustion, are about as useful as waving sticks at a hurricane, and every attempt to scream for help is swallowed by the cacophony of mocking voices around him. The sounds blur together—

laughter, jests, sharp words spat with venom. It's as if they've turned cruelty into an art form, and Ade is the unfortunate canvas. Amidst the brutality, Ade clings to the hope that this will end—surely, at some point, one of them will tire. Or, dare he think it, Yinka might find a shred of humanity and call them off and declare this some twisted joke gone too far. But the minutes stretch on, and the violence continues unabated. No one comes, no rescuer, no knight in shining armour. His hopes fades, and in its place, a crushing despair begins to take root, slowly settling over him like a suffocating blanket.

Another voice cuts through the fray. "*Da òpá èyìn yen si enu e*—pour the local gin in his mouth."

They force it down his throat, the foul liquid burning like acid, soaking into his hair, his clothes, his skin. All the while, they continue their cruel, relentless barrage, as if determined to beat every last shred of dignity from him.

"Eeya, and na fine boy oh."

"E con get money join."

"Why you go be gay?"

"E fit even be gay, but e go find one girl marry."

"And the girl no go sabi."

"Even if e sabi, money dey."

"Na true, she no go talk."

He doesn't recognise these voices, but Yinka is quiet until someone prompts him. "Bia, Yinka. How you sabi am?"

"I been wan use toilet for one party I go last month. Na there I hear him and hin friend talk," he says, his voice is unsteady as if something is constricting his throat.

"Na only last month you sabi am?"

"And e don buy you phone?"

"Maybe na house e go buy you next."

After what feels like an eternity, one of them says, "Leave am, make we go."

Ade raises his head with a sheer force of will, every part of him begging to stay down, to just let the pain take him. Through his blurry vision, he watches the four men walk away, their mocking laughter trailing behind them like a bad smell. They walk as if they've just had a lovely evening's football game, not a brutal, cowardly assault. Each step they take feels like a dagger twisting in his gut, not just because of the pain, but because of the downright, galling insult of it. Weakness, indignity, humiliation—each word pricks at him like a needle.

With a grimace, he forces himself to rise. Everything hurts, every muscle screams, but he's not about to lie there like a discarded rag doll. He plants his hands against the ground, arms trembling, willing his body to obey as if pain is a mere suggestion. He heaves himself up, gasping as his ribs howl in protest, but he's up. Mostly. He staggers, but he's standing, and that's half the battle won. Then, the task of limping back to the car. It's only a few steps, but it may as well be Everest. Every movement sends a jolt of pain through him, sharp enough to make his vision blur all over again. But Ade, stubborn to the last, grits his teeth and forces one foot in front of the other.

Taiwo flies out of the car, eyes wide. "Ade *kílóselè?*"

Ade, in a state of disoriented silence, can't quite summon his voice. Taiwo helps him into the backseat, then calls Ade's parents, explaining that Ade is bleeding and bruised all over and to meet them at the hospital. By the time they arrive, Ade's parents are already there, their faces a study in raw anguish, as if every blow he's endured has been distributed to them as well. As the nurses wheel him in, Ade's father, chief Adebola, reaches out, his fingers brushing against Ade's battered cheek with a tenderness that barely masks his seething anger. Chief Adebola's chest heaves beneath the intricate patterns of his agbada and the veins on his neck stand out like tight ropes. The weight of his fury as discernible as the oppressive heat of the Nigerian sun.

Wordlessly, Ade hands his mom his phone, open to Yinka's chat. She accepts it, her attempt to hold back tears a valiant, if ultimately futile effort. The nurses get to work, cleaning and dressing his wounds, and Ade remains a stoic statue, his expression a mask of determined calm. Each flick of the bandage and dab of antiseptic is met with an internal promise not to crumble. He shoves the attack to the back of his mind, where it is relegated to the status of a footnote in the otherwise orderly script of his life.

Or so he thinks.

🏃

Sunday, 26th June 2022.

Abuja.

"I'm gay," Ade says, the words suspended in the air like a defiant kite on a windy day.

It's the week after the attack. Ade, feeling a peculiar mix of grim determination and apprehensive hope, calls his family to the living room. There's no reason to hide anything now. He perches on the edge of his chair, his fingers fidgeting with the edge of his sleeves. He hadn't precisely planned for this conversation—he's more of a go-with-the-flow kind of person, but this flow is decidedly rough. He understands that reactions to such revelations can vary. Parents, after all, are not always equipped to handle their children's differences with the ease of flipping a switch.

"Did you just know?" his dad asks, curiosity rather than condemnation colouring his voice.

Ade inhales deeply. "Since I was seventeen," his gaze skittering like a distracted butterfly.

His dad's face falls. "Why didn't you tell us then?"

"I don't know. I'm sorry."

But Ade is acutely aware of an underlying current of anxiety that refuses to be ignored. Despite his parents' open-mindedness, he can't shake the feeling that he's somehow letting them down, not quite living up to the shining image of the child they had envisioned. This disquieting thought—that they might quietly distance themselves from him, even unintentionally—haunts him. And in his efforts to starve off this looming dread, Ade resorts to procrastination.

"Teniade, you are my son," his dad says, crossing the room to him. "I love you just as you are." He kisses Ade's head and draws him into a hug.

The hug becomes a group hug. They've all learned from Nathan, almost squeezing the life out of him. At this rate, Ade will possibly *come out* and *go out* on the same day.

"If you had told us at seventeen, or even fifteen, our response would've been the same," his mom assures him. "Ayò ati ìdùnú nìkan ni mofé fún e omo mi—I only want joy and happiness for you, my child."

Ade exhales deeply, relieved. In this moment, he realises something he's always known on some level: there's a rare and precious kind of love here, one that not everyone is fortunate enough to experience from their family. It's a love that wraps around him like a comforting embrace, offering acceptance and understanding in a way that feels both generous and deeply validating. But the relief brings with it a tinge of regret. He thinks about all the moments he might have shared with them sooner, but even amidst that, there's also a quiet gratitude.

Temmy clears his throat, a signal Ade knows too well. "We think you should leave. Come to Newcastle and get away from them."

Ade stares at his family, disbelief on his face. "Leave? I did nothing wrong. I didn't approach him. I don't even know the others," he turns to his mother. "I can't leave. I have a job to start. Can't you do something?"

Justice Remilekun's eyes glisten, her lips pressed into a thin line as she fights back tears. "I wish I could, Ademi. You know the laws of the country we live in. I wish I could change them, and I hope as a people, we become more accepting. But we have to shield you from this. That boy... he texted when you were at the hospital, and he was making threats. Things we cannot fight now. They are trying to hold this over your head, and we don't want that."

Everything she says stings but one point lands like a slap across the face: the country they live in. A nation so deeply entrenched in its prejudices that people can launch attacks with the assurance of widespread applause and support. If the incident were to make headlines, Yinka and his accomplices would be celebrated as heroes, their bravery rewarded with fame and fortune.

But what about the oppressed? When do they get to fight back? Why is it considered normal to ponder escape after such brutal injustice? And what happens to the less fortunate in minority groups, those who don't have the option to flee? What is the fate of the average Nigerian if, as one of the elites, the only solution they can fathom is for him to pack up his life and leave? Ade's heart pounds with a mixture of anger and despair.

"Ade, try to understand where we are coming from," Temmy says. "I don't think they plan to stop there. Like mom said, think about their bloody law."

Ade surveys the faces around him, seeking dissent, but finds it in scant supply. His father's eyes offer a glimmer of defiance, but it's a mere blip in the sea of consensus. The majority has spoken, and Ade's fate is sealed. For something that wasn't his fault at all, he is being banished. Protection and safety, they call it. To him, it is exile. His dreams, his plans, everything he's worked for—gone in an instant. Without a word, he storms into his room, the door slamming shut behind him like a final verdict.

Jola walks in moments later, climbs on the bed, and wraps an arm around him. "I understand you don't want to leave. But we are scared, Ade. I am scared. This could have ended much worse. We could have lost you, and my heart cannot take it for you to stay here where it is so dangerous, where you are exposed." She sniffs, her voice breaking. "When dad called us, what came to my mind was two years ago. I thought the worst had happened and I—"

Ade turns to face her. "Jughead."

He remembers the day, vividly—his frantic rush to the hospital amid a pandemic, the horror of the news, the terror that gripped him. His unconscious sister in his hands, the cold, impersonal lights of the emergency room. The moment when time stood still, and the gaping hole that ripped through their family.

"I know you couldn't control what happened. And I know they are different scenarios, but if Diego had a choice, what would he have chosen?"

Diego. The name hangs like an unspoken ghost, a whisper from a past shrouded in pain. It's a name they haven't mentioned for nearly two years, a period marked by silence. But it's a name that Jola screams in the dead of the night, when the darkness seems to close in, and her nightmares take on a life of their own.

"I know," Ade sighs, seeing the desperation in her eyes, the silent plea for him to understand, to choose safety over principles. "I just don't want to leave mom and dad. The plan was to stay here, follow my dreams, at least until they retire."

"They want you to be safe. We all do. If you stay and something else happens to you, how do you think they will feel?"

"Okay," Ade shrugs, then adds: "This wasn't how I planned to come out, by the way. I had a whole thing planned."

A faint smile touches Jola's lips. "Will I be talking out of my arse if I say I kind of suspected?"

"I thought you surely knew. Or that Nathan might have slipped."

"Oh, that boy was iron-clad about it. And I might be a bit envious that you both didn't let me in on this." She smacks his arm. "I have a session with Sparks this evening. He says you can join and talk to him, if you want."

"It is one thing for me to agree to leave but I am not talking to anyone. Never."

Jola shakes her head but doesn't press further.

16
THE MEETING

— Cardigan by Taylor Swift.

Friday, 2nd March 2018.

Stockholm

STEFAN'S EIGHTEENTH BIRTHDAY MARKS MANY FIRSTS in his life. It's his debut performance where he finally steps out of the metaphorical closet to reveal his true self to his family and friends. On this milestone day, he wades into the hedonistic waters of a nightclub for the first time. It's also the first time he tries alcohol—a rite of passage he's been looking forward to. Stefan even takes it up a notch and has his first kiss. And if—only if—it is worth a mention, the first time he meets Honza Rychlý.

Stefan wakes up to the irresistible aroma of baking, a smell that announces his birthday with all the subtlety of a brass band. His mom, Sara, is in full baking-mode; it's a tradition for her to bake him cakes on his birthdays—a

Swedish speciality with layers of sponge cake, pastry cream, and a thick doomed layer of whipped cream covered with marzipan. It's the kind of cake that could make a pastry chef weep with envy. With a groggy stretch and a yawn that could rival a lion's roar, Stefan shuffles downstairs on a quest for his gifts, which, as usual, are arranged in their designated corner of the dining room. Each present is wrapped with the kind of care that suggests his mom views gift wrapping as an art.

"*Här är födelsedagsdarnet*—here's the birthday boy," his dad, Leon, announces with the air of a game show host.

"*Grattis på födelsedagen, min älskade*—Happy birthday, my love," his mom coos, showering him with her customary barrage of kisses.

"Happy birthday, son," his dad adds, delivering a hug that's reassuringly solid.

They settle in for cake and hot chocolate, a tradition that has become a comfortable routine over the years. Unlike most families, no one in the Wickström household drinks coffee or tea—perish the thought. It's a peculiar little quirk that stretches back generations. Even his uncle, God rest his soul, who always seemed like the type to enjoy a strong brew, and his grandparents, who might have been expected to favour tea in their later years, never touched the stuff—Stefan hopes they're all having a nice mug of hot chocolate in heaven. The Wickström, it seems, are immune to the charms of caffeine or tannins.

"I have to tell you both something," he announces after breakfast, his voice a mix of nervousness and resolve.

His parents turn to him at once, giving him their full, undivided attention, as if everything else in the room has ceased to exist. It's always like this with them—utter devotion, no matter the subject. He could announce the weather or muse about a squirrel he saw, and they would lean in as though he's unveiling the secrets of the universe. It's not performative, either. They genuinely hang on to each word simply because it's *him* doing the talking.

"I've known about this for some time, and I want you to be the first ones I tell because you are the most important people in my life." He takes a deep breath. "*Jag är bisexuell*—I'm bisexual."

"*Min kärlek,*" his mom sighs with relief. "I thought you wanted to go live alone or something."

"What?" Stefan places a hand on his chest dramatically, "and not have you fuss over me?"

His parents hug him, their love and acceptance a comforting balm to his soul. "*Tack för att du berättade för oss*—thank you for telling us," his dad says.

"*Vi älskar dig över allt annat.*"—we love you above all else—his mom says, attacking him with another round of kisses.

"*Här träffar vi din pojvän?*—so, when do we meet your boyfriend?" his dad asks.

"*Eller flickvän?*—or girlfriend?" his mom adds.

"*Jag har inte en pojvän*—I don't have a boyfriend," Stefan replies, helping himself to a slice of cake. "*Eller flickvän,*" he chuckles. "Maybe now, I'll find one."

"You must bring him or her to us once you do," his dad instructs, mock sternly.

"Don't tell me you plan to investigate who I date?"

"Well, not investigate," his mom says, unconvincingly. "But we have to make sure they will treat you well."

Excellent point, Stefan has to agree.

"Okay... if I get to Edwin and Żaneta's level with someone, I'll bring them home."

After unwrapping half of his gifts, Stefan returns to his

room to talk to his friends on FaceTime. As he settles into the familiar comfort of his own space, he's overcome with a surprising lightness in his chest—an unexpected freedom that feels like a particularly pleasant afterthought. His parents' acceptance is like a grand, unspoken applause, a signal that he's finally stepped into the stage of his true self, and the audience is delighted. This newfound clarity of heart and mind is not just a fleeting pleasure, but a deep, reassuring calm that permeates his very being.

Ludvin joins their call briefly before he disappears, and Edwin's younger sister, Elin takes the phone from him.

"His girlfriend is calling him," Elin supplies. "Happy birthday, hon."

"Thanks, E. When did Lud get a girlfriend?"

Żaneta cackles on the screen. "Get? Like he bought her from Stradivarius?"

"He just met a Czech lady," Edwin reports mid-laugh. "Her name is Yaroslava."

"Isn't that a Ukrainian or Russian name?" Stefan asks. "Or Serbian?"

"I think it's an old Slavic name," Edwin replies. "She's beautiful. Lud wants us to meet her soon."

"We'll be at yours by four," Żaneta says. "Be ready and tell Marcus."

"What are we doing?"

"Every year, he asks, knowing we won't tell." Żaneta rolls her eyes.

On each of their birthdays, the other two always plan fun activities if there's no party. This year, however, Stefan had drawn a firm line, adamantly rejecting his parents' ambitious plans for an over-the-top eighteenth birthday party—a soirée that promised to be the most extravagant in Sweden's history.

His reasons were apparent, if not a bit disillusioning. In past years, Stefan had been trapped in grand parties, overflowing with faces he barely recognised and didn't particularly wish to. These gatherings had been less about genuine connection and more about flaunting inherited wealth, as if the only achievement was being born into affluence. For Stefan, the grandeur of these parties only underscored the emptiness of social climbing and shallow pleasantries. This year, he wants something authentic and meaningful—the simple, unadulterated joy of spending time with his friends, far removed from the insincerity of his social circle. With them, he could savour the uncomplicated joy of being himself, away from the ostentatious pretences and hollow interactions that had so often marred his celebrations.

By four in the evening, Marcus is driving the trio to an undisclosed location—well, only undisclosed to Stefan. Żaneta had already discreetly whispered their destination to Marcus. After about thirty minutes of winding roads and scenic detours, Marcus finally steers into the parking lot of Gröna Lund—Stockholm's famed amusement park. Stefan steps out of the car, ready for a day brimming with whatever adventures lie ahead.

And the day is a rollicking adventure from start to finish. They begin with the go-kart track, where they zoom around corners and challenge each other to not-so-friendly races, unleashing their inner speed demons. Next up is a stint at the skjutbanan, the shooting range, where Stefan discovers Żaneta's hidden talent for marksmanship—she may not be the most graceful on the go-kart track but her aim at the range is something to behold. Stefan will do well not to incur her wrath. The laser tag arena transforms them into a band of neon warriors, darting and dodging in a vibrant maze of light and sound. Skeeball follows, each of them vying to land the highest score while exchanging whimsical jabs. At some point, they wander into the House of Nightmares, where the scares turn out to be more farcical than terrifying, but it doesn't stop Stefan from quickly retreating. His favourite activity, surprisingly, is the Flygande Mattan—flying carpet. After the ride, they huddle together checking their pictures which captures them in all their absurd glory: mouth agape, hands flailing like windmills, and eyes popping out of their heads. Stefan is having the time of his life.

They move on to a restaurant, where Żaneta casually suggests, "Maybe we should go to a gay club."

"Wanna go, Stefan?" Edwin asks. "There's one called Backdoor."

"Sure. I follow them on IG," Stefan says, accepting their orders. "We'll eat in the car, so I can give Marcus his food."

Marcus drives them to Backdoor after their meal but insists on waiting in the car. "You can leave, Marcus. I'll grab a cab home," Stefan says.

"I need to stay with you." Marcus counters, his protective instincts on high alert.

Stefan sighs. "I can call you when we're ready to leave," he persuades. Marcus reluctantly agrees and leaves. "Having him around will make me too cautious," Stefan complains. "He's like a bodyguard."

"Well, you need one to avoid being kidnapped," Żaneta quips.

"No one is interested in kidnapping me," Stefan says, heading towards the club's entrance. "I'm eager to drink."

Edwin laughs. "I'm eager to see how you handle alcohol."

As they step into the throbbing heart of the club, Stefan

immediately questions his decision. The club is a sensory assault of epic proportions: flashing lights that seem to have a personal vendetta against his sense of equilibrium, casting ever-shifting shadows across the packed dance floor. The bass-heavy music pulses through Stefan's chest with such intensity that it feels almost like a physical presence, thudding in time with his heartbeat. The air here is a mix of raucous laughter, shouted conversations, and the occasional high-pitched screech that rises above the general noise. Stefan weaves his way through the crowd, feeling both invigorated and slightly daunted by the commotion, and he can't help but wonder if he's bitten more than he can chew.

What do people enjoy in clubbing?

The bartender lines their ordered shots, and they raise their glasses. "Happy birthday, Stefan," Żaneta practically shouts.

"Happy birthday!" Edwin echoes, clinking his glass with Stefan's.

Five shots later, Stefan is starting to grasp, albeit vaguely, why people flock to the clubs. His initial disorientation begins to fade, and he starts to feel the loosening grip of inhibition that alcohol provides. The music still pulses like a living entity, but now it feels more like an energising heartbeat rather than an assault. They remain at the bar, patiently awaiting their Moët & Chandon —a wait that feels interminable—when a man in his mid-twenties approaches them. His gaze flits over their faces with a casual curiosity before landing squarely on Stefan.

He smiles and introduces himself. "Name's Honza Rychlý. And who are you guys?"

"Edwin," his friend replies with polite detachment.

"Żaneta," she says with a grin.

Stefan hesitates, feeling Honza's intense scrutiny. "Stefan."

At that, Mr. Rychlý scrunches up his nose. "Do you have another name?"

Stefan's brow arches in confusion. "Uh, Omar?"

Honza's smile widens. "Now, that's a pretty name for such a pretty boy."

Stefan is not sure, but he thinks he hears Żaneta snort.

Friday, 16th December 2022.

Newcastle

Stefan sits at DINE, absently twirling his fork through the remnants of his risotto, when the soft scrape of a chair being pulled out snaps him from his reverie. Someone has settled into the seat opposite him, uninvited. He doesn't need to look up to know who it is—he can feel the unwelcome presence like a change in the air, the perfume is also a dead giveaway. But still, out of some morbid curiosity, he raises his head, and there it is: Honza's face, his smile so wide and cartoonish it could belong to a villain in a children's comic.

Stefan sighs internally, his stomach already twisting itself into knots, like it knows what's coming. A flash of irritation stirs in his chest, but he tamps it down, pressing the rim of his glass to his lips instead. Water. Calm. He wills the cool liquid to settle the uneasy churn in his gut, but it does little to soothe the rising tide of discomfort. Without a word, Stefan lowers the glass and returns his attention to his plate, resolutely continuing with his lunch as though the man sitting across from him were nothing more than a mild inconvenience. Maybe, if he concentrates hard enough on his food, Honza will simply vanish. Stranger things have happened.

But of course, Honza doesn't vanish. He never does. "It is great to see you, Omar," he says, reaching to take Stefan's hands. "I've missed you."

Stefan drops his hands to his lap, his fingers tapping rhythmically against his thigh. Honza's smile falters for the briefest second, his face flashing with anger before his grin snaps back into place—just as ridiculous as before. "Can I get you more drinks? Dessert, maybe?"

Honza ordering for *anyone*? Stefan raises a brow but continues chewing, curious in spite of himself. The Honza he remembers would've flagged down a waiter and ordered an entire feast, demanding Stefan partake whether he liked it or not. Progress, or something resembling it?

"I'm full," Stefan replies, voice flat.

Honza's smile tightens by degrees. "Alright. I won't get anything myself either. Even though I'm *starving*."

Ah, the classical guilt trip, finely tuned over the years. If Honza wants to starve himself out of noble sacrifice, Stefan thinks, so be it. In fact, that would make Stefan's life easier.

"What do you want?" Stefan keeps his voice low, to avoid drawing attention.

Honza reaches across the table, that annoyingly familiar glint of self-righteousness in his eyes. "Omar, I love you. I want you back. I understand now, everything you said. I'm ready to be the man you deserve."

Can you fucking believe this guy?

Stefan leans back, his suppressed irritation pressing against his ribs. "You do not understand at all," he says slowly, just in case Honza's hearing is as poor as his grasp on reality. "You followed me here. Or does your company happen to have a branch in Newcastle?"

Honza's brows twitch as he forces a look of wounded innocence. "What choice did you leave me with? You blocked every number I call you with. You didn't tell me you were leaving Stockholm. I had to find out from someone else! That's not *fair*."

Is he for real? The nerve of him.

"I broke up with you," Stefan says, dragging out the words, like explaining quantum physics to a toddler. "I owe you nothing. Certainly not information on my whereabouts, and definitely not an invitation to stalk me."

"Omar, *Zlato*,"—gold, spoken in the syrupy sweetness of Czech—"I was worried about you. I needed to know you were okay. Maybe you're right, and I shouldn't have done that, but I wasn't trying to stalk you. You shouldn't use words like that."

Ah, yes, now we arrive at the manipulation part of the programme. Stefan wonders briefly, despairingly, if this really is how he's spending his afternoon.

Heaven, help me.

"What are you doing in Newcastle?"

"To see you. I told you, I missed you."

"So, you came only after you somehow knew I was here? And did I ask for you to come?"

"I don't see how this is important," Honza says tartly. "Most people would find it romantic."

Romantic? Stefan bites down on a laugh. If this is romance, then Jane Austen must be turning in her grave. "You don't have to worry about me, Honza. I've been clear. I just want the past to remain where it belongs. I didn't involve the authorities, against *very* strong advice, mind you.

But this?" He gestures vaguely at the table, at Honza. "This has to stop."

Honza's smile finally crumbles, giving way to the sneer underneath. "It's the *black* boy, right?" his voice sharpens, spitting the word 'black' like a curse. "You are leaving me for that mon—"

Stefan's fist slams onto the table before he's aware of it, rattling the glasses. His eyes flash with a fury he rarely lets loose, and his voice is low, dangerously so. "Do not finish that sentence."

Honza balks. For the first time, he doesn't meet Stefan's eyes, his petulance melting in the face of something he clearly didn't expect—*resistance*.

"Omar, you cannot leave me," Honza tries, voice slipping back into a childish whine. "Not for him."

Stefan's lips curl. "*Javel*," he mutters under his breath. *Motherfucker*. "I left you four years ago, and it has *nothing* to do with him. What we had," he pauses, searching for a word, "couldn't even be called a relationship."

"You're in love with him," Honza states, a sneer still laced through his tone as if the idea is the most preposterous thing in the world.

"It is none of your business if I am."

"You don't deserve me," Honza snaps, "or anything I could give you if—"

"*What* do you give me, Honz?" Stefan's voice is a growl now, his anger simmering. "All you've given me is this ridiculous charade." He leans in, voice steady. "I ask for *nothing* from you but to leave me the fuck alone."

They stay silent for a few minutes, regarding each other. Finally, Honza leans back, a look of disgust warping his features. "Fine. You were only ever worth anything when I knew I was the only one who had ever touched you." His words drip with spite. "Now that you're sullied, I want nothing to do with you."

Stefan throws his head back, shoulders shaking as a deep, hearty laugh bursts forth. He clutches his stomach, tears springing to his eyes as the absurdity of Honza's words cracks something wide open.

Honza, momentarily flustered, rises. "You can laugh all you want. You'll never hear from me again." And with such great last words, Mr. Rychlý leaves.

Stefan wipes his eyes, still laughing. He flips his phone over, and sends the recording to his group chat. Prosecco seems in order, something crisp to match the sparkling satisfaction of Honza's long-overdue departure. The silence that follows is delicious, the kind that lets your thoughts stretch out luxuriously, like a cat in a sunbeam. And naturally, Stefan's relentless mind drifts back to Ade.

Lately, they've been talking, though mostly about *Shadowhunters*—a shared obsession now, which seems fitting, considering their own tangled history. There've been a few polite phone calls and the odd fleeting moments when their paths crossed during group hangouts. At Ben's, for example, Stefan had maintained a careful distance from Ade, as if space could somehow mute the ache he felt for him. Spoiler alert: it didn't. No amount of distance would. In truth, and in the privacy of his own mind, Stefan would much rather close the gap entirely. Rip Ade's clothes off, as Jason had so artlessly pointed out last Saturday. Jason, bless him, always went straight for the jugular of awkward truths. Stefan hadn't commented at the time, but yes, Jason was right. Very right.

Stefan has replayed the events of the Halloween party like an Instagram reel he can't stop watching, hoping each time for a different outcome. He'd overthought everything to the point of irrationality, convincing himself that Ade's behaviour was a deliberate rejection when, in fact, it had been quite the opposite. In hindsight, it's all so obvious, so embarrassingly simple. Ade had been trying, *really* trying, to be better for him. And someone trying to make themselves better for you should be the highest form of compliment. It shows strength and courage. But Stefan, in all his stubborn glory, had been too busy fortifying old defences to notice the olive branch in Ade's hands. He remembers now, with almost painful lucidity, the tremble in Ade's fingers as he tried to explain himself, the quiet desperation in his kiss. The guy had practically worn his heart on his sleeve, and what had Stefan done? Slammed the door in his face.

"Idiot," he mutters under his breath, tipping back his glass. It's a scolding directed inward. And regret—the slow, insidious kind that sneaks up on him after he's had too much time to think.

The past month has been a miserable one and Stefan knows exactly who's to blame. Himself. But now? Now, things are different. He doesn't care about the past, the obstacles, or even the potential for disaster. He wants Ade. No, more than that—he needs him. And if life throws a few hurdles in the way? Well, Stefan's decided he's quite up for the challenge. After all, as Celine Montclaire so wisely concluded in *The Wicked Ones*, strength isn't about avoiding suffering—it's about enduring it. Stefan smiles to himself, the Prosecco fizzing pleasantly on his tongue. He's ready. Ready to endure whatever comes his way for the chance to be with Ade. Ready to weather the storms, if need be. Because, as ridiculous as it might sound, Stefan finally understands what he's been too blind to see before.

Love, real love, is worth fighting for—even if he's fighting against his own fears.

THREESOME 🙂
Today at 06:56 PM

▶ •ıl|ı|ıl||||ııı|ıl|ıı|||ııı| 59:41

JULIET

Omg! Omg!! Omg!!!

I'm so proud of you, put him in his place.

ROMEO

This is very well done. He got the message this time.

Such a twisted guy.

JULIET

Come home in December. I owe you a thousand kisses.

ROMEO

I'm right here Żane.

But true, we'll kiss you.

Threesome finally or I'm not coming.

ROMEO

Okay, we'll make a video of us three fucking. And send it to Mr. Rychlý.

March 2018.

Stockholm.

Stefan's head spins as he stumbles away from the bar, the alcohol painting the world in slightly blurred strokes. The evening is a haze of laughter, lights, and the peculiar euphoria that only comes from being just the right amount of tipsy. He slides into a chair at the table with his friends only to realise with a slight start, that Honza has followed him like a stray cat that's found someone with food.

"So, what's a gorgeous boy like you doing here?" Honza's voice cuts through the noise, each word laced with far too much excitement for Stefan's liking.

Stefan, attempting nonchalance, gives a short laugh. "It's my birthday."

Honza's face lights up, his enthusiasm so exaggerated that Stefan wonders if the man has ever experienced a birthday before. "That's amazing! It's your *narozeni!*" he declares, throwing in the Czech word for birthday with such pride it might as well have been his invention. Honza raises his glass high, toasting the moment as though they were in the final act of some grand opera. "Happy birthday, Omar. How old are you?"

Stefan glances at his friends, seeking some rescue, but they're too engrossed in their own conversation to notice. "Eighteen. How old are you?"

Honza laughs. "I'm twenty-six, my dear boy." And before Stefan can say anything further, Honza grabs his hand with the eagerness of a child pulling their parent to see something marvellous. "Come, let's dance!"

Stefan barely has time to process what's happening

before he's being yanked toward the dance floor. "Guys, let's dance!" he calls back to his friends.

"I have never seen a gorgeous boy like you," Honza yells into Stefan's ear over the pulsing music. "You must be made of something special."

Stefan forces a polite smile. "Thank you," he mutters, while mentally calculating how long this dance needs to last before it becomes socially acceptable to escape.

And then, just like that, Honza leans in closer. "I want to kiss you," he announces, as if declaring his intention to board a train.

Before Stefan can gather his thoughts—or even muster a response—Honza's mouth is on his, and suddenly, Stefan is part of a kiss that feels more like a concussion. Stefan has no list of references, but he can tell there's far too much tongue; an alarming proximity to his nose, and the overall sensation that Honza is trying to lick the inside of his face. He's been told before that kisses—especially the first kiss—can make the world spin, make your knees weak, but this? This is just... damp. As the kiss continues, his body remains resolutely unimpressed—it's awkward, clumsy, and devoid of any spark he's been led to expect. This is no romance novel or movie kiss. No Magnus and Alec's chemistry here.

Stefan pulls away, blinking, slightly dazed but mostly relieved. Deciding this night has been quite enough, Stefan signals it's time to leave. His friends gather their things, and as they say their goodbyes, Honza leans in once more. "I want to speak with you," he whispers, as if they're in on some grand conspiracy. He follows them outside, where Marcus is waiting. Stefan steps aside with him as his friends walk to the car. "Why don't you come with me to my hotel?" Honza proposes, his voice urgent. "I can take you home in the morning."

Stefan hesitates, glancing towards his G-wagon idling nearby. "I can't. I didn't tell my parents," he says with a half-shrug. "Our driver is waiting."

Honza's face falls slightly, but after exchanging phone number and a promise to meet again, Stefan climbs into the car with his friends.

"What did he want?" Żaneta asks the moment Stefan settles into his seat.

"A date."

"He wastes no time, does he?" Edwin comments.

Żaneta isn't finished. "How was the kiss?"

"You saw?"

"I did, and now I *have* to know."

Stefan considers the best way to sum it up. "Let's just say it wasn't life-altering," he says, finally.

"And you agreed to a date *after* that?" Edwin's voice is filled with disbelief.

"It may not be in the kiss, you know," Żaneta muses thoughtfully. "Hyacinth and St. Claire didn't have the best first kiss either, and look how that turned out."

"*Bridgerton*," Edwin mutters, rolling his eyes.

Stefan laughs. "We'll see how it goes. If I don't like him after the date, I'll stop seeing him. Simple."

The next day, as promised, Stefan meets Honza for their date. It's fine, perfectly pleasant even, but it still lacks the spark he's hoping for. Honza, for his part, is brimming with earnestness. "I wish I'd met you the moment I arrived," he says wistfully. "I want to get to know you better so we can be together. Can we keep talking until I visit you again?"

"Sure." Stefan agrees.

Their long-distance arrangement begins innocently enough, like most things that tiptoe quietly towards calamity. It starts with a flurry of texts, midnight phone calls, and the occasional video calls that Stefan half-enjoys, half-tolerates. There's a certain novelty at first—Honza's eager questions, the way he speaks about the future as if it's already written, the promises of adventures yet to come. It's flattering, Stefan tells himself. Who wouldn't be charmed by someone so utterly smitten? By August, when Honza returns to Stockholm, Stefan quickly realises that their reunion is nothing like he's hoped.

If anything, it marks the beginning of his problems.

17

RUNNIN' NO MORE

*— Runnin' (Lose it All) by Naughty Boy
ft. Beyoncé & Arrow Benjamin.*

Tuesday, 20th December 2022.

ADE STRIDES INTO JOLA'S CLUTTERED OFFICE AND HE'S instantly greeted by a sight that nearly makes him question his surroundings. Jola, the model of poise and professionalism on any ordinary day, is bouncing around like a child who's just been handed all the sweets in the world, clapping her hands together in barely contained glee.

"What's up, Jughead?" Ade asks, stepping inside with Nathan and MT in tow.

Jola spins on her heel, a light blue gift bag practically thrown into his hands. "Open it, open it," she demands, eyes glittering with a mixture of excitement and pure mischief.

"Alright, alright," Ade laughs, tearing into the wrapping. "But what's this?"

"Don't be slow, Ade," Jola says, her grin widening. "It's from him."

At that single pronoun—*him*—Ade's heart somersaults in his chest. His hands freeze for a moment before he pulls away the wrapping paper and sees the AirPods Max box inside. But it's not the headphones that seize his attention; it's the folded piece of paper resting on top, as if waiting patiently to change everything. Ade carefully unfolds the note, eyes scanning Stefan's unmistakable handwriting. The words are few, but they may as well be gospel.

Téní,

I miss you very much

-Stef.

The air leaves Ade's lungs in a rush, and his knees, the traitors, give way. His body sags, a flood of relief, joy and hope washing over him—hope he's avoided since that October night. He blindly feels behind him and slumps into a chair. He's dimly aware that his sister and friends are watching, but the world has shrunk to the size of this note. Stefan misses him. *Stefan*—the person whose absence has corroded Ade's very being for weeks, the love of his life—*misses* him.

Jola's voice cuts through like a record scratch. "Check your messages, mister," she prods, nudging him back to reality.

He finds his phone, hands shaking as he opens iMessage. And there it is, Stefan's text. He reads, and suddenly, everything fades away again, the magnitude of it all threatening to suffocate him in the best possible way. He stands abruptly, gathers the headphones, the wrapping paper, and the gift bag, then turns to the door. "Nathan will drive you home!" he calls over his shoulder, barely hearing his own voice above the roar of blood in his ears.

STEFAN 😎 >
Today 06:05 PM

> ▶ Runnin' (Lose it All) - Naughty Boy feat. Beyoncé & Arrow Benjamin

> I want you to listen to this first.

Where are you?

> OMW to the airport.

What time is your flight?

> 8:45PM

Jola's voice follows him with a grin he can practically hear. "He will never live this day down till the day I die."

She's absolutely right, but it doesn't matter. Nothing matters except one thing. He needs to get to Newcastle Airport. Now.

He climbs into his bZ4X, but his hands are still trembling so much to even start the car. He manages to open the box, connects the headphones to his phone, and hits play. The moment Beyoncé's voice comes on, he feels peace wash over him. It's as though Stefan is speaking to him through the music, each lyric a balm to his soul.

"So where are you?" Beyoncé sings.

"Coming to you, my Stef," Ade whispers, his voice barely audible as he joins her in the refrain.

He drives out slowly, careful not to let his impatience get the better of him, though the urge to put his foot down and fly down the A19 is almost overwhelming. Images of Stefan flood his mind—Stefan's face, Stefan's smile, Stefan's voice, Stefan writing that note. Stefan, Stefan, Stefan. Every mile he passes is one step closer to the guy he thought he might lose forever. When he encounters traffic, he swears loudly and quickly texts Jason: *hold him in the car* 🫠🙏.

Jason's response is as swift as it is irreverent: *Brb, getting rope* 🙄.

When the traffic finally thins, Ade exhales in relief and presses down on the accelerator, cutting through the miles like a mad man. The sprawling car park of Newcastle Airport looms into view, buzzing with the usual chaos of arrivals and departures. Ade parks, heart in his throat, and quickly types another message to Jason: *Where are you?*

Jason's reply is immediate: *Get down and open your arms* 😎.

Ade knits his brow, but there's no time for overthinking now. He climbs out of the car, scanning the lot as he dials Jason, the phone pressed to his ear.

Then, he sees him.

Stefan. His *Stef*. His heart's desire, racing towards him with the same wild urgency burning in Ade's veins. His phone falls silent in his hands as he lets it drop.

And Ade opens his arms.

🏃

Ade saunters into their living room with the self-assured swagger of someone who's just discovered the secret to eternal youth. "*Ekú ìròlé,*" he greets, prostrating to his parents and then swivelling towards Ken and Annette

Bower—Sophia's parents—with a cheerful nod. "Good evening."

His dad chuckles. "*Báwo ni ìrìnàjò e?*—how was your trip?"

"What did they tell you?" Ade's scowl is an impressive feat of facial gymnastics.

"How did it go?" Sophia asks, failing to keep the curiosity out of her voice.

Ade flops onto the couch. "Have to wait till he's back to know," he replies, his lips pulling into a smug smile.

"You look lovesick, tueh," Jola remarks from her perch by their dad's couch, her head resting on his lap.

Temmy chuckles, then clears his throat as if preparing for a grand declaration. "Firstly, I'd like to apologise to you," he begins, addressing their parents. "For going against your instructions, but I couldn't just sit and do nothing when one lowlife thinks he can hurt my brother and get away with it. Ade is already working hard in therapy to heal from this, and I can't let them mess it up by contacting him again in the future. Their actions cannot go unchecked."

Ade's head snaps up from his phone, his eyes wide with alarm. He and their parents speak in unison. "Temmy, what did you do?"

Temmy's lips curl into a cunning smile. "Nothing yet," he reassures. "MT got the guy's information from someone called Halima. After that, it was pretty easy. I spoke to him as Ade's brother, who's scared for him not to be outed. For our family not to be put in," he air-quotes, "shame."

The entire family is keenly aware that Chief Adebola and Justice Remilekun Adeowo couldn't care less about societal judgments. Shame holds no sway over them; their sole concern is ensuring their child's well-being and shielding him from Nigeria's cruelty.

"I told him I might have some cash," Temmy continues. "If it meant getting him to leave Ade alone, and I arranged to have it ready for him today." He pauses for dramatic effect, laughing so hard he nearly falls off his chair. "I told him," he wipes his eyes, "I couldn't transfer the funds because our parents monitor my Nigerian bank account."

Their parents' eyes meet, mirroring Ade's tightened expression. "You want to pay him off?"

Temmy shakes his head, dismissing the idea. "Pay him off ko. *Sísi, kòní rí*. He's getting nothing," he says. "Taiwo and Bolanle have him right now, and we're going to say hello to the dumbass."

Temmy taps away on his MacBook, dialling Bolanle, their mom's orderly (judges in Nigeria come with police escorts like VIP packages). Sophia, Jola, MT, Nathan, and Ay huddle around him. Once the call connects, Nathan's reaction to Yinka's face is more colourful than a fireworks display. He curses under his breath and joins Ade, who watches the scene unfold with a mixture of dread and detachment.

"So, you are Mr. Olayinka Oguns?" Temmy asks, his voice measured.

Yinka sounds as if he's about to launch himself from a moving vehicle. "Y-y-yes sir," he stammers.

Ade braces himself as Yinka's voice crackles through the speaker, expecting a deluge of emotions—rage, dread, perhaps even an existential crisis. Instead, he's met with an unnervingly flat void. There's no surge of anger or pang of anxiety, just a vast, echoing emptiness that seems to swallow up any potential feeling—truly a masterclass in emotional anticlimax.

"In June, you attacked my brother with three other men. Is that true?" Temmy's voice drips with contempt.

Yinka's response is a barely audible whisper. "No, sir," he says, "I mean, yes. But I didn't want to. They made me do it, I swear."

Temmy's eyes narrow, his patience wearing thin by the second. "Why?"

Yinka's words tumble out in a frantic rush. He explains —rather, he stammers—that he is indeed the very person he claimed to be. His initial approach to Ade, he insists, was driven not by rancour but by a sense of kinship. But, on that fateful day, his cousin had snatched his phone and read through his conversations with Ade. When he was faced with the threat of exposure to his parents, Yinka's courage evaporated faster than a puddle in the Sahara. So, he concocted a flimsy story about merely baiting Ade to extort him. And when his cousin rallied the others, Yinka was helpless, unable to halt their scheme for fear they would turn on him and spill the beans to his parents, who, he feared, would cast him out.

"I'm so sorry, I just had no choice," he cries.

Jola's temper flares. "You're a liar," she snaps. "If that's true, why did you send him disgusting pornos just weeks ago?"

Yinka continues, revealing that his cousin made him contact Ade, and subsequently sent the vile videos and pictures himself. Temmy's voice remains acrid, though tinged with resignation, as he demands names and information about the other attackers. Ade knows his siblings like the back of his hand. He knows what Temmy, Jola, and Sophia must be feeling, similar to how he now feels. Not sympathy, but pity and a deep sorrow. Pity for this guy who would never be who he truly is. Who may never have a chance at happiness, entrapped by the shackles of societal standards, and ruled by fear.

Fear so strong, it could easily be tipped into vileness. It could be exploited into violence. Fear, Ade realises, is a formidable force. It can be weaponised to warp the mind, twist the soul, and drive even the most innocent to commit acts of cruelty. What is wrong here, he wonders, in simply loving who you want? In two consenting adults deciding to be with each other? In being true to oneself, regardless of societal norms?

As Yinka recites the details of his co-accomplices, the regret in his voice is evident, but it offers no solace. The damage has been done, and it is irreversible and lasting. Ade looks at Jola, sensing as her fury simmers beneath the surface. And he can tell that she may pity Yinka, but it's a shallow sentiment compared to the anger that consumes her. "Take the phone from him," she instructs Bolanle. "Delete Ade's number, then remove his sim for him. And drop him in Ajah, that Sangotedo side," she adds with a wicked grin. "Love you. Muah."

MT and Ay erupt into fits of laughter that they topple off the armrest of the chair they're perched on. Sophia explains to her parents the distance between Ajah and Iyana-Ipaja, or even his hostel in Akoka, likening it to a journey between two states. He will face considerable difficulty returning home.

"Don't take the phone from him, Jughead," Ade protests.

Jola turns an icy look to him. "It is this or I have him roughened up. Trust me, Ay has a guy," she retorts, her tone brooking no argument.

"If you tell your friends about this call, we'll find out, and it won't be good for you," Temmy warns with authority. "I am being lenient with you because our parents raised us properly, unlike you. You should also know we have incriminating evidence against you, should you think we're bluffing. He never sent you anything admissible." He rises to his feet, gesturing to Ade. "Now, you're going to apologise to my brother."

Ade tries to protest but sits down with a resigned sigh as Temmy gives him a warning glare.

"I'm so sorry, Ade. I know what I did is unforgivable, but I'm very sorry," Yinka says, tears streaming. "I agreed to meet today not for the money. I was hoping whoever I meet will let you know how sorry I am."

"*Lórí iró*," MT mutters. "Lies."

Ade rises silently, and Nathan immediately envelops him in a tight hug, patting his back before Ade makes his way to sit with their parents, who embrace him.

"ASSHOLE," Jola slams down the laptop with a triumphant thud. "Revenge is sweet."

A surge of vindication courses through Ade, which feels as strange as it is weirdly comforting. He knows that what has just transpired won't magically mend the wounds or erase the scars of his past, but it's not the kind that's about justice in the conventional sense; it's more about the steadfast loyalty of those around him. His family and friends have rallied around him with an intensity that goes beyond mere support. Their dedication is so thorough, it's practically a full-blown show of loyalty. And it's not just about confronting his adversaries, but a reminder that he's got a whole squad behind him. This fervent support might not fix what's broken, but it does offer a delightful assurance that he's not stumbling through this battle alone.

"What'll happen to the names you took?" Ken asks.

"Ay's guy will deal with them," Jola replies.

"What does that mean?" Annette asks.

"They will be beaten up," Nathan supplies helpfully. "Tit for Tat."

"Good then," the Bowers agree. Sophia turns a stunned look at them. "What? Sometimes, the high road has to be abandoned," Ken says.

MT and Ay collapse into peals of laughter, falling back to the floor.

18
HOMECOMING

*— Hypnotized by Purple Disco Machine
& Sophie and the Giants.*

STEFAN SITS IN THE BACKSEAT OF JASON'S QX80, THE scent of raw leather and overpriced aftershave swirling in the confined space. He unwraps his Christmas gift with the kind of caution usually reserved for disarming a bomb. And, in a way, it is—emotionally speaking. His fingers pause as he peels away the last shred of festive paper to reveal the shiny PS5. A folded note, barely tucked between the console and the box, flutters like a fallen leaf. "Forgive me, please," it reads. Classic Ade.

The gift had been delivered earlier by Jola, fresh out of her class, after Stefan had awkwardly handed her Ade's present. And she made it abundantly clear that her career aspirations did not include being a courier woman.

"Do you like it?" Lina asks from the front seat, eyes sparkling with curiosity.

"Of course, he likes it," Jason answers from behind his phone, without even bothering to look up.

Stefan manages a sheepish smile. "I do," he admits.

"I miss seeing both of you being cute together," Lina sulks, as if she's personally been robbed of a Netflix romcom subplot.

"I miss us being cute together," Stefan murmurs, flipping open his copy of *Vagabonds!* in an attempt at distraction. Not that he could concentrate with the elephant-sized PS5 sitting next to him, figuratively poking him in the ribs. He snaps the book shut with an exaggerated sigh. "So, do you guys have anything planned for the holiday?"

"Thesis," Lina replies, her tone resigned.

"That's true. I don't have that problem until next year," Stefan offers a sympathetic pat on her shoulder. "What's it on?"

"Soil chemistry."

"Yikes." Stefan grimaces, offering another reassuring pat. He then turns to Jason, who is snickering to himself. "What funny, J.?"

Jason's fingers are busy flying over his phone screen, typing like he's on some covert mission. "Oh, nothing at all," he says, in the least convincing tone imaginable.

They lapse into a casual discussion of holiday plans, none of which are particularly groundbreaking. Christmas, it seems, has settled into a predictable groove for all of them. But then Lina nudges Stefan, and before long, the pair are enthusiastically belting out the chorus to "Nothing Breaks Like a Heart," turning the parking lot of Newcastle Airport into their own private concert hall. Lina sings like someone auditioning for The Voice, while Stefan mumbles the lyrics like he's afraid someone might notice.

Jason, typically unimpressed, interrupts their impromptu karaoke session. "Lovely. Lin, do you want Maltesers?"

Lina spins around mid-note, ready to respond, but then freezes, her gaze locking onto something beyond the car window. She jabs her hand in the direction of the far side of the parking lot, her voice suddenly sharp. "Isn't that Ade's car?"

Stefan's heart lurches in his chest. Without another word, he jumps out of the car.

Thick winter air clings to the night, a heavy, icy mist that Stefan cuts through as he sprints across the Newcastle Airport parking lot, the cold biting his exposed skin. His breath comes in quick, sharp bursts, but there's a warmth building inside him that defies the chill—the kind that only flares up at the sight of someone who makes his pulse race and his heart ache in the best way.

Ade starts forward, hands already reaching out, but Stefan is quicker. They collide, and for a moment it's as if the world holds its breath. Ade lifts him off the ground with that effortless strength, their bodies moulding into each other like pieces of a puzzle finally slotting into place. The cold? What cold? It disappears the moment Ade's hand finds Stefan's hair, fingers combing through it as though reassuring themselves that this, all of it, is real.

"Stef, Stef," Ade whispers, his breath a ghostly vapour in the frigid air. And they just stand there, a pair of statues carved from need, unmoving but for the sound of their breathing, refusing to let go.

"I miss you," Stefan murmurs, his words muffled against Ade's coat. He shivers a little. "I miss you so much."

Ade pulls back just enough to stare at him, wide-eyed. "Stef, you don't have a jacket!" he exclaims, the practical part of his brain kicking in. In a swift motion, he shrugs off his coat and drapes it over Stefan's shoulders. "Come," he says, with the confidence of a man who knows exactly how to take care of what's his, pulling open the back door of his car.

Stefan buries his face in the collar of Ade's coat, inhaling deeply—Tobacco Vanille, coconut, and just Ade. Once Ade slides into the back seat, Stefan doesn't hesitate, climbing onto his lap like it's the most natural thing in the world. Their eyes lock, full of things unsaid but felt so strongly, they could fill a library. Just as Stefan leans in, ready to erase the last painful weeks, there's an obnoxious tap on the window.

Jason and Lina stand outside, grinning like cats who've caught the canary. Jason opens the front door and deposits Stefan's bag, jacket, and phone with a grin that practically screams *caught you*. "Well then. Goodbye, Stefan."

"Hi, Ade. Bye, Stefan. Have a good flight," Lina adds cheerfully.

Stefan blows them a kiss, Ade waves—his royal wave, Stefan calls it—and Jason shuts the door, leaving them once more in the cocoon of warmth, quiet, and something achingly close to bliss.

"Hello," Stefan says, turning back to Ade.

"Hello," Ade replies, pulling him closer until there's not a breath of space between them.

And then they're kissing—no tentative peck, but a deep, all-consuming kiss, the kind where every second counts, where they pour everything they've been holding back into the other person's mouth. Stefan drowns in the feel of Ade, in the way his body presses into his own. Ade lets out a low, throaty grunt, and Stefan smiles against his mouth. Who knew one could miss the sound of someone's grunts?

"You can't just tell a guy you miss him... and then leave the country, Stef," Ade pants between kisses.

"I'll be back," Stefan promises, nipping at Ade's lower lip, drawing out another low grunt.

After what feels like both an eternity and no time at all, Ade pulls away, his forehead resting against Stefan's. "You'll miss your flight if we keep this up," he says, though it sounds more like a reluctant warning than a real concern.

"I don't care," Stefan whines, settling his head against Ade's chest, listening to the steady thrum of his heartbeat.

Ade chuckles, pressing a kiss to Stefan's hair. "I love it when you talk like that. Stef, I want—"

But Stefan silences him with a finger, pressing it gently to Ade's lips. "Not today. When I get back... I have something to tell you as well."

Ade's eyes soften as he kisses the tip of Stefan's finger. "What time do you return on the fifth?" he asks, his voice more measured, though his arms tighten around Stefan as if he's afraid to let go.

"You remember my return date?" Stefan asks, a little incredulous, though not really surprised. "Should be landing around six in the evening."

"Of course, I remember," Ade says, leaning in for another kiss. "I'll be here by noon." They walk to departures. "Call me the moment you get to Stockholm. And give me your flight number. I'll track it."

"Okay," Stefan laughs, forwarding his return ticket to Ade's phone. He starts to slip out of Ade's coat, but Ade stops him.

"I want you to have it," Ade says, pulling him into another tight hug. "I'll miss you."

Tuesday, 5th January 2023.

Stefan floats through the vast expanse of space—or at least, that's how it feels. Everything within him is lighter, buoyant with a rush of happiness so potent it might just send him spinning off into the stars. Love is coursing through him like some rare, intoxicating elixir—sweet as nectar, heady as champagne, and with far less chance of a hangover. It drowns out the last faint whispers of doubt that once cluttered his mind like moths around a fading bulb.

There was a time, not long ago, when those doubts ruled him, their voices sharp and insistent, convincing him that love was something fragile, something to be mistrusted. Fear and anger, twin tyrants, had clouded his vision, warping the world around him, making him believe that he wasn't worthy of what was being offered. But now, as he floats here, heart light and free, he looks back and wonders how he could've been so dumb.

What he wouldn't give to go back in time, just for a moment, and whisper in his own ear—*Stop. Open your eyes. You're about to throw away the one thing that matters*. But of course, life rarely affords such luxuries. There are no do-overs, no rewinding of time. And yet, Stefan realises now that maybe—just maybe—that's part of the beauty. He wouldn't have appreciated the sheer, breathtaking gravity of what he has now if he hadn't come close to losing it. Thank God, he thinks, with a quiet breath of relief, thank God it's not lost. It's his—all of it.

With a contented sigh, Stefan readies himself to leave for the airport. He makes his way to the living room to bid his parents goodbye, fully aware of what awaits.

"*Stefan inte en pojkvän!*" his mum trills with the enthusiasm of a Eurovision contestant.

"Stefan has a boyfriend!" his dad joins in, adding a percussive accompaniment with his hands, the rhythm questionable but the heart very much in it.

"Honestly, the Barden Bellas could never," Stefan quips, embracing them both. "I'll miss your duets."

"We can sing it to you and Ade when we call," his mom suggests, all too eager.

"Or we save it for when he visits at Christmas," his dad adds.

Stefan's mind flashes back to that infamous first call. Without warning, he'd handed the phone to his parents so they could speak with Ade. He ambushed the poor guy—his voice had trembled throughout. Still, somewhere in the midst of the conversation, Ade had promised to join Stefan on his next trip home. And Stefan, for his part, managed to keep it together when introduced to Ade's parents—at least outwardly. Inside, it had been an entirely different performance.

Stefan shudders with mock horror. "Or we could, you know, *not*."

Shortly after, he leaves for the airport with Marcus, but his mind is already flitting like a sparrow through the memories of the past two weeks. Ade and him sharing everything shareable, except Stefan still somehow neglected to tell him about Honza when they talked about exes. He had wanted to tell Ade—really, he had—but then thought better of it. It's hardly a topic that he can drop into casual conversation over the phone, is it? "By the way, I had a disastrous relationship with a man who now stalks me" is not a tale to be told between "I miss you" and "I can't wait to kiss your mouth off."

Still, the irony of it doesn't escape him. Honza—*of all people*—being the one to make him realise just how much he loves Ade. It's almost laughable. Somehow, in the midst of that rollercoaster conversation, Stefan was forced to face the truth. What he wanted, what he needed was Ade—steady, reliable, with a smile that could calm a storm and a heart as kind as it is patient. And so, despite every fibre of his being wishing he could erase Honza from his mental scrapbook, Stefan has to admit—even if only to himself—that Honza did serve a purpose. An accidental, painful, but entirely necessary purpose.

Stefan arrives at the airport with the kind of focus that could put a laser beam to shame. He's early—ridiculously so—bouncing on his heels with the kind of impatience that makes fellow travellers shoot him curious glances. Once boarding is announced, he's up like a shot, dodging and weaving through the slow-moving clusters of travellers like a man on a mission. He's the first to board, and even the cabin crew member who greets him at the door can't help but give him an amused nod. Stockholm, with its cobbled streets and familiar skyline will always be home. It's where his roots stretch deep into the earth, where his family lives, and a decent chunk of his fortune lie, where the story of his life has, for the most part, unfolded in neat, predictable chapters. The city holds his past, cradles it like an old friend, each corner imbued with memories that plays like old film reels.

But Newcastle—that's different. Newcastle is where his heart beats a little faster. Where the future lies, unknown and thrilling, because Ade is there, a beacon that pulls Stefan across oceans, making a foreign land feel like the most natural place in the world. It's a curious thing, this realisation that home isn't a place—it's a person. And wherever Ade is, that's where Stefan belongs. It's where he feels most alive, most at peace, as though all the pieces of his world slot into place the moment he steps into Ade's orbit.

After take-off, he listens to Miya Folick's "Talking with Strangers", there's something about the lyrics—something about the messy, wonderful, terrifying thing called love, that resonates deep in his bones now. Who knew love could feel this... transformative? The flight drags on, as flights do when one is counting down the seconds. He skims *She Called Me Woman*, but his mind is already ahead of him, touching down long before the wheels hit the tarmac. The second the seatbelt signs flicker off, he's up, shrugging into Ade's ridiculously oversized coat. He moves through the airport with purpose, thankful he has no checked baggage to slow him down. Time is a luxury he doesn't have—not when Ade is waiting.

And there he is.

Ade, standing tall in a chauffeur's hat, holding a sign that reads simply, **Welcome home, my Stef.** Nothing more, nothing less. But to Stefan, it might as well be the first words ever written in the history of love.

He doesn't walk—he barrels into Ade's arms, inhaling the familiar scent of home, of love, of the familiarity that grounds him more than any city or street could, of everything he's been counting down the minutes for. "I missed you so much," he murmurs, into Ade's chest, his words muffled but no less true for it.

"I missed you," Ade says, placing a gentle kiss on top of his head.

And there they stand, locked in what can only be described as the longest, most unapologetic hug to ever grace this airport. Any onlookers who dare wonder why two grown men are glued together can feel free to lodge their complaints with airport security. Stefan certainly doesn't care.

"My God, you got even more beautiful," Ade eventually says, pulling back just enough to drink in the sight of Stefan's face.

"I can say the same about you," Stefan replies, a smile playing at the corner of his lips.

Nice jacket," Ade remarks, pointing to the oversized monstrosity Stefan's wearing.

"I know, right? It's a treasure."

Ade places his bag in the backseat before turning to Stefan with a smile so warm it could defrost a glacier. With a dramatic flourish that could rival any stage performer, he swings open the passenger door and gestures for Stefan to take his seat. As if this isn't enough, he reaches behind the driver's seat and produces a bouquet, like a magician revealing his final trick.

"Sunflowers." Stefan says, his smile spreading as he takes in the vibrant blooms.

"Don't you mean *solros?*"

Stefan nods and leans in, his hands looping around Ade's neck as he presses a tender kiss to Ade's lips, the bouquet dangling from his grasp. "You're romantic," he murmurs, unable to hide the admiration in his voice.

Ade intertwines their hands. "You make me romantic," he replies, kissing the back of Stefan's hand. "You hungry? We can get takeout."

Stefan's stomach provides a timely rumble in agreement. "Yes, please. Let's get those wings I love from Wendy's."

"Why didn't you say so before?"

"Seeing you made me hungry for something else."

"You shall have what you're hungry for." Ade deadpans.

Stefan swallows.

When they walk into Wendy's, they're greeted by the rich, intoxicating aroma of fried chicken and spicy sauce. "You said takeout," Stefan reminds, half-heartedly protesting.

Ade, seemingly unbothered, drags him to a booth. "We're here. We might as well eat," he says, leaning in with a conspiratorial whisper. "I can hear your stomach from here."

"Okay," Stefan whines.

"Only do that when we're alone," Ade whispers, his breath hot in Stefan's ears. "It has an effect on me."

Stefan swallows again.

About thirty-five minutes later, they're scouting for a free space in the parking lot of Number Eight Collingwood Street.

"You're staying the night, right?" Stefan asks.

"Nights," Ade grins, clearly in a good mood.

Stefan looks around, and a wave of nausea rolls over him as his eyes land on a red Ford. The world around him seems to slow, the air thickening with a density that makes it hard to breathe.

There, slouching in the driver's seat, smirking with an unsettling familiarity, is Honza.

August 2018

Stockholm

Stefan meanders through the city centre, Edwin and Żaneta flanking him as the sun bestows its golden kisses upon their skin. Their routine is predictable: scooters, then bicycles, with Edwin winning one round and Żaneta the next. Stefan, the good observer, lacks any competitive bone, preferring to cheer than compete.

"Best summer ever," Żaneta declares, a sentiment Stefan finds trite. It's the same script they followed last summer, and the summer before that.

"I agree," Edwin chimes in, brandishing his cup. "The caramel iced latte is better."

They've toyed with the idea of travelling, but summer's onset has seen them in a deadlock. When Edwin proposed Paris, Żaneta and Stefan scrunched up their noses in unison, denouncing it as a 'dirty city'. Marseille was swiftly vetoed by Edwin, while Spain was cancelled for its many beautiful options because they couldn't decide between Barcelona, Madrid, or Ibiza. Finally, they settled on Poznan —Żaneta's city—for late August, securing tickets and rooms at the NH hotel on Ludvin's recommendation.

This summer may mimic its predecessors in predictable routine, but this year hums with a different tune. University starts next month, and Stefan can hardly contain his excitement. While Edwin and Żaneta will commute from home, Stefan will step into a new world at Lappkärrsberget SSSB—a dormitory of Stockholm University. He eagerly looks forward to the independence of dorm life—a welcome departure to the well-meaning but intrusive staff who currently attend to his every need. However, Marcus with his dedication of a fanatic bodyguard, insists on accompanying Stefan to campus.

"You're both absurd," Stefan remarks to his friends just as his phone rings. "Hey Honz."

"Hi love. Guess what?"

"You know I'm hopeless at guessing."

Honza sighs. "I'm in Stockholm, just arrived."

Stefan's pace falters, a touch of alarm creeping in. "You didn't mention this." He glances at his friends, mouthing, "Honza's in town." Żaneta peers around, scanning for Honza as if expecting him to materialise out of thin air. Stefan adds, "Not here here, but in Stockholm."

"That would've ruined the surprise, Omar. I want to see you. Come over."

Stefan checks the time, feeling queasy. "Where are you?"

"Radisson Blu."

A cold sweat beads on Stefan's forehead. The waterfront hotel is a mere fifteen minutes from their house on Lidingö. "Okay," he says after a pause, "but I can't stay long."

"What?" Honza's voice bristles with irritation. "You're not staying over?"

Stefan knows Honza's temper well. "Honz, this is sudden. I need to inform my parents."

"You can't tell them you are with those two friends of yours?"

"Our parents know each other," Stefan points out, then ponders. "How about this? I go home and tell my parents I'll be out the whole day tomorrow. We can hang out then."

Honza's tone softens. "Only tomorrow? I came here for you, Omar, nothing else. I didn't even buy a return ticket."

This is an effort from the guy, Stefan has to admit. He can hang out with him daily; it's not a problem. Maybe Edwin and Żaneta can join them. They can take Honza to all the cool places in Stockholm, which is everywhere, in his unbiased opinion.

"We can discuss all that tomorrow."

"Okay, love," Honza agrees. "See you tomorrow."

"See you, Honz."

"No roaming about for you tomorrow?" Edwin teases.

"Hot sex instead," Żaneta chirps.

Stefan laughs, but his mind is elsewhere, wondering if he even wants to sleep with Honza. Despite their constant communication, he's yet to develop anything more profound than a polite indifference. Stefan had imagined he'd be swept off his feet by now, but five months in, his thoughts are still stubbornly unperturbed. Their conversations often feel like small talk at a dull dinner party, and every attempt at intimacy is about as effective as trying to ignite a fire with wet wood. And Stefan has been aroused a lot from watching porn—not that he will admit it to anyone—so he knows he doesn't have a problem in the dick and arousal department.

Or even just now, the news of Honza's arrival barely nudges his pulse. Instead, a vague sense of unease coils around his chest, like an overzealous boa constrictor. He can't help but wonder if he's someone who takes an extraordinarily long time to connect, or if his connection with Honza was never destined to catch fire in the first place.

"I don't know, guys," he sighs. "Maybe kiss him, make out a bit, but I don't feel attracted to him."

Żaneta nods sympathetically, patting his arm. "You might feel differently when you see him again."

"Yeah," Edwin agrees. "Keep an open mind,"

They have one more scooter ride, which Stefan miraculously wins, before he calls Marcus to drive them home.

By noon the following day, Stefan ambles alongside Honza, their fingers laced together as they make their way to Honza's room, the corridor stretching before them and the polished floor reflecting the soft light filtering through the windows.

"I've ordered us an early lunch," Honza announces, gesturing grandly towards the table laden with food.

Stefan forces a smile. "I'm not particularly hungry," he admits, settling onto the couch. "How was your flight?"

"It was tolerable," Honza replies, guiding Stefan to his feet. "I've missed your pretty face, Omar." He ushers Stefan to the table. "You have to eat something. You're too skinny."

"We FaceTime every day," Stefan points out, reaching for a croissant. "This is fine, thanks."

Honza snatches the croissant away with an air of righteous authority. "These junk foods you eat are not good for you," he declares, depositing a plate of pasta in front of Stefan.

Stefan raises an eyebrow, surprised. They've never broached the subject of his diet, and his indulgences are reserved for when he's out with his friends. "I assure you, I'm fine. Ate before coming," he mumbles, taking a few reluctant forkfuls. "Happy?" He rises and returns to the couch, casting about for a change of subject. "What do you wanna do?"

Honza masks his annoyance before kissing him, drawing Stefan towards the bed. But when Honza's hands stray to the band of his jeans, Stefan hesitates, tapping his arm with a hint of trepidation.

"Wait, Honz."

Honza halts, casting Stefan a puzzled look. "Wait? Why?" There's a trace of impatience in his voice, a glimpse of something perverse beneath the surface.

Stefan's heart pounds, sensing a shift in the atmosphere. "I just... uhm, I don't think I'm ready."

"Well, I want to," Honza insists, moving to unzip Stefan.

Stefan freezes for a microsecond, his mind grappling with shock. At eighteen, he's a lanky, unassuming figure, starkly outmatched by Honza's physical presence. The unexpectedness of the moment sharpens his senses, and with a surge of adrenaline, he summons all his strength to shove Honza away. Honza, caught off guard, flops onto the bed in a somewhat undignified heap, like a puppet with its strings cut. Stefan scrambles to leave, but with a sudden, powerful yank, Honza slams his back against the wall. The impact jars Stefan, leaving him temporarily disoriented as he finds himself pinned, his hands held firmly above his head.

"You're not ready?" he mocks, his voice dripping with scorn. "I came here for you, and I'll have you."

Stefan's mind reels as Honza's grip tightens. "But I didn't ask you to. I never expected... I never wanted..."

Stefan struggles to comprehend the sudden change in Honza's behaviour. He doesn't understand what's happening—or rather, he does—but cannot relate the person he's been talking to for about five months to this maniac in front of him.

"You did not ask me?" Honza sneers, his voice laced with bitterness. "So why have we been talking all this while? Why are we dating?"

Stefan immediately regrets ever engaging in conversation with Honza. It was a moment of misplaced trust, a decision that now feels like a monumental misstep. He should have kept his distance and maintained boundaries, but it's painfully obvious that he couldn't have predicted this turn of events.

"I've been in this fucking city for two weeks," Honza barks. "Watching you go around with those two. Are you fucking them?"

"Edwin and Żaneta? They are my friends. Honz, let me go, and we can talk."

"Friends?" Honza's laughter is sharp, tinged with malice. "I've seen you three together. No way you aren't fucking. Isn't that why you're claiming to be bisexual? So, you can fuck anything that moves, and you're here telling me you don't want to?"

Stefan recoils as Honza tugs insistently at his jeans. He hadn't even had the presence of mind to zip up, his sole focus consumed by the frantic need to leave. Now, Stefan is thrown into a maelstrom of chagrin and bewilderment. Nothing had suggested Honza was this kind of person. Or was Stefan blind to the signs?

As Stefan's mind scrambles to piece together the fragmented puzzle, he replays past interactions with a dawning, disconcerting clarity. He remembers when he told Honza he is bisexual, and Honza's cool "Indeed" in response. Stefan now realises that he had completely misunderstood the significance of that flat reply. Then there were the subtler hints: dictating what Stefan should and not wear, the attempts to curtail his socialising with his friends, the constant nitpicking of his choices, the demands for real-time updates on his whereabouts. Even the seemingly minor flashes of anger, which Stefan had previously dismissed as quirks of his personality; everyone has a temper now and then. But now, standing on the precipice of horror, he's piecing them together that those are the signs of a controlling person.

With a speedy, almost casual motion, Honza pulls down Stefan's boxer shorts, his face contorting with rage as he stares down at Stefan's unresponsive state. "What's this?" Honza's voice is sharp and accusatory as if Stefan owes him an explanation for his lack of arousal.

Before Stefan can process this violation of being reduced to nothing more than an object to be scrutinised, his cheek stings. Honza's hand connects with brutal force, leaving behind a burning imprint that throbs with agony. *What the hell just happened?*

With a peek towards the door, Stefan calculates the distance and the precious seconds it will take to make it there. Honza unzips his trousers and forcibly grabs Stefan's right hand to hold himself. "See how stretched I am for you?" Honza's voice oozes with venom, squeezing Stefan violently. "Are you impotent? Even that wouldn't excuse this."

Stefan's mind spins like a tornado of terror and confusion. He knows he needs to escape, to flee from this grotesque situation, but fear roots him in place, immobilising him until he can figure out his next move. He keeps his attention on Honza, steadying himself. With a sense of grim determination, he uses his left foot to remove his right shoe and steps gingerly on his jeans pooled at his ankle. Each movement is a careful ballet of stealth, aimed at avoiding Honza's notice as he readies himself for action.

Honza turns his face towards the wall, his hands tightening on Stefan's waist. Stefan wills himself not to fidget, every muscle in his body tense with the riskiness of his plan. Without warning, he pivots with all the finesse of a matador and delivers a decisive kick to Honza's groin. The scream that erupts from Honza is almost musical in its agony as he crumples to the ground, hand clutching at the source of his pain. Without missing a beat, Stefan channels every ounce of strength he can muster into another kick, and then another. Stefan darts out of the room, his breath coming in jagged bursts. Half-dressed and clutching his jeans and shoes, he dashes down the hallway, abandoning the elevator for the stairs. By the time he reaches the reception area, Stefan is trembling uncontrollably. He fumbles for his phone, dialling Edwin's number with shaking hands, his entire body aching.

"Stefan, what happened?" Edwin demands, eyes wide as he sees Stefan's bruised face and dishevelled appearance.

"I'll tell you on the way," Stefan says. He spots Ludvin approaching them, his expression a mix of concern and anger.

"What's his room number?" Ludvin asks, his tone brooking no argument.

Stefan leads them to Honza's room, the door still ajar. They find Honza sitting on the bed, typing on his phone, his face twisted in a scowl of pain and rage.

"If you ever come near him again, I'll kill you," Ludvin says, punching Honza's face. "Mark my words."

Before Honza can respond, they swiftly exit the room. As they make their way down the corridor, Stefan begs Ludvin to take him to his apartment. His face, now marred by the unmistakable evidence of the abuse, tells a story of its own—one he's desperate to shield from his parents. He knows that seeing him in such a state would shatter their hearts into pieces, a prospect he can't bear to imagine.

January 2023.

Stefan swears loudly, the word crackling through the car like a whip. His knuckles blanch as he clutches the door handle, the cold metal imprinting its sharp edges into his palm. The initial shock—that brief moment of disbelief—vanishes, melting like a snowflake landing on hot stone. In its place, anger flares beneath his skin, pulsing like a second heartbeat.

"What's wrong, Stef?" Ade's voice carries a note of concern, the kind that twists Stefan's stomach with guilt.

He turns to Ade. "Can you stay here for a minute? I have to deal with something."

Ade nods, a shadow of worry flitting across his face, but he holds steady as Stefan leans in for a slow, lasting kiss before exiting the car, bouquet in hand. Across the lot, Honza emerges from his Ford with the kind of purposeful stride one might expect from someone convinced they're still relevant.

Stefan's muscles coil with restrained fury, but his voice remains unnervingly calm. "What? Still couldn't stay away?"

"I thought your little stint with him was over?" Honza drawls, managing to inject both boredom and arrogance into his tone.

"My stints aren't your problem. Thought I didn't," he air quotes, "Deserve you."

"I changed my mind."

"Well, that's fascinating. Should I alert the press?" Stefan's eyes flick back to the car, where Ade sits, blissfully unaware. "Do you want me to report you to the police, Honza? Because honestly, I will do it."

"I heard you," Honza smirks, his face twisting with a

predatory grace. "But if I can't have you, I'll make sure no one does."

Stefan snorts, eyes flashing with dry amusement. "You are overestimating yourself, Honz. Who are you in the grand scheme of things, huh? Just some balding guy I won't fuck?"

The man is, without question, more delusional than Stefan initially gave him credit for. Truly, the nerve.

Honza shrugs, unperturbed. "Maybe. Let's see what your black boy thinks about this."

"About what—"

Before Stefan can even finish the question, Honza lunges, his hand grabbing Stefan's face, his vile mouth crushing against Stefan's. Stefan's entire body stiffens with revulsion, his mouth snapping shut as if his very dignity depends on it. He shoves Honza away, hard enough to make his point, but not enough to topple him over.

"You think your show will do anything?" Stefan spits, wiping his mouth with the back of his hand.

Another infuriating shrug from Honza. "Who knows? He's coming, though, and he doesn't look happy."

Stefan's stomach drops as he turns to see Ade approaching, wheeling his luggage like a man who's ready to collect what's his, and there's a sternness to his face. Stefan reaches out, taking Ade's hand with a confidence he doesn't quite feel. "Let's go in."

"Won't you introduce me?" Honza's ridiculous smile widens. "I'm Honza, by the way. Omar's boyfriend."

Ade eyes Honza's extended hand with thinly veiled disgust. His eyes, usually warm and inviting, are now pools of smouldering intensity. Stefan catches the look, and despite everything, it brings him a small measure of satisfaction.

Sick to death of entertaining Honza delusions, Stefan gives a dismissive shake of the head and turns to Ade. "Come on."

They leave Honza in the parking lot, where he belongs—his presence barely worth a passing thought. Stefan doesn't spare him another glance as they stride towards the building, his hand still clasped securely in Ade's. The lobby door gives a polite click as they step through, the kind of door that never feels the need to slam. The elevator arrives with a genteel ding, and they step inside, the small space is immediately filled with an awkward quiet. Stefan leans back against the wall, glancing at Ade, whose face is set in a mask of unreadable calm. He could break the silence—he should—but he opts to say nothing. Instead, he brushes his thumb over Ade's knuckles in what he hopes is a gesture of peace and not just a nervous twitch. Ade doesn't pull away, which is victory of sorts, but he doesn't react either, his eyes fixed forward as the floors tick by in slow succession.

Stefan unlocks his door and waves Ade inside, though the loft itself does most of the welcoming. Stefan methodically removes his jacket, hangs it on the wooden coat rack by the door, and slips off his shoes, placing them neatly on the rack. The small automatic routine feels grounding, almost ritualistic, as if by organising his space, he might somehow restore order.

"Who's he?" Ade's voice slices through the room, sharp and clean, leaving no space for evasion.

"He's a nobody," Stefan replies quickly, turning to face Ade, who stands by the door like a sentinel, unmoving and, judging by the look in his eyes, unconvinced. "Come on in, Teni. Let's sit and talk," Stefan tries, his tone veering dangerously into 'customer service voice'—too smooth and rehearsed—as he walks towards him.

"I don't want to sit," Ade grounds out, voice hard as granite. "Who the fuck is that guy?"

Stefan halts mid-step, his confidence evaporating like mist in the morning sun. He opens his mouth, but nothing comes out.

Ade's eyes narrows, unimpressed by the silence. "He said he is your boyfriend," he spits, offering Stefan a lifeline that feels more like a noose.

"He's lying," Stefan blurts, too fast. "He's an ex. If you can even call him that," he adds, hoping the clarification might save him.

Ade's eyes flash, reflecting a fire that threatens to erupt. He fists his fingers, the sound of his knuckles cracking resonating in the tense air, and his nostrils flare with each heavy breath. When he finally speaks, his voice is a low, thunderous rumble. "He kissed you," enunciating each word with deliberate precision. "He cupped your face and kissed you."

Stefan shrinks under Ade's glare, feeling as though the walls themselves are closing in. "I... I didn't kiss him back. We can't talk like this, Teni, come in," he pleads, his words tumbling over each other, pointing desperately towards the living room as if comfort might be found in a change of scenery.

But Ade's focus is relentless, locked on that one fact. "He *cupped* your face," he repeats, the disbelief curling around his tongue. As if that, out of everything, is the most unforgivable part.

"Teni, don't be like this."

"Like what?" Ade snaps, his eyes bloodshot, and Stefan suddenly feels very small. "Each time I tried to touch your face, you flinched from me." He looks down at his hands, his eyes darting from palm to palm. "I thought y-y you d-d don't like it. So, I stopped." He draws in a ragged breath, the kind that tears through the soul. "But *he* cupped your face," his voice shakes now, "and you let him."

Stefan's knees threaten to buckle, his legs turning to water beneath him as a hollow ache settles deep in his chest. How had he missed it? *Flinching?* Stefan replays the accusation in his mind, searching through his memories, trying to pinpoint a moment, any moment, where he might have recoiled from Ade's touch but comes up blank. How could he have been so oblivious? *Why didn't Ade say anything sooner?* Why had he let it fester, silently enduring the rejection he thought he saw, the imagined repulsion Stefan had never meant to convey?

Stefan takes a step forward, his steps slow and hesitant —he's walking on eggshells, and every crack underfoot threatens to make the floor fall out beneath him. He's desperate to bridge this fissure that has opened between them, to reassure Ade that his touch is always welcome. They need to talk. No, they need to *fix* this. Ade's arms remain crossed, his body stiff, though his eyes—those stormy eyes—change, just for a second. Stefan thinks he sees something there, something softer, but it's gone before he can hold onto it.

"I can't believe this," Ade mutters, more to himself. "Is this... is this some sort of revenge?"

"Revenge?" Stefan halts, and for a moment, he's genuinely lost. "Teni, what are you talking about? Revenge for what? Let me explain. Please, don't give him what he wants. Don't let him get in your head."

But Ade's already shaking his head, his jaw set like iron. "I need air," he mutters, and before Stefan can stop him, he storms out.

Stefan stands immobilised, watching as the door slams

with a finality that feels like a guillotine dropping. He's half-expecting Ade to walk back through it, but he doesn't. And suddenly the silence feels deafening. His chest burns with the kind of rage that doesn't flare up—it builds, slow and hot, until it consumes everything. With a guttural yell, he hurls the bouquet to the floor, petals scattering in a frenzy. *Honza won't let me be free. I have to kill him.* Tears blur his vision, but it's not enough to wash away the image of Ade walking out, eyes red with betrayal.

There's a compulsion stirring within him, a fire he can't extinguish. He grabs the nearest vase off the coffee table, feels the cool glass in his grip for just a second before he sends it crashing to the floor, shards cutting into his skin. The sound is satisfying, but the pain doesn't register. It's not nearly enough. He stumbles towards the kitchen, leaving a trail of red, grabs the other vase and hurls it at the wall. The shattering is louder this time, reverberating through the loft like some kind of twisted applause.

"*Javel!*" he screams, voice cracking as he sinks to the floor, shards of glass around him like a broken crown. He clutches his chest, heaving, "H-h he is r-r right."

December 2018.

Stefan has come to enjoy dorm life more than he ever thought possible. His small room in Lappkärrsberget, with its familiar scent of books, laundry detergent, and a faint hint of last week's Chinese takeout, already feels more like home than his actual house. The thought of leaving it for the Christmas holiday feels distinctly unwelcome, even though he's still here, waiting for Marcus to drive him home.

It's only ten minutes away, for God's sake. But no, trust Marcus—the dedicated driver and part-time overbearing bodyguard—to insist on picking him up. The man is practically allergic to the idea of Stefan doing something as unthinkable as taking a cab. Is it possible to fire someone for caring too much?

A knock on the door interrupts his thoughts. Stefan strolls over, already forming a wry smile. "Honestly, Marcus, I can carry my own bag. I'm not a ch—"

The words freeze in his throat as he opens the door. It's not Marcus at the door. It's a face Stefan thought—hoped—he'd never have to see again. Yet here stands Honza, breathing the same air as him. Stefan's heart thumps in his chest, and a cold and clammy sting creeps across his skin. This is a scene straight from his worst nightmares—the ones that dragged him to a therapist's couch for months. His stomach knots itself into something tight and uncomfortable.

"Hi, Omar," Honza greets, that sinister smile plastered on his face as he forces his way in. "Long time no see."

"Why are you here?" Stefan asks, his voice faltering despite his attempt to sound firm.

Honza has been pestering him for months, calling from different numbers like a particularly determined scam artist. Stefan blocked them all, of course, but deep down, he should've known. Honza was always the kind to force his way back in. Like a bad rash.

"Can't I come and see my boyfriend?" Honza's tone is deceptively casual, but his eyes gleam with something veiled.

"I'm not your boyfriend," Stefan grips the door handle so tightly that his fingers ache. "We broke up."

"Did we?," Honza steps closer, and the atmosphere

becomes stifling. "I don't remember that. We had a fight, sure, but couples fight, don't they?" His eyes dart around Stefan's room, as if inspecting a property he's considering buying. "And I apologised. A dozen times, actually." He cups Stefan's face, and Stefan blanches at the touch, his skin prickling with unease.

"I ignored you because you assaulted me," Stefan manages, each word feeling like a battle won.

Honza tilts his head, an exaggerated expression of innocence crossing his face. "Omar, love, that's not what happened." His fingers trace Stefan's cheek, as if that's going to erase the past. "I was angry. I didn't mean to hurt you."

Anger and fear collide inside Stefan, swirling into a frantic mess. "Leave," he says, trying to inject firmness into his voice, but it barely comes out above a whisper. "Before I call the police."

"I love you," Honza presses a kiss to his lips. Stefan flinches but remains still, crippled by dread. "Can't you understand that? We can be happy together. Tell me what you want, and I'll do it."

Stefan's thoughts run amok, desperately searching for an escape. He knows he isn't strong enough to fight Honza off, not physically. But if there's one thing Stefan's good at, it's bluffing. He forces a smile, even as his insides twist. "Okay," he says, running a hand through Honza's hair, feigning affection with a stomach-churning revulsion. "But... let's talk later. Our driver will be here soon," he adds, hoping Marcus arrives soon and does not stay in the car like he asked. *If there is any time Marcus shouldn't listen to me, it's now.*

"Are you sure?" Honza's smile is wide, almost unnerving. "You'll meet with me?"

"Yeah," Stefan forces a smile so wide it feels like his face might crack. "You can call me. We'll talk."

To sell the lie, Stefan unblocks Honza's number, bile rising in his throat as he does.

Marcus, where are you, please?

As if on cue, there's another knock at the door, and Marcus's familiar voice calls out. Relief floods through Stefan, almost embarrassingly so. He opens the door, nearly dragging Marcus into the room with the force of his gratitude. His trusted driver stands there, a picture of calm efficiency, with that air of mild exasperation he seems to reserve just for Stefan's life choices.

"Ready to go?" Marcus asks, barely acknowledging Honza.

Stefan nods mutely, more out of necessity than anything resembling composure. He gestures towards his bag—his trusty excuse for avoiding eye contact—and Marcus moves to grab it, wasting no time. The space between Stefan and Honza suddenly feels both infinite and far too small. Honza, with his revolting smile, leans in and places a kiss on Stefan's forehead. A kiss that, in any other world, might have been sweet. But in this one? It feels like a stamp of possession. Stefan suppresses a shudder, holding his breath as if it might erase the touch.

The car is his safe haven. Marcus doesn't ask questions; he knows when to drive in silence and when to play therapist. Today is, mercifully, a "don't ask" kind of day. As they pull away, Stefan lets his head fall back against the headrest, feeling the hum of the engine vibrate through his body like a lullaby. He reaches for his phone, already ringing with a call from the last person he wants to speak to. Without hesitation, he declines it and quickly types out a text: *I am breaking up with you. Leave me alone.* No room for interpretation this time. The words hang there, stark and blunt, before he presses send. Then, with a satisfying tap, he blocks Honza's number again, hoping against hope that this time it'll stick.

Stefan doesn't return to the dormitory after Christmas break. Instead, he opts for the slightly absurd ritual of commuting to campus, chauffeured to and from by Marcus. It's a routine that feels oddly Victorian, as if he's some sort of brooding aristocrat being whisked back to his estate after an exhausting day of academia.

For three blissfully quiet months, Stefan manages to avoid Honza entirely, like dodging an inconvenient storm cloud that refuses to rain itself out. Honza makes his next unwelcome appearance on Stefan's birthday—of all the days in the calendar to resurface. Stefan's solution is simple: ignore him, like one would a distant cousin who insists on talking about a pyramid scheme. But, of course, Honza isn't the type to be brushed off that easily.

By December, just when Stefan thinks he might have slipped through Honza's net for good, there he is again, cornering Stefan in a restaurant. This time, Stefan tells him outright—point blank and to his face—that he doesn't love him. If Stefan expected Honza to crumple at those words, to finally accept defeat with some shred of dignity, well, he is clearly being far too optimistic. Instead, Honza doubles down, as persistent as an Amazon delivery notification, reminding Stefan that he's not going anywhere.

Not even a global pandemic could stop Honza. As the world locks down and everybody is busy panic-buying toilet paper, Honza is busy flooding Stefan's phone with calls and messages. Each notification is a fresh jolt to his already fraying nerves. He blocks the numbers with the methodical efficiency of someone whack-a-moiling an infestation, but like some sort of twisted hydra, for every number he cuts off, two more seem to pop in its place.

The once-familiar comfort of routine now feels like a trap, and fear becomes Stefan's constant companion, casting long, ominous gloom over his daily life. He finds himself glancing over his shoulder with increasing frequency, a habit borne of mounting paranoia. By May 2022, with no end in sight, Stefan finally snaps. He informs his parents of his grand plan to relocate to England. He imagines Honza's confusion when he doesn't find him in Stockholm and hopes that he might finally take the hint and give up.

But as Stefan soon discovers, he's gravely mistaken.

19
THE REQUEST

*— Somewhere Only We Know
by Keane.*

January 2023.

ADE TURNS BACK TOWARDS STEFAN'S LOFT, JUST A FEW steps from the elevator, hands stuffed in his pockets, shoulders hunched like the weight of the world has personally singled him out for torment. His heart, traitorous thing that it is, hammers loud enough to drown out any external sound.

"Fuck my life," he mutters.

That sight—damn it, what's his bloody name—kissing Stefan, *his* Stef, feels like a tractor ploughing through his chest, leaving his insides raw and exposed. He blinks, but the image remains, stubborn, burning itself onto the back of his eyelids. He forces a laugh, the kind one makes when trying to convince oneself about not caring. He's being daft, ridiculous even. They're just cheeks, and it's irrational to be behaving this way. He should grow the fuck up. But still, *they're mine*, damn it. Stefan's cheeks, his smiles, his everything—they're supposed to be his. Not some random bloke waltzing in like he owns the place, kissing Stefan as if it's the most regular thing in the world. No one else should get the liberties Ade doesn't dare reach for himself.

What's-his-name is courting death. That's what he's doing. Death by idiotic kissing.

Ade lets out a long breath as his mind drifts to their kiss in the car. Not just any kiss—it was *their* kiss, the kind that takes its time, tender and unhurried, like the world had decided to pause just for them—like Stefan was trying to tell him something without actually saying it. Ade can almost hear the quiet between them, the kind that felt like safety. His anger, fiery and bristling just moments ago, begins to lose its edge, cooling into something softer. Something far more complicated. Hurt, yes. But also a creeping uncertainty, the kind that refuses to be reasoned away. He knows Stefan is telling the truth—he's not the sort to lie, not like that. He trusts him, *wants* to trust him. But why hadn't he mentioned this ex before? Two whole weeks and not a whisper.

And they had time. Oh, they *definitely* had time. They had somehow managed to squeeze in two movie nights despite the distance, watching *Maurice* and *Brokeback Mountain* over Tele-party. If they had time to dissect tragic gay love stories, to share their thoughts, feelings and opinions about it all, surely Stefan had *plenty* of time to mention this ex—something as simple as a "By the way, my ex still kisses me sometimes." It wasn't like he was short on opportunities. But no. Instead, it gets sprung on him like this—unannounced, as if it's nothing. As if it's normal to sit there and watch someone from Stefan's past casually grab his face and kiss him—on the mouth, for that matter—like they're still in each other's lives, like that's allowed.

As Ade nears Stefan's door, a sharp, jarring crash erupts from within the apartment, shattering the quiet of the hallway. It's the kind of noise that sends a spike of adrenaline through his veins—loud, chaotic, the unmistakable sound of something valuable meeting an untimely end. Before his mind has a chance to catch up, Ade's legs are already moving, launching him forward in a mad sprint. Then, another crash, louder this time—more violent. Ade's mind spins. Maybe it's nothing. Maybe Stefan is just... redecorating? A bit aggressively? Unlikely, given Stefan's neat-freak tendencies, but he clings on to the thought for a fleeting second as he grabs the door handle. Inside, it's a war zone. The loft now looks as if a hurricane has torn through it. Glass shards are scattered across the floor, like glittering confetti from the world's worst party. And then he sees him.

Stefan.

Stefan—his Stef—lying in the middle of the wreckage, curled in on himself like a delicate shell, and there's blood. Too much blood, pooling around him—a dark, spreading stain that sends Ade's brain into a frenzy.

"Stef, Stef!" Ade drops to his knees beside him. "*Baby...*" it slips out unintentionally, unable to reflect on calling Stefan "baby" for the first time.

"You let him win," Stefan heaves between dry sobs. "He said he wouldn't let me have you, wouldn't let you have me."

"You have me. I'm yours," Ade reassures him, his voice quaking.

He lifts Stefan with the care of someone carrying a priceless relic, mentally willing his arms not to shake. As he hoists Stefan up, he expects some protests—anything—because Stefan has never been the quiet, damsel-in-distress type. But no, silence, which scares Ade more. Ade forces a breath and shifts into action. First things first: get him patched up. He heads straight for the staircase, moving like a man who's been here a hundred times, because, well, virtually speaking, he has. The countless hours of video calls, Stefan's casual apartment tours, his constant "Oh, I'm just going up to my room" like it was his favourite place on earth, have clearly drilled a mental map into Ade's brain.

When he reaches Stefan's bedroom, he gives the door a nudge with his elbow and crosses the threshold, heading to the bathroom, where he gently lowers Stefan into the tub, which seems the least of a bad idea compared to the alternative of the floor.

For a second, Ade allows himself to look at Stefan. His face, usually the picture of poise and beauty, is streaked with blood and tears. It's a sight that twists Ade's heart in ways he doesn't like to admit. Stefan, of all people, reduced to this fragile, crumpled version of himself? It doesn't seem real. But there's no time for poetic melancholy now. No, this is business time.

Ade rummages through the bathroom cabinets and locates the first aid kit. Holding the kit aloft like a prize, he returns to the tub, where Stefan lies, looking like he's had a run-in with a particularly vindictive Picasso. Years of being patched up by Temmy have turned Ade into a makeshift medic. He'd always told Temmy to keep the medical tips to himself but now he's grateful for every bit of that unsolicited expertise.

He gently wipes Stefan's face with a damp towel, removing the blood and to his relief, there are no deep cuts, only bruises, which he covers with small plasters. He checks

Stefan's hair next, carefully parting it for shards or cuts. The blood is there and has matted his hair into sticky clumps but, thankfully, there are no cuts.

"Stef, I have to remove your clothes."

Stefan nods, granting Ade permission with a faint, pained smile as Ade carefully peels off his shirt. The fabric comes away to reveal wounds on his arms that look worse than they are. Ade grabs the methylated spirit, dabbing it on a cotton pad before pressing it against the wounds. The sting of it makes Stefan wince and Ade can't help but murmur, "I'm sorry," as if that could make the pain disappear. He applies iodine next and then wraps each hand with bandages, making sure they're tight enough to keep the gauze in place but loose enough to avoid cutting off circulation.

He turns his attention to Stefan's lower body and begins to unfasten his jeans, his movements quick but cautious. As he carefully removes the denim, he finds the source of the bleeding: a deep, open gash near Stefan's ankle. Ade's heart nearly leaps out of his chest, and he barely manages to suppress a scream. Panicked, he dials Temmy's number twice, but the call goes straight to voicemail, so he calls Sophia next and explains that a vase mishap led to Stefan's injuries. It feels like a clumsy excuse, but it's the best he can do under the circumstances.

"Can you come or talk me through what to do?" Ade pleads.

Sophia asks to see the first aid box and the cut, assessing the situation over the phone. "He doesn't need stitching. I can come after I leave the hospital, but you have everything. You don't have to wait."

With Sophia's guidance, Ade cleans and dresses the

wound, applying the gauze bandage with an adhesive bandage to hold it close. "Thanks, Sugar."

"You'll start fixing the rascals from now on," Sophia says. "Take care, Stefan, darlin."

Ade fetches Stefan's pyjamas from the closet. "Do you think you can stand for a minute?"

With Ade's support, Stefan manages to change into the pyjamas. Ade washes Stefan's blood-matted hair at the sink and dries it before leading Stefan to the bed. Tucking Stefan under the covers, Ade dithers, reluctant to leave him alone even for a moment.

"Are you leaving?" Stefan's voice is soft, vulnerable.

Ade kneels by the bedside. "No, no, I won't leave you."

Stefan opens his eyes, lassitude and torment evident in them. "Thanks"

"Rest, baby," Ade presses a tender kiss to Stefan's forehead. "I need to clean downstairs."

Stefan nods, a ghost of a smile on his face. "Kiss me before you go."

Unable to resist, Ade murmurs, "summertime sadness." They chuckle as Ade leans in, brushing his lips against Stefan's.

About one hour later, the living room and kitchen are sparkling. Ade fills a bowl with water for the flowers, carrying it into Stefan's room. He strips off his blood-stained clothes and tosses them into the washing machine with Stefan's before taking a quick shower. Dressed in an oversized t-shirt, he climbs into bed beside Stefan, who is already asleep and curls closer to him.

Wednesday, 6th January 2023.

Ade opens his eyes to the dim light of dawn filtering through the drapes, a sleepy embrace warming him. He turns to look at Stefan, a wave of comfort enveloping him to be here, holding him. Stefan reaches out, his fingers threading through Ade's tightly coiled hair, the soft curls springing back with each touch as if alive. "You're up," Ade murmurs, his voice a low purr.

"Good morning," Stefan whispers, leaning in for a kiss.

"Morning baby," Ade whispers back against Stefan's mouth before pulling away slightly. "I need to check your leg."

"I'm fine," Stefan whines but lifts the covers.

"I'll have to redress it after you shower," Ade says, settling back and facing him. "Does it hurt?"

"Not as much as yesterday," Stefan responds with a faint, almost mischievous smile. "I'm sure I won't even limp."

"I was terrified yesterday, Stef. When I got back and saw all the blood, I—"

"I'm sorry. I just... I felt so helpless."

"It's one thing after another, isn't it?"

Stefan leans in, their forehead nearly touching. "It's my fault. I should've told you about him. I just wanted to do it in person. I can tell y—"

Ade interrupts him with a slight, playful smile. "No. Not now. Check your email."

"What will I find there?" Stefan asks, reaching for his phone.

"An invitation," Ade grins, his eyes twinkling.

"There is something I want to do before I check," Stefan says, setting his phone aside.

"What's that?"

Stefan takes Ade's hands and gently draws them towards himself, his eyes glimmering with a silent request. Ade instantly comprehends Stefan's intent. "Stef," he starts, but Stefan hushes him, pressing Ade's hands to his cheeks.

"There's not one part of my body that's off guard for you. And I'm sorry you had to see that yesterday," Stefan says quietly.

Ade's thumbs stroke his cheeks as if in a trance, a tender caress that sends a soothing lustre radiating through Ade himself. "Stef," he breathes with relief.

"I never noticed flinching from you," Stefan starts. "It must have been subconscious, not intentional. But yesterday, I realised you've never cupped my face to kiss me. And, believe me, I remember every kiss we've shared as vividly as a recurring dream. I'd forget my own name before forgetting the days, times, and places where I kissed you."

Stefan has also never touched Ade's face, he realises now with a hint of bemusement. It's a curious thought, given that Stefan had once remarked that Ade's cheeks were among the first things he noticed when they met. It's almost as if their physical interactions have followed a playful dance of mutual restraint, each waiting for the other to make the first move. It seems Stefan's understanding of affection achieves a balance, as if he was playing by the rules of reciprocity.

Reverently, Ade manoeuvres Stefan into a sitting position. He then kneels before him, their eyes meeting in an unspoken dialogue rich with intimacy. Ade cradles Stefan's face in his hands, his touch as delicate as if he's handling the most precious of porcelain. He leans in and kisses Stefan with an elegance that could make even a sonnet feel inadequate. The kiss unfolds like a perfectly timed waltz, each movement imbued with a tenderness that swells Ade's heart with pure joy.

Ade savours the kiss, and his happiness blooms like a garden in midsummer, infusing him with glee. The familiar thrill of Stefan's lips on his, the gentle pressure of his hands, and the affection spreading through him—all blend seamlessly into a harmonious symphony. It feels as if each sensation is a note in a grand composition of contentment. Ade knows this moment, this exact way of touching Stefan will be etched in his memory with the clarity of a favourite melody—an indelible reminder of how delightful and profound Stefan makes him feel.

BLACKPOOL

From: Teniade Michael Adeowo tadeowo@tees.ac.uk
To: Stefan Omar Wickström swickström@tees.ac.uk
Date: 05.01.2023 at 11:21 AM

-fotgiw me Stefan, I'n vwty soeey-
    Stef, My Stef.

On the 29th of October 2022, I started this email to you. I was extremely drunk that night, so all I managed to type were those six words above. But even in my drunken haze, I knew I needed to reach out to you and seek your forgiveness for the pain I've caused you. For you to know it was never my intention to hurt you, and I'm willing to do whatever it takes to prove that to you, even if it means carrying this burden until the end of time.

I've spent every day since October reflecting on everything that has happened between us, and it weighs heavily on me. There are moments I look back on, and I wish I could change them. But I want you to know my decision wasn't because I didn't love you. It was because I didn't know how to love you properly, and I thought I was too broken to try.

But now, as I complete this email, I realise I want something different. I want to take you somewhere special, somewhere that holds a piece of my heart and introduce you to it. Because, Stef, with you, I've found a sense of peace that I've never known before.

You have a way of calming my heart, of making me feel whole and thrilled. And I miss those moments we shared; those memories are a constant reminder of what I hope to rebuild with you.

I remember one of those TV shows Jola made me watch over the years, and I'm glad I grudgingly watched it with her. It's called One Tree Hill. There was this moment in season four, episode nine, where Lucas Scott walked up to Peyton Sawyer after their school won the state championship. As he stood there, surrounded by cheers, he told her, "When all my dreams come true, the one I want next to me is you."

It's a line that has always stuck with me, not just because it's one of the best lines on TV, but also because it speaks to the depth of love and connection between two people. And I've also borrowed this particular line because as Lucas declared himself to Peyton, "Heartbeats" by Jose Gonzales played in the background. I know it's in your top five favourite songs.

And speaking of dreams, Stef, I have so many of them. But the first dream that's come true for me is meeting you. You've filled the empty spaces in my heart and in my future, and now I can't imagine a life without you by my side.

I know you love road trips as much as I do. There's something about the open road that makes me feel free, and I think it'll make it easier for me to talk to you. I want to share all with you, away from where we have experienced sadness.

If you're willing to take a chance on me and make me the luckiest guy in the world, we will return to Newcastle after leaving behind all the pain and uncertainty and start anew.

Lastly, I love music. I think it's the first thing I told you. So, I made you something to express some of the things in my heart, things I may not have the words for yet: https://music.apple.com/uk/playlist/MyStef

Will you come with me to Blackpool, baby? Say yes, please.

Wholly Yours,
Téní.

20
BLACKPOOL

— Taste by Sleeping At Last.

Wednesday, 6th January 2023.

S̲t̲e̲f̲a̲n̲ j̲u̲m̲p̲s̲ o̲n̲ A̲d̲e̲, d̲i̲s̲r̲e̲g̲a̲r̲d̲i̲n̲g̲ t̲h̲e̲ s̲t̲i̲n̲g̲i̲n̲g̲ cuts that crisscross his body.

"Of course, I'll come with you," he declares, planting a series of exaggerated smooches on Ade's face. "We'll detour at yours to pack you a bag?"

Ade grins, his eyes radiant with mirth. "I already have a bag packed."

"But how?" Stefan's eyebrows draw inward. "Didn't you say you just changed plans yesterday?"

Ade's grin widens to cheeky proportions. "I've had a bag packed since October."

"For SP42?" Stefan asks, pressing their noses together in a playful nuzzle.

"You remember that?"

"Of course," Stefan blurts out, a smile breaking through. "I prepared my bo—" He covers his mouth.

"You prepared what?" Ade murmurs, pressing a soft kiss to Stefan's neck.

"Not telling," Stefan retorts, sticking his tongue out before rolling off the bed. "Let's make breakfast."

"We can order in," Ade suggests, pulling him back with an insistence that's hard to resist. "What do you wanna eat?"

"I can make us something, maybe kroppkakor? We'll have to go to Tesco, though. I don't have everything needed."

"No cooking," Ade decrees firmly. "You shouldn't be on your feet."

Stefan laughs and mock salutes. "Okay, sir. No kroppkakor, got it. How about pancakes? I want you to try the traditional Swedish ones."

Ade sighs, knowing he cannot win. "Alright then." He stands up, watching Stefan closely. "How's your leg?"

"It's fine, or do you want to carry me downstairs?" Without warning, Ade lifts Stefan effortlessly, swinging him over his shoulder. "Teni!" Stefan squeals as he dangles in Ade's grip.

"You asked for it," Ade chuckles, setting him down in the kitchen. "What do I do to make the pancakes?"

"I haven't forgotten Sophia's comment," Stefan says, his body shaking with suppressed laughter. "Sit, I'll handle it." He heads to the counter, pulling out flour and other ingredients.

"What is Krop—? I can't remember what you called it."

"Kroppkakor," Stefan replies, removing the nonstick griddle. "It's Swedish potato dumplings and it's delectable." He smacks his lips and gestures to the door. "Tesco isn't that far."

"Another day." Ade insists, surveying the countertop. "I

don't want you stressed today. Surely, there's something I can do."

Stefan hands him a bowl. "Beat four eggs."

Stefan finds solace in the act of cooking, viewing it as a serene ritual that imbues his day with a sense of purpose. The rhythmic chopping of vegetables, the sizzle of ingredients in a hot pan, and the comforting aroma that fills the kitchen are his form of meditation. But, he never imagines that this tranquil pursuit could be made better simply by Ade's presence, transforming it from a quiet hobby into a shared joy. The kitchen soon fills with the irresistible scent of pancakes, and Stefan plates them with artistic flair, draping his in lingonberry jam and a lavish swirl of whipped cream for Ade. And soon, they are caught up in a culinary game of tag—stealing from each other's plates and smearing whipped cream on their faces with glee as "Tears in Heaven" plays.

After breakfast, they retreat upstairs, their steps light and content. They flop on the bed and wrap themselves in the warm cocoon of the fluffy duvet, snuggling as they watch *My Policeman* on Prime. Stefan lounges against the mattress, his heart doing a happy dance as he luxuriates in the moment. The day is unfolding just as he had meticulously planned months ago, and he revels in the serendipity of it all, realising that sometimes, the universe's idea of a second chance is better than any plan he could have imagined.

"They didn't deviate from the book much," he comments, feeling the warmth of Ade's body against his.

"Harry Styles is hot," Ade remarks, nearly drooling.

"He's in the top ten," Stefan agrees. "I miss his long hair."

"Who's your celebrity crush?"

"I have about a hundred, but first on the list is Troye Sivan," Stefan grins. "I know who yours are."

"Of course you do. Jola and Sophia downloaded me to you," Ade says, pouting adorably.

"If I ask you to choose," says Stefan, putting his laptop aside, "between Tyler Blackburn and Matt Bomer, who would it be?"

"Yes," Ade responds with a cheeky grin.

Stefan collapses in laughter. "That's not an answer."

"That's my answer," Ade insists, wiggling his finger. "I refuse to choose. I'm Oliver Twist."

After their shower, Ade tends to Stefan's cut with the exactitude of someone who has done this many times. "This isn't looking as scary as it did yesterday," he says, pointing to the cut by Stefan's ankle.

"Thank you."

"Anytime," Ade replies, kissing the top of Stefan's head. "We can leave now. I want us to get there when it's dark, but not too late."

In another twenty minutes, Ade stows Stefan's bag next to his own in the boot, and with a final check to ensure everything is in place, they climb into the car. The car's engine purrs with a low, contented rumble, its steady hum melding with the rhythmic cadence of streetlights flashing past their windows, creating a soothing backdrop to their journey. As they drive away from Newcastle, the city's skyline gradually receding into the distance, Ade's tone shifts from light-hearted to sombre. Stefan, sensing the shift, straightens in his seat, ready for whatever comes next.

"First thing you have to know is that it's illegal to be gay in Nigeria. It's punishable with up to fourteen years in prison."

Stefan fumes but he stays quiet, listening intently as Ade continues.

Ade recounts meeting a guy at MT's party in May, unknown to him he overheard their conversation. "So, when we got talking, it was cool. I had no close male friends in Naij, just guys I went to school with, who were homophobic. They don't know about me, but being in their company is just gross with what they say, so I stayed away." Ade explains, his voice steady. He then continues with how their conversations grew, the guy's confession, and the subsequent plan to meet. "I liked him enough, I think. So, I told him we'd meet once I was back in Lagos."

Finally, Ade describes the harrowing ambush by four men, each word revealing a new layer of the brutality he endured. As the story unfolds, Stefan's eyes fill up and before he can stop it, the tears begin to flow. His heart aches with every detail, each new revelation feeling like a personal assault, as if he's experiencing the violence vicariously. In a state of panic, Ade pulls the car sharply into a nearby parking spot, jostling them. Stefan, overcome by offering comfort, shifts Ade's seat back and clambers into his lap, enfolding him in an embrace as though he might protect him from the trauma with sheer willpower.

"Stef, don't cry," Ade murmurs, caressing Stefan's back. "I'm alright now."

Stefan's tears, however, show no sign of abating. "I'm so sorry, baby. I'm so sorry you had to endure that," he sobs, his voice breaking. In a moment of unexpected introspection, he wonders why they reserve endearments only for moments of distress—perhaps it's a peculiarity of their love. Regardless, Ade will always be his baby, now and forever. "I'm so sorry I didn't listen when you tried to tell me."

Ade wipes his face. "You're listening now. That's what counts."

Stefan's fury is a tempest of such magnitude that he fantasises about exacting vengeance not just on the guy who harmed Ade, but also his ineffectual cronies and their entire wretched family. The thought of obliterating them feels almost poetic in its cruelty. Even before Ade confirms it, Stefan knows with chilling certainty that this tormentor is the very same miscreant who called him back in October.

Ade, still maintaining his calmness, talks about the day Stefan left for Stockholm and the plan orchestrated by his siblings and friends. Stefan can practically see it—the lot of them, gathering like a band of conspirators, plotting their revenge. And the confrontation of the other three attackers? As brutal and swift as the reckoning of gods. Ade removes his phone and plays the videos for Stefan. Those fools thought they could get away with it. Now, they're on video, not so cocky anymore—no, now they're begging for mercy. The favour had been returned, and Ay made sure they knew it. Stefan can't help but admire it, in a twisted sort of way and he makes a mental note never to end up on Ay's bad side; it appears to be a particularly unpleasant place to find oneself.

"I still can't believe the country is that homophobic," Stefan says, incredulous.

"It is. Reporting to the police would've meant praise for my attackers. It's that bad."

"Good riddance," Stefan sniffs. "I love what Jola did. It's a better form of justice."

"You and Nathan are the same," Ade says, cupping Stefan's face. "Hey, I'm okay. The day after you left for Stockholm, I declared myself healed to Sparks."

Stefan chuckles. "What did he say?"

Ade scoffs. "He asked if I wanted to sit on the chair or lie on the couch."

Stefan collapses on Ade's chest, laughing. When he looks up, Ade is scowling. "You're okay?" Stefan asks, searching Ade's face.

"I'm fine," Ade says, running his hands through Stefan's hair. "I won't dismiss Sparks' work. He's been a great help, and there's much I understand better now." He pulls Stefan closer. "And you helped me, Stef. I—"

Stefan kisses him. They are on the E05 almost in Leeds, and they're kissing, because they can, because they want to, and because they are in love.

Stefan settles back in his seat, stretching out with the nonchalance of someone who's used to long journeys but never quite patient for them. "We should keep going. I'm eager to see this place. Or we can change, and you'll become the passenger prince."

Ade smirks, resuming the drive. A few minutes later, he points out the window. "This is Lancaster we are passing through."

Stefan yawns, watching the scenery blur past. "The only nice city on this route."

Ade glances over. "You tired?"

"No, just bored. We should play something to pass the time."

"Your wish is my command," Ade grins, hitting play on "What You Waiting For". "We've got less than an hour to go."

Fifty minutes later, they are belting out the chorus to

"Thunder" at full volume, as if they're the headline act at Wembley. By the time Ade pulls into a parking lot, they are breathless from singing. Ade leaps out of the car with a boyish energy, rushes to Stefan's side, and practically yanks him out of his seat.

"Come on!" Ade exclaims, taking Stefan's hands and guiding him towards a towering structure in the distance. His excitement is contagious, spilling over like champagne on New Year's Eve. "It's the Blackpool tower."

Stefan takes in the sight before him, wind tousling his hair like an unseen hand. He stands, utterly entranced on the windswept promenade, his eyes fixated on the tower. Its iron frame stretches elegantly into the night, as if it's aware of its own importance. There's something about its graceful lines that speaks to Stefan of a love story written in steel. Somehow, this towering structure has managed to bottle the essence of romance, and Stefan half-wonders if it might have been built just for moments like this. If it starts serenading them, he wouldn't be entirely surprised.

To Stefan, this isn't just a landmark. No, it's a symbol, a testament to something far deeper. The tower stands as a metaphor for the resilience of their love—unyielding, unshaken, despite whatever storms may have tried to wear it down. He smiles at the thought: they might not have the most conventional story, but then again, neither does Blackpool Tower look like it's ready to follow convention.

Stefan's eyes lands on the river beyond, where the moonlight stretches like liquid silk across the water. The shimmering reflection of the tower ripples in the current, shinning like a ghostly apparition, teasing the edges of reality. The way it sways on the surface is almost too perfect, like the whole scene has been staged just for them. Stefan knows, without a trace of doubt that no matter where life leads them—through challenges, through victories—their love will persist. Just like this tower. It is timeless, resilient, and unbothered by time. And if he's being honest, maybe a little showy. But then again, so is he.

"Wow," Stefan breathes out, taking in how the tower stands as a beacon of modernity and history intertwined, and the light from the tower that seems to take on a life of its own. "It's... it's so beautiful, Teni."

"Just like you," Ade murmurs from behind, wrapping his arms around Stefan's waist, his voice warm against the cool night air. "Just like you. Look at how the light brightens the place and sparkles off the river." He gestures towards the water. "That's what you do for me, Stef. You cut through the darkness and illuminate my life. Your presence hones my life more than I ever thought it could. Ever since I found you again, it feels like fate. I've always known deep down that I was made for you. I—"

Stefan turns to face Ade, the power of the moment settling around him like a velvet cloak, heavy yet comforting. The night air, crisp and tinged with the scent of salt and sea, seems to still, as if even nature is rooting for them. Ade's eyes are wide, soft, and dangerously earnest—like he's about to say something monumental, the kind of thing that shifts the ground beneath you.

But Stefan isn't ready for all of it. Not yet.

It's not that he doesn't want to hear it; in fact, he suspects that when Ade finally lets those words spill out, they'll be the very thing his heart has been waiting for. But, and this is a rather large but, Stefan isn't ready to receive that until he's standing on equal footing. For now though, he knows something with a surprising amount of clarity: they have a real chance at this. A proper, unflinching chance to build something remarkable.

They're moving in the right direction, like a ship finally catching the right wind, and the sails are set. They don't need to rush the words. They already know. Ade is his, and Stefan? Well, Stefan is absolutely his. And for the first time ever, Stefan feels like he's standing exactly where he's meant to be—on a windswept promenade, staring at the love of his life.

"Don't cry, baby," Ade murmurs, his thumb gently brushing away the tear that's slipped down Stefan's cheek. "It hurts me when you do."

Stefan laughs softly through the tears, shaking his head. "Happy tears. You just... you make me happy."

Ade's eyes soften, and he leans in for a kiss, his voice tender. "That's all I ever want to do."

Minutes later, they pull up at the Hampton by Hilton. Ade checks them in with his usual efficiency, while Stefan, feeling a bit cheeky, watches him lug both their bags towards the suite. "You're like Marcus," Stefan remarks, eyes twinkling. "Never lets me do a thing."

Ade chuckles, setting the bags down. "What do you feel like eating tonight?"

"Pasta should do," Stefan says, exploring the suite. "And there are two rooms?"

Ade rubs the back of his neck, a touch of shyness creeping into his otherwise confident demeanour. "I thought... you might want some space. You know, just in case."

Stefan does and he can't help but wonder if Ade has somehow mastered mind-reading. It's quintessentially Ade—thoughtful and intuitive. And Stefan appreciates it more than he can say, because it gives him exactly what he needs: space. Space to breathe, to think, to let the events of the past day catch up with him. He needs time to process everything and prepare for the conversation that's inevitably coming. A conversation he knows will change everything.

Now that they're here, in this impossibly quiet hotel room with only the distant murmur of the city beyond the window, there's a dash of something more unsettling. Not fear exactly, not the kind that sends you running for the hills, but a nervousness, a jittery sort of excitement that simmers just under the surface. But he feels slightly scared. A bit like standing on the high diving board, peering down into the pool below, knowing he's about to leap but not quite sure if he's ready to feel the splash. It's not love that scares him—not that. That's as certain as the sun rising in the east. It's the talking part.

"You're always so considerate," he smiles, encircling Ade's waist.

After dinner, Stefan retreats to the bathroom, emerging a while later feeling more relaxed, his earlier fears reduced to a minimal point. He glances around. "Where's my bag?"

"In there," Ade points towards one of the rooms.

Stefan picks up his phone from the table and heads towards the room. He pauses at the doorway, throws a cheeky grin back over his shoulder and says, "You have mail."

Re: BLACKPOOL
From: Stefan Omar Wickström swickström@tees.ac.uk
To: Teniade Michael Adeowo tadeowo@tees.ac.uk
Date: 06.01.2023 at 10:13 PM

YES! YES!! YES!!!

A thousand times yes to you, Teniade. I will follow you anywhere.

I had this in my drafts before, so I'll just copy and paste it here. xo.

Téníadé.

You know how much I love the *Shadowhunters* books, and it made me happy, still makes me happy to know you're reading them. Even after all that's happened, you didn't stop reading. They are amazing books, that's a fact, but I know you read them for me too. So, I'm going to speak strictly in *shadowhunter* and try not to spoil much from the books you've not read.

I am starting with Jem and Tessa, which, to me, is the most iconic love story of all. If you get to be with the one you love after a century and a half, it is iconic indeed. If you get to be with them after most of their heart almost turned to stone for nearly one hundred and fifty years, after you've watched them love another year after year. It is the most iconic indeed.

Next is James and Cordelia. By now, you've read that the evilest enchantment woven by a prince of hell himself snapped cleanly into two halves because James Herondale's love for Cordelia Carstairs couldn't be touched, subverted or altered. Although Jame's horniness might have factored in, seeing as he was kissing his wife at the time of said snapping. But you get the gist.

The story of Helen and Aline in The Mortal Instruments and Dark Artifices books is another one that shows the extent of love. Remember when I said the shadowhunters also have humans' limitations? Just as there are small-minded people in the world today who think different means bad, they hate it if you look different or love differently, forgetting that love is love. Helen Blackthorn was banished to the coldest place in Wrangel Island because of her faerie blood, and what did her girlfriend, Aline Penhallow, do? She packed up and followed her. She followed her to some place that can only be described as the end of the world without a word of complaint.

Now to my personal favourites: Magnus Bane and Alexander Lightwood. Alec was closeted until he met Magnus and couldn't get him out of his head. He was eighteen and shy, but he went all the way to Magnus' apartment to ask him out. Do you understand? He was closeted, scared to be who he was, but he met a guy, and that propelled him to take his fate into his own hands. And he didn't stop there, by the way. He went further to have two kids with the warlock and marry him.

The closeted, shy kid grew up into a bold, strong and powerful man because he didn't lose love when he found it. And the only thing he wants to be remembered by is that he loved one man so much, he changed the world for him.

WOW. MINDBLOWN.

And when you look at Magnus Bane, an immortal warlock who has lived hundreds of years, he has loved and lost, but until he met Alec, he never had surety of such an immense love. A love so monumental, it gave him faith. A faith so great, it made it possible for him to make a whole family happy. To make him know that what others may call the presence of God, Magnus called it Alec.

Teniade, what I'm saying is quite simple. I know love, and I'm not just talking about fiction. I've seen love around me. I recognise it, value it, and know I am in love.

With you.

I will wait centuries for you, break enchantment for

you, follow you to the end of the world and change the entire world for you, my love.

And I will love you until the end of time, baby.

PS: Because I know how much you love music: (https://music.apple.com/uk/playlist/mylove)

Entirely Yours,

Stef.

21

LOVE AND LANGUAGES

*— Fly Me To The Moon
by The Macarons Project.*

ADE FEELS THE SOFT, WARM PRESS OF LIPS ON HIS forehead. A featherlight kiss, barely there, but it sends ripples down his spine, awakening something deep in his chest.

"Teni?" Stefan taps him, softly yet insistent.

"You're awake?" Ade's voice is a sleepy rasp as he peels open his eyes. Stefan lies beside him, all soft hair and sleepy eyes, watching him in a way that makes Ade feel like the only person on earth. "What's the time?"

"Almost midnight. And I wasn't sleeping."

"You're good at fake sleeping. You even snored."

"Liarrrr," Stefan pouts. "But I've had practice. Do you remember when I was sick in October?"

"You were pretending to sleep?"

"Well..." Stefan gives a mischievous grin that could rival a fox caught in the chicken coop.

"Stef," Ade groans, burying his face into the crook of Stefan's neck, breathing in the familiar scent of him. "I deserved that, though."

"No, you don't," Stefan whispers, kissing his hair. "But we need to talk, babe."

"Sure," Ade says, lifting his face to meet Stefan's eyes, which glimmer with something unspoken. "After this," he adds, pressing his lips to Stefan's in a kiss that promises love and understanding before anything else.

Stefan breathes deeply, steadying himself as though he's about to wade into deep waters. "I need to tell you about Honza and his absurdity."

Ade frowns, a teasing smile tugging at the corner of his lips. "Thought his name was Hooker."

"Baaaaabe."

"I'm listening," Ade says, now serious, though his heart aches at the nervousness flickering in Stefan's eyes. He rolls onto his back, pulling Stefan's head onto his chest, his fingers threading through soft curls.

Stefan begins to talk, his voice trembling as he recounts his eighteen-year-old birthday—the park, the club, the kiss, and meeting Honza. He continues with how they started texting, Honza's visit, and eventually, the horror of it all. "He, um," Stefan falters, his voice dropping to a whisper, "he hit me. On the face."

Ade feels his heart shatter, the kind of pain that leaves him hollowed out. He shifts, pulling Stefan astride him, cradling his head to his chest. "Stef, I'm so sorry."

He feels broken, the heaviness of his guilt hanging about him like an ill-fitting coat. He hates himself for yesterday, for the ridiculousness of it all. Complaining— honestly, of all things to throw a fit over, that had to be the one? It's absurd now, as if his frustration had clung to the nearest, silliest excuse. He cringes at the memory, at the stupidity of his outburst. But then, Stefan lifts his head and there's no reproach waiting in his gaze, no cool distance or bruised ego. Instead, those eyes—so clear, so steady—are brimming with love, affection, and something even better: trust. That quiet, unshakable trust that knows, without doubt, that Ade isn't Honza, that he would never be Honza. Stefan knows that Ade loves him fiercely, even when Ade can barely stand himself. He knows it and believes it in a way that leaves Ade feeling both stripped bare and inexplicably safe. And isn't that just like Stefan? To make even Ade's crumbling bits feel like they're still worth holding onto.

As Stefan speaks of the stalking and the threats, Ade's mind sharpens. "When we get back home, you will register a complaint with the police," he says firmly, his hand cupping Stefan's face with gentle insistence. Stefan tries to dismiss it, but Ade doesn't waver. "Do it for me, please?"

Stefan gives a small nod. "You know I'll do anything for you."

They fall into a comfortable silence, the kind shared between people who know each other's scars. But when Stefan lifts his head, his vulnerability is evident. "You know, after him, I avoided meeting new people. I couldn't bear anyone touching me. But I met you and you knocked me off my feet. With your ridiculous smile and chubby cheeks."

Ade understands this too well, their first meeting playing in his mind. The way he couldn't form any words at first, blindsided by the collision and Stefan's face. "Ridiculous smile? You don't say," he arches a brow. "But I told Sparks something similar during one of our sessions. That day at Heathrow, I was instantly pulled to you."

Stefan laughs, soft but genuine. "Same for me. When

we met again, I knew I wanted you, and I thought," he trails off, hiding his face in his hands like a bashful schoolboy.

"Tell me," Ade urges, taking his hands.

"It's stupid," Stefan says, his cheeks flushing.

Ade leans in to kiss his neck. "Pretty please?"

Stefan swallows. "I thought if we had sex, I'd forget all he did." He tries to hide his face again, but Ade still has his hands in captivity.

"That day of the party in my room?"

"Yeah. I was scared, I guess, of you touching me. I thought if we had like actual sex first, then I'd be more comfortable with other things. But when you gave me the playlist at Ben's, I knew there isn't anything we do that I won't be comfortable with," he says in a confessional state.

Ade cups his face. "There isn't anything you *do* to me that I won't be comfortable with."

Stefan grins, his usual mischievousness sneaking back in. "Oh baby, I'd like to *do* quite a lot of things to you."

"I love you," Ade says, and it feels like exhaling after holding his breath for too long. Since fucking October, the words have been waiting to tumble out, and now they flow freely, like a river finding its course. "When I decided to start therapy, it was so I could be better for you, but I was also scared. Scared that you may not want me if you know. It was easier to think me working on myself is why we aren't together."

"*Teni.*"

"I was already in love with you. I wanted you in every way imaginable, more than I could ever admit. But the fear of rejection, of not being enough, made me think I needed to distance myself, to become better, because you deserve something more than me. I wasn't running away from you, I would've been running from myself because you," his voice breaks, but he steadies himself, "you're the best of me."

A tear escapes from the corner of Stefan's eye, and before it can travel too far, Ade's thumb is there, sweeping it away. "Baby."

"I love you so much," Ade continues. "My love for you... it knows no bounds. It's not something that can be measured or contained." He pauses, searching for the words to capture something that feels too vast, too all-encompassing. "It's woven into every fibre of my being. Like a thread running through me, binding me to you in ways I can't even begin to explain. You are not just someone I love. You're *in* me. In my thoughts, in my breath. Every day, all the time." His voice catches and he swallows. "You're the essence of who I am, Stef. Loving you isn't just something I do. It's what I *am*. You're not just a part of my life, love. You *are* my life."

Stefan pulls him into an impassioned kiss, one so sudden and full of longing, the kind that makes Ade feel like he's stepped off the edge of a cliff and is falling, weightless, into something utterly irresistible. Stefan's lips are silken but urgent, conveying everything words have failed to capture, and Ade melts instantly. Stefan's hands begin to roam, sliding over Ade's back, his sides, as if charting every inch, curve, and dip of him. A soft moan escapes Stefan, the sound vibrating into Ades mouth; a sweet intoxicating melody that unravels him, piece by piece. And Ade dissolves with each touch, as he always does, fully at Stefan's mercy, lost in the dizzying blend of lips, skin, and breath.

Ade's fingers move to Stefan's pyjama shirt, managing to pop the first button with a certain haste, feeling Stefan's chest beneath. He's about to move to the second button when—just like that—the kiss breaks. Stefan pulls back, gulping, but his hand wraps firmly around Ade's wrist, halting his progress with a smile that's almost too knowing. Ade blinks, lips still parted as if the kiss might continue if he stays perfectly still.

"Patience, baby," Stefan says, biting Ade's upper lip. "I, um, have something else to tell you."

Stefan takes a deep breath. "I'm going to tell you I love you in twenty-three languages," he announces.

Ade's brows knit together in a comical mix of curiosity and dubiety. "You speak twenty-three languages?" The question escapes before he can filter it, even though it sounds as outlandish as asking if Stefan could juggle flaming torches.

"No, but I learned to say 'I love you' in them. Well, twenty-two, minus Swedish."

Ade's jaw drops, disbelief encasing him in a moment of stunned silence. The sheer scale of Stefan's devotion is staggering. To know that someone loves him so intensely they've gone through the effort of learning to say those three words in multiple languages is deeply humbling. Ade, who has been told he should be beheaded for his identity, whose homeland criminalises his existence, and who has faced violence simply for being himself. And yet, despite all the adversity he has faced, here stands someone who cherishes him deeply and sincerely.

In this extraordinary moment, Ade is reminded of his favourite Bible passage: "The stone the builders rejected has become the cornerstone." It's the first passage he ever memorised in Yoruba, the beauty of its meaning magnified by the operatic cadence of his mother tongue. The verse gives him a sense of calm and purpose that is both profound and comforting. Like a cherished melody, it symbolises resilience and transformation, reflecting the hidden strength within him. It speaks to the ability to rise above rejection and emerge as something essential and foundational.

The passage is more than mere words; it is, like Stefan himself, a guiding light through life's vagaries. It's a reminder that every challenge harbours the seed of something greater. "Stef, I-"

"Shhhh. All you have to do is listen. Just listen to me."

Ade nods, feeling his heart swell with a love that seems almost too large for his chest. Stefan's eyes are alight with deep devotion as he prepares to dazzle Ade. His kisses dance across Ade's skin, a symphony of delicate and enamouring touches. Starting from Ade's forehead, Stefan whispers, "In Swedish, *jag älskar dig.*" He moves to the bridge of Ade's nose. "Turkish, *seni seviyorum.*" A kiss lands on Ade's right cheek. "Polish, *kocham cię.*" Then, his right ear. "French, *je t'aime.*" Stefan's tongue traces from Ade's nose to his cheek. "Japanese, *aishitemasu.*" He moves to his left ear. "Swahili, *nakupenda.*" Down to his neck. "Italian, *ti amo.*" And at the base of his throat. "Croatian, *volim te.*"

Stefan expertly unbuttons Ade's shirt, and Ade watches, captivated and enchanted, as each button falls away. Stefan continues his serenade, his voice a gentle hum. "In German, *ich liebe dich.*" Another button undone. "Danish, *jeg elsker dig.*" Another. "Indonesian, *aku cinta kamu.*" Another. "Shona, *ndinokuda.*" With a casual shrug, he discards the shirt, his eyes, once cerulean, darkening with ardour. "In Romanian, *te iubesc.*" His kisses travel to Ade's right shoulder. "Spanish, *te amo.*" To his left shoulder. "Czech, *miluju tě.*" To his chin. "Finnish, *minä rakastan sinua.*" And to his jawline. "Chinese, *wǒ ài nǐ.*" Down to his chest. "Nepali, *timīlāī māyā garchu.*" He takes one of Ade's nipples in his mouth. "In Thai, *chan rak khun.*" He moves to the other nipple. "Ukrainian, *ya tebe iyubiyu,*" he whispers before biting down.

Ade shivers.

Stefan kisses Ade's right arm. "In Norwegian, *jeg elsker deg.*" He kisses his belly, making playful bubbles with his mouth and laughing softly. "Korean, *salanghaeyo.*" He looks back at Ade, eyes alight with love.

And all Ade can do is stare, his mouth slightly agape, as Stefan recites "I love you" in an array of languages from around the globe. Each phrase, each tender utterance, is like a brushstroke painting their affection across continents. The languages may be foreign, the countries distant and unknown, but in this moment, they are connected through the universal language of love.

Stefan's voice morphs with charming dexterity—from the romantic lilt of French to the rhythmic charm of Swahili, and Ade finds himself swept up in this globe-trotting declaration. Their love is being woven into the fabric of the world itself, reaching far beyond the confines of their immediate surroundings. The idea that their love could ripple through diverse cultures, touching every corner of the earth is profoundly moving. It's as if Stefan's words are tiny, radiant messages in bottles, floating out into the vast ocean of humanity, connecting them to a sprawling, invisible network of hearts.

"Shhhh," Stefan coos, wiping Ade's face clean before kissing him. "In Yoruba, *mo ní ìfé re.*"

Fresh tears spill down Ade's face, his lips quivering. "I love you, Stef," he whispers, holding him tightly, like clinging to a life raft in a stormy sea. But it feels woefully inadequate. It feels like a teardrop in an ocean after listening to Stefan declare in a whooping twenty-three languages, no less. "I love you," he repeats. "I may not be able to tell you in as many languages, but I'll spend the rest of my life showing you how much I love you."

Stefan presses something cool against Ade's cheek. "Show me," he says, voice low, eyes smouldering.

Ade stares in wonderment. "When d—"

"You can't bring a guy on a romantic getaway and not have condoms, Teni."

"They've been in my bag since October, though."

Stefan wrinkles his nose. "From the five hundred in your drawer? Ewww, they'd have expired by now."

Ade laughs. "You saw them?" he asks, brushing his fingers over Stefan's cheeks with a light, ethereal touch.

Stefan nods, eyes glazing over with desire, his body arching into Ade's touch like he's been waiting for it, like he's craved it. Ade can't help but marvel at the way Stefan responds to him—how even the smallest touch sends a tremor through his limbs, how those soft, breathy gasps fall from his lips like confessions. It's intoxicating, seeing him like this: wanting, and all his.

Ade leans in and captures Stefan's mouth in a kiss so searing, it threatens to melt the last fragments of air between them. It's the kind of kiss that rewrites history, the sort that demands its own chapter in any future conversations about great, world-altering moments. Ade's mouth moves with purpose, sketching the curves of Stefan's mouth, neck, collarbone, chest—branding the taste and feel of him into his very soul. He manages to unbutton Stefan, peeling back the fabric as if it were wrapping on a gift he hadn't earned but was absolutely keeping. With a deft, practiced movement—one that somehow feels like instinct—he rolls

Stefan onto the bed, positioning him beneath him, and they are both whispering against each other's mouths.

"Baby."

"You're perfect."

"Can't get enough."

"I love you."

Both their trousers are gone in a heartbeat, leaving them gloriously naked. He lies back on Stefan, winded. "You're so beautiful."

Stefan's lips curl into a teasing grin as he trails his tongue over Ade's neck, fingers wandering downward with devilish intent. "You know," he teases, brushing against Ade's erection, "I thought there's no way this thing's going to fit."

Ade inhales sharply. "It has to," he whispers, nuzzling into Stefan's neck.

Stefan laughs beneath him, the sound vibrating through their bodies like the sweetest, most dangerous music. "How do you go about with this?"

Ade, almost undone by Stefan's caress, manages to keep it together. Barely. "I shall keep it to myself, then," he jokes, feigning an attempt to stand.

But Stefan yanks him back down, lips curling into a wicked smile. "You shall not."

Ade's whole body feels aflame—charged, alive, desperate. "Where's it?"

Stefan hands him the condom. "Lube's in the drawer," he adds, matter-of-fact.

Ade reaches into the drawer, his hands only slightly steadier than the rapid thrum of his heart. The bottle pops open with a soft click, and he leaves it perched on the edge. He tears the packet with a quiet rip, arms himself, and slicks his fingers with lube. The cool, sticky sensation a stark contrast to the heat simmering between them. For a split second, he thinks: *I can't believe he's all mine.* "You're perfect," he breathes as he presses his fingers into Stefan, preparing him. Every movement is deliberate, measured, as though he's handling something precious, irreplaceable. And, in truth, he is. "I love you."

Stefan's eyes flutter shut, his head tilting back as a low, breathless moan escapes him. "I love you. I want you," he murmurs, voice laced with need that matches Ade's own.

Inch by inch, Ade eases himself in, his every movement as slow and cautious as he can manage, checking in with Stefan at every shift of their bodies. "You okay?" he asks, voice rough with both concern and desire. Every soft nod, every whispered 'yes' from Stefan, gives Ade the courage to keep going, to move forward. Once fully in, Ade stills, the overwhelming sensation nearly too much to bear. "Baby, you okay?" His voice is strained, almost pleading, because he needs Stefan's reassurance just as much as Stefan needs him.

"Yes." Stefan's breath is ragged, quivering. "But you have to move." His voice is a husky, starving rasp. Starving for Ade.

Ade starts moving.

He feels his own restraint fray at the edges, but he starts slowly, fastidiously. His hips roll in gentle, careful thrusts, the rhythm of their bodies like a new language they're learning together. Stefan's hands find Ade's shoulders, gripping tightly, his breath hitching as Ade fills him completely. Ade moves within Stefan, slowly but steadily, his body begging for more, his instincts urging him to go faster, harder. But he resists. This moment is too important, Stefan is his—completely, undeniably his. There's a sacredness to it, this act of surrender, as if the entire world has contracted to the space between their bodies. No future, no past. Just now. Just them—bodies and hearts, bound by a desire that no words, however lyrical, could hope to express.

His hand tangles in Stefan's hair, the other cradling his face as their mouths meet again, swallowing every pant, every moan, every whispered affirmation that slips between them. The sheer intimacy of knowing they're each other's first, that this is new, uncharted territory for both of them, adds a sense of something greater than just need. This isn't just sex—it's the beginning of something profound, something that binds them together in a way neither of them had anticipated.

"Look at me," Ade pants between kisses. "I just want you to look at me, to see me."

Stefan's eyes flutter open, hazy with lust but clear in their affection. "I see you," he whispers, and in that gaze, Ade feels as if the entire world has distilled into this one, perfect moment.

Ade's world reduces to this—this singular, stimulating feeling of being in Stefan. Each thrust, each brush of skin against skin, weaves them closer, intertwining their very souls. Ade knows he never wants to stop moving in Stefan, never wants to stop fucking him, never wants to stop making love to him.

"I'm going to have to go a little faster."

"*Yes*," Stefan breathes, the single word thick with need.

Gosh, this is far beyond anything Ade had ever imagined. Nothing—not even his countless wanking—could have prepared him for this. For the way Stefan feels around him, for the intoxicating closeness that feels like the only thing that matters. "Are you close?" he whispers, his voice tight with the effort of holding on. He's teetering on the edge, the pressure inside him building, but he won't let go until Stefan does. *Not before him.*

"Yes," Stefan whispers back. "*Don't stop.*"

"Never," Ade vows, and he means it. There's nothing in this world that could make him stop now. He captures Stefan's mouth again, his kisses just as urgent as his thrusts, plunging into Stefan with a rhythm that sends them both hurtling towards the inevitable. The sound of their bodies meeting, the heat between them, the feeling of Stefan wrapped around him—it all pushes him closer.

Minutes later, Stefan's fingers dig into Ade's back. "Yes," he pants hoarsely, his body tensing beneath Ade's. "*Yes, Teni.*"

And then Ade feels it—a warm, sticky fluid streaking across his thigh, and that's all it takes. He explodes, a crescendo of pleasure that leaves him trembling, shattering. Stefan quivers beneath him, their bodies collapsing together as the last pulses of their shared climax ripple through them.

"Gosh, Stef. That was..." Ade pants, utterly spent. He tries to summon a word, any word, but his brain refuses to cooperate.

Stefan, equally out of breath, lets his hand lazily roam to Ade's arse, giving it a slow, satisfied squeeze. "It was," he agrees, the tiniest hint of a grin in his tone.

22
BOYFRIENDS

— Oceans by Seafret.

STEFAN IS NO LONGER AN *OSKULD*.

Though he doesn't have an extensive list of comparisons, he's willing to wager his entire fortune—and even throw Jason in—that he just had the best sex, exceptional even. Deserving of a Guinness Book of World record for breathtaking coitus. The sheer pleasure of being with Ade had whisked him away to an entirely different realm, a place where every thrust seemed to amplify the ecstatic current coursing through his veins. Now, Stefan is insatiable. His hunger has shifted from mere need to a ravenous longing. He aches for Ade with an intensity that feels almost perilous. How did Ade learn to make love like this? It must be an innate gift. Stefan chuckles at the thought, imagining Ade as some kind of cosmic sex guru.

"What's so funny?" Ade asks breathlessly, lifting his face from the crook of Stefan's neck.

Stefan grins. "I was just contemplating where you acquired your impressive skills."

Ade cackles. "I took a crash course in sexology 101."

"*Stepdad turns brother-in-law gay* on Pornhub?"

"More like Xvideos. Pornhub kept insisting I meet horny dudes in my area," Ade quips, brushing a stray lock of hair from Stefan's forehead.

"I'm the horny dude in your area," Stefan replies, his tone dripping with mock seriousness.

"And what a delight it is to meet you," Ade says, his voice softening as he caresses Stefan's cheek. "But seriously, was it as good for you as it was for me?"

"You set my entire body on fire. It was pure flames," he murmurs, pressing a kiss to Ade's jaw.

"I love you," Ade says, kissing the tip of Stefan's nose. "And you've got to tell me how you managed to master all those languages. I'm still trying to wrap my head around it."

Stefan's smile widens. "For Yoruba, I called Temmy."

"Temmy?" Ade echoes in disbelief. "As in, my brother?"

"Yep, I was like 'Hi Temmy, could you teach me to say, 'I love you' in Yoruba?' He laughed for ten minutes straight and then told me I needed to learn how to say Yoruba properly first. He sent me a couple of voice notes. I spent days learning."

"God, I love you," Ade says, kissing him again. "I'm honestly speechless. Learning languages for me is just incredible."

Stefan shrugs modestly. "Lina taught me Croatian, Italian, and Romanian," he continues, tracing patterns on Ade's shoulder with his fingertips.

"Wow."

"I picked up Indonesian from *City of Lost Souls*."

"Is the Chinese from Jem?"

Stefan laughs. "Yes, our one and only Jem. For Japanese and Korean, Rosh and Peng helped me. Peng gave me a hard time because she thought I mixed up her nationality. It took me ages to convince her I knew she spoke Korean."

"Sounds like her."

"For the rest, I relied on Google Translate," Stefan admits, kissing Ade's chin. "Oh, and Żane taught me Polish, and Yaro taught me Czech. I actually got the idea from hers and Lud's wedding."

"You were raving about their vows!" Ade's hand finds Stefan's, intertwining their fingers. "You're quite the fast learner."

"I almost told you on the phone," Stefan admits. "I can't keep a secret from you."

"I should reward you by sullying you even more," Ade says with a laugh, his body shaking.

"I should never have mentioned that," Stefan groans, dragging a hand down his face as if wiping away the mortifying memory.

Ade's laughter spills out, a low, filling sound that seems to dance in the air between them. "Oh, you love it when I sully you, don't you?"

There's something in Ade's tone—a mixture of mischief and challenge—that shoots straight through Stefan like a spark, lighting him up in ways he'd rather not admit. The shiver that follows is more betrayal than reaction. His body has always been far too honest, far too quick to respond. "You're going to have to switch," he replies, his tone taking an almost daring edge.

"Am I?" Ade's eye gleam, like a fox who's just found an unlocked henhouse, and Stefan can't decide whether to be thrilled or terrified by that single, loaded question.

Ade is still inside Stefan, and he can already feel the

renewed firmness in Ade. After swiftly grabbing a serviette to clean them up earlier, Ade had collapsed on Stefan with an air of sated exhaustion. Ade begins to withdraw himself, his lips, now a shade rosier, curl into a languid seductive smile.

"You're eager to be sullied, aren't you?" Ade's voice drops to a husky murmur.

"Stop saying sully," Stefan chides, licking Ade's neck.

"I won't," Ade pouts. "Sully, sully, sully." He repeats the word as he disposes of the condom and squirts lube into his hand, then takes hold of Stefan's dick. "I'm going to sully you with my hand until you sully my hand with your nectar," he says, dead seriously, before he starts stroking.

Stefan's body tenses, every muscle singing as Ade sets a steady tempo with his hand—neither torturously slow nor overly brisk, but perfectly paced to drive Stefan to the brink. Ade's lips trail from Stefan's neck down to his chest, his kisses light yet enthralling. As he nibbles on each nipple with a teasing attention, Stefan feels a surge of need ripple through him, an insistent pulse that grows with each deliberate touch.

Returning to Stefan's mouth, Ade asks, "Tell me how it feels."

"It feels incredible," Stefan pants. "Immaculate."

Ade laughs into his mouth, a sound filled with joy and affection. "Immaculate? I love that. I love you. You are immaculate, baby."

Ade grunts, his tempo picking up as if driven by some inner metronome, just as Stefan's arousal reaches a fever pitch. Stefan loses all restraint, caught in the rapture of it all. "Yes," he cries out, pressing harder against Ade, kissing him with more fervour. Each movement, each stroke, creates a flood of sensation that overwhelms him, surpassing anything he's felt before. And in record time, he sullies Ade's hand as per instruction, gasping for breath as he murmurs, "You're going to ruin me, baby."

He had said it before, but the certainty in his words is now absolute. He's experiencing what he once could only dream of, and he knows he'll crave Ade every minute of every day. What's even better? He knows, without doubt, that Ade will always be there to meet his needs, every damn time. Stefan opens his eyes to Ade cleaning his hands and Stefan's belly with an almost ceremonious air, grinning with the satisfaction of a job well done.

"I just love the way you say 'yes'. Sounds through me," Ade says, rolling onto his back.

"You," Stefan pants, "are talented." His throat is dry. But God help him, he's barely able to move.

"You know how to make a guy feel ten feet tall, Stef."

"Water," Stefan croaks.

Ade leaves the room and returns with a bottle of water. Stefan gulps it down gratefully. "You're already not that far from ten feet," he grins.

Ade settles back in bed beside Stefan, lying on his side. "I'm not much taller than you," he says with a smile.

"Now, who's making who feel ten feet taller?" Stefan asks, sidling closer to Ade, their lips meeting once more in a tender kiss.

Stefan gasps, and honestly, who wouldn't? Ade's hand is on his backside, exploring with all the curiosity of a man who's just discovered a rare treasure. "How's your arse so soft?" Ade mutters, with the kind of wonder reserved for stargazing.

Stefan's hands return the gesture with equal enthusiasm. "Yours is softer," he replies. "I was watching it jiggle when you walked out."

"The jiggling turns you on?"

"Oh, love, your entire existence turns me on," Stefan declares, his tone so utterly sincere that it would be saccharine if it weren't absolutely true.

"I stand no chance, do I?" Ade leans in, their forehead touching, his voice filled with faux defeat. "You're going to romance the shit out of me."

"I'm going to romance the shit out of you, baby," Stefan promises, before dragging Ade into a kiss that's all heat and fire.

As their lips meet, Stefan is transported back to that first kiss in Ade's room, a kiss so tentative, so new, it still rings in his memory like a sacred chord. The moment their lips touched, Stefan knew—kissing Ade is the best thing in the world. It's an unassailable truth, right up there with gravity and the fact that no one looks good eating a banana. There's nothing, not even the most gourmet tiramisu, that could compare to Ade whispering "You're perfect" to him. Nothing, not even the grandest of world wonders, could match the bliss of being kissed, touched, or, let's be honest, utterly ravished by the love of his life. This—this—is love, true and unparalleled, the kind that eclipse everything else.

Stefan rolls Ade onto his back, straddling him with the grace of a man who's done this before, his lips plot a familiar course—mouth, cheek, ear, chin. He peppers kisses like breadcrumbs, ensuring Ade could always find his way back. There's a packet in his hand, foil crinkling—the harbinger of intent. But Ade, always attuned to the undercurrent of things, shakes his head slightly. "Your leg isn't healed," he says, trying to guide Stefan back down, his fingers grazing the bandaged ankle in a gesture that feels more like love than caution.

But Stefan is nothing if not determined. "It's fine," he insists, mad with need.

Ade remains sceptical, his eyebrows quirking in that endearing way of his. "We can wait, you know."

"I want to now," Stefan whines.

Ade, ever the indulgent partner, can't resist that whine. "Fine, but go slowly, yeah?"

Stefan wastes no time, reaching behind to roll the condom onto Ade while Ade's fingers prepare him. Soon, he lowers himself, Ade's grasp firm but tender on his hips, guiding him down until Stefan takes him fully. And, oh—oh, the sound that escapes him is unlike anything he's ever made before, a raw, unfiltered cry of passion. This—this position—is something else, a revelation. It's better than anything he's experienced before. It's more delicious—no, immaculate.

Being in control like this, sitting on Ade, his thighs trembling, feels like the most exquisite thing in the world. It shifts something deep within him, a satisfaction so profound it nearly brings tears to his eyes. And Stefan knows, oh, he knows, that once he moves, they won't last long—it'll take mere minutes, perhaps only seconds. But that's half the beauty of it. Burning bright and fast, like a star collapsing magnificently into itself.

"My God, Stef," Ade grunts from beneath him, voice roughened by desire.

Stefan begins his ride, their bodies falling into that perfect harmony of push and pull, give and take, as though they've rehearsed this a thousand times. Stefan is drifted closer to that wonderful realm of bliss, the place where nothing else exists except for the two of them. It's a place he knows well by now, but it never ceases to amaze him—how easily Ade takes him there, how simple and profound it is.

And as he drives them both forward, Stefan feels something deeper unfurl in his chest—Happiness. Real, unfiltered happiness, filling him like sunlight pouring through the cracks. To be here with Ade, away from trauma, tears, and exes. Just Ade. Just the man who stayed, who loves him in ways no one else ever had. Here, with Ade beneath him, there's no pain—well, alright, maybe a bit of sweet, delicious pain. It's just them—Stefan and Ade—and the love they share, a love that has not only endured but thrived. A love that is steady, unwavering, and powerful enough to push back the darkness that once threatened to overwhelm them both.

"Choke me," Ade growls, his hands still firmly on Stefan's arse. Stefan obliges, wrapping a hand around Ade's throat, his hold tightening as Ade whispers, "Tighter."

Ade thrusts up into Stefan and his brain fries, but the rush is unstoppable, inevitable. The delight coils tighter inside him, winding and winding until it's a storm ready to break. And break it does. Stefan's body shakes with the severity of it all, his orgasm tearing through him in a wave of heat and light, and the only sound in the room is his gasping cry as he topples over the edge, taking Ade with him. He collapses onto Ade's chest, panting, quivering, totally worn, but gloriously happy. As the world slowly knits itself back together, Stefan can't help but think: *Yes, kissing Ade is the best thing in the world, but this—this isn't far behind.*

Ade opens his eyes, filled with worry. "I'm sorry, baby," his voice shakes. "Did I hurt you?"

Stefan strokes his hair, his breathing slowing. "No, love. You didn't. It was... perfect."

Ade breathes in relief, and holds Stefan tighter. "How's your leg?"

Stefan rolls his eyes, his hand sliding down Ade's waist. "It's fine. Ask me something else."

Ade pretends to think, his brow furrowing. "Alright, then. Why twenty-three languages?"

"It's obvious, love. It's your age," Stefan says, as if it's the most logical thing in the world.

Ade chuckles. "I made the playlist twenty-two."

"I noticed," Stefan replies, his heart swelling with fondness. "To think I once thought we were so different. But here we are. The playlist is twenty-three songs."

Ade's smile softens, his hand brushing Stefan's cheek. "We're ridiculous, aren't we?"

"We're in love."

"And we're boyfriends," Ade adds, kissing him once more.

23
COMFORT ZONE

— Everything by Michael Bublé.

Tuesday, 10th January 2023.

Ade wakes, half-searching for Stefan, whose head is evidently not occupying Ade's chest. With one eye still shut, he pats around aimlessly. "Stef?" His voice is hopeful but laced with the tiniest hint of panic—the kind that only comes from memories of that awful Sunday morning when Stefan had disappeared without a trace. But before his anxious thoughts can overcome, Stefan's voice floats through the suite.

"In here, babe."

Ade exhales, rolling his eyes at his own melodrama. Of course, Stefan's still here—where else would he be? He pulls on his pyjama bottoms, the fabric cool against his skin, and heads towards the living room. In there, Stefan is not just eating breakfast; no, he's making an *event* of it. He's warbling through the chorus of "Lost on You" as if he's auditioning for some ill-advised musical, all while jabbing at his scrambled eggs like they've personally wronged him. Ade leans against the doorframe, arms folded, amused and totally besotted. This is his boyfriend, a delightful mess of contradictions and talent, and the sight makes his heart do a little jig.

Stefan catches sight of him and, without skipping a beat in his performance, whines, "Stop staring!"

Ade crosses the room, planting a kiss atop Stefan's messy hair. "Good morning, baby."

"Um," Stefan taps his index finger against his lips like he's waiting for payment in the form of a real kiss. Obligingly, Ade leans in, their lips meeting in a slow, lazy kiss, his hand instinctively tangling in Stefan's hair. One kiss turns into two, then three, and suddenly they're in full "ravage mode", as if they haven't seen each other in a decade.

When they finally break apart, Ade grins and breathes, "Why were you butchering LP?"

Stefan pulls back with the mock indignation of someone who's just been snubbed at the Grammys. "Excuse me, I *have* a great singing voice. I could totally be their backup singer."

Ade nearly falls off his chair, laughing. "If you insist."

Stefan ignores him with the regal dignity of a dethroned king. "You are cocky now that you've seen me naked."

Ade wipes a tear from his eye, doing his utmost to stifle another laugh. "Oh, I've *earned* that right, love." He pulls Stefan into his lap, holding him close. "So, how about we get out of here today? I want to show you the town properly. We haven't even scratched the surface."

"Well... You've been doing a great job zapping my energy."

"Zap?" Ade echoes, mimicking Stefan's exasperated

tone from last night. "Yes, *yes*, Teni. *TENI.*" His impression of Stefan, lost in the throes of passion is spot on, and Stefan crosses his arms, full-on sulking mode activated. "Did I lie?"

Stefan stands, giving the room a quick sweep, searching for an invisible audience before plopping back down. "Who are you even talking to?"

Ade leans in, his hands creeping up Stefan thighs. "Refuel, my love. You'll need it soon."

Stefan feigns a serious expression. "I am on strike."

"Oh, are you now?" Ade murmurs, trailing his lips from Stefan's cheek to his ear, his hand finding Stefan's evident arousal. "Are you quite sure?"

Stefan lets out a reluctant groan, already surrendering to Ade. "Betrayal," he accuses, glancing pointedly at his own treacherous anatomy before pulling Ade in for a kiss that quickly melts any notions of a strike. He turns Ade so his back is against the table, drops to his knees, pulls Ade's bottoms down, and has him for desert.

After breakfast—and ahem, dessert—they venture out to a snowy hill, sled at the ready. Snow falls gently, coating the ground in a picturesque blanket of white. Stefan, wrapped in a purple parka like some sort of woollen marshmallow, protests but still can't hide the smile on his face. "I can't believe you talked me into this," he mutters, settling himself at the front of the sled.

Ade, looking striking in his navy blue jacket and matching scarf, grins. "You'll thank me later," he quips, giving the sled a push.

The sled takes off with a jolt, their yelps of surprise turning into peals of laughter as they hurtle down the slope, wind whipping their faces. For a brief, marvellous moment, they're just two idiots in love, careening through the snow without a care in the world. They tumble off at the bottom in a tangled heap, snowflakes dotting their faces. Ade wipes one from Stefan's flushed cheek, smiling. "You look like a snow angel."

"More like a snow gremlin after that landing."

Ade kisses his cheek. "Gremlin, goblin—whatever, you're my angel."

The glow of the afternoon seems to follow them as they take a leisurely walk through the town, poking their heads into quaint little shops, laughing at random trinkets, and making up hilarious backstories for each item. Stefan is in his element, picking up knick-knacks and mock-inspecting them with the seriousness of an art critic. "What do you think of this?" he asks, holding up a ceramic figurine of what can only be described as a dog caught mid-sneeze.

Ade peers at it, tilting his head. "Honestly? It's hideous."

"I'm buying it."

The sun is beginning its slow descent as they arrive at the iconic Blackpool Tower, casting everything in a soft amber light. At its base, the town lights start to twinkle in the encroaching dusk. Hand in hand, they ride the lift to the observation deck, the gentle hum filling the quiet between them. They step out onto the observation deck and the view unfolds before them like a postcard come to life. The Irish Sea stretches out, vast and shimmering, while the town below twinkles like something out of a fairy tale. But up here, it feels like they're in their own world, detached from everything except each other.

Ade points out familiar landmarks with the enthusiasm of a child showing off his favourite toy. "Look, you can see the whole town from here. There's the pier, and over there's the beach..."

Stefan is barely listening, his attention more on Ade than the town below. "It's beautiful."

Ade catches him staring and, unable to resist, pulls Stefan in for a kiss, the cool wind from the sea whipping around them. The world below forges on, unaware that for these two, time has stilled. Stefan wraps an arm around Ade, who leans into the embrace, feeling the steady beat of Stefan's heart.

"This has been the best day," Stefan whispers.

"It has. And I'm the luckiest guy in the world."

Sunday, 15th January 2023.

Ade's initial plan for their romantic getaway was a modest one—just a few days—but here they are, ten days in and nowhere close to wanting it to end. Ade would've let it stretch into a luxurious ten months if it weren't for their pesky exams.

"You have to bend down. We're not in the tub," Stefan commands with the authority of a seasoned stylist.

Ade obeys, head dipping under the water like a well-trained pupil. This liturgy, of Stefan washing his hair daily has become almost revered, and Ade finds himself surprisingly attached to it. He chuckles inwardly, remembering a tweet he's seen once—something about time flying when you're 'enjoying penis.' He hadn't quite understood it then. Now? Oh, now it makes perfect sense. Ten days of bliss, the best ten days of his life.

"All done," Stefan grins, fully aware of his reward.

"Thanks, love." Ade leans in, kissing him, hands already weaving through Stefan's hair. Stefan's hands, like clockwork, find Ade's waist, pulling him closer with a soft squeeze. "Give me," Ade says, with a knowing glance, hardly surprised when a condom appears as if by magic. It's a trick Stefan has perfected, producing them at moments of maximum heat—be it post-breakfast, mid-tour, or halfway to the couch, as if Durex had somehow made a pact with him.

"How do you always have one ready?" Ade asks, half-curious, half-amused as he turns Stefan around.

Stefan's laugh is light, but breathy. "You have your innate talents with sex. I have mine with Durex," he quips, gasping as Ade makes his entrance.

Ade grins, hands tightening on Stefan's hips. "What? You don't think my crash course helped?" he teases, his voice quivering ever so slightly.

Stefan can barely get the words out. "No amount of *Hot Plumber Fucks Twink* can teach you this."

Ade snorts mid-thrust. "How do you even have these titles?" he purrs, licking Stefan's ear.

Stefan stifles a groan. "I... used to... Oh, damn... used to masturbate a lot. Certified professional."

Ade laughs loudly. It's not just the sex that's perfect, though. It's the way they talk through it, laugh through it, as if every part of their relationship, even the most intimate, is a conversation—sometimes ridiculous, often profound. Two days ago, when Stefan said, "Your dick is a steele marking my soul." Ade came immediately.

"Stef. Baby. Now?"

"Yes...*Now*."

Ade's pace intensifies, his hands firm on Stefan's hips as their bodies move in sync. When they finally crash together, it's with a force that leaves them gasping, clinging to each other, leaning against the fogged-up walls. They stand there for a while, chests heaving, bodies weak, until Ade pulls out, both grinning like schoolboys who've gotten away with something. After regaining their stamina and finishing their shower, they step out.

Ade hands Stefan a hairbrush with a knowing smile. "I have to bend, I know." They swap places, each brushing the other's hair in companionable silence. "Ever thought about straightening your hair?"

"No," Stefan replies, casting him a glance. "Do you want me to?"

Ade shakes his head. "Nah. I love it just the way it is."

After breakfast, they pack their bags with the dull efficiency of men who aren't quite ready to leave but know they must. It is bittersweet leaving this place that has been more than just a suite to them. It's been a sanctuary. But they're leaving as a couple, something Ade had only dared to hope for when they embarked on this journey.

As they're about to leave, Stefan holds out a velvet-covered box, suddenly looking bashful, a rare sight. "I got it for you in Stockholm," he says, scratching the back of his neck.

Ade can hardly believe this is Stefan, after all the obscenities he's heard from him. It is a surprising look for him, considering the guy has no issue saying, "honey's sweetness is overrated. Your dick is the real honey," and "fuck me till I forget where I come from." He opens the box, and his jaw drops—he has a feeling that his jaw will not leave the floor in this relationship. Inside the box is a cute gold pendant with three symbols: a capital 'T', joined to a heart, and a capital 'S'. It's simple but impossibly beautiful.

"Wow," Ade breathes, blinking back the urge to let his mouth hang open permanently. "Wow, Stef. This is... Wow." He removes his chain, slides the pendant on, and hands it to Stefan to clasp. There's something spreading in his chest that has nothing to do with the jewellery, everything to do with the guy standing in front of him.

"Do you like it?" Stefan asks, fastening the chain around Ade's neck.

"I love it. Thank you, baby," Ade says, pulling him in for a tight hug. "I love you so much."

Stefan's grin returns full force. "I had it customised at Efva Attling. One of Sweden's best."

"It's perfect."

Ade leans in to kiss him, his fingers already moving to undress Stefan. They may be cutting it close for checkout, but some things simply can't wait. Late checkout fee? Ade will pay it promptly. Right now, there's only one thing on his mind—showing Stefan his appreciation and exactly how deep his love runs. The rest can wait.

24
CHAIN OF THORNS

— Valentine by Jim Brickman
& Martina McBride.

Tuesday, 14th February 2023.

"That," Ade declares, pointing to his spotless plate, "was perfect." He gives his belly an exaggerated rub to pass his message across.

Stefan chuckles, his eyes crinkling into crescents. "What's the belly rub for?"

"Visual representation," Ade explains, taking a sip from his glass. "The Kroppkakor was that good. Thanks baby."

Stefan grins as he gathers their plates. "Glad you liked it," he says, heading for the sink. He's about to load the dishwasher when Ade appears behind him, adding their glasses to the pile, his breath ghosting along Stefan's ear.

"Leave it," Ade whispers, spinning Stefan to face him with a look that could melt glaciers. "I've missed you." His teeth graze Stefan's lower lip before pulling him into a kiss that demands everything and promises even more.

"I've missed you more," Stefan murmurs, arms winding around Ade's waist, pulling him close like he's been holding on to absence for far too long.

And it's been far too long—no thanks to exams and a month of reading with their study groups. Ade holed up with Nathan and the other data guys, while Stefan slogged through with Lina. But now, right now, all those days apart feel like a distant dream. And the one thing he knows for certain? He's missed Ade. Missed the feel of him, the taste of him, and—to be completely honest—he's missed Ade's dick like a man misses oxygen after a dive into deep water. Ade grunts, threading his fingers through Stefan's hair as their kisses grow hungrier, and Stefan swears he can feel his heart hammering in every inch of his body.

Ade pulls back just long enough to mutter, "I want you," his voice a low rumble as his tongue skims Stefan's ear, his neck. The teasing path of Ade's tongue is nothing short of torture, but the best kind, the sort that leaves Stefan dizzy and desperate for more.

"Upstairs," Stefan suggests, struggling to keep his bearings.

"Too far," Ade mutters, already kissing him again, lips pressing firm and unrelenting.

"But the con—" Stefan swallows his protest as something cold presses against his neck.

"I'm prepared this time," Ade whispers, his face alight with playful intent.

Stefan's pulse kicks up a notch, his hands unbuttoning Ade's shirt in a hurry, the desperation of want overtaking all semblance of finesse. He's almost running mad; his craving for Ade is undeniable, as is how Ade makes him feel alive and wanted. The shirt hits the floor. Then, in swift succession, so does Stefan's polo. Bare skin meets, and it's like a match to kindling, a crackle of heat that should come with a warning label. Stefan's hands roam over Ade's chest, savouring every plane, every inch. Without ceremony, Ade guides them to the breakfast counter, unzipping himself with practised ease. He never breaks eyes contact, rolling on the condom like it's second nature, before swiftly turning Stefan, pressing him against the cool countertop. Ade kisses a line down to Stefan's shoulder as he unzips him, then wanders lower, leaving reverent kisses on Stefan's buttocks before returning to stand behind him.

Stefan has barely any time to think before cool, sticky fingers slide into him, he lets out a surprised laugh, delight already hazing his thoughts. He's about to make some smart remarks about Ade carrying condoms and lube around campus when he feels Ade, hot, hard, and needy, pressing into him. The words die on his lips, replaced by a guttural "fuck," that slips out like a prayer.

"That's right, baby," Ade's voice is a sultry whisper against his ear. "I'm going to fuck you."

And fuck him he does. There's nothing gentle about the way Ade moves—nothing slow, nothing restrained, but with the kind of ferocity that only comes from weeks of pent-up need. Stefan clutches the counter as if it's the only thing keeping him tethered to earth. Ade moves, harder, faster, with a hunger that's almost feral, and Stefan is out of his mind with ecstasy—this is beyond anything he imagined. And he doesn't want it to end: he wants it like this all the effing time.

Ade's hand grips his waist with a firmness that borders on possessiveness, his other hand grabbing a fistful of Stefan's hair, pulling just enough to weaken Stefan's knees. "Gosh, Stef, you're going to be the end of me. You and your delicious arse."

Stefan's mind is a haze, every nerve aflame, every sound and touch amplified to a point where he's convinced that pleasure has donned a cricket bat and is walloping him with reckless abandon. He thinks of Blackpool, of the way Ade had said, with all seriousness, "God specifically constructed your arse for me." It was absurd, ridiculous, and yet at the time, it had sent Stefan over the edge. Or the time when Ade said that Stefan's arse should have its own religion—right now, Stefan is ready to believe. There's nothing he loves more than these rough whispers in his ear.

Stefan barely holds himself together, the pressure building to an almost intolerable height. "You are already the end of me."

Ade's lips press against his neck, his breath hot and heavy. "Do you want to come for daddy?"

"Yes," Stefan whispers—a desperate plea.

"Say it," Ade demands, his voice a growl.

"I... want to come for... daddy," he breathes out.

Ade smacks Stefan's arse, a sharp, exhilarating sting. "That's my good boy."

Stefan sees stars. Not just any stars—no, these are the kind of twinkling bastards that dance at the edge of his vision. "Do it again," he demands, his voice hoarse, hardly recognisable as his own.

Ade lowers his head, lips brushing Stefan's ear in that way that makes his knees feel about as stable as a jelly on a trampoline. "Do what again, love?" His tone is anything but innocent.

"Smack me again," Stefan practically begs.

Ade doesn't need asking twice. His palm lands with a delicious crack, harder this time, leaving fiery trails across Stefan's skin that only fans the flames of his need. Ade's hand then wraps around Stefan's dick, stroking him with a pace that matches the rhythm of his thrusts. "I can't hold off for longer, baby," he pants, moving with the kind of precision that makes Stefan wonder—briefly, between gasps of breath—*where exactly did Ade learn to fuck like this?* Stefan's mind shatters, not in a slow, graceful crumble, but with the force of a dam breaking, his senses flooding under the relentless speed of Ade's thrusts, his hand, his everything. It's too much and nowhere near enough. He's on the brink, every nerve in his body feels alive, buzzing with a kind of pleasure that is borderline unbearable but entirely addictive.

Ade leans in again, his breath hot against Stefan's ear, a whisper that feels more like a command from a deity. "Come for daddy, baby."

And really, what choice does Stefan have? There's no stopping this. Heaven help him. His body convulses, pleasure detonating from the core of him like a star going supernova. A cry tears from his throat, raw and uncontrolled, as he spills over the edge.

Ade and Stefan sag to the floor in a heap of tangled limbs, sinking into the softness of their discarded clothes. A shared exhale escapes, the kind that's let out when words are too heavy and yet too light. Ade pulls Stefan into his lap, nuzzling into the crook of his neck with the lightest of kisses —to say, *I've got you.*

"You okay, babe? Ade murmurs, lips brushing Stefan's shoulder in between kisses, like punctuation marks on a love letter.

Stefan, for his part, is rendered speechless. He nods, tapping Ade's lap, but no words come—just a contended sigh. Ade holds him tighter, their breaths syncing, and Stefan melts into him. And for a moment, they stay like that, basking in the closeness and quiet satisfaction of skin against skin.

After a few minutes, the floor ceases to be comfortable so they gather themselves—reluctantly—ready to make their way upstairs. Stefan turns and tilts his face. "You left me breathless," he whispers, and Ade gives him a kiss that's both an apology and a promise to do it again.

Stefan scoops up their clothes, ambling up the stairs as Ade stops to retrieve his backpack from the couch. By the time Stefan emerges from the closet, Ade is already sprawled on the bed—on a spot Stefan now mentally calls *Ade's side*, and he laughs at the label. How had this guy so thoroughly claimed not just a side of his bed, but his whole heart?

"That's for you, babe," Ade says, nodding towards a white box tied neatly with a crimson ribbon, atop the drawer. He taps his phone, and "Breathless" by The Corrs starts playing, because subtlety is for the weak.

Stefan's brow quirks. "And this," he says, handing Ade his own box, "is for you. And you're a complete fool for playing that song."

Ade moves to the edge of the bed on his knees, looking pleased with himself, and wraps his hands around Stefan's waist. "A fool, maybe. But one who *very much* plans on leaving you breathless again." He hums as he opens his gift, a low, almost off-key rendition. He lifts the box lid, and then freezes, his jaw practically hits the floor. "Babe!"

Stefan's grin is wide. "You like it?"

"Like it? *I love it*," he says, one hand reaching for the Air Force 1 Low VLONE 2017 nestled in the box. "Thanks, baby." He points eagerly at Stefan's drawer, like a boy ready to share his best secret. "Now, open yours, babe. Open it."

Stefan can barely sit still as he sets the box in his lap. The moment he lifts the lid, a gasp escapes his lips. "It's *The Red Scrolls of Magic!*" His voice rings out in pure, unabashed astonishment. "You *found* it! I've been searching *everywhere* for this." He clutches the book to his chest, as if it might try to make a run for it, or worse—disappear like it never existed at all.

But just as he's about to unceremoniously drop the box, Ade shakes his head with a knowing smile. "You should keep looking," he says, pointing towards the box. "Lift that."

Stefan, now completely curious, carefully lifts the cardboard divider as if unearthing treasure—and treasure it is. "*The Lost Book of the White!*" he exclaims, voice rising again in glee. He lifts the next divider and uncovers the next book, realising Ade got him the three additional *Shadowhunters* books he doesn't yet own. "And *The Shadowhunter's Codex!*" He's really bouncing now, showering Ade with kisses, laughing between each peck. "You are *unreal*, you know that?"

Ade chuckles, enjoying Stefan's reaction with the calm of someone who knows the best is yet to come. "Lift the next divider, babe."

Stefan pauses mid-kiss. "There's *more?*" He's breathless now, as if the mere possibility of more books might be too much to handle.

Ade nods, clearly enjoying himself.

Stefan reaches back into the box, lifting the next divider, and his gasp is nothing short of theatrical. His hand flies to his mouth as if it's the only thing keeping a full-blown scream at bay. His eyes shine with barely contained joy as he takes in the sight of the book, its cover adorned with a young woman in a sweeping green ball gown, red roses in her hair, holding a lamp as she gazes into a shadowy entryway. It is the book three of Cassandra Clare's *Last Hours* series.

"*Chain of Thorns!*" he exclaims in a low voice, as if speaking the title too loudly might summon a thunderclap. The book is more than just a book. It's a miracle in hardcover. He stands up so abruptly the box tumbles to the floor, but he doesn't care. He's trailing his fingers over the cover. "It's *the collector's first edition*," he whispers. "It's sold out *everywhere*. I pre-ordered, but even then, nothing. I even called the bookshops in Stockholm, but they don't have it either." He climbs back into bed, hugging the book tightly to his chest like a long-lost love finally returned. "It's the collector's first edition," he repeats, still in awe. "I love you. I love you," he murmurs, the words now as much for Ade as for the precious treasure in his arms.

Ade, who has been watching his entire display with the patience of a saint, leans in and kisses Stefan's forehead. "Open it."

Stefan, now enchanted, does as he's told. Inside he finds an illustration, a young man dressed in crisp black trousers, waistcoat, and white shirt, shadows swirling behind him like a cape. "This must be James," he mutters. And then there's a small piece of paper tucked between the pages. "Page 579?" he reads aloud as he flips to it. When his eyes land on the underlined words, they widen, and for a moment, all air seems to leave the room. "*Kheli asheghetam*," he whispers, his voice barely audible.

Ade cups his face. "It's Persian," he says, voice gentle. "For I love you."

Stefan stares at him for a moment, heart full to bursting, then at the book, as if trying to decide which of the two he's more in love with. After a long pause, he sets the book aside —gently—before pulling Ade into a kiss so searing it might as well ignite the room. He pushes Ade down onto the bed, climbing atop him, his hands and lips moving with a fervour that suggests the books might have to wait just a little longer. "I'm going to love you forever."

And the truth of it is so simple, so solid, that there's no need to say more. But as Stefan reaches into the drawer, Ade lets out a scream that echoes through the house, shattering the silence with all the grace of a dropped teacup. He scrambles off the bed, hands slapped to his face like a man who's just seen a ghost.

"What's wrong, Teni?" Stefan asks, caught somewhere between bemusement and concern.

Ade's fingers wobble as he points at Stefan's waist, like he's trying to locate something invisible. "Y-y-you're bruised," he stammers, the words barely making it out of his mouth. "You said you were okay."

Stefan glances down, inspecting himself. Sure enough, a couple of dark red patches have appeared on his waist, but instead of alarm, a small smile tugs at his lips, like it's all a bit of an inside joke. "Babe," he says, stepping closer, "it doesn't hurt. I wouldn't have even noticed if you don't."

Not convinced in the slightest, Ade spins him around, his eyes scanning Stefan's backside like he's inspecting a priceless artefact for damage. A hoarse cry escapes him, ragged and raw. "I need to call Temmy."

Before Stefan can react, Ade is in a frenzy, rifling through the sheets for his phone. Stefan, now finding this whole ordeal far too amusing, saunters over to the mirror. He eyes the deep redness on his right buttock, shaking his head. "Babe, call your brother for what, exactly?" he asks, a trace of laughter threading through his voice. He mimics holding a phone to his ear. "Hey Temmy, I accidentally injured Stefan during sex? Or Temmy, I fucked Stefan too hard?" He wipes a tear from the corner of his eyes, body shaking. "You're overreacting."

"Overreacting?" Ade's voice breaks, eyes wild with guilt. "I never want to see a bruise on you. Not after—" He swallows hard. "Not after cleaning you up in January, scared out of my mind..." His voice trails off, the words too painful to finish. "And now, to think I caused this..."

Stefan pauses, thrown. January? Why would Ade think this is anything like January? And why does he look so guilty? A bit of harmless passion has never killed anybody.

Ade's hands are shaking as he finally finds his phone. "I-I hurt y-you and you think I'm j-just... overreacting?"

Before Ade can punch in a single number, Stefan swipes the phone from his hand and gently shoves him back onto the bed, straddling him. Ade stays put, hands flat against the mattress, eyes wide.

"I told you, I'm fine." Stefan's arms snake around Ade's neck, his voice soft, coaxing. "Would I lie to you?"

Ade says nothing, his silence a stubborn wall.

"Answer me, babe."

"No," Ade finally murmurs, nuzzling into Stefan's neck like a weary cat. "You wouldn't lie to me." He lifts his head, eyes searching. "But I can't stand seeing you in pain. I—"

"I'm not in pain," Stefan interrupts, his lips brushing against Ade's forehead. "So, stop acting like I'm at death's door." He lifts Ade's hands from the bed and wraps them around his waist. "Remember. There's nothing we *do* to each other that I don't enjoy. I'm comfortable with everything."

Ade's hands begin to massage Stefan's waist, concern

softening to tenderness. "Are you sure you're okay?" he asks, his voice quieter now.

"I'm okay," Stefan reassures him, pulling Ade closer into bed. "You know, it's a good thing we're together," he adds, rummaging through the drawer.

"Why is that?" he whispers against Stefan's skin.

"Because, darling," Stefan says, tearing the packet, "I would've happily slept with anyone who bought me *Chain of Thorns*."

Ade lets out a hushed laugh, shaking his head. "I love you, Stef," he breathes, pulling Stefan into a kiss that feels like the only truth that matters. He pushes Stefan gently onto his back, his voice a soft chant. "I love you... I love you... I love you."

And each time, with a smile that could light up the darkest of days, Stefan whispers back, "I love you."

25

ADVENTURES OF A LIFETIME

*— Adventures of a Lifetime
by Coldplay.*

Thursday, 2nd March 2023.

THE PRIVATE DINING ROOM AT NEELY'S IS PACKED, ITS ambience wrapped in a cosy, celebratory spirit. Ade had meticulously orchestrated this gathering for Stefan's twenty-third birthday, even flying in Żaneta and Edwin as a surprise, because nothing says 'I love you' quite like ensuring Stefan spends the day with his best friends.

"Happy birthday, Stefan," Jola beams, enveloping him in a sisterly hug.

"Thanks, big sis," Stefan grins, his eyes bright as sunlight on water.

The party soon settles into easy laughter with the pulse of "Cheap Thrills" floating through the room. Jola slips into a seat next to Ben, who is watching her like she's the sun in his solar system. His green eyes gleam with something so intense that even Ade, the master of observation, can't quite put his finger on—adoration? Worship? Or possible indigestion, but Ade goes with romance.

"You shine at birthdays," Ben whispers to Jola, as if the words are a secret meant for no one but her."

Jola shifts slightly in her seat. "You did also at your party last week."

Ben, tracing the rim of his glass, almost absentmindedly, shrugs with a quiet smile. "That's because you were there. I—"

Before Ben's epiphany can fully bloom, Stefan's excited voice cuts in, loud and buoyant. "So many gifts!" He eyes the wrapped boxes like a kid in a sweet shop. "I love you all."

Ade clears his throat rather pointedly.

"Oh, right. I love you *more*, baby," Stefan corrects with a grin, before planting a quick, show-stopping kiss on Ade's mouth.

Peng, never one to reserve her comment, points accusingly at them. "I get why those two are kissing, but what's going on with *them*?" She nods towards Kurt and Rosh, who are mid-clinch, thoroughly absorbed in their own little world.

Rosh flashes a cheeky grin, his arm still firmly around Kurt. "Gays celebrating Stefan's birthday, obviously."

After dinner, the room descends into the sentimental ritual of birthday tributes, each person taking turns to say what they adore about Stefan.

"Everything about him," Ade declares without a shred of hesitation, his voice full of certainty.

Peyton snorts. "Oh, come on. Shouldn't it be his..." she raises her brows suggestively, gesturing downward. "His d—"

"*Peyt!*" Priya shrieks, slapping a hand over Peyton's mouth, trying to salvage what's left of their dignity.

Undeterred, Peyton's muffled voice continues, "What? I like your wet pu—"

"PEYT!" Priya clamps her hand tighter over Peyton's mouth. "Sorry guys, she's American."

"Hey!" Chad chimes in. "We are not all like that."

Peng is beside herself with laughter, nearly toppling from her seat as the rest of the room follows suit, stifling giggles or full-blown cackles. But before any more suggestive remarks can fly, Elvis Presley's "Can't Help Falling in Love with You" starts playing, shifting the mood like magic.

Ade rises, offering his hand to Stefan with a flourish. They move to the dance floor, their bodies naturally synchronised, their movements as fluid and effortless as their love. Ade's hand finds Stefan's waist, guiding him gently, and they sing along—flawlessly. At the "Take my hand" line, Stefan spins out of Ade's arms, only to be reeled back in, much to the delight of their audience, earning them an applause. Ade pulls him close, sealing it with a kiss that is equal parts adoration and possession. Their fingers entwine, always so naturally, as if they were designed to fit, like the final pieces of a puzzle.

Peng scoffs good-naturedly from the sidelines. "They're supposed to be *dancing*. Why are they kissing again?"

Before anyone can chime in, the unmistakable opening of "Man's Not Hot" thunders through the speakers, and in a flurry of whoops and cheers, everyone rushes onto the dance floor. Stefan's phone, of course, picks the worst possible moment to ring. With an apologetic smile, he slips out to take the call, leaving Ade momentarily adrift.

After what feels like mere minutes, Sasha leans over,

eyes scanning the room. "Where's the birthday boy?" she asks Ade.

Ade, trying and failing to sound casual, sighs dramatically. "He's taking a call in the car. Too loud in here. I miss him already."

Temmy, shakes his head, laughing at his lovestruck brother. "*Ífé ti yí orí e.*"

Jola eyes Temmy, smirking. "Oh, please, if he's crazy in love, then what are you? Like you didn't teach him everything he kn—."

"What the fuck?" Edwin suddenly swears, eyes fixed on something outside the window, his face darkening with anger. He shoots to his feet like a loaded spring.

Ade's head swivels to follow Edwin's gaze, and the rage that fills him is volcanic. Fury rises in him, coursing like wildfire, and before he can even register the sight, he's on his feet. "I'll kill him," he growls, the words spilling out with lethal intent. His body moves on instinct, charging for the door with Edwin and Nathan hot on his heels. "Ben, call Detective Koffi!" he shouts over his shoulder, anger propelling him forward.

Outside, in the cool night air, the scene that greets them does nothing to quell the rage inside Ade. Quite the opposite, in fact. Honza, all brute strength and bad temper, has Stefan shoved up against the bZ4X, his hand knotted in Stefan's shirt like he's about to throttle him—or worse, kiss him. Ade doesn't slow his pace. He strides up, his focus singular as he separates Honza from Stefan. Honza doesn't even see it coming. Without a second thought, Ade delivers a thunderous slap to his face, the sound sharp and precise as a conductor's baton hitting the podium.

"Do you have a fucking death wish?" Ade snarls, his

voice low but dangerous. He keeps his hand raised, just in case Honza fancies testing the theory.

Stefan, still leaning against the car, is frozen like a rabbit caught in headlights, his breath coming in shallow gasps as if he's not quite sure whether to be more terrified of Honza or Ade.

Temmy pulls Ade away from Honza just as Nathan grabs Honza by the throat, while Jason and Edwin form a protective wall around Stefan. Honza, the reckless fool, has the audacity to smirk, as if the entire fiasco is a comedy staged purely for his entertainment.

"Let me go to Stef," Ade insists, wrenching himself free as Jola, Ben, and Żaneta join them outside. He rushes to Stefan, pulling him into a tight embrace, kissing him with all the relief in the world. "You okay, baby?"

"I am," Stefan whispers, holding on like Ade's the only solid thing left in the world. "Now that you're here."

"Restrict him by the hands," Ben instructs Nathan. "The detective's on his way."

Honza, the insufferable twit, doesn't resist in the slightest. Instead, he speaks. "Omar, does he know you're fucking those two?" He lazily gestures towards Edwin and Żaneta.

Ade detaches from Stefan with a speed that could only be described as feral. Before anyone has the chance to intervene, he swings twice at Honza, landing both punches squarely in his gut. Honza's smirk vanishes, replaced by a cry of pain as Ade glares down at him, fists still clenched. "Don't you dare talk to him, you bastard."

"Teni!" Stefan yelps, pulling Ade back, wide-eyed but not entirely displeased, just as Detective Koffi arrives with two uniformed officers.

Ben gestures for Stefan to explain the situation. Stefan, poor thing, looks like he'd rather wrestle a grizzly bear than rehash the events. He takes a steady breath and keeps his hand firmly in Ade's. "I came out to the car to talk to my parents. When I got out, he grabbed me and shoved me against it, saying I had no choice but to go with him. He's been following me for weeks, trying to get me alone. Just like the voice notes I gave you in January."

The officers swiftly cuff Honza, whose earlier bravado is now fizzling out. There's something intensely satisfying about seeing the smirk finally wiped from his face, a small victory. As they lead him away, Detective Koffi turns back to Stefan. "Are you okay?" Stefan nods, but Detective K isn't quite finished. "You should get a restraining order. We can hold him until morning, issue a formal harassment notice, and conduct an interview. If you want him charged—"

"No charges," Stefan interrupts, shaking his head, weariness creeping into his voice.

Ade turns to him, his eyes softening as he reaches out, gently placing a hand on Stefan's arm with a quiet plea in his voice. "Babe, *please*. We have to do this."

Stefan pinches the bridge of his nose, letting out a long sigh. "He knows now not to come near me. I don't need to do anything else."

Ade's heart aches as he listens, knowing Stefan is trying to be strong, trying to convince himself that he's safe now. But Ade sees the cracks in that façade. He can't just sit by and hope for the best. "I can't bear it if he lays a hand on you again," Ade's voice breaks slightly, his grip tightening on Stefan's arm. "And I can't live with myself if he does and I'm not there to stop it." His words are filled with the fear he feels whenever Stefan is out of his sight, the helplessness that comes with knowing the person he loves is vulnerable.

He knows, of course, that if he asks Stefan directly, ask him to do this for *him*, Stefan will fold like a cheap deckchair. He'd file the paperwork, sign on every dotted line, just to put Ade at ease. But that's not the point. This isn't about Ade's nerves or his ability to sleep at night—it's about Stefan. This is about Stefan's safety, his autonomy, his peace of mind. Stefan doesn't have to live like this, doesn't have to accept unwarranted attention from Honza when a legal document could push the man right out of his life forever. This decision needs to be Stefan's, and no one else's.

"I'll get the restraining order," Stefan finally concedes.

Detective Koffi nods. "Come to the station tomorrow morning," he instructs before departing.

"Come," Ade says, opening the car door." Let's go home."

But Stefan shakes his head, the fire in his eyes returning. "No way. I'm not letting him ruin my day."

His defiance is met with whoops of approval from the others. Ade, however, isn't celebrating just yet, his fists still clenched at his sides.

Stefan cups Ade's face. "Besides, I would've fought him off if I hadn't drunk so much. I wasn't scared of him. I'm fine, okay?" He then kisses Ade, pushing him against the bZ4X.

"I think he's truly fine. Let's go back up," Ben suggests.

"*Fine* doesn't cover it," Ade mutters, still bristling with leftover adrenaline. He shakes his head, running a hand through Stefan's hair. "What was he even *thinking* coming here?"

Stefan smiles faintly, but there's a weariness in his eyes. "Let's just focus on the party. I don't want to give him more space in my head."

"You sure?" Ade's voice softens now, concerned but resolute. Stefan gives a small nod, dragging him gently back toward the entrance.

As they enter the room, the group parts like the Red Sea, clapping and whooping like they've just won a round on *Strictly Come Dancing* rather than facing off with an actual menace.

"You really know how to throw a party, Ade," Chad says. "Dinner, dancing, a bit of light brawling... what's next? Fireworks?"

"Don't give him ideas," Sophia quips.

"You don't even need my guy, Ade," Ay says, grinning.

As if on cue, "Take My Breath" blares through the speakers, and with another collective cheer, the party resumes in full swing.

Friday, 16th June 2023.

"You can't seriously tell me you don't see it," Ade declares, jabbing an indignant finger at the TV screen. *Young Royals* plays on in the background, glowing with the unmistakable drama of Scandinavian royalty. "He's your twin!"

"You're blind," Stefan chuckles, the sound light as air, glancing briefly at Omar Rudberg's chiselled face. "I look nothing like him."

"Ugh, you never let me have *anything*," Ade huffs, throwing his hands up like he's just been dealt a cosmic injustice. His dramatics are not lost on Stefan, who watches, amused, as his boyfriend pouts like a sulking prince.

"Well..." Stefan says, voice dropping an octave as his fingers start a slow journey down Ade's torso. "Since it's your graduation..." His voice is a whisper now, warm against Ade's skin. "You deserve to celebrate."

Ade shifts, a half-grunt escaping him. "We'll be late, but I can't say no now, can I?"

Stefan's grin is practically criminal as he leans in, lips brushing against Ade's, slow and tantalising, like he's savouring each second. He then wraps his hand around Ade's dick.

"Congratulations, love," he whispers, each stroke of his hand designed to set nerves alight.

Ade's mind splinters, as it so often does when Stefan touches him, flashing through memories of their blissful months together. Honestly, their love is so disgustingly perfect it could make anyone queasy. The days had unfurled with an ease that made them nauseatingly happy, the kind of love that makes onlookers roll their eyes and mutter envious things behind closed doors.

Ade practically revels in the routines they've sunk into, like an old, domesticated couple. They debate the finer points of the *Shadowhunters* series with the kind of intensity usually reserved for world politics, but Ade swears Stefan sometimes takes absurd positions just to wind him up—just to see that fire light in his eyes. Or maybe Ade's obsessed with Stefan. Just a smidge. He's even come to love Stefan's TV obsessions, begrudgingly at first. He might've grumbled about Stefan being a 'boy Jola' with his endless watchlist of *911: Lone Star, Shameless, Lucifer, Person of Interest*, and more, but he stuck around. To be fair, Stefan had devoured Ade's shorter list—*Madam Secretary, White*

Collar, and *Roswell: New Mexico*—with equal enthusiasm. Balance, after all.

And the sex? Ade can barely form coherent thoughts on that, let alone words. It's beyond electric, the kind of connection that leaves you questioning if magic is a real thing. It's the kind of mind-blowing that turns ordinary nights into fireworks.

Stefan pushes Ade onto his back, ready to straddle him, when a knock at the door makes him halt mid-mount. "Uncle Ade, grandma *sopé ó yá*," Enny informs.

Ade groans, feeling every inch the thwarted lover in some tragic romance. "To be continued," he mutters, hoisting Stefan off the bed and steering him towards the bathroom.

The living room is buzzing by the time they rejoin the world of the fully clothed. Ade's mother is already mid-sentence, gleefully pinning Stefan to her side. "I've got more *àádùn* for you," she beams, pressing a wrapped snack into his hand like some grand offering.

Stefan has somehow charmed Ade's parents—miraculously, really. His face lights up accepting the snack from her. He's become a sort of delicacy connoisseur since meeting Justice Remilekun and Chief Adebola Adeowo, sampling Nigerian treats with varying degrees of bravery. The *àádùn* had been a hit. *Kúlíkúlí?* Less so—tears had been shed that day. Ade snickers at the memory.

He watches Stefan unwrap it, and as he takes the first bite, Ade leans in slightly, waiting for that inevitable reaction. And there it is—his brows lift in what can only be described as pure delight.

"Well?" Ade asks, already knowing the answer.

Stefan makes a soft sound of approval. "It's like... sweet

caramel, but with a kick, melts right in my mouth and leaves this... warm, nutty flavour. This... this is genius."

Time skips ahead, and soon they're in the backyard, the ceremony in Middlesbrough fading into the past. Stefan, unable to resist, prods Rosh. "Why are you still wearing this?" he asks, feeling the graduation gown.

Rosh grins, sly and full of mischief. "Kurt wants the honour of taking it off."

Peng, the faux voice of propriety, sighs. "There are *parents* here," she says, eyebrows climbing somewhere into her hairline.

Stefan turns to Ade, eyes gleaming with new ideas. "Put your gown back on. I'm suddenly very inspired by Kurt."

Ade leans in, unbothered by the watching parents. "How about the cap?"

"Oh, absolutely. You should wear it."

Before they can enact any further plans, the unmistakable clink of spoon against glass halts their chatter. Jason stands, poised to make a toast—except instead of raising a glass, he drops to one knee in front of Lina, diamond ring in hand.

Ben spits his drink.

"Lin, my love," Jason begins, his voice shaky yet sincere. "I have rehearsed what to tell you, what to say to make you know how much I love you. But what I feel for you can't be rehearsed."

Ade leans in, ready for some grand declaration of love.

"You've shown me a new world, one with endless possibilities, a better world." Jason continues, smiling at Lina, who has one hand on her small bump, her eyes glittering. "I remember thinking if you ever leave me for someone else, I'd follow you to that relationship, and we'd be like that throuple in *The Dark Artifices*. I-"

Jola chokes on her drink. "Did you just... reference a fictional throuple? In your proposal?"

"I mean, why not?" Priya jumps in, defensive. "Mark, Christina, and Kieran are hot."

Stefan looks around, surprised. "Wait, you guys read the series?"

"We read them with Peng," Peyton explains nonchalantly. "We'll read anything with a throuple in it."

"Oohh," MT claps gleefully. "Are you guys going to be a throuple?"

Jason, still on one knee, sighs with the exasperation of a man whose big moment has been thoroughly hijacked. "Ladies, your impending throuple sounds cute, but I'm trying to propose here."

"I read them," Lina is saying to her pregnant buddy, Sophia. "Although for Kit and Ty, but they nev—"

"*Lin*," Jason laughs, shaking his head. "It's *you* I'm proposing to."

"Right!" Lina turns back to him, eyes soft and full of love. "Sorry, baby. Carry on."

Jason exhales, visibly regrouping. "I forgot where I was."

"The throuple," Nathan supplies helpfully.

Jason spares a second to glare at Nathan, then takes Lina's hand. "Lina, will you make me the happiest man in the world by marrying me?"

"Yes!" Lina all but tackles him before looping her hands around his neck and kissing him until her father, Johnny Čizmić, coughs pointedly. Ade stifles a laugh as Jason, like a schoolboy caught passing notes in class, stops kissing Lina just long enough to slip the ring onto her finger, the diamond catching the sunlight in a brilliant display.

"That reminds me," Jason grins, his voice loud enough

to reach every corner of the canopy. "I'll never hurt you because I love you. Also, your dad threatened me."

Laughter ripples through the crowd like a gentle wave, the kind that comes when everyone's in on the joke. And then it's a flurry of hugs and congratulations, the Čizmić and Browns folding into each other in a tangle of limbs and teary smiles.

"The wedding will be in Zagreb," Johnny declares with the finality of a man accustomed to making decisions, not suggestions. Jason nods like a man who knows better than to argue with his future father-in-law.

Ade can't help but marvel. Jason, once Newcastle's resident playboy, now completely subdued by love—it's enough to make anyone believe in miracles. He's never seen Jason so compliant. If Johnny had announced the wedding would be held on the moon, Ade suspects Jason would have already been browsing spacesuits.

Ade's attention shifts to Ben, who is sweeping Lina into a bear hug. "Welcome to the family, sis."

There's something about Ben—an unshakeable sincerity that always gets to Ade. The kind that just pours out of him without pretence or performance. He remembers Ben back in March, standing outside their driveway, presenting Jola with a brand new Mercedes Benz GLP 250 SUV for her birthday, looking like a proud but nervous puppy. Jola had initially refused, her expression hovering somewhere between disbelief and a lecture, but the crestfallen look on Ben's face had been enough to make even the strongest hearts falter.

Ade steps into the embrace, arms stretching out to gather Stefan, Jason, and the rest of the Gen Z crew into their tight-knit circle. There's something comforting about the lot of them, huddled together, a band of misfits turned family.

As "Marry You" plays from the speakers, Ade and Stefan edge towards the dance floor, a gentle pull of invisible strings drawing them closer.

"So," Ade begins, his hands settling on Stefan's waist, "do you want a throuple discussion during our proposal?"

"How are you sure," Stefan grins, cupping Ade's face, "I won't be the one to propose?"

"I wouldn't mind a throuple discussion, baby."

Their lips meet in a kiss that always makes the rest of the world fade away. Once again, it's just them, wrapped in each other's arms, dreaming of a future filled with love, laughter, and maybe, just maybe, a throuple discussion of their own.

Monday, 19th June 2023.

Ade and Stefan find themselves in Paris, the City of Lights, a place where the scent of freshly baked pastries seems to wrap itself around them like an expensive scarf. It's their first stop en route to Bangkok, with a five-hour layover at Charles de Gaulle. Naturally, instead of languishing in the sterile confines of the airport, they decide to take in the city. Stefan wrinkles his nose as they wade through the tourist-thick tide at the Eiffel Tower and the Louvre—he has opinions about cities, and Paris is decidedly a "dirty city," and he keeps repeating it, as though declaring it will somehow tidy up the streets.

By the time they recline in their plush double suite aboard Singapore Airline, Stefan's judgement of Paris remains unshaken. "Dirty city," he mutters again, sinking into the kind of luxury that makes one wonder if maybe first class is where the world should spend more time.

"We're leaving the 'dirty city' now," Ade chuckles, helping Stefan fasten his seatbelt.

Up in the air, the earth a forgotten blur beneath them, Ade buries his nose in *Red, White & Royal Blue,* which he started reading after Stefan's successful campaign. Even Jason had been recruited to give his two cents on the book, with the father-to-be declaring it "such a beautiful story."

"His royal highness, Prince Henry of Wales, should avoid Newcastle," Ade huffs, half lost in the pages already.

Stefan, of course, is beside himself with laughter. "Why are you threatening a child of the crown?"

Ade fakes outrage, eyes wide with mock indignation. "Can you believe the guy? Hops back and forth between England and America just to sleep with Alex. Ditches Germany to meet him in Paris, invites him to Wimbledon, calls him 'love', shares all sorts with him, and then had the audacity to say—" Ade pauses for effect, throwing in air quotes. "'I never imagined you would love me back.' I mean, seriously? Who no go fall in love?"

Stefan wheezes, wiping tears from his eyes. "You're so sexy when you speak pidgin."

"But really!" Ade persists, his faux indignation gaining steam. "Who wouldn't fall in love with all that?"

"Prince Henry is deeply, deeply sorry," Stefan says, his voice mock-serious, as he smooths down the front of Ade's shirt. "*Máa bí'nú oko mi*—don't be angry, my husband."

The last of Ade's outrage evaporates as quickly as it had arrived. He tosses Stefan a pair of pyjamas, his voice dropping to a warm whisper. "You know what you do to me when you speak Yoruba." They slip into the bed, the cabin dimly lit, cocooned in cosy, luxurious silence, the outside world irrelevant. Ade takes in the sight of Stefan—his Stef—eyes filled with that same soft wonder they held the first time he ever saw him. Ade's fingers glide over Stefan's cheek with the lightness of a passing breeze, like tracing the edges of something fragile and beautiful. And he is, Stefan is beautiful.

"We're going to Bangkok," Ade whispers, though it sounds less like a statement of fact and more like a promise.

Stefan's smile is the kind that could power cities. "Technically, we're en route to Singapore," he corrects with a teasing smirk, "but we're going to Bangkok, baby." His grin widens just before he leans in, lips brushing Ade's with a playful nip before giving way for a kiss.

Ade remembers seeing the date on their tickets, it was one of those moments when time tilts, and the past sneaks in, uninvited. But before he could spiral, Stefan was there, as always, slipping his arms around Ade from behind, pressing close. "I want you to have a new memory of the date," Stefan had whispered softly, "a better one." And in that instant, if it hadn't been clear before, it certainly was then—Stefan is his anchor, the steady hand that pulls him back from the edge when the waters churn and threaten to drown him. His saving grace.

Ade had once tried to explain this to Sparks during one of their sessions, though no words ever seemed quite enough. But he had told the therapist how Stefan's unyielding presence had become the bedrock of his healing. Stefan's steadfastness has been the very thing tethering him to his own healing. And let's be honest, if love were a competition, Stefan would be winning by miles. There's no denying it: the guy's patience and support have been nothing short of heroic. He hasn't just watched Ade heal;

he's actively helped piece him back together, bit by bit, without a flicker of doubt.

Not that Ade's been slacking, of course. He's more determined than ever to continue his progress, to keep healing, to never miss a session, even if it means skyping from Bangkok, because growth doesn't take holidays. He's resolute in his promise—his unspoken vow—to love Stefan deeply, wholly, and with all the messy, beautiful humanity he can muster. Stefan deserves nothing less than Ade's best, and for him, that's precisely what Ade intends to give.

"It's good we saw Craig before leaving," Stefan says, his fingers deftly working open the buttons of Ade's shirt, a smile tugging at his lips.

Ade chuckles, recalling their recent doctor's visit. "All clear," he grins, mirroring Stefan's movements, his hands slipping under the fabric of Stefan's shirt, trailing kisses down his chest as he works him out of his trousers. "Hello there," he greets Stefan's dick with a cheeky grin, before returning to kiss him, fingers tangling in Stefan's hair. "I love you."

"I love you," Stefan murmurs, his hands just as quick to shed the remaining layers between them.

Ade shifts, positioning himself above Stefan, his lips hovering just above Stefan's. "You ready, Adeife?"

That name—Adeife is the Yoruba name the Adeowos gave Stefan. Or rather, Ade gave him and informed the others, just like Jola did those years ago. The name means 'crown of love' and Stefan wears it with pride.

Stefan, crowned with love, grins up at him. "Always, Olólùfé," he winks, the Yoruba slipping from his lips with ease.

Ade taps their travel playlist, setting it to shuffle, and with impeccable timing, "Love Tonight" fills the air.

Ade takes his time, moving slowly and deliberately, reintroducing himself to Stefan's body like an old, beloved song played on a newly tuned instrument. No barriers now, no barricade—just them, skin to skin, where they should be. Flesh meets flesh in an intoxicating dance that feels new and familiar all at once, stirring something deep, exhilarating, and untamed. The plane hums gently beneath them, but it's their own rhythm that carries them—steady, raw, and alive.

"How does it feel?" Ade asks, his voice betraying a slight tremor. His gaze flits over Stefan's flushed face, taking in every detail—the glint of his dark, desire-clouded eyes, the sheen of sweat on his skin, the rapid rise and fall of his chest.

Stefan's response is ragged, breathless, as though Ade has quite literally stolen the words from his lungs. "You're going to send me out of my goddamn mind," he manages, fingers tracing the contours of Ade's body with reverence and longing.

They had been running from something, both of them—from their pasts, from fears they hadn't yet learned to name, from the quiet ache of loneliness that settles in the soul from wandering alone for too long. They were sprinting through life in opposite directions, each convinced that if they just kept moving, the past would never catch up.

But, as it often does, fate had other plans. It stepped in with a subtle hand, weaving their parts together on that fateful August day, under a sky so impossibly clear, it felt as though the heavens themselves had paused to watch. And at first, they believed their encounter was fleeting, one of those brief flashes of connection that are beautiful in their own way but never meant to last. But the whims of destiny reunited them, bringing them back into each other's orbit with a quiet insistence as if to say, *This is meant to be.*

And the universe, in its infinite grace, and surprising sense of generosity, had given them a gift—a love that transcended the obstacles life threw at them, a love that refused to be boxed in by the usual limits of time or distance. It defied expectations, shattered any preconceived notions they had about what love was supposed to look like. This is not the kind of love they had read about in books or seen on TV. It is richer, messier, more complex—and more real. It holds within it both the beauty and the flaws of their individual journeys, and somehow that only makes it more perfect.

It's not lost on either of them—the delicious irony of it all. Once, they were running from life, from love, from the world that seemed too harsh, too cruel. And now? Now they're running no more. Instead, they are moving forward, hand in hand, with the sky wide open before them.

A year ago today, Ade had faced the ugliest side of the world, a brutal reminder of the prejudice and hatred that still plaques humans. But today is a different story altogether. Today, he stands in a place of light, wrapped in the unwavering love of Stefan. The contrast is almost dizzying—the difference a year can make. He is no longer the person defined by that horrible day, no longer caged by the trauma that once seemed insurmountable. He is no longer alone. Today, he finds solace in the arms of the guy who loves him fiercely, in the eyes of someone who sees him not as a target, but as a treasure. The world has expanded again, full of bright possibilities, and Ade is right there, at the centre of it, held fast by a love that refuses to falter.

And they had each faced their own battles—some fought in silence, others in the harsh light of day. The scars from those struggles, both seen and unseen, were etched deep into their souls, remnants of pain and fear. But now, those once-heavy marks seem to fade, replaced by something far more powerful: a sense of belonging, of acceptance that neither of them had dared to believe possible before.

Here they are, soaring nearly forty thousand feet above sea level, the world beneath them, far away and small, the clouds rushing by. And they're making love, because they can, because they want to, because they are in love.

Afterword

In the heart of Nigeria, the criminalisation of love is a dark stain on the fabric of society—a law that transforms the very essence of identity into an offence. The 2014 Same-Sex Marriage Prohibition Act was not merely a legal decree; it was a sentence handed down on love itself. With a stroke of the pen, it declared that to love someone of the same sex is to transgress the very bounds of what is considered "proper" in a world already suffocated by societal expectations. It cast a shadow over the lives of countless individuals, demanding that they shrink, hide, and abandon the truest parts of themselves.

This law, born of fear and misunderstanding, did not simply criminalise an act; it criminalised the right to exist. It rendered invisible those who have long been forced to walk through a world that tells them their love is unnatural, unworthy of existence, or worse, criminal. To live under such a law is to exist in the margins of your own humanity, to feel the weight of every gaze, the quiet cruelty in every whispered word, the unspoken rejection that ripples through a society that insists you be other than you are. It is not only the heart that is imprisoned in such a world; it is the soul.

What this law ignores is the inherent truth of love—that love, in all its beautiful and infinite forms, is not a crime. It is a force that binds us, heals us, and makes us human. When love is shackled by fear, when people are made to feel shame for their own hearts, it is not just those individuals who suffer—it is all of us. For when we deny someone their right to love freely, we deny ourselves the gift of empathy, connection, and understanding.

In writing this book, I drew inspiration not only from the imagined worlds of my characters but from a much grittier muse—the lives of real people who have dared to love beyond the cramped margins society often imposes. Across Nigeria and far beyond, LGBTQ+ individuals confront a world that too often greets their truth with violence, prejudice, and, in some cases, even death—for the audacity of existing in full colour.

One such person was Ifeanyi Chuckwu-Agah Benedict (AKA Abuja Area mama) who was brutally murdered on August 8, 2024 in Abuja, Nigeria, for being open about their identity. This, sadly, is not an isolated incident. Every day, queer people in Nigeria are subjected to similar forms of hate and violence, driven by laws that demonise their very existence. These real lives, taken away and torn apart by hatred, are the hidden truths behind the statistics we too often overlook.

The consequences of this law erode the very foundations of trust, safety, and belonging that any society should offer its people. It breeds a culture of silence, one that tells individuals they are not worthy of the simplest, most universal human right: to love without fear.

But laws, as history teaches us, can change. They must.

Change will come when we, as a society, stand together and declare that love is not a crime. That the right to be seen, to be heard, and to exist authentically is not up for debate. The fight for equality is not just about the law; it is about dismantling the prejudices that haunt the corners of our culture and replacing them with the light of compassion and justice.

Acknowledgments

I began writing last year, caught in that rare pocket of time when the hours stretched wide, and I found myself with more hours than I knew what to do with. So, I did something unexpected. Although this story had been with me for so long, I hadn't dared believe I could actually write it.

But then I told my husband, and in an instant, he was all in—immediately, wholeheartedly on board. His enthusiasm was the spark that allowed Ade, Stefan, and the other Adeowos to step into the world—he loved them first, and that love sustained me. My deepest thanks, Adedeji, for being not just the love of my life but the one who believed first. You may be the only man who could make a writer feel her dreams are hardly wild enough.

To my friends and family, who support my brazen choices with unwavering loyalty and humour, and who always seem to know that, at the heart of it all, I mean well—thank you. I'm grateful to have such an audience for my quirks.

To my first set of readers, who were both my fiercest critics and my greatest cheerleaders: thank you for your unfiltered honesty, your impassioned debates over Stefan's motives, and the long calls dissecting every nuance of the characters. Olene, Omotola, Bukunolami, Demi, and countless others—you all brought this story to life in ways only true book lovers can.

A special shout-out to Karo for her iconic tweet all those years ago—I never knew it would be so pivotal. And to Kiki Mordi, a generous queen: I'll never forget how you immediately pulled together a PR campaign the moment I called. Your unwavering support has been nothing short of legendary.

And finally, to my readers, if you take anything from these pages, let it be this: love, in all its messy, unexpected, and often absurd forms, will always find a way.

About the Author

G.T. Dípè is a fourth-year doctoral student in environmental science who spends more time watching TV shows and reading novels than actually working on her research (please, don't tell her supervisor!). She is currently traveling across Europe—unlike her characters, she is not running, just avoiding too much lab time. She is married and has a daughter. This is her debut novel.

Sign up for her newsletter (www.gtdipe.com) to be notified of new releases, books going on sale, bonus chapters, and other news.

Follow her on TikTok, X, & Instagram: @thegtdipe

Contact her via email at grace@gtdipe.com

Scan to enjoy Ade and Stefan's playlist on Apple Music 🤍

Apple Music

Scan to enjoy Ade and Stefan's playlist on Spotify 🩶

Spotify

Teniade may be done running, but his sister, Jolade, is only just starting.

When memories fade, can love still find it's way home?

RUNNIN' FROM GUILT

G.T. DÍPÈ

COMING SOON